*A husbandless suburban mom, Cindy Jones was willing
to admit that the battle-scarred bodyguard sprawled
helplessly on her bed was handsome. But he was also
lethal. Not just because he knew how to kill.
But because he knew how to love...*

**Sparks fly between
THE BODYGUARD & MS. JONES
in this keeper by Susan Mallery.**

"Susan Mallery is warmth and wit personified.
Always a fabulous read."
—*New York Times* bestselling author Christina Dodd

* * *

*She was a suspect under investigation. He wasn't
supposed to like her. Respect, admire even, not like.
But, man, standing there, looking at her,
he found an awful lot to like.*

**In this memorable novel
from bestselling author Suzanne Brockmann,
a HERO UNDER COVER finds himself caught
between duty...and desire.**

"The hottest author going in series romance today."
—*Romantic Times Magazine*

SUSAN MALLERY

is the bestselling author of over forty books for Silhouette. Twice, she's earned nominations for the prestigious Romance Writers of America RITA Award. In 1995, her novel *Marriage on Demand* was awarded Best Special Edition by *Romantic Times Magazine*.

Susan finds herself in the unique position of living out her own personal romantic fantasy with the new man in her life. She lives in sunny Southern California with her handsome hero husband and her adorable-but-not-bright cats.

SUZANNE BROCKMANN

lives just west of Boston in a house always filled with her friends—actors and musicians and storytellers and artists and teachers. When not writing award-winning romances about U.S. Navy SEALs, among others, she sings in an a cappella group called Serious Fun, manages the professional acting careers of her two children, volunteers at the Appalachian Benefit Coffeehouse and always answers letters from readers. Send her an SASE along with your letter to P.O. Box 5092, Wayland, MA 01778.

SUSAN MALLERY

SUZANNE BROCKMANN

HER GUARDIAN

Silhouette Books

Published by Silhouette Books

America's Publisher of Contemporary Romance

SILHOUETTE BOOKS

ISBN 0-373-21714-5

by Request

HER GUARDIAN

Copyright © 2001 by Harlequin Books S.A.

The publisher acknowledges the copyright holders
of the individual works as follows:

THE BODYGUARD & MS. JONES
Copyright © 1996 by Susan W. Macias

HERO UNDER COVER
Copyright © 1994 by Suzanne Brockmann

CONTENTS

Dear Reader,

The Bodyguard & Ms. Jones is one of those very special books that grows out of real-life experiences. No, I did not have a handsome bodyguard drop into my life unexpectedly, but I did move from California to Texas. After growing up in the craziness of Los Angeles, I found myself in a Houston suburb, where neighbors spoke to one another, high school sports were as important as national politics and people thought *I* was the one who talked funny!

I loved everything about Sugar Land. My three years there were terrific and I have long-lasting friendships to prove it. One day, when I'd been in Texas for about a year, I started thinking about all the adjustments I'd made. Then I started thinking about how interesting and funny it could be for someone else to make the same adjustments. Maybe a person who could fit into every situation imaginable...except possibly the Sugar Land suburbs. My macho bodyguard, Mike, was born.

Enjoy!

Susan Mallery

THE BODYGUARD & MS. JONES
by Susan Mallery

To Christina Dodd—
with thanks for teaching me to survive the wilds of
Houston, for explaining that I really do need to
unplug my computer during a bad thunderstorm
and for generally being a wonderful friend.
Here's to incredible success!

Chapter One

"**M**ister. Mister! Are you dead?"

The voice was insistent and faintly whiny. Mike Blackburne tried to block out the noise, along with the pounding in his head and the painful throbbing that pulsed through his body. He failed miserably on both counts.

"I think he's dead," the voice proclaimed.

"He's not dead. He's sleeping."

"No way. I can't wake him up. See?"

Mike felt a jab in his side. The poking continued, hitting right above the bruise on his ribs. The pain increased, and the black haze he'd been fighting for God knows how long began to descend.

"Leave me the hell alone," he roared. Or at least it was supposed to be a roar. Instead, his mouth barely opened and he mumbled something that sounded like "Ve m'll own."

There was a moment of blissful silence. The jabbing

against his ribs stopped. Then his peace was shattered by a high-pitched call.

"Mo-om, he's not dead."

Whatever he was lying on shook slightly, as if it had been bumped. There were footsteps, then silence again.

Mike told himself to sit up. The pain flowing through his body like liquid torture warned him that wasn't advisable. Trying for a lesser goal, he started to open his eyes. His lids felt as if they'd been glued shut.

He tried again and this time was rewarded by a sharp stab of light. He blinked, attempting to bring something, anything, into focus, then wished he hadn't. Some ugly green creature with flaming eyes was staring at him.

He jerked back, causing his head to swim and the cadence of agony to increase. He felt like roadkill. Blinking again, he studied his guardian.

"Hell," he muttered. It was a two-foot-long statue of a dragon, about the ugliest piece of art he'd ever seen. It was just as well he wasn't dead, because he expected the good Lord to have better taste than that.

One corner of his mouth curved up, pulling at his split lip. He grimaced and raised his hand to touch the spot. Tender but not bleeding. Besides, who was he to assume that on his death he was going north?

Footsteps caught his attention. He tried to turn toward the sound. He could see a massive marble fireplace, wing chairs that looked more decorative than comfortable and a small lacquered table supporting a smaller version of the dragon staring down at him. However, he couldn't locate the owner of the footsteps. He hoped it wasn't that kid again. He was in bad enough shape without being poked and prodded.

His eyes closed involuntarily. He didn't want to sleep anymore. He didn't know how long he'd been out. He didn't even know where he was, although something about the room was familiar.

"Mr. Blackburne?"

Soft, sweet tones recalled him to consciousness. She didn't sound like any nurse he'd ever met. But then, he wasn't still in the hospital. Maybe she knew where he was and what he was doing here.

He forced his eyes opened. As everything swam around, he felt a cool touch on his forehead. He blinked.

Directly in front of him were a pair of long, curvy legs. Her honey-colored thighs were about two feet from his face. He could see the bare skin, a freckle above her right knee and a faded scar, probably from some run-in she'd had years before with a curb.

"Mr. Blackburne?" she repeated.

Did angels go around naked? He raised his gaze slightly, hoping to encounter more bare skin. Much to his disappointment, she was wearing pale blue shorts with a white gauzy shirt tucked into the waistband. Leaning over him the way she was, her shirt gaped slightly. He saw the curve of her breasts. A weak but nearly audible flicker of male interest told him he was not only alive, but more than likely on the road to recovery.

Before he could move his head back far enough to see her face, she moved closer and sat next to him. The action took her legs out of his range of vision, but now he could see her features without straining.

She had shoulder-length light brown hair with a fringe of bangs falling to her eyebrows. Her mouth was wide and turned up at the corners, as if she was on the verge of smiling. Her eyes were green, with a hint of gray smoke. He'd never seen her before.

"I hope you feel better than you look, Mr. Blackburne, because you look pretty bad."

"Where am I?" he mumbled. The words came out garbled.

She frowned, a faint line appearing on her forehead. "I can't understand you, but you probably shouldn't be talking, anyway. My name is Cindy Jones. Your sister, Grace, is my neighbor. You're in Grace's house now. You arrived sometime last night, but I wasn't expecting you for another week. If you hadn't left the front door open, no one would have known you were here."

She touched his face again. Her fingertips were cool as she traced a line from his temple to the corner of his mouth. "You've got a fever, and you're bleeding. I don't think you should have left the hospital."

"Hate hospitals."

"Now you sound like Jonathan." He must have looked confused. She smiled. Her lips parted and curved up, exposing white teeth and a dimple in her right cheek. "Jonathan is my oldest. He's nine. He hates anything to do with the doctor. Last summer he broke his arm. You should have heard him complaining every time we took him in to be checked."

Now he knew where he was. He didn't remember much about getting here, although the faint memory of a plane trip made sense. Last time he recalled being fully conscious, he'd been in a hospital in Los Angeles. Grace lived outside of Houston. Why had he gone there? He had his own place....

"Earthquake," he mumbled.

That damn earthquake a couple years back had destroyed his apartment building. He'd meant to find another place, but he'd been too busy working. The memories were coming back faster now. Grace had come to see him in the hospital and had offered her place. She was going to be gone for the summer, anyway. He could recover in peace.

"So who are you?" he asked.

"I told you. I'm Cindy Jones. Your neighbor. Grace asked me to look after you until you were on your feet."

"I don't need any help." He would be fine. As soon as the pounding in his head subsided to a tolerable level and the bullet wound in his leg stopped throbbing in time with his heartbeat. So much for his recovery. "I feel like I was run over by a train."

"Actually, I believe you fell off of a building."

He must have glared at her because she quickly added, "According to Grace, it was a very small building. Some bushes broke the fall."

"They should have done a better job." He concentrated all his strength on getting upright. If he could just swallow a handful of pills that his doctor had prescribed, he would be fine. But first he had to sit up.

He braced his left hand on the sofa cushion and pushed with all his strength. He got about halfway toward sitting before the room started spinning and the shaking in his arm got so bad he collapsed.

"What are you trying to do, Mr. Blackburne?"

"Sit up." He could feel the sweat on his face and back. He hoped it was from the exertion and not a fever. That was the last thing he needed right now.

"Why?"

"Pills." He motioned to the floor, knowing he would have dropped his duffel bags on his way in. His eyelids were getting heavier.

She stood up. He heard her faint footsteps as she crossed the room. There was barely any sound on the hardwood floor, so she must be wearing soft-soled shoes, he thought. A useless piece of information provided by a brain trained to keep him alive. Sometimes, knowing the kind of shoes someone was wearing could save a life. Good to know he still had it, even though he didn't have the strength to use it.

"Is this all your luggage, Mr. Blackburne?" Cindy asked.

"Mike," he mumbled. Everything he owned in the world fit into two duffel bags. If the flight wasn't full, he didn't bother to check them. That way, he could carry them off the plane and not have to wait.

He heard the rattle of pills and knew she'd found the bottles. But instead of handing them to him, she crossed the room toward what he supposed was the kitchen. "Jonathan, keep an eye on Mr. Blackburne. I want to call his doctor."

Mike opened his mouth to tell her not to bother, but no sound came out. Seconds later something poked his injured side. He groaned.

"You really shot?" a voice asked. "Did somebody fill you with lead?"

He forced his eyes open and glanced at the boy staring down at him. He had blond hair, long on top, but trimmed short around his ears. Bright brown eyes peered at him curiously. "Go 'way," he said.

"Can I see the bullet hole? Did you bleed a lot?" The boy looked over his shoulder toward the kitchen, then bent toward Mike's face. "Are you packing a gun?"

Too much TV, Mike thought.

Cindy returned to the living room. From the look on her face, she wasn't happy.

"I spoke to your doctor," she said, holding out a bottle of pills. "He said you were supposed to stay in the hospital another four days. You could spike a fever or worse."

"Uh-uh. I'm fine."

"You don't look fine. You look like—"

"Garbage?" Jonathan offered helpfully.

"Jonathan."

The boy's shoulders dropped. "Sorry, Mom."

She shoved the pills into her shorts pocket. "Go check on your sister. I'll be home in a few minutes, as soon as I figure out what to do with Mr. Blackburne."

He was having trouble concentrating on what she was saying. "Mike," he told her again. "Call me Mike." At least that's what he thought he said. He had a feeling the words that passed his lips bordered on unintelligible.

"Mike," she repeated. "You shouldn't have left the hospital. I'm not sure what to do with you. We've got a great facility here. I could take you there."

He shook his head. Instantly, black spots appeared. He closed his eyes and rubbed them, but the spots didn't go away. He cleared his throat and spoke slowly, more for his benefit than hers. "I'll be fine. Just get me a glass of water, and I'll take my pills."

"I can't do that."

"Why not?"

"I promised your sister I would take care of you while she was gone. I can't just give you pills and leave you here. You need medical attention. At the very least, you need to be watched. The nurse on the phone said you'd hit your head."

"Listen, lady, I don't need anything but a damn glass of water." He got the whole sentence out clearly.

"Uh-huh. Sorry, but I'm not impressed by your temper."

"Why not?"

She smiled. As smiles went, it was a nice one, he

thought, then knew for sure that a fever had kicked in. When did he bother noticing a woman's smile?

"I've got two kids, Mike. I'm used to crankiness in the sickroom."

"I'm not cranky."

"You're doing a fair imitation. I'll make you a deal. If you're strong enough to walk to the bedroom so you can lie down properly, I won't make you go to the hospital."

"Fair enough." He thought about sitting up and wondered if he could do it. "Where's the bedroom?"

"Lucky for you, it's downstairs."

"No problem. Give me a minute."

He concentrated all his attention on his arms, willing them to be strong. After taking three deep breaths, he pushed himself into a sitting position. The room tilted and spun, but he didn't dare close his eyes. Focusing on Cindy, who seemed to be moving slightly less than everything else, he began to rise. His thighs trembled, his knees refused to lock and he felt himself start to go down. At the last moment, he ducked left. The last thing he needed was to be impaled on that damn ceramic dragon.

Cindy thought Mike might actually make it to his feet. He was almost there, when he started to topple like a half-assembled tower from one of Jonathan's games. She lunged forward, catching him before he fell. She grabbed him around the waist. His left arm encircled her shoulder.

It didn't do any good. He outweighed her by about sixty pounds, and he was unconscious. It was like trying to hold up a large, male sack of flour. Her legs buckled, and she found herself pinned under him on the sofa.

His head rested on her chest, his right hand slipped between her thighs. His torso settled across her hips. She couldn't move. The intimacy was almost as unsettling as the heat she felt from him. He had a fever.

"Mike?" she said.

He didn't budge.

"Mike?" She shook him. Nothing. Not even a hint that he could hear her.

A strand of hair settled on her face. She blew it away and studied the situation. Her left foot barely touched the ground. If she could push off with that leg, she might be able to roll him a little and slide out from under him. Her right arm was caught between him and the sofa; her right leg bent awkwardly and was likewise captured.

She glanced at the dragon resting on the glass coffee table in front of the sofa. "You could help," she said.

The dragon didn't answer.

Cindy pushed and wiggled and only succeeded in pulling her shirt out of her waistband and bunching her shorts up around her rear.

"I'm not making progress here," she said, then giggled. Who exactly was she talking to?

"Jonathan?" she called as loudly as she could. "Allison? Mommy needs your help."

She figured the odds of her children hearing her were slim, but she had to try. She wasn't sure how long they would wait before coming to investigate. If they got interested in a show on TV, it could be an hour or more.

"I can't wait that long," Cindy said. She wiggled to get free, and instead managed to wedge Mike's hand tighter between her thighs. "If you knew how long it's been since a man touched me there." She giggled again. She had been reduced to talking to inanimate objects and unconscious men. "At least they're not talking back. I do still have a slender hold on my sanity."

The giggle turned into laughter. She again tried to push

Mike off her, but she didn't have any strength. She laughed until tears trickled down her temples and into her hair.

"I never have my camera with me when I should."

Cindy turned toward the voice and saw Beth standing in the foyer. "Help me," she said.

Beth raised her eyebrows as she took in the scene before her. "I understand about getting them a drink to relax them, but Cindy, honey, I think you went too far. And, if you're going to have sex with a stranger, try to remember to close the front door."

"But if he's not a stranger, I can leave the door open?" Cindy shoved against Mike, but he didn't budge. "Would you help me, please?"

Her friend sauntered across the room. She was slim, with dark red hair and brilliant blue eyes. She bent close. "He's handsome. Does he have a name?"

"Mike Blackburne. Grace's brother."

"Oh, my. The bodyguard. Very nice. Grace didn't mention he was so good-looking. I like that in a man."

"Beth! I can't breathe here."

"Stop whining. I'm going to help." Beth grabbed him by the shoulder and raised him slightly. At the same time, Cindy pushed off and managed to slide out from under him. She shimmied off the sofa and plopped onto the floor on her backside.

"He was so overcome by lust that he passed out?" Beth asked.

"I think it was the fever. He's sick."

"Most men are."

Cindy shook her head. "No, I mean he's ill. Grace told me he'd been shot and fell off a building. I spoke to his doctor's office. He left the hospital too early. His doctor said he needs to take his medication and rest."

Beth eyed him. "If you ask me, he needs a new line of work."

"Help me get him to bed."

"You're going to keep him?"

"He's not a puppy. I can't send him back where he came from."

"Take him to the hospital."

Cindy looked at the unconscious man sprawled out on the sofa. The doctor had given her instructions on how to care for Mike. As long as she got his pills and some water down him, all he really needed was a little rest. He sure hadn't wanted to go back to the hospital and she couldn't blame him.

"I promised Grace I would look after him while he was here," she said. "I owe her."

"I'm sure she didn't expect her brother to be so ill."

"Probably not," Cindy agreed. "But she's already gone. I want to try and take care of Mike. If he gets worse, then I'll take him over to the hospital."

"Mike?" Beth raised her eyebrows. "You two have met?"

"Yes, before he passed out."

"And is there a Mrs. Mike?"

"I didn't ask." Cindy stood up and brushed off her shorts. "Don't start matchmaking, Beth. I mean it. Mike Blackburne is a professional bodyguard. He goes from job to job. He's here because he doesn't have a place of his own. I'm not interested in a man like that, and he wouldn't be interested in me."

"I'm not saying you have to marry him," Beth said, tilting her head so she could study Mike's features more clearly. "I'm just saying that once he's on his feet, maybe the two of you could—"

Cindy cut her off. "I'm not that type."

Beth smiled slowly. "Honey, we're *all* that type. It's just that some of us get a little more of a chance to prove it than others."

"Cheap talk for a woman who's been married to the same man for fifteen years."

"I know, but a girl can dream." She touched Mike's cheek with the back of her hand. "He's burning up. If you're serious about taking care of him, there's no point in putting him in Grace's bedroom. You'll just have to run back and forth between the two houses. Let me go get Darren and the three of us can wrestle Mike into your place."

"That makes sense," Cindy said. "I'll take his things over."

"Be right back."

Beth left the house and crossed the street to her own place. Cindy heard her calling for her husband. Thank goodness it was Saturday. There was no way she could have moved Mike on her own.

Cindy picked up the two duffel bags on the floor, went out the front door and cut across the green lawn. She walked down the driveway and into her own house through the back door.

"Mommy, Mommy, is he really dead?" seven-year-old Allison asked. "Jonathan says he's dead, but Shelby and I don't believe him."

"He's not dead, but he's sick. He's going to stay with us for a little while."

Jonathan eyed the duffel bags. "You think he's got a gun in there?"

Cindy clamped her lips together. The thought hadn't occurred to her, but Jonathan could be right. "I think the two of you should stay out of the way for the next few minutes. Mr. and Mrs. Davis are going to help me bring Mr. Blackburne over here.''

Allison's big green eyes widened. ''Where's he going to sleep?''

''In my room. It's downstairs.''

''Daddy won't like that.''

Cindy didn't bother pointing out that Daddy had given up his right to complain when he'd walked out on his family nearly two years ago.

''Daddy doesn't care about us, stupid,'' Jonathan said.

''He does care, and I'm not stupid. Shelby says *you're* stupid.''

''At least I'm not dumb enough to talk to invisible people.''

''She's not invisible. She just doesn't want mean boys like *you* seeing her.''

''Children!'' Cindy said loudly. ''Please. No name-calling. I mean it.''

They both looked at her. Cindy raised her gaze toward the ceiling. It was only the first weekend of summer vacation. It was going to be a long three months.

''Sit,'' she said, pointing to the floral-print sofa in the family room. They both sat.

Cindy picked up the duffel bags, walked through the formal living room and into the master bedroom. After Nelson had moved out, she'd redone her room in cream and rose. The heavy oak furniture he favored had been replaced with bleached pine and lacy curtains. She put down the bags and, working quickly, she pulled back the decorative pillows and comforter, then smoothed the sheets. Thank goodness she'd changed them that morning.

When that was done, she approached the two duffel bags. She hated to go through Mike's things, but Jonathan had a point. She couldn't keep a gun in the house with her children. Mike was a bodyguard. It made sense he might carry a weapon with him. Sending out a mental apology, she unzipped the first bag.

Five minutes later, she knew that Mike Blackburne wore only button-fly jeans, had an eclectic taste in reading material, owned one pair of dress shoes and had a passport that had been stamped by every country she'd ever heard of and several that she hadn't. But he didn't carry a gun.

She exhaled the breath she hadn't known she'd been holding. A week ago, her neighbor Grace had asked her to look after her older brother while he recovered from his injuries. After all Grace had done for her, Cindy was pleased to finally have an opportunity to pay her friend back. At the time, however, she hadn't thought looking after Mike would turn her life upside down.

Beth stuck her head in the room. "Darren's ready, if you are." She pointed to the bed. "Where are you going to sleep?"

"Upstairs in the guest room."

"You are so conventional. As my only single friend, I count on you to allow me to vicariously experience the thrill of the mating game. I must tell you, I've been very disappointed in your performance to date."

Cindy pushed her friend from the room. "I'll try to do better."

"Starting when?"

Cindy ignored her. As they passed her children, she said, "We'll be right back."

When they were outside, Beth leaned close. "Are you going to take his clothes off?"

"I hadn't really thought about it."

"Can I watch?"

"I thought I might ask Darren to do that."

Beth pouted. "And you call yourself a friend."

Cindy led the way into Grace's house. Darren was already raising Mike into a sitting position. Even unconscious he looked dangerous. His brown hair was short, with an almost military cut. His muscles were powerful, his body as much a weapon as any firearm. All he owned fit into two duffel bags. She was willing to admit he might be handsome, but he was also lethal. Not just because he knew how to kill, but because he knew how to leave. Cindy had learned early in life that men who left were the most dangerous of all.

Chapter Two

Mike opened his eyes because he could hear breathing. It was faint but there. In the moment before his vision focused, he wondered what he would see. Maybe a nurse. Certainly a stranger. He wouldn't have been too shocked to see the devil himself. Instead, the person next to him was a child. A little girl.

"'Morning," he said and was pleased that his voice worked.

She wasn't very tall or very old. He didn't know enough about children to guess their ages, but figured this one was more than five and less than ten or eleven. She had short blond hair that was curly on the ends and big green eyes. She wore a ribbon in her hair—a blue one that matched her blue-and-white T-shirt. When she smiled at him, he knew exactly who she was—the daughter of that woman. Cindy Jones. The dimples were identical.

"I'm Allison," she said. Her voice was faintly singsongy, and high-pitched. If he'd had a hangover, he would have winced at the sound. But surprisingly, the pounding in his head had reduced from a jackhammer pounding to a dull knocking and he was able to ignore it.

"Hi, Allison. I'm Mike."

"Mommy says you're hurt. That we have to be real quiet while you get better. Mommy said you fell off a building. You shouldn't do that."

"Gee, thanks." Advice always came too late to do any good. He glanced around the room. This wasn't his sister's living room, and if his memory was working any better than his body, it wasn't her bedroom, either. "Where am I?"

"Mommy's room." Allison held a doll clutched to her chest. Her green eyes regarded him solemnly. "She had to go to the store, and she asked me to watch you. You've been sleeping."

"You're watching me?"

She nodded. "I've never watched anyone big before."

He wondered if Cindy had meant for her daughter to stand at his side staring. "You seem a little young to be baby-sitting."

Allison dimpled. "I'm seven. Jonathan's watching TV, and Mrs. Davis is watching us. She was here until a minute ago, but she had to go start her dinner. The front door is open and she screams across the street all the time. Mr. Davis has a seizure if his food isn't on the table at six. But he has other 'deeming qualities." She paused to draw in a breath. "Do you know what 'deeming means?"

"Sorry, no." He didn't know what she was talking about. Or why a seven-year-old had been left in charge of him. He also wondered what day it was and how long he'd been out. He'd arrived on Saturday morning. So today was... "It's Sunday, right?" he asked.

Allison shook her head. "Tuesday. You've been asleep for a long time." She tilted her head. "You say bad words in your sleep. And you get all twisted up in the covers. You had a fever, too. Mommy had to take care of you and I was very quiet."

Tuesday? What the hell happened to Sunday and Monday? He couldn't have been asleep that long. He reached up and rubbed the stubble on his face. Only the innocent stare of the child kept him from grinding out another bad word. He'd been out of it for over seventy-two hours. Then he wondered what else he'd said.

"Could I have a glass of water?" he asked.

She smiled. "I'll get it." She placed her doll on the bed and ran out of the room. "He's awake, and he asked *me* to get him a glass of water," he heard her call as she ran through the house.

Footsteps clattered on the hardwood floor. Mike tried to sit up. His body didn't want to cooperate. He compromised, stuffing a couple of pillows behind his head so he could see more. He did a quick survey of the room. It was spacious, maybe twenty feet square, with a big bay window at one end. The walls were a pale pink, trimmed in cream. The light-colored furniture was large, but simply designed so the big pieces appeared more feminine. An armoire sat across from the foot of the bed. A dresser was next to that. Opposite the window was a doorway that led to a bathroom. Beside the door stood a highboy.

Someone approaching the room interrupted his inspection. The footsteps didn't sound like Allison's so he wasn't surprised when a boy entered the room. He was bigger than his sister and looked older. Something tugged at his memory, the faint impression of the boy prodding him into consciousness.

The kid had blond hair like his sister, but brown eyes.

The shape of his face was different, as well. He must look like his father. Mike glanced around the room again and wondered if Mr. Jones lived elsewhere.

The boy shoved his hands into his shorts pockets. "Can I see the bullet wound?"

Until that moment, Mike had been able to ignore the pulsing pain radiating from his thigh. The memories crashed in on him. The ambush on the rooftop garden terrace, the madness in the assassin's eyes, the sudden slowing of time as Mike had shoved his client to the ground and pulled out the Beretta he carried with him. The assassin's first round had missed, the second had caught Mike in the thigh. Mike had shot the assassin, and had then been attacked by the man's assistant. In the struggle, Mike had gone off the side of the building. He'd taken the assistant with him. The client escaped unharmed, the bill was paid and Mike was left to move on. Only this time it had been to a hospital instead of another job.

He shook his head to clear it and only succeeded in blurring his vision. The kid was still staring at him expectantly. What did he want? Oh, yeah. To see the bullet wound. "Not right now, sport."

The boy's mouth twisted with disgust. "My name's Jonathan. I just want to look."

Allison entered, carefully carrying a glass of water in both hands. Her pale eyebrows drew together in concentration. When he took the glass from her, she smiled proudly. "I didn't spill any."

"Thanks."

He tried to sit up again, but he didn't have a prayer. The spirit might be willing, but his body was still whimpering and broken. He tilted his head forward and drank the water down in four long swallows.

The liquid was cool and about the best-tasting drink he'd had in weeks. When he was done, he sighed and offered the glass back to Allison. Now both kids were staring at him, their mouths open, their eyes big.

"You drink fast," Allison said.

"I guess," he said, feeling vaguely uncomfortable.

"You ever kill anybody?" Jonathan asked.

Allison grabbed her doll and took a step back. Mike set the empty glass on the nightstand and looked at the boy. "No. My job is to protect people. I'm hired to keep my client safe."

"But someone shot you."

"It happens."

"Was it a bad man?" Allison asked. Her voice was soft and concerned. She continued to keep her distance.

"Yes, he was bad," Mike told her. "He's in jail now. He can't hurt anyone again." For some reason, he wanted to reassure the little girl. He didn't like seeing the fear in her eyes. He tried smiling at her. His lips felt dry and his face was tight. Still, it must have worked, because the wary expression faded and she approached the bed again.

"Shelby thinks you're nice," she said shyly.

"Who's Shelby?" He glanced around searching for yet another kid.

Jonathan rolled his eyes. "Allison, don't be such a baby. Stop talking about Shelby. She's not real."

The girl tightened her grip on her doll. She ignored her brother and leaned closer to Mike. "Shelby's my bestest friend in the world. She doesn't like Jonathan and won't let him see her."

Mike didn't know what to make of this. He was saved from having to answer by the sound of a car pulling up the driveway.

"Mommy's home, Mommy's home." Both kids went

flying from the room. Their feet thundered on the wooden floor.

"Stop pushing," Allison ordered.

"Then get out of my way."

"Mo-om, Jonathan's pushing."

"Am not. Quit being such a baby."

"I'm not a baby."

"Are, too! Allie's a baby. Allie's a—"

The voices were abruptly cut off when the back door opened. For the next few minutes, there were only low murmurs, then Mike heard the woman approaching.

She walked into the room and smiled at him. "I'm afraid to ask if you woke up on your own, or if the children are responsible."

"I think it's a little of both."

She bent over the nightstand and pulled open the top drawer. After pulling out a thermometer, she shook it down and placed it under his tongue. She expertly took his pulse, then leaned close and studied his eyes. While she looked at him, he looked at her.

She was as he remembered her. Today she wore a headband to keep her hair off her face, but the color was still light brown and it fell almost to her shoulders. Her eyes were smoky green and the corners of her mouth tilted up. A red T-shirt clung to her breasts. White shorts hugged her hips and exposed long, tanned legs. She didn't look like any nurse he'd ever had, but he wasn't about to complain.

"Your eyes are clear," she said. She touched his forehead, then his cheek with the back of her hand. "You feel cool, too." She removed the thermometer and studied it. "Normal. Finally. So, Mike, how do you feel?"

"Not bad for a guy who fell off a building."

"You've been asleep for three days. According to your

doctor, that's exactly what you needed." There was a shuffling at the door. She glanced over her shoulder. "Jonathan, Allison, your ride for swim team will be here in about fifteen minutes. Go get ready."

He heard footsteps on the stairs and the sound of childish voices. "They don't do anything quietly, do they?"

"Not if there's a way to do it loudly." She perched on the edge of the bed. "I can't tell you how relieved I am to have you awake. I've been worried." Her skin was smooth and slightly tanned. When she smiled, there were faint lines around her eyes. He guessed she was close to thirty.

"Are you a nurse?" he asked.

She laughed. The sweet sound caught him off guard, and he felt himself smiling. It was the second time in less than fifteen minutes. Before now, he probably hadn't smiled twice the entire year.

"Hardly. I teach math at the middle school."

"Excuse me for asking, but if you're not a nurse, what the hell are you doing looking after me in your house? This is your house, isn't it?"

She leaned back against the footboard. After drawing one knee up toward her chest, she clasped her hands around her calf. "I'm friends with your sister Grace. She lives next door." She tilted her head. He recognized it as the same move Allison had made. "Grace has lived here four years. If you're her only brother, how come we've never seen you here before?"

"I don't have much time to see family." Grace was always inviting him. And she made him feel that she really wanted to see him. But Mike could never bring himself to visit. He'd always been a loner. It was easier, and in his profession, safer. "You still haven't explained why you didn't just dump me in the hospital."

"I owe her. My kids get out of school about an hour and a half before I get home. Grace looks after them. She won't let me pay her. I can only buy her so many lunches. When her husband found out he would be spending the summer in Hong Kong, she wanted to go with him. Then you got in touch with her. She didn't know what to do. Going to Hong Kong was the opportunity of a lifetime, but you needed a place to recuperate. That's where I came in. I said I would look after you until you were back on your feet."

"Just like that?"

"Of course. She's my friend." She seemed surprised by the question, as if opening her house to a sick stranger was commonplace.

"What does Mr. Jones think about this?"

Her mouth twisted down at one corner. "I didn't consult him. We're divorced."

"I'm sorry."

"It happens. He left me for a trophy wife."

She leaned forward slightly. The movement caused her shorts to gape slightly by her thigh, exposing a hint of white, lacy panties. Mike told himself he was a bastard for looking and forced himself to concentrate on the conversation.

"Trophy wife? You mean a woman he won somewhere?"

"Exactly. A trophy wife is younger, prettier, blonder. Now that Nelson is successful, he wants someone new to share that with. I'm surprised you're not familiar with the phenomenon. It's very prevalent in the suburbs."

"I've never been in the suburbs before."

"You're in for a treat. It's a different world here. One of four-door cars and families. This is the American dream in progress." Her eyes brightened with humor. "I sometimes think I'm the ultimate cliché." She shifted on the bed and sat cross-legged. It made his knees hurt just to look at her. She held up one hand and began counting off on her fingers. "I'm divorced, and I was left for a younger woman. I'm a teacher, a traditionally female profession. I live in a bedroom community, I drive a minivan, I use coupons and I have two-point-four children."

He folded his arms over his chest and grinned. "Let me guess. The point-four child is Shelby, Allison's imaginary friend."

"You've met?"

"She's met me. I wasn't sure where she was standing."

Their gazes locked. Something leaped between them. Something hot and alive—like electricity. Mike felt warm all over, even though he was practically naked under the sheet. His skin prickled and he had the strangest sensation of taking a step off a bridge, or a building. Only this time, instead of falling, he was suspended there.

Cindy's green eyes darkened as her pupils dilated. Her breathing increased. He could hear the rapid cadence in the silent room. His blood quickened and he felt the second flickering spark of desire around her.

Then, as if someone had snapped his fingers to break the spell, it was gone. They both looked away. Mike didn't know if Cindy was feeling the same sense of loss, but he noticed a splotch of color on each of her cheeks.

She cleared her throat. "The only difference between me and most women in my situation is that I got to keep the house. Aunt Bertha, bless her heart, died and left me enough money to pay down the mortgage, pay off Nelson and refinance. You can't keep a place this big on a teacher's salary."

He didn't know what to say, so he blurted out the first

thing that came to him. "Why did you marry someone named Nelson?"

She laughed. "It's a question I've asked myself again and again." She leaned forward and lowered her voice. "He wasn't much of a husband. Good riddance."

He tried to remember the last time he talked with a woman. Just talked. Not as a prelude to sex, or because they were working together. Except for his phone calls with Grace, he didn't know that he ever had.

"What about you?" she asked. "Ever married?"

"What makes you think I'm not now?"

"Because you would have gone home to her instead of coming to Grace's."

"Good point. No, I've never been married." It wasn't his style. He didn't believe in getting that close.

"And you've always lived in the city?"

He nodded. "I had a place in New York for a while, then I got a lot of work in Los Angeles. I kept an apartment there until it was damaged by the earthquake a couple years back. Since then I've been working steadily and haven't found anywhere I liked."

She stood up. He couldn't help watching the graceful way she unfolded her legs. He'd dated a couple of models while he was in New York, but he didn't like their bony torsos and straight legs. Cindy's calves and thighs curved as if trying to lead a man astray while tempting him to paradise. He grimaced. He was thinking some strange thoughts. Maybe he'd fallen on his head harder than he'd realized.

"You live a very odd life, Mike Blackburne. You're about to get a crash course on how the other half lives," she said. "Welcome to the world of children and Middle America."

A car honked. She walked to the door and yelled, "Allison, Jonathan, your ride is here."

The two children ran down the stairs and over to her. She bent down and kissed them both. "Be good."

They called back that they would, raced across the floor, then slammed the door shut behind them. Cindy drew in a breath. "Ah, blissful silence. You hungry?"

At her question, his stomach rumbled. "I guess so," he said.

"I'll make you some soup." She glanced over her shoulder. "Think you can manage to get to the rest room on your own?"

He eyed the door. "Yeah."

"I have chicken soup with round noodles, noodles shaped like dinosaurs and alphabet noodles."

"You're kidding."

"Obviously you've never had to feed children."

"I guess not. You don't have any plain flat noodles?"

"Sorry. They're not exciting enough."

She was right. He had entered a strange and different world. "Surprise me."

Cindy set the soup bowl on the tray, shifted the water glass over and stared at the crackers. Dry toast might be better. She hesitated for a moment, then figured the man was unlikely to finish what she'd brought him, as it was. She picked up the tray and headed for the bedroom.

Mike was back in bed but sitting up this time with the sheets and blanket bunched around his waist. His hair had been brushed, although he still needed a shave.

"You look pale," she said.

"I just about had to crawl on the return trip but it was worth it." He pointed to the bowl. "What did you decide?"

"Dinosaurs. I thought they would make you big and strong."

The look he shot her told her he wasn't sure if he believed her or not. She bit back a grin. Better for her if she kept him a little off-balance. Having Mike Blackburne in her house wasn't doing much for *her* equilibrium.

She settled the tray over his lap. The wooden legs held it up off his thighs. "Would you rather have juice than water? I didn't think coffee would be a good idea. You need sleep more than anything, and I don't have any decaf."

"I don't drink decaf," he said, picking up a spoon. "The taste of coffee is bad enough, but at least it has caffeine. If it doesn't keep you up, why bother? Water is fine."

He dipped his spoon into the bowl, then stared at the miniature pasta dinosaurs floating in the chicken broth. After a shrug, as if to say "What the hell," he downed a mouthful.

"Tastes the same," he admitted.

"What did you expect?"

"I'm not sure. Maybe little crunchy bones?"

She smiled. "Tomorrow, when you're stronger."

While he ate, she moved around the room, opening the drapes, then smoothing the folded comforter at the foot of the bed. Anything to keep from staring at Mike. It had been easy to take care of him while he was only semiconscious. She'd awakened him enough to get him to swallow his pills and make him drink water, but they hadn't actually spoken before. Sleeping, he'd been good-looking. Awake, he was sinfully handsome and dangerously intriguing.

In an odd way, he reminded her of Nelson. The statistics were the same. Both men had brown hair and brown eyes, and were six feet two inches tall. However, that's where the similarity ended. Nelson's face was ordinary. Glasses hid his eyes, which were his best feature. Her ex-husband was pale, slightly flabby, at least he had been the last time she'd seen him naked, and had the beginnings of a bald spot on the top of his head. His chest was furry to the point of making her wonder if his family tree held the evolutionary missing link.

Mike was broad and strong, tanned with rippling muscles that made her wish he never had to put a shirt on again. His smooth skin made her fingers tingle and her palms itch. He had a strong nose and a square chin. He could have used a couple more inches of hair—she wasn't fond of the military cropped cut—but what was there was thick enough to make him the star of a shampoo commercial. Altogether, he was an impressive male specimen and she didn't know what on earth she was going to do with him. Fortunately, except for helping him get well, nothing was required.

"I unpacked a few of your things," she said, pulling open the top drawer of her dresser and taking out shorts and a T-shirt. "I thought you might like to get dressed."

"That would be great. Maybe later."

When she turned around to look at him, he'd already set the spoon down and was leaning against the pillows. He'd finished all the soup and two of the crackers.

"Do you want some more?" she asked.

"No. I'm weaker than I thought."

"You've been through a lot. What with being shot and all."

He rubbed his chin and grimaced. "You got this funny look on your face when you said that."

"Said what?"

"Shot."

"Not many people around here have much experience with that. We don't get a lot of terrorist activity in the suburbs."

"It's not a lot of fun."

"You've got painkillers," she said, walking toward one of the duffel bags. "Do you want one? And please, don't try to be macho and impress me. I've got children, I'm immune."

"Yeah, okay."

She dug around for the pills, then shook one out onto her palm. "You know, I find it fascinating that you travel with so little luggage. Do you have things in storage somewhere?"

He took the pill from her and downed it with a single gulp of water. After wiping the back of his hand across his mouth, he shook his head. "No furniture or anything. I have my work clothes. Suits, shirts, that sort of thing. I dropped them off at a cleaners in L.A. and he keeps them until my next job. But I don't need a whole lot."

"You're just like my dad. He traveled light, too. If something was too much of a bother, he didn't want it around. It was one of the reasons we never had a dog." She leaned against the footboard post and folded her arms over her chest. She knew men like Mike traveled light emotionally as well as physically. "One day his family got to be too much bother, so he left us behind, too."

Mike grimaced. "That's one of the reasons I never married. In my line of work, it's a mistake."

"You never wanted a home life? Something stable, something of your own?"

"Nope." His brown eyes held hers. "Not my style."

In her heart, she knew exactly what Mike's style would be. He had the looks to turn any woman's head. He would seduce her easily, then move on. He seemed nice enough to issue a warning first, but women too often believed they could change a man, maybe even make him want to stay. Cindy knew better.

"My stepfather was just like my dad," she said. "I guess my mom was attracted to the type."

"Where did that leave you?"

"Alone."

"Is that why you're a teacher with two-point-four children?"

"I guess so. I wanted them to have what I never had. A stable home life. Two parents who really cared about them. I was determined to marry someone sensible. Unfortunately, I picked Nelson." She moved closer to him and reached for the tray.

"Better luck next time," he said.

"Right." Next time she was going to do the leaving so it wouldn't hurt so much. "You're looking pretty tired. Why don't you try and get some rest?"

Mike shook his head. "I was going to tell you I'm fine, but I can't keep my eyes open. I appreciate this, Cindy. I'll get out of here tomorrow."

"Don't be foolish." She started walking toward the door. "According to your doctor, you're going to be here for at least another week. You haven't been any trouble. Besides, it's summer vacation. Having you around keeps the kids from being bored."

She turned back to him. Mike was sprawled out on the pillow, already asleep. A short lock of hair fell over his forehead. His tanned torso contrasted with her pale sheets. The bed and linens had been purchased since the divorce, so Mike was the first male to sleep there.

"Ah, Cindy, you live a wild life," she told herself as she walked into the kitchen. "What would the neighbors think if they knew you had a nearly naked man in your bedroom in the middle of the day?''

The way her luck with men ran, Mike was about as good as it was going to get. She was fooling herself when she said she planned to be the one leaving next time. There wasn't going to be a next time. It was so much easier not to get involved at all.

Chapter Three

Cindy looked up when she heard the knock on her back
door. Beth waved and turned the knob.

"I came by to say hi," Beth said.

"Sure you did." Cindy added the flour mixture into the
wet ingredients and stirred. "You wouldn't be the least
bit interested in how Mike is getting along."

Beth stuck her finger in the bowl and scooped out a
taste. She licked off the batter. "You make the best peanut
butter cookies on the block. You must be adding something I don't know about. And you have to admit, life is
certainly more interesting since your young man came to
stay with you."

"He's not a young man, he's close to forty. He's also
not mine. And to answer the question I see burning in
your eyes, yes, last time I checked he was asleep."

Beth grinned. "Oh, goody!" She slipped off her san-
dals and walked quietly across the floor. "Yesterday he

had his sheet all bunched up around his waist. Do you think it's still like that?''

Cindy rolled her eyes. ''Beth, he's been up and sort of staggering around since then. I doubt he's in exactly the same pose. While we're on the subject, I'm sure he wouldn't appreciate knowing you come to look at him like he's some animal on exhibit at the zoo.''

''Don't be a stick-in-the-mud. How often does a handsome man just fall into our lives? We must take advantage of the situation. Strike while the iron's hot. Seize the day. Begin as—''

''How many more clichés?''

Beth grinned again. ''You don't appreciate me, Cindy. And you should. I'm not just a good friend, I'm highly entertaining.'' She tossed her head, sending her spiked bangs dancing across her forehead, then turned and headed for the bedroom.

It was several minutes before she returned. Cindy had already filled two cookie sheets and stuck them in the oven. She was filling a third when she heard an exaggerated sigh.

''He's incredibly gorgeous.''

She glanced up and saw Beth leaning against the doorway to the dining room. She had a hand pressed against her chest. ''I swear I got palpitations just looking at him. Feel.''

''Thank you, I'd rather not.''

Beth walked over to the kitchen table and pulled out a chair. ''My Lord, how do you stand it? He's just lying there, naked.''

''He's not naked.''

Eyebrows nearly as red as her hair raised slightly. ''How would you know?''

"I put out clean underwear every morning, and it disappears."

"How disappointing." Beth leaned back in the chair and sighed once more. "Still, it's just you and him alone. Night after night."

"The kids are here," she reminded her friend. "You're trying to make this into something it's not. Mike is Grace's brother. I'm doing this for her, not him. As for him being attractive…" Beth looked at her. Cindy held up her hands in a gesture of surrender. "Okay, I'll admit he's pretty good-looking."

"Good-looking? The man could jump-start a person in a coma."

"Beth!"

"Well, he could! I just wish he'd wake up so I could see his eyes. What color are they?"

"Brown."

"Oh."

Cindy looked up from the cookie batter. "You sound disappointed."

"I was hoping for something more exciting. Gray maybe, or a nice—" She broke off and frowned. "You know, there aren't many colors for eyes to be, are there? Okay, brown."

The timer on the oven beeped. Beth stood up. Like Cindy, she was dressed in shorts and a T-shirt. The Houston summer heat required a minimum of clothing, even in the air-conditioned house.

Beth grabbed the pot holders resting on the counter and took the baked cookies out of the oven. She set them on the cooling racks on the edge of the island, then grabbed the filled pans Cindy had prepared.

Cindy smiled. This was one of the things she liked about where she lived. Being friends with her neighbors and sharing time with them. She, Beth and Grace had canned fruit together, baked pies and even prepared holiday dinners. They ran back and forth when ingredients were low, the days too long or something bad happened in their lives. Both women had been there for her when Nelson had walked out. She would never forget that.

Beth closed the oven, then tossed the pot holders on the counter next to the cooling cookie sheets. She grabbed a spatula, slipped a cookie off and picked it up. "Hot!" she said, bouncing it from hand to hand and blowing. When it was cool enough, she took a bite. Her eyes closed and she smiled. "Perfect." She offered half to Cindy.

Cindy tasted the cookie and had to admit, she had a way with peanut butter. She took the glass of water Beth had filled and sipped. "I miss Grace," she said.

"Tell me about it. I miss her, and I miss my kids." Beth returned to the kitchen table and sat down. "I know, I know. I'm the one who couldn't wait for them to leave. They annoy the hell out of me. I mean, they're practically teenagers. That's their job. When they said they wanted to go to camp I was thrilled. But it's only been a few days and the house is so quiet and boring."

Cindy smiled. "I thought you and Darren were going to plan things for the two of you to do."

"We are. It's kind of fun, actually. But I still miss the kids. I guess this is what the empty nest is like. I'll end up like those old women who keep their children's rooms as shrines. Everything in its place."

"I don't think so."

"Yeah, me neither." Beth looked up and shook her finger. "Don't try to trick me into changing the subject. How's it going with Mike?"

Cindy thought about pretending ignorance, but there was no point. Beth was like a bulldog. Once she got hold of something, she never let go. "It's not going anywhere. I don't want it to go anywhere. He's just a houseguest. Grace's brother, nothing more."

"He's a single, good-looking guy."

"I'm not interested in getting involved with him or anyone."

"We only want you to be happy."

"We?" She didn't like the sound of that. She picked up the last two unused cookie sheets and began scooping dough into neat rows. "You and Darren, or you and Grace? You haven't been trying to set me up, have you?"

Beth's eyes widened with exaggerated innocence. "Set you up how? The man fell off a building, Cindy. As much as I want you to have a date, I wouldn't send a man close to death just to get you alone with him."

"I suppose." But she was going to grill Grace the next time she spoke to her.

"It's been two years." Beth wasn't smiling now. Her blue eyes were dark with concern. "It's time to let go."

Cindy shifted uncomfortably. When the cookies were laid out neatly, she dipped a fork into a small bowl filled with flour and began making crisscross marks. "I have let go," she said. "I don't want Nelson back. In the last few months, I realized I hadn't loved him for a while. Even before the divorce. But I thought we would stay together forever. I thought we would be friends and offer a stable home to our children. Dating is so—" She shuddered. "I don't even want to think about it. I'm not ready."

"What are you waiting for?"

"Inspiration." Cindy smiled.

"Someone to fall into your lap, so to speak?"

"Don't start on Mike again. I barely know the man." She set the fork down and faced her friend. "It's not as easy as you think. Not many men want a woman with children. Even if I was interested, where am I supposed to meet these guys? I work at the middle school. I'm surrounded by kids all day. I love my job, but it doesn't make it easy to socialize. It's not as if I'm going to meet some cute man at the water fountain.''

Beth rested her elbows on the table and cupped her chin in her hands. "I see your point. No offense, Cindy, but you're not really the bar type.''

"I agree." She shuddered again. She'd been to a bar once, with a friend from work. Another single teacher. It had been hideous. "Check on Allison and Jonathan, will you?''

"Sure." Beth leaned toward the window. "I can see them playing in the yard. It looks like a game that involves far too much running for the time of day.''

Cindy glanced at the clock on the oven. It was nearly two. "The swim meet is at five. I should probably bring them in to rest for an hour or so." She walked to the window and stared out.

Their house was at the end of the cul-de-sac. Beyond that was a wide expanse of grass and trees with a walking path down the center. The greenbelt was the main reason she and Nelson had bought this particular lot when they'd had the house built. It gave the kids a great place to play. The area was quiet and secluded, safe.

"Don't you ever get tired of being alone?" Beth asked.

"You mean lonely?" Cindy glanced down at her friend. She shrugged. "Sure, but I don't want the kids hurt again. It was hard enough for them when their dad left.''

"Maybe they're not the only ones you're scared about. Maybe you're also worried about yourself.''

"I can't deny that. I've been hurt, too. I'm beginning to think it's easier not to try.''

The timer went off. Cindy moved to the oven and pulled out the cookies. She couldn't imagine herself dating. When would she have time? Nelson only took the kids every other weekend. She wanted them to remember their childhood as happy, not a collection of baby-sitters because their mother was too busy trying to have a social life.

"We've had this conversation before," Beth said.

"Yes."

"You're being very stubborn."

"Probably."

"I care about you because you're my friend."

Cindy set two trays in the oven and set the timer again. "I know you do. I also know you're sweet enough to change the subject."

Beth pursed her lips as if she wasn't going to agree, then she nodded. "Just this once. Now we can talk about Mike some more."

Cindy groaned.

"Darren and I are having a barbecue a week from Saturday. You're invited. Bring Mike."

"What if he doesn't want to come?"

"He has to. Everyone wants to meet him. It will be fun. You'll see. Besides, you have to show him around sometime. You can't imagine the phone calls I've been getting."

Actually, Cindy could. She'd gotten a few of her own. Everyone was curious about "Grace's bodyguard brother." "I can't decide if it's the fact that he's single or if it's his career that has everyone so curious," she said.

"It's both." Beth rose to her feet and walked to the refrigerator. "Is it all right?" she asked, motioning to the door.

"I'm sorry. I should have offered. Grab me a soda, too, please."

Beth pulled out two diet sodas. She handed Cindy one, then popped the top on the other. After taking a long drink, she set it on the counter and began sliding cooled cookies into a plastic container.

"Mary Ellen called to find out if I thought she should offer to cook him meals," Beth said.

Cindy snorted. "Yeah, right. Does this mean she's done having her way with the delivery guy?"

"Probably not. But I would say the affair is winding down. You know how she likes to have someone waiting in the wings."

"Mike is in a weakened condition," Cindy said. She finished spooning out the last of the cookie batter and set the bowl in the sink. "I'm going to have to protect him from Mary Ellen. That brunette bombshell could kill a man."

"That's not all," Beth said. She sauntered over to the sink and turned on the hot water. "Everyone is very intrigued by the fact that he's staying here with you."

"What?" Cindy spun around and turned off the faucet. "What's that supposed to mean?"

"Don't get mad at me. I'm not making up the rumors, I'm just telling you. After all, it's been two years since Nelson left and you haven't been on a single date. Now you have a naked man living in your house."

Cindy leaned against the counter and sighed. "He's not naked," she said weakly, then wondered if it really mattered. She knew how people talked in small communities. Gossip spread faster than fire ants. Nothing was as interesting as what everyone else was doing.

"I hope you're telling everyone he's been injured," she said. "My goodness, he can barely walk to the bathroom unescorted. We're not having wild sex. My children live here.''

"The sex doesn't have to be wild, if that would help."

Cindy just stared at her.

"Fine. Disappoint all your friends. See if I care." Beth squeezed soap into the large mixing bowl and swished it around. When the water was sudsy, she picked up the measuring spoons and cups and dropped them in. She reached for a dishcloth. "It hasn't even been a week, so I'll forgive you for not having had sex yet. But you have to give me something. Have you at least seen him naked?"

"Beth!"

"Oh, please say you have."

"I can't believe we're having this conversation."

Beth looked at her, then at the dishes. "If you see him naked, will you tell me?"

"I'm not going to see him naked."

"But you have to."

"Why?" Cindy stared at her friend. "You've finally slipped over the edge, haven't you? You've lost your fragile hold on reality."

"Of course not. It's just…" Beth drew in a deep breath. "I met Darren in college. I hadn't dated much in high school and he was the first man I, you know, did it with." A spot of color appeared on her cheeks. "I talk big, but the truth is, I've only been with Darren. I've never even seen another man's…" She cleared her throat. "I just want to know what he looks like."

Beth was up to her wrists in soapy water. Cindy took a step closer and gave her a hug. "You're a terrific friend. I was a virgin when I met Nelson, too. So I haven't seen anyone else naked, either."

"It's just so unfair." Beth glanced at her, blue eyes

dancing. "Men see women naked all the time. It's in magazines, in the movies. Maybe we should take advantage of that for the next school fund-raiser. We could hire men to walk around naked. Think of the cover charge to get in. It could be a couple hundred dollars. We could buy a lot of sports equipment with that."

Cindy released Beth and stepped back. "You *are* crazy."

"It's a great idea."

"No."

Beth finished washing the measuring cups and rinsed them. "Can I at least go check and see if Mike really has on underwear?"

"No."

"But if I peel the covers back slowly, he won't even—"

"No! I mean it, Beth."

"You're no fun." She rinsed her hands and grabbed a towel.

"Where are you going?"

"Home."

Cindy walked Beth to the door. "You want some cookies?"

"Save them for Mike. He'll need his strength to survive around here. Don't forget. Next Saturday. Say, six o'clock?"

"I'll ask him, but if he doesn't want to come, I can't make him."

"Of course you can. Bat your eyes. If that doesn't work, try a low-cut T-shirt."

"Sorry, they're all like this." She fingered the neckline of her crewneck shirt.

"So disappointing. If you're not going to be a little more wild, I might have to find another single friend."

Before Cindy could answer, Beth gave her a hug. "Take care of yourself and that hunk of yours."

"I will."

As Beth crossed the street, Cindy glanced around the house toward the greenbelt. About eight children were playing together in the shade of a pecan tree. She wondered where they got their energy. It was about ninety-four degrees and the humidity was nearly that high. Just standing in the open doorway was making her sweat.

She stepped inside and shut it behind her. The timer on the oven dinged.

After taking out the last batch of cookies, she put a couple of cool ones on a plate, then poured a glass of lemonade. A quick glance at the clock told her it was almost time for Mike to wake up. In the last couple of days, they'd settled into a routine. He slept for an hour in the morning, then right after lunch. He spent his afternoons reading or watching TV. Every day he was getting a little stronger, but he wasn't going to be back at work anytime soon.

She carried the plate and glass into the bedroom. He was sitting up against the pillows.

"I thought you'd still be asleep."

"Oh, really? But the conversation you and your friend were having was so interesting."

She started to set the plate down, then froze. Heat burned her cheeks as embarrassment flooded her. "You heard us?" she asked, her voice a squeak.

"I don't know if I heard all of it, but I heard enough." He studied her. "I never knew what women talked about when they were alone. I think it was better that way."

She cleared her throat. After setting the plate and glass on the nightstand, she brushed her hands against her shorts. Her conversation with Beth had been completely innocent, she reminded herself. And private. It wasn't his business.

Except Beth *had* asked about seeing him naked.

Cindy glanced at his bare chest, then raised her gaze higher to his face. He'd shaved that morning, although he hadn't had the strength to stand. She'd had to bring a chair into the bathroom for him. She could see the strong lines of his face and the slight tilt at the corner of his mouth. One eyebrow raised expectantly. She didn't know if he was annoyed or mad.

"It's Friday," she said at last. "If it makes you feel any better, on Monday we generally discuss women being naked. We try to be fair about it."

Mike grinned. Cindy returned his smile, her relief tangible.

"Beth sounds like a scary lady," he said.

"She's really very nice. Oh, did you hear about the barbecue?"

"Just a word here and there." He'd been asleep until a strange woman had tiptoed into his room. Their conversation had carried to him in the quiet house, although when they ran water in the kitchen, it drowned out the sound of their voices.

"Everyone will want to meet you," she said. "You're something of a local celebrity. Not just because you're Grace's brother, but what with your work and the injuries..."

He remembered his sister's instructions to be nice to her friends. "I'll go," he said, and knew he would hate everything about the evening.

"It's not until a week from Saturday. I'm sure you'll be better."

"I hope so." He flexed his sore leg and winced.

"I need to change the bandage," she said.

He nodded and flipped back the covers. Cindy went into the bathroom and came back with a small box containing her supplies. She took her nursing very seriously. As he scooted over to give her more room, she settled on the edge of the mattress. He grabbed his leg below the healing bullet wound and raised it while she slipped a towel underneath.

"We're getting to be quite a team," he said.

"Practice." Her hands were small but sure. She gave him a quick, apologetic glance, then carefully removed the bandage.

She studied the hole in his thigh. It was sort of lumpy and still red but it wasn't infected and didn't bleed anymore.

"I think it's better," she told him.

He leaned back as she continued her treatment. Over the smell of disinfectant, he caught the fragrance of her perfume. In the last four days, he'd accepted the fact that she was only ever going to wear shorts and a T-shirt around him and that he'd better get used to long honey-colored legs taunting him at every turn. He wondered how men in the suburbs got anything done with all these half-naked women around. Maybe they became immune, or didn't bother noticing. If so, they were fools.

Having Cindy bend over his injury, with her light brown hair falling loose and her face all scrunched up with concentration, was the best part of his day. Her friend across the street might be all hot to see him naked, but he didn't think Cindy ever noticed he wasn't wearing anything but briefs. To her, he was simply Grace's brother. Almost a eunuch.

Of course, if he kept noticing the way her breasts moved, she would soon have proof he was very much a man. Instead of indulging himself, he forced his thoughts elsewhere. In the last four days he'd learned two things. First, Sugar Land, Texas, wasn't like anywhere he'd ever been before. Even sleeping half the day away, he sensed the difference. Second, Cindy Jones wasn't for him. He might admire her legs, and the way she filled out her shirt, but she was as off-limits as his best friend's wife. If he had a best friend. She'd just admitted she'd only been with one man in her life. He'd never dated anyone for more than a month. He didn't believe in relationships, she needed to be married.

She applied a fresh bandage. "The kids are outside playing," she said and stood up. She reached for the pair of jeans she'd folded earlier and placed on the footboard. "If you can get dressed and out to the family room before they come inside, that means you get to control the TV remote. If you don't, they have the power."

He shuddered at the thought. "Do you know what's in those cartoons?"

"Yes, that's why I try to be out of the room." She tossed him the jeans, then bent over his duffel bag and dug out a T-shirt. "Think of it as your aerobics exercise for the day. A race for the remote control."

His heart was already getting a workout, he thought, watching the way the fabric of her shorts pulled tight around her derriere. The feminine curves tempted him. He didn't know what the problems had been in her marriage, but he was willing to bet her husband hadn't left because he wanted someone better-looking. If Mike was wrong, her husband was a fool.

Cindy tossed him a T-shirt then started for the door. Before she left, she glanced back at him. "About Beth," she said, then nibbled on her lower lip. "She's just talking. She tries to be very worldly and all, but she's in love with her husband. She'd never actually do anything."

"I know."

"I just didn't want you to think that she was like that."

"Maybe when I meet her, I should offer her a quick look."

Cindy laughed. "Only if I can be there to see the expression on her face."

"Deal."

"Get dressed, eat your snack, then head for the family room. The kids will be outside for another half hour or so."

With that, she left. He found it humorous that she would tend to the wound on his thigh but she always left him alone to dress. She treated him with amused tolerance. He couldn't remember the last time he'd joked with someone, or bothered to relax. He'd been working too hard, without a break between jobs.

If nothing else, this forced time off would give him a chance to regroup. As soon as he was able, he could move into Grace's house. Once there, he would think about what it was he wanted to do with his life. His recent encounter with death had him wondering about different career options. He was pushing forty. Next time he might not be so lucky.

He grabbed his jeans and started to slip them on his good leg. Before he'd pulled them up past his knee, there was a scream from outside.

"Mommy, Mommy, Allie's been hurt."

"Allison!"

Mike heard Cindy race through the house, open the front door and call for her daughter. He jerked on the jeans, and about lost his balance when his head started to swim. He grabbed the footboard and held on. The room twirled and darkened, then slowly returned to normal. He pulled the trousers up over his hips and quickly fastened the buttons. He started out the door in a slow shuffling step.

Pain radiated from his bullet wound. Darkness nipped at the edges of his vision. He could hear conversation and someone crying. As he reached the entryway, Cindy came in carrying Allison in her arms.

The little girl was sobbing. She clung to her mother as blood oozed from a scrape on her knee. Behind them, Jonathan and a couple of other kids he didn't know trailed in. Cindy looked up and saw him.

"Mike, could you bring that box of medical supplies into the kitchen, please?" Before he answered, she looked over her shoulder. "Billy and Ashley, you're going to have to go home now. Jonathan, shut the door."

Mike headed for the bathroom. By the time he got to the kitchen, he was breathing hard and hanging on to walls for support. Jonathan stood by the entrance to the family room, just watching. Cindy had settled on one of the kitchen chairs, with Allison's injured leg propped up on the one next to it. Using a damp washcloth to wipe away the dirt, Cindy cleaned the still-bleeding wound.

Mike shuffled forward and placed the first-aid kit on the table. Cindy glanced up at him. Her green eyes widened. "You look like you're going to pass out. Take a seat."

He sank onto the chair across from hers.

Allison's cries had quieted to sniffles, but she still kept her face buried in her mother's neck. She winced as the washcloth touched her scrape.

"Hush, baby girl," Cindy murmured. "It's going to be all right."

She reached for the antiseptic and dampened a cotton ball. Mike flinched, knowing what was coming. He'd treated some bad wounds before, but those had been on adults. This was seven-year-old Allison who came to visit him every morning and told him about her imaginary friend, Shelby. He hated to see her face streaked with tears.

"Take a deep breath," Cindy warned, then touched the cotton to the scrape. Allison shook all over. She sucked in another breath, then let it out in a hiccuped sob.

"I know," her mother told her. "Almost done. You're going to be fine, although I don't think you'll be swimming this afternoon."

"Can I still have cookies?" Allison asked, then sniffed.

"Sure." Cindy opened a bandage and placed it over the scrape. After smoothing it in place, she hugged her daughter close.

Mike stared at the pair. He felt something odd inside. A hollowness, as if he was just now noticing a piece that had been missing from his life for a long time. The ache felt old and bitterly familiar. It came from being on the outside looking in.

As Cindy held her child and rocked her, light brown hair fell over blond. Her voice was soft as she hummed tunelessly. He could hear Allison's breathing calm.

The girl opened her eyes and looked at him. A single tear dripped onto her mother's shoulder.

"Better?" he asked.

Allison nodded.

It was as if a giant fist were squeezing his heart. Maybe it was seeing all he'd never had. Not just the house, although his family had been poor. He'd grown up in a one-bedroom apartment, sleeping on the sofa, or the floor of his mother's room if she was entertaining. He'd always felt passed over in the business of her life. First she'd been working so much, then she'd remarried and had

Grace. Her new child had claimed her time. Funny, he'd never blamed his half sister for that.

Watching Cindy hold Allison reminded him of all he'd missed. The caring, the bond between a mother and child. The love. Until that moment, he'd forgotten the emotion even existed.

Chapter Four

Mike braced his hands against the tiled wall of the shower and let the hot water run over him. He breathed in deeply, noticing it didn't hurt so bad to inhale. Pretty soon he would be able to cough and sneeze like a normal person.

When he'd rinsed the shampoo from his hair, he reached for the bar of soap and lathered it leisurely. As he rubbed the bar over his body, he noted which parts still hurt like hell and which were healing. The bullet wound would take the longest. The entry hole was just about closed, but the exit wound was still nasty looking. In the next day or so, he was going to have to start rehabilitation. As he rinsed off the soap, he grimaced. Rehabilitation was a fancy way of saying he would spend the next three months sweating in a gym, slowly bringing his torn and injured muscles back to normal.

He turned slowly under the spray, then pushed in the

knob to turn off the water and stepped out of the shower. The bathroom was large enough that the steam simply floated away. The wide mirror opposite didn't fog up. Instead, it reflected his image clearly. He snapped up the towel he'd left hanging on the hook and ran it over his chest and arms. After passing it over his legs, he rubbed his hair, then wrapped the towel around his waist.

Mike limped toward the double sinks. Cindy had left his shaving kit next to the one on the left, so that's where he brushed his teeth and shaved.

The silence of the house sounded odd on this weekday morning. Usually, one or both of the children were inside playing, running or shrieking. He'd grown used to dozing between the calls of various games or the thunder of feet on the stairs. Cindy tried to keep them quiet when he was resting, but he'd quickly learned that a grown-up's and a child's definition of quiet were extremely different.

He'd had a bad night, with the pain keeping him awake, even after he'd taken his pills. As he bent over the sink and splashed shaving cream off his face, he felt the twinge in his leg. It was better today. He'd been shot before so he knew the drill. There would be bad moments, and good ones. Eventually, it healed and only the weather would remind him of the injury.

This morning, Cindy had taken the children to the grocery store with her. Mike had asked her to pick up a few things for him. He wondered if she was getting tired of nursing him, but every time he mentioned leaving, she insisted he stay until he was more mobile. He didn't mind being here. The kids were kind of fun and Cindy was prettier than any nurse he'd ever had. Between her shorts and those snug T-shirts she wore, he was about ready to—

The sound of the doorbell cut through his thoughts. He finished wiping his face, then limped to the front door.

The marble tiles in the entryway were cold on his bare feet. The beveled-glass window in the wooden front door allowed him to see the shape of the person on the other side, but not her features. He turned the lock and pulled open the door.

The woman in front of him was in her sixties. Despite the already rising temperature of the Houston summer morning, she was wearing a long-sleeved dress in a blue-and-green floral print, with a little straw hat on her head. Tight gray curls marched across her forehead. A purse hung over her left forearm and she was clutching a clipboard to her chest.

"Yes?" Mike asked when the woman didn't say anything.

She stared. Her small blue eyes widened and her mouth opened. There wasn't any sound.

"Were you looking for Mrs. Jones?" he asked.

The woman nodded. She was short, maybe an inch over five feet, with the matronly roundness of a grandmother. Her face paled, until the powder she was wearing seemed colorful by comparison.

"Is she here?" the woman asked, her voice high-pitched and shaking. Her gaze, which had swept over him thoroughly, now settled on his bare feet.

"Not right now. She's at the grocery store. I expect her shortly. May I give her a message?"

"And you are?"

He frowned. "A friend."

"I see." With that, she handed him a sheet of paper. At the top, a banner reminded the reader of the annual blood drive at the local church. "If you could give this to her, please."

Mike glanced down at the towel he was wearing and

groaned silently. Damn. He was flashing the local church lady.

"Ah, ma'am? Cindy, ah, Mrs. Jones, is a friend of my sister's. I was recently injured on the job and she's been taking care of me. It's not what you think."

The woman turned smartly and started down the walkway, never once looking back. He thought of continuing his explanation, then figured she wouldn't believe him, anyway. He swore again.

Before he could close the door, he heard a call from across the street. As he looked up, he saw a woman standing in her front yard. She had short, dark red hair and the kind of chest that made a man act like a fool.

"Hello," the woman called. "You must be Mike. I'm Beth, Cindy's friend. How are you feeling?"

Beth? The same Beth who had wanted to see him naked? "Fine," he called back.

"I see you're up and around."

And flashing the neighborhood. "Yes. Thanks. See you soon." As he closed the door, he had the fleeting thought that he could solve Beth's problems by dropping the towel, but then figured she would like it too much. As he made his way back to the bedroom, he wondered how he was going to explain the incident with the church lady to Cindy.

By the time Cindy and the kids returned, he'd pulled on jeans and a shirt. He carried in one load of groceries, then had to sit down before his leg gave out.

Allison set a sack of potatoes on the table in front of him and smiled shyly. "Shelby says you're going to get sick again if you do too much."

"Tell Shelby she's a very smart little girl."

Allison dimpled.

"How are you feeling?" Cindy asked as she carried in

the last armful of groceries. Jonathan trailed behind her, shutting the doors of the minivan.

"I'm going out to play," he said, hovering by the back door.

"Me, too," Allison added. Her knee was better with only a small bandage covering the worst of the scrape.

"Go ahead," Cindy said, then laughed as they closed the door. "They'll do anything to avoid putting away the groceries. Even play outside in the heat."

"They do that, anyway," he said.

"You're right." She glanced around at the kitchen. "Do you think we have enough food?"

He followed her gaze. The countertops were in the shape of an L. Bags of groceries covered the white surface. There were twelve-packs of soda, cartons of detergent and double packs of cereal.

"Expecting a famine?" he asked.

She chuckled. "It's triple-coupon day. You should have seen the lines. And soda was on sale, along with a great cut of meat. The grocery store does this a couple of times in the summer. I suppose it's to get people out in the heat."

Money was tight. He should have figured that out already. She'd explained that most divorced women couldn't afford to keep their houses. "How much do I owe you for what I've eaten?"

She placed her hands on her hips and glared at him. He supposed she was trying to intimidate him, but all she did was draw her shirt tighter over her breasts. He'd already had two highly erotic dreams about her. He looked away and forced himself to think of something else.

"I was making conversation, not hinting," she said. "I could feed you for a month and not even get close to what your sister has given my kids in snacks and meals. So I don't want to hear another word about paying me for your food."

"Yes, ma'am." He rose to his feet. "At least let me help put the groceries away."

"Don't be silly. You'll fall flat on your butt." She leaned over the table and pushed on his chest. He was still tired from carrying in two bags, so he didn't argue. He took the glass of juice she offered and watched her put away the food.

She moved around the kitchen with graceful ease. Her movements were almost a dance, the smooth lifting and bending. She kicked off her shoes and he saw she painted her toenails pale pink. Her shorts were red and her T-shirt had a drawing printed on the front that proclaimed her to be Queen of Everything. Small gold hoops dangled from her earlobes and a red headband held her hair off her face.

He supposed there was nothing unusual about Cindy Jones. In this neighborhood, hundreds of women just like her wore T-shirts and bare feet as they put away groceries. Yet, he'd never sat in a kitchen and observed the ritual.

She pulled three pink-paper-wrapped packages out of a bag and sighed. "Pork roast, roasted potatoes and salad. My favorite meal."

"Sounds great."

She placed two of the packages in the freezer and one in the refrigerator, then tossed him the empty bag to fold. "It is. Nelson never appreciated my cooking. He often wanted to go out. But I like eating at home. Which do you prefer?"

Mike was startled by the question. "I don't cook much."

"Of course you wouldn't when you're with a client or subject or whatever you call them. But what about when you're off work? Or did you leave that for your lady friends?''

''Sometimes women cook for me.''

She was putting away cereal, raising herself on tiptoe and sliding the new boxes behind the old. As she came down on her heels, she glanced at him and smiled.

''Why is it men can take care of themselves perfectly well when they're alone, but the first second they live with a woman, they suddenly become helpless?'' she asked.

''I've never lived with a woman.''

The smile faded as her eyebrows drew together. ''Really? I knew you hadn't been married, but I just assumed...'' Her voice trailed off. She reached into the full bags on the kitchen table and drew out canned beans.

Until she questioned him, he hadn't really thought about it. ''My life-style isn't conducive to long-term relationships.''

''I guess not.'' She reached in the bag for more canned goods. ''No roommates?''

''I told you I travel light.''

''Ah, yes. Extra baggage weighs you down. Fight hard, fight lean.'' She paused and shrugged. ''For a long time I blamed the marines when my father left, but as I grew older, I saw that lots of other officers managed to balance a career and family. They were terrific fathers.'' She looked in the bags on the table, then picked one up and started folding it. Her green eyes focused on something above his head. ''When my father missed an important event at school or forgot my birthday, I used to wish one of the other families would adopt me. My friend Lorraine had a wonderful family. Warm, loving, everything I wanted. I remember thinking it wasn't fair.''

Mike was startled when he realized he could picture Cindy as a child. She would look a little like Allison, only

The Bodyguard & Ms. Jones

her eyes would be dark with pain. "Life's not fair," he said.

"I figured that one out on my own," she said. "Although I still thought I could make it fair when I married Nelson."

She finished folding the bag and slipped it into an open one, then moved to the long counter and started putting away fresh vegetables.

"Why did you get married?" he asked.

"The usual reasons."

"Which are?"

She looked at him over her shoulder. "You don't know?"

"I never married. Never saw the need." Or felt the compulsion. He liked women. Sex was great, but aside from that, he didn't get the point. Why would anyone want to share quarters with someone else? He'd heard the fights, listened to his buddies complain. It was better to be alone. It was certainly easier.

"You ever been in love, Mike?" she asked.

"No." He didn't want to think about the loving part. That was the one piece of the puzzle that eluded him. Without wanting to, he remembered Cindy holding Allison in her arms after the little girl had been injured. The child had clung with the trust of someone who knows they're loved and will be taken care of. Cindy hadn't asked for anything in return, she'd simply given. He believed love existed—he'd seen it. It just didn't live in his world. He hadn't loved anyone, and no one had ever loved him, except maybe his sister.

She leaned against the counter and tilted her head to one side. "It's lovely. Your heart beats fast, your palms get all sweaty."

"Sounds like the flu."

"Funny. When I first met Nelson, I just knew he was the one."

"Because you felt all tingly inside?" The question was meant to come out sarcastic, but instead he sounded curious. And he was.

"Actually, no. That should have been my first clue. With Nelson, the love grew more slowly. I was attracted to him because he was so different from me. His family has lived in Houston for three generations. He was stable. Until college, he'd never been out of the state. I thought he was the answer to my prayers. I was wrong on that one."

"I'm sorry."

"Me, too, but it's done. I'm going to do the best I can with my kids. They're going to have everything I didn't. Stability, a sense of continuity. A chance to grow up in one place. That's one of the things I like about living here. I know our neighbors, and they know us."

Mike had lived in his L.A. apartment for five years and hadn't known even one of his neighbors. Of course, he was gone a lot, but even if he'd come home every night, he still wouldn't have made friends with anyone. He preferred to be alone.

"This is a different world for me," he said.

"I'm sure it is. Minivans, schools, churches on every corner."

Damn. He'd forgotten. "Cindy, some lady came by while you were out and left you something." Using the table for leverage, he pushed to his feet, then limped toward the foyer. The sheet of paper was where he'd left it on the hall tree. He limped back and handed it to her.

She scanned the flier. "I'm glad she stopped by. I'd nearly forgotten." She grinned at him. "I guess you don't have any blood to spare."

"Not this week. Ah, Cindy, I didn't think when she rang the doorbell."

Her eyes widened. "Oh, Lord, you didn't pull a gun on her, did you? Was she about five feet tall, kind of round with gray curls and wearing a hat?"

"That's her and no, I didn't threaten her with a gun."

"Thank goodness. Miss Vanmeter is one of the most conservative members of the church. She's a spinster and not very forgiving of us 'young people,' as she calls anyone under forty."

He swallowed and leaned against the island for balance. "I'd just gotten out of the shower. I was shaving. I came to the door in my towel. I didn't mean to flash the church lady."

Cindy covered her mouth with her hand, but he could tell she was giggling. "The woman won't go to a movie that isn't rated G. I'm sure she'd never seen a naked man in her life."

"I wasn't naked. I was wearing a towel."

"It was probably the highlight of her year."

"She thinks we're living together."

That sobered her up. "Oh, my. Okay. I'll call the church secretary and explain." She drew in a breath. "I've never been involved in a scandal before."

"There's more."

"The towel fell off? She made a pass at you?"

"I met Beth. She was standing in her yard while Miss Vanmeter was avoiding eye contact. We waved and said hello. Actually, she's the one I thought about flashing."

"Oh, I hope you didn't. She would have enjoyed it too much."

"That's what I thought."

Light color stained her cheeks. Little lines crinkled by her eyes. He was close enough that he could inhale the faint scent of her perfume. He liked the fragrance, and the way her laughter made him want to smile. He lived in a world of shadows, dodging death and trying to outwit assassins. Cindy lived in a world of normalcy and light.

Without thinking, he reached out and touched the tip of her nose. "I'm sorry for making trouble with Miss Vanmeter."

Electricity arced up his arm, through his chest and settled low in his belly. He couldn't pull away fast enough. Cindy's humor faded and she caught her breath as if she, too, had been burned.

He backed up and took his seat at the table. She continued to put away groceries. They talked, but the connection had been broken, severed by a physical awareness he couldn't shake.

"I should probably be leaving," he said. Usually, he couldn't wait to get away, but this time, even though he mouthed the words, he didn't want to move out of Cindy's house. Which meant it was past time to go.

"You can't even carry two bags of groceries in from the car," she said, opening the refrigerator and putting away margarine. "Wait until Monday. That's another four days away. If you try to do too much before you're ready, you'll just end up sick again."

She had a point. "Okay, I'll leave Monday."

She tossed him another empty bag, then leaned against the counter and folded her arms over her chest. "The kids are going to miss you."

"Why?"

"You play games with them, watch those horrible cartoons and tell them great stories. Why wouldn't they miss you?"

He wasn't sure that anyone had ever missed him before.

"They've been coming in my room," he said. "I wasn't trying to—"

She held up her hands, palms out. "You don't understand. The fact that they're going to miss you is a good thing. It means they like you."

"Oh. I like them, too." He frowned. He liked children? When had that happened?

"Don't look so concerned. I'm sure it will wear off. Soon we'll all be a distant memory."

"How long has Allison had Shelby?"

"Since about six months after Nelson and I separated." Cindy carried the cartons of detergent into the laundry room, then closed the door. "It was about the time I told her that her daddy and I were getting divorced." She bent down and reached into one of the cupboards. After pulling out a tall machine, she set it on the counter, then added tea leaves and water. She flipped the switch. "I've spoken to a counselor about it. I even took Allison in a couple of times. The woman told me it was pretty normal. When Allison is ready, she'll let her imaginary friend go. In the meantime, it gives her some security."

She pulled out the chair across from his. "I never had an imaginary friend, so it doesn't make sense to me."

"Allison is a good kid."

"You know this because you've had so much experience?"

"I know people."

She sighed. "I hope you're right. She's my baby girl. I just want her to be happy."

He wanted to comfort Cindy, but he didn't have any words. Nor did he want to risk touching her again. Lusting after her in the privacy of his own mind was one thing, touching her was quite another. Besides, she'd felt the spark, too, and the last thing either of them needed was the messy entanglement of a relationship.

The sound of the tea machine was loud in the silence. Cindy bit her lower lip. The ringing of the phone rescued them both.

She jumped up and grabbed the portable from its cradle mounted on the wall. "Hello?"

He watched as her concern faded and she smiled. "Grace! Are you really in Hong Kong? This is an amazing connection." She paused, then winked at Mike. "He's doing great. When I came home from the market, he was bench-pressing the sofa in the family room." She listened. "Uh-huh. No, it's going fine. He hasn't been any trouble. He's right here. Why don't you talk to him yourself?"

He took the phone. As usual, before he could say hello, Grace was off and running.

"Michael? Are you okay? I called last week, but Cindy said you were pretty out of it. If I'd known you were hurt that badly, I would have stayed home. When I visited you in the hospital, you made it sound like a scratch."

He eyed the outline of the bandage visible through his jeans. "It is a scratch. It just happens to go through to the other side."

"Eeewww, that's gross." He could picture Grace wrinkling her nose. His sister looked nothing like him. She was short and blond, with bright blue eyes. He didn't care that they had different fathers or that she was almost ten years younger than he. She was the closest thing to family that he had. Being around Cindy and her kids made him realize that was important.

"Are you being nice to Cindy?" Grace asked.

"Of course. I'm very polite." He glanced at the subject of their conversation. She was pulling out bread and luncheon meat for sandwiches.

"That's not what I mean and you know it. She's very sweet and she deserves better than being dumped by her husband. So look out for her. Also, don't hide out all the time. Go outside. Sit in the sun."

"It's nearly a hundred degrees here," he reminded her. "The humidity is almost as high."

"Stop whining. I'm just saying you shouldn't stay in the house alone all the time. My friends are going to be checking on you. Be nice."

The doorbell rang. Cindy left the kitchen.

"I'm going to want a full report when I get back," Grace said.

"From me or your friends?"

She laughed. "Both. By the way, what do you think of Cindy?"

The curiosity in her tone belied the casualness of the question.

"Grace," he growled.

"She's very pretty," she went on, ignoring him. "Smart, a great mother. I think you'll like her."

"She's amazingly virtuous," Mike agreed. "But I'm too old to be set up with one of your friends. I'm fine. Go back to your husband and run his life."

"Mike!"

"Say goodbye, Grace."

"I'll call next week. I love you. Bye."

With that, the line went dead. He stared at the portable phone for several seconds before pushing the off button. She always said the same thing at the end of every conversation.

"I love you."

How easily she spoke the words. As if saying them was simple. As if the thought of love was something she could grasp.

He stood up and limped to the wall, then hung up the phone. He wondered if Cindy knew Grace was matchmaking. Not that it was going to make a difference. Cindy wasn't his type. Hell, he didn't have a type.

Cindy walked into the kitchen and handed him a business card. He glanced at the small pink card and frowned. "What's this?"

"Mary Ellen is our local representative for this line of cosmetics." She pointed to the gold-embossed name curling across the card. "Her company has just started a line of men's skin-care products, and she stopped by to offer you a free facial."

"Why?"

Cindy returned to the refrigerator and pulled out jars of mayonnaise and mustard. "You're a single, good-looking guy, and Mary Ellen is…" She looked at him. "Let's just say I wouldn't recommend turning my back on her if I were you."

He tossed the card on the table as if it had burned him. "This is a scary place."

"Sorry, Mike. You'd better get used to it. Face it, you're about the most exciting thing to happen around here since they filmed a toilet-paper commercial at the local grocery store. You've got a very romantic profession, you've been shot. All the maternal types want to baby you, the single women want to marry you, the unfaithful wives want to sleep with you. You're a hot commodity."

He almost asked what *she* wanted. But that would have been stupid. He was occasionally a jerk, but he rarely acted without thinking. "I feel like a minnow in a pool of piranhas."

"Not a bad analogy." She picked up two packages of luncheon meat. "Roast beef or turkey?"

"Beef."

"Don't worry," she told him. "Somehow I think you can take care of yourself."

"We're about to find out. I don't even know the rules here."

"They're simple. I'll explain them as I go. Rule number one—don't wear a towel when you answer the door."

"So it's better to be naked?"

She grinned. "It would certainly be memorable. Although you might want to wear clothes to the barbecue Saturday. After all, Beth is going to be there."

He shuddered. "I'm counting on you to protect me."

She tore off several pieces of lettuce and handed them to him. "Go wash these, please."

As he took them, their hands brushed. The electricity leaped between them again. Their gazes locked for a moment, then they both looked away. Cindy might be willing to protect him from Beth, but who was going to protect him from himself?

Cindy stood in the upstairs guest room and studied her outfit in the mirror. It was only eight-thirty on Saturday morning, but she was up, had showered and put on makeup and was now trying to decide what to wear. She hated herself for caring.

"It doesn't matter," she said out loud. "He's not even going to get out of the car."

It wasn't as if she wanted Nelson back. She wasn't trying to impress him. It was just a matter of pride. She glanced at the clock and swore. She'd wasted the better part of an hour trying to look her best, when Nelson was simply going to honk the horn. She was a fool. Worse, she was pathetic.

With that, Cindy stuck her tongue out at her reflection

and left the room. She turned right and walked to the two bedrooms at the end of the hall. There was a bathroom between them. Both doors stood open.

"Are you guys about ready?" she asked.

Allison stepped out of her closet. "I'm packed, Mommy, but Shelby doesn't want to go. She likes Mike and wants to stay with him."

"It's important for you to see your father," Cindy said. "I'm sure Shelby would miss you if she stayed behind."

"Shelby will come with me," Allison said quickly, her green eyes widening. "She was just wondering if we could stay home this one time."

"Sorry." Cindy moved into the room and checked her daughter's suitcase. "You have a toothbrush in there?"

"I still have to brush my teeth."

"Then go do it."

Cindy moved through the bathroom, into the second bedroom. Allison's room was all ruffles and lace with stuffed animals filling the corners. Jonathan's room was spare by comparison. He kept most of his sports equipment in the garage. The built-in shelves in the closet kept his toys tidy. On his ninth birthday, Cindy had bought him a computer and several software programs. It sat on the desk in front of the window and that's where he spent a lot of his time.

"Are you packed?" she asked.

Jonathan didn't look up from the screen. "Uh-huh. I packed my toothbrush. You don't have to ask."

"Good." She bent down and kissed her son's head. "You have a good time with your dad. Be polite to him and to Hilari."

Jonathan put down the joystick and looked up at her. Brown eyes, Nelson's eyes, stared at her. "She's just a dumb old girl," he said.

She smiled. "I love you, too."

With that, she left the room. She hated alternate weekends. First there was the rush of getting the children ready, and then they were gone. She couldn't even spend her morning cleaning up the kitchen. Nelson took the kids out to breakfast, so she didn't have to prepare anything.

She walked down the stairs, turning at the landing in the middle and following the staircase that led to the kitchen. The stairs were in the shape of an upside-down Y, with one leg leading to the living room and the other going to the kitchen. The smell of coffee greeted her.

"I hope you don't mind," Mike said, motioning to the already full pot.

"I think it's wonderful." She poured herself a cup, then glanced at the plastic containers, bowls and frying pan. "Are you cooking?"

"Pancakes. It's about the only thing I can make well."

"Sounds great."

He'd been in the house nearly two weeks and mobile for about nine days, but she still wasn't used to coming downstairs and seeing him in the kitchen. For one thing, he was too good-looking. A man like him should be saved for special occasions. She was used to something slightly more ordinary in her everyday life.

Now that his bullet wound had almost healed, he'd replaced his jeans with shorts. While she admired the tanned expanse of muscled leg, she wished he would go back to the denim. It was easier to concentrate when he wasn't so exposed.

He motioned to the empty bowl. "I don't know how many to make."

"I can probably force myself to eat four small ones," she said.

"What about the kids?"

She put her coffee on the counter and shrugged. "They won't be eating with us. It's their weekend to go with their father."

"And you're leaving, too?"

"No, why?"

"You're sort of dressed up."

She stared at the shorts and shirt she'd put on. The silk outfit had been on sale, otherwise she wouldn't have bought it. She was wearing makeup and she usually didn't bother. Her hair was curled. No wonder Mike thought she was going somewhere.

"Ignore me," she said.

He moved close to her. "What's wrong?" he asked.

The overhead lights caught the various shades of brown in his hair. The colors ranged from dark blond to gold to chestnut. His military cut was growing out. In another couple of weeks he would pass for a civilian. His T-shirt emphasized his strength. She desperately wanted him to hold her. Just for a minute, until the feelings of inadequacy went away. A foolish wish. Mike was just passing through. It wasn't his fault that every time he touched her, her knees turned to marshmallows.

There was a clatter on the stairs. Both kids came running down, banging their small overnight suitcases against the railings.

"Careful," she called.

They skittered to a stop when they saw the open containers. "Whatcha cooking?" Jonathan asked.

"Pancakes," Mike answered, limping back to the island and picking up the flour. "Your mom said you'd be having breakfast with your dad."

"But I want Mike's pancakes," Allison wailed.

"Hey, I'll make them next week," he said.

"Promise?"

He bent over and tugged on her blond braid. "Cross my heart."

"You guys aren't going to do anything fun while we're gone, are you?" Jonathan asked.

"We'll be as boring as we are old," Cindy said. "Besides, we're going to Mrs. Davis's for a barbecue tonight. If you guys stayed, you would have to come."

She heard the sound of a car engine and looked out the kitchen window. A sleek red convertible pulled up in front of the house. Nelson honked the horn, then stepped out of the car. The children grabbed their suitcases and raced toward the door. Cindy followed more slowly.

At the front door there were frantic kisses and calls of goodbye. Nelson waited by the now-open trunk and waved to his children, but he didn't glance at Cindy. She knew they would be back tomorrow promptly at four-thirty. If there had been a change of plans, Nelson would have had his secretary call and tell her.

Without wanting to, she peered at the front passenger seat. She couldn't see much of Hilari except for her long, dark curls. Cindy had seen the woman close up once. She was startlingly beautiful with long legs and a perfectly flat stomach. She was also very young. Maybe twenty-two. Nelson was nearly forty.

As the kids climbed into the car, they stopped to hug Hilari. Cindy felt a stab of pain in her heart. She knew her children loved her, but watching them with bimbo number two was difficult.

She waved until the car turned on the cul-de-sac then sped off. She closed the door and slowly walked back to the kitchen.

"I hate her," Cindy said as she grabbed her coffee and sat down at the table. "I suppose it's transference. I don't want to hate Nelson because I might say something to the children, and I don't want to make it harder on them. So I hate her." She took a sip of the hot liquid and grimaced. "I wish he would pick them up Friday night so I could get drunk or something, but what is there to do at nine on a Saturday morning?" She shook her head. "I sound pretty pathetic. Did you see her?"

Mike was measuring milk. "Who?"

"Nelson's girlfriend. Hilari. One *L,* and an *I* instead of a *Y.*"

"You're kidding? Yeah, I saw her. So?"

"She's very beautiful. Even younger than the woman he left me for. Nelson kept his trophy wife for nearly a year, but they've separated now."

He cracked an egg, then looked at her. "Let me get this straight. You're upset because your ex-husband is dating some skinny teenager who can't even spell her name? Cindy, you're a beautiful woman, you've got great kids. Nelson is obviously a fool as well as a cad. Forget him." He picked up a fork and began stirring the batter.

She stared at him. His words floated around in her brain, then sort of settled in place. Mike thought she was beautiful. He'd said it casually, as if it was an obvious fact. The way most people would comment on the color of her eyes, or her hair.

She sipped her coffee and grinned. The most gorgeous man she'd ever met was standing in her kitchen, cooking her breakfast, telling her that her ex-husband was a jerk and that she was beautiful. If Mike kept that up much longer, she wouldn't have any choice—she would have to fall for him.

Chapter Five

"I thought it would look like Tara from *Gone With the Wind*," Mike said as they pulled up to the country club.

Cindy glanced at the large white building in front of them. It sprawled out on either side. To the left was the swimming pool where the kids' swim team practiced and had meets, beyond that, the tennis courts. On three sides was the private golf course. She suspected living close to the golf course was one of the few things Nelson missed about their marriage.

"Southern Gothic would have been too obvious," she said. "They went for a sort of art deco look, instead. More contemporary." She left the keys in the ignition and took the parking stub the valet handed her.

Mike had already opened the side door on the passenger's side. She grabbed her small gym bag. "It's pretty crowded on weekends," she said, pointing to the cars filling the parking lot. "When you come on your own, you don't have to use the valet. I thought it would be easier today."

Mike picked up his bag and slid the door of the minivan closed. "I appreciate it. I wouldn't want to use up all my strength walking to the gym only to collapse once I got there. I appreciate your bringing me."

"It's no trouble. We'll get you signed up. Grace has a family membership, so you can easily be added for the summer. In addition to the gym, there's tennis and golf. Oh, the restaurant's pretty good, too."

He held open the front door for her. As she walked past him, she noticed her eyes were level with his throat, just as they had been with Nelson. But somehow, Mike seemed larger than her ex-husband.

"I've never understood the purpose of golf," Mike said, following her to the reception desk. "It seems like a perfectly good way to ruin a walk."

She laughed. "You need to say that quietly around here. People take their golf very seriously. There are seven courses within a fifteen-minute drive."

When they reached the reception desk, the young woman there smiled at both of them. Her gaze drifted over Cindy, then settled on Mike. Cindy almost heard her intake of air. "Good morning," she said, her voice nearly a purr. "How may I help you?"

Cindy leaned on the countertop. "My friend, Mr. Blackburne, is staying at his sister's house for the summer while she's away. He would like to use the facilities here. His sister has a family membership. I have the card right here."

She held it out. The woman, barely out of her teens, couldn't seem to tear her gaze away from Mike. Cindy waved it in front of the receptionist's face. "Miss? The card?"

"Oh." The woman blinked. Her smile broadened. "It will be no trouble, Mr. Blackburne. Would you like a tour of the facilities? I would be happy to take you myself."

Mike shook his head. "Cindy's going to take me around."

The younger woman flashed Cindy a look of pure hatred. Cindy couldn't help it. She slid close to Mike and looked up at him. "It's simply no trouble," she said, staring into his brown eyes.

Suddenly, what started out as a childish bid to claim a relationship that didn't exist quickly turned into something else. As he met her gaze, she realized his eyes weren't brown at all. They were all colors. Flecks of gold and hazel and brown and tiny dots of blue. His pupils dilated and her knees weakened. Without wanting to, she placed her hand on his forearm. The tingling began in her fingertips and worked its way up to her shoulder, across her back and down her chest. It was difficult to breathe, and she could have sworn she heard music.

He'd shaved that morning and his jaw was smooth. Her fingers itched to touch his skin, to feel the heat there. His mouth was firm. What would it feel like against—

Cindy jerked her hand away and bit back a yelp. What on earth was she thinking about? This was insane. She glanced at Mike out of the corner of her eye, but he was signing a form the receptionist had given him. It was as if the incident had never happened. At least not to him.

A few moments later, she was still fighting the effects. The skin that had touched his was both hot and cold. Her breathing was rapid, her breasts achy. Hormones, she told herself firmly. It was just a weird time in her monthly cycle. Or maybe Beth was right and she'd been living too innocently for too long. Maybe she should think about dating, or therapy. Whatever the solution to her problem, it sure wasn't Mike Blackburne.

"If you need anything, Mr. Blackburne, I mean anything at all, please let me know." The receptionist picked up a card and wrote something on it, then handed it to him. "Enjoy your stay."

"Thanks," Mike said.

They turned away from the desk. Cindy headed them toward the stairs. "The locker rooms are down here," she said. "Along with the weight room and the aerobics classes. You probably don't want to take a step class anytime soon."

He shook his head. "I've got to build up the muscles slowly. They've been ripped pretty bad."

She shuddered. "Maybe you need a new line of work. What you do sounds scary."

"Not as scary as this." When they reached the bottom of the stairs, he handed her the business card the receptionist had handed him.

She scanned the printed words. They named the country club, stated the hours it was open and gave a number to call. "So?"

"Turn it over."

She did. On the back, someone had written: *I'm Heather. Call me anytime. For anything.* The last word was underlined three times and followed by a phone number. Cindy felt her eyes widen. "My goodness, she was hitting on you."

"Yeah." He tugged at the collar of his T-shirt.

He looked so genuinely surprised and uncomfortable, she laughed. "Oh, Mike, she's just a kid. Maybe twenty. I'm sure a big, bad bodyguard like you could handle her."

"I'm not so sure. Kids are maturing earlier these days. She could probably teach me a few things."

The hallways downstairs were more narrow than the spacious upper rooms. As they were talking, several people passed. All the women eyed Mike, then said hello. At first, Cindy thought she was imagining it, but by the time the third woman paused to smile and greet, she knew it was real.

"You're very popular," she said.

Mike swallowed. "Why?"

"I'm not sure. You can't be the only good-looking guy in the building."

"Gee, thanks."

She glanced up at him, then covered her mouth. "Sorry. You know what I mean."

"Uh-huh. Sure. Why don't you show me where the locker rooms are."

She walked to the end of the corridor and turned the corner. There was a large door marked Men, and across from that was the ladies' locker room.

"Are you going to work out?" he asked.

She hesitated. She walked regularly, although it was difficult in the summer because of the heat. She'd been fighting five pounds for about two months and currently the extra pounds were winning. "I thought I might use the treadmill," she said.

"Great. Let's meet here in five minutes."

Before she could answer, the door to the ladies' locker room opened and a stunning brunette stepped into the hallway. She was closer to forty than thirty, but had the face and figure of a beauty queen...or that actress who had played Wonder Woman on television. Cindy sagged against the wall. Timing. It was all about timing. Two minutes later and they would have missed her. But no. Here she was—in the flesh.

Dark blue eyes met hers. The woman smiled. "Cindy.

How good to see you. At the grocery store yesterday, I remember thinking you hadn't been to the club in a while. I'm so glad you're back." She patted her own flat stomach. "We can't let gravity win."

The so-called niceties taken care of, she swung her head toward Mike. The smile that had been merely pleasant became predatory. Her teeth were white enough to read by, Cindy thought grimly, still smarting from the dig about her weight.

"You must be Mike," the woman said, her voice low and sultry. "I'm Mary Ellen. Did you get my card?"

Mike looked blank for a moment, then he nodded. "Cindy gave it to me. It's really nice of you, but I'm not interested in—"

She raised her hand to cut him off. "I know. A man like you doesn't need any help. You're handsome enough on your own. But have you considered the fact that you'll be forty in another five or six years? Skin can be very unforgiving." She stepped closer and reached her fingers up to touch his cheek. "I'd hate to see all these good looks hidden behind some nasty wrinkles."

Cindy resisted the urge to stick her finger in her mouth and make gagging noises.

"Not today," Mike said and reached behind him. He got hold of the doorknob and turned it, then disappeared into the men's locker room.

"He's quite something," Mary Ellen said.

Cindy smiled tightly, then did a disappearing act of her own. As she peeled off her shorts and T-shirt and shimmied into a green Lycra leotard, she decided that bringing Mike to the club had been a bad idea. She should have just dropped him off at the curb and returned later to pick him up. There were too many women around. She felt like the kid who got a pony for her birthday and it arrived during the party; everyone got to ride it but her.

She shoved her clothes into a locker, then walked over to the mirror. Several women were on either side of her. She saw them looking at her, but none of them said anything. Thank goodness. A few hours ago, Mike had made her feel special when he'd told her she was beautiful and Nelson was a fool. Now she just felt dowdy and unnecessary. Like a shriveled-up appendix. Not that she wanted his attention. She didn't. It was just—

She sighed. She didn't know what it was anymore. Nothing made sense. She slipped a headband over her head, then pulled her hair back into a ponytail. It wasn't very long, so the ends only stuck out a couple of inches. She adjusted the headband so her bangs were off her face, then frowned at the reflection in the mirror. She was still wearing her makeup. She was going to sweat it off in about fifteen minutes.

"An attractive look for summer," she muttered as she left the locker room. "Raccoon eyes and streaked cheeks."

Mike was waiting in the hallway, speaking to a blonde. As soon as he saw her, he pushed off the wall and moved close.

"Get me out of here," he whispered into her ear.

"The gym is this way."

They entered the mirrored room. About half the equipment was in use. "I'll be over there," Cindy said, pointing to the row of treadmills at one end.

Mike nodded. "I'm going to use the weights. It'll take about forty-five minutes."

Great. He could lift weights longer than she could walk on the treadmill. And he hadn't even seemed to notice the way her sleeveless leotard clung to her body. Of course, judging by Mary Ellen's cracks about her weight, he probably didn't want to. *I need this day to start over,* Cindy told herself.

"Why don't we meet out in front in an hour?" she said.

"Perfect."

He turned toward the machines. She waited, hoping he would wave, or watch her walk to the treadmill, but he seemed absorbed in the equipment. She gave a sigh of defeat and moved down the center aisle. She wondered if she looked like Allison did when she pouted.

Mike glanced around the gym and wished it weren't so new. He was used to seedy places with concrete-block walls and dirty windows. Here the lighting was concealed, the mirrors sparkling clean and the carpeting nicer than anything he'd had in his apartment.

He was also dressed all wrong. He saw that right away. His tattered shorts and cutoff T-shirt made him stand out even more. The women were wearing matching outfits that clung to every curve. On some of them, like Cindy, it looked great, but a few of the women looked as if they'd been starving themselves.

He walked over to the leg press and adjusted the weight down. His right leg was strong, but his left would have to be built up slowly. It would have been easier if it had been his arm. Then he could have used free weights.

He settled in the seat and began to press. Instantly, pain shot from his thigh to his ankle, then up to his groin. He breathed slowly and worked through the discomfort. After a few repetitions, it faded to a manageable ache. Slowly and steadily, he told himself. It was going to take three months to build up his strength again.

He ignored everyone around him. It was safer. In the two minutes he'd spent waiting for Cindy, three women had approached him, offering everything from a home-cooked meal to a massage. More unsettling than their invitations was the fact that they all knew who he was. It made him nervous. He was used to being in the background. In his line of work, he blended with the other men in suits. When someone looked at him, they didn't know if he was an assistant, a superior or the bodyguard, and that's how he liked it.

He stood up and adjusted the weight a little higher, then repeated the exercise. This time he glanced around. He found if he turned his head just so, he could watch Cindy in one of the mirrors without looking anywhere near her. Of course, he could only see her from the rear, but it was still a great view.

She had a perfect butt. Not flat, but round. He imagined holding it, squeezing it, nibbling it. Her hips flared out from her waist. She was curvy. He didn't understand women who wanted to look like teenage girls. Women were supposed to be soft and yielding. The bumps and dips were the best part. Of course, who was he to judge?

He finished his reps, then stepped over to another machine. The door opened and two men came in. One had a beerbelly and both had thinning hair. From the way they ogled the women exercising, Mike figured they were here just for the view. He ignored them and set the weight on the leg-curl machine. He could feel the sweat popping out on his back. It hurt like a sonofabitch, but he kept going.

One of the men—the one wearing a T-shirt advertising a local dance club—walked to the leg-press machine. He glanced at the weight and did a double take. "Someone let their kid in here?" he asked no one in particular.

Mike ignored the comment and continued working. He massaged the muscle between reps and reminded himself it couldn't be healed in a day.

He walked over to the next piece of equipment. Beer-belly followed. He glanced at the weight, then Mike. His thick eyebrows drew together, then he made a big show of moving the weight higher. Much higher.

They repeated the procedure twice more. Mike was starting to feel as if he was in a contest. Everyone was watching him. He wanted to tell the guy he'd been shot in the leg and fell off a building and that's why he was working light weights. He wanted to tell himself it didn't matter. But his ego wasn't listening. Occasionally, he glanced at Cindy. When she saw him, she waggled her fingers at him. Her breasts moved with each step. That was enough to distract him from his bad temper.

It had been a mistake to come here on a weekend. He would skip tomorrow, not only because it would be crowded, but because the muscle would need to rest, then he would limit his workouts to the middle of the week. He didn't need the aggravation.

Cindy stepped off the treadmill and grabbed a towel to wipe her face. He glanced at his watch, then limped over to her. "Are you done?" he asked.

"Yeah. Twenty-five minutes is all I can do today." She was flushed and sweating.

"I'm about done, too," he said.

"I thought you said it would take you forty-five minutes."

He glanced at the crowded room. Most people looked away when he caught them watching him, although a few of the women continued to stare boldly. Beerbelly was adjusting the weights up, yet again, on a machine Mike had used.

"I'm tired out," he said. "And I don't dare take a shower here. They'll probably sell tickets."

"I'm sorry."

"It's not your fault."

He glanced at the bench press, then at her. "I'll meet you in the hall in a couple of minutes. I have to do one more machine."

After she left, he went over to the bench press. He adjusted the weight, then got in position. He focused all his attention on raising the bar. His muscles protested, but he did twenty slow reps. Then he grabbed a towel and started for the door.

Once there, he paused. Beerbelly had followed him to the machine. He looked at the weight, then at Mike. His eyes widened with disbelief. Beerbelly settled on the bench and tried to lift the bar. It didn't budge. Mike gave him a mocking salute, then left the room.

When he was settled in the passenger seat of the minivan, he acknowledged to himself that he'd behaved like a child. Damn, it had felt good, too.

"You okay?" Cindy asked.

"Yeah. Just a little overwhelmed. I know you mentioned there weren't a lot of single guys in the neighborhood, but I was afraid for my life in there."

"I think it's your career." She stopped at the bottom of the slight hill and made a right by the fountain. "It's very romantic, if you don't mind your significant other risking his life. Face it, Mike. You're a hot prospect."

He didn't want to ask for what. "Why don't you date, Cindy?"

"How do you know I don't?"

"I heard you talking with Beth."

"Oh. I forgot." She cleared her throat. "Yes, well, it's difficult for a woman with children. A lot of men aren't interested, for one thing. For another, dating requires a certain amount of time and energy. I don't want to miss my kids' best years because I'm trying to have a social life. It's hard to balance what I want and my needs with what's best for them. Right now, I'm giving them more and myself less. I think in time that will change."

"I admire your dedication," he said. "Your kids are lucky to have you."

They'd turned onto the main street, but instead of studying the familiar road, he pictured his own empty childhood. How would things have been different if his mother had been a little less concerned about herself and a little more concerned about him?

"I'll ask you to repeat your praise the next time they're furious at me for something," she said.

"Be my guest."

He glanced at her. She was smiling. He could see her dimple and the curve of her cheek. She'd thrown a T-shirt over her green leotard. Her long legs were bare. He wanted to run his fingers along her thighs and feel her silky skin.

It was the wrong thing to think about, so he focused on her hands, the smooth short nails, the delicate wrists. Why had Nelson left her? Cindy had said something about a trophy wife, but why would any man want someone other than her? She was funny, bright, incredibly sexy and a great mother.

"What are you thinking?" she asked.

He slid his gaze away and stared out the front window. "I was wondering about lunch."

"We have to eat light. The barbecue is tonight, and the food is always amazing."

He'd forgotten about that.

"Get that panicked look off your face," she told him. "These people are my friends. You'll be safe."

He wondered what it would be like to have friends. He knew people, but he didn't spend time with many. What would it be like to live in one place, to come home to one woman? What would it be like to belong? He couldn't imagine. He'd never belonged anywhere in his life.

Cindy handed Mike a covered cake plate, picked up a bowl of potato salad from the hall table, then closed the front door behind them.

"Aren't you going to lock it?" he asked.

"We're just going across the street," she told him.

"You should at least make someone work if he's going to break into your home."

"If you insist." Shifting the salad bowl to her left hand, she opened the door, pulled the key out of the lock, closed the door, turned the key until the bolt shot home then looked at him. "Happy?"

"Very."

Cindy chuckled. "This is Sugar Land, Mike. Nothing bad happens here. I swear."

"You never know." He checked the cul-de-sac before stepping out onto the street. "I'm glad we're walking and not driving tonight. This cake looks lethal."

She glanced at the container he was holding. "It's called Black Russian Cake and it's wonderful. Be sure to take a piece. I got the recipe out of a romance novel I read last year. I think the author lives somewhere in town, but I'm not sure."

Despite the fact that it was after six, the air was still steamy. They hadn't had rain in a couple of days so the humidity had fallen below ninety percent, but the sun beat down unmercifully.

"I'm glad Beth has trees in her yard," she said. "It's going to be hot."

Mike grunted.

She looked at him. "What's wrong?"

"Nothing." But he was staring at the house in front of him as if he'd never seen it before.

She could hear voices from other couples already in the backyard. If she didn't know better, she would swear Mike was nervous. "Everything is going to be fine," she said.

He didn't answer. Before Cindy could question him more, Beth spotted them and came to the gate.

"You're here. I'm so pleased." With one smooth movement, she reached for the cake plate and held out her other hand. "You must be Mike. I'm Beth."

Mike shook hands with her. He smiled tightly as she chattered, then shot Cindy a look. She knew he was wondering if she'd told Beth that he'd overheard their conversation last week. She hadn't. She figured if she did, Beth would never dare show her face again.

Before she could intervene, Darren came forward and urged Mike into the backyard. The men had congregated around the two grills. There were six men, counting Mike. He was handed a beer and introduced.

Cindy thought about rescuing Mike but figured he'd been in more dangerous situations than this. After all, she knew these men and they were basically nice guys. She followed Beth into the kitchen.

The other four women were already there. They poured Cindy a glass of wine and instantly bombarded her with questions.

"So what's he really like?" Sally asked.

"He's a serious hunk," Christina said.

"What do the kids think of him?" Mary asked.

"Wait, wait." Beth held up her hands. "I want to go first. I have two questions. One, have you seen him naked yet? And two, how hard are you resisting temptation?"

Cindy set her container of potato salad on the counter

and took the wine Sally offered. She settled on the stool by the bar. "I have nothing to say on the subject."

The other five women groaned in unison.

"You have to tell us something," Karen said, leaning close and poking her in the ribs. "I mean, we're all boring married ladies. You're the only one who gets to have any fun."

"Being divorced is a real blast," Cindy said. She felt her good mood slipping away.

Beth caught her eye and gave her a sympathetic smile. She quickly put the women to work, rolling paper napkins around plastic utensils. Soon Cindy's houseguest was forgotten amid the usual chatter and gossip.

She sipped her wine slowly. She knew these women. She carpooled with them, had been to their houses and had entertained them at her own. But in those few minutes of questions, she realized she was different. She was single and they were married. Funny, she'd never put that together before.

After the divorce, they'd all stood by her. It wasn't unusual not to have a husband at a social function. Most of the men in their circle traveled quite a bit, sometimes for months at a time. But she wasn't one of them anymore and it was unlikely she ever would be again.

She reached for a package of paper plates and began counting them. Beth came over and leaned against the counter. "Sorry about that," she said. "I didn't know they'd all jump on you."

"It's okay. They're curious." She glanced at her friend and smiled. "*You're* curious."

Beth lowered her voice. "Have you seen him naked?"

"Not yet, but when I do, you'll be the first to know."

"Gee, thanks."

Beth gave her a quick hug, then walked over to the

oven. The ribs were being baked first so they would cook quicker on the grill. While the women were talking, Cindy slipped out the back door. She glanced at the men but didn't see Mike. She walked to the edge of the fence and stared at the sky.

The sun hadn't set yet and wouldn't for another hour or two. Heat rose from the sidewalk. Candles in glass jars had been placed around to ward off bugs, although she and Mike had sprayed themselves with insect repellent before leaving her house. She dropped her gaze to the pecan trees, then lower to children playing in the green-belt.

She hadn't felt this alone since she'd been a teenager.

What had gone wrong? Why hadn't her marriage worked out? She grimaced. She knew the answer to the last question. Nelson was a jerk. Unfortunately, it had taken ten years and his walking out on her for her to see it. But that didn't explain how everything got so messed up. She'd had her whole life planned.

"You look serious about something," Mike said, coming up to stand next to her.

She shrugged. "What were you doing? Casing the joint? Checking out the perimeter?"

She'd been teasing, but Mike looked sheepish. "Some habits are hard to break."

"It's been several years since the last terrorist attack, soldier," she said. "Maybe you could not be on alert tonight."

"Maybe." He took a sip from his bottle of beer. "What's your excuse?"

"I miss my kids."

"What else?"

"I thought I'd be married forever." He offered her his bottle and she took a swallow. As a rule, she didn't like beer, but tonight the biting yeasty flavor tasted right. "I suppose that's what I get for trying to plan out everything. I was tempting fate."

He leaned against the fence, bumping her elbow with his. She could smell the faint scent of his skin. He was warm and tempting. She found herself wondering how she could get their bare legs to brush together without making a complete fool of herself. She couldn't come up with a plan and figured she would have to settle for looking at his legs. Bless the summer heat, she thought with a smile.

"There are always variables," he said. "You've got to learn to go with them. No matter how well I plan a job, there's always something. Some kid steps out in front of the car, the electricity goes off. When you least expect it, life throws you a curve."

"The ribs are ready," Beth said, coming out the back door and carrying a large tray. The men parted to let her through to the grill, then Darren took the tray from her.

"Mike, why don't you take the first watch?" Darren said, holding out the tongs.

Mike started toward the other man. When he reached the grill, he looked back at her and winked. Low in her belly she felt a flutter of awareness, of need and something slightly more dangerous. A tugging that went all the way to her heart.

It wasn't just that Mike was gorgeous, had a smile that could melt aluminum and a body worth worshiping. It was that he was also a nice guy. She had a feeling, a very bad feeling, that life had just thrown her a curve.

Chapter Six

It didn't take Mike long to figure out he didn't like barbecues. Grown men standing around an outdoor grill on a hot, muggy summer evening burning meat and fighting off bugs wasn't for him. If they wanted to go camping, *that* he could understand. He liked being away from civilization, pitting his skills against the wilds of nature. But this suburban ritual made no sense to him. The grills were gas, for God's sake, and the meat had already been partially cooked in an oven.

He took another swig of beer, then shrugged. Everyone else was having a good time. He didn't have to understand what they saw in it. In his business, he was used to watching other people do odd things. What made him nervous this time was that everyone knew who he was.

He liked his life in the shadows. When he guarded a political figure or a celebrity, all eyes were on the client. But here, in Beth's backyard, they knew his name, what he did for a living and the fact that he'd served in the military.

"I wish our football team had a chance at a winning season this year," Sam said. "It's Jeff's last year."

"He's going to play?" Darren asked.

"Running back. First string. But he's not going to try to make the team in college. He wants to keep his grades up. You follow football much, Mike?" Sam asked.

"I don't have the time."

"Too bad." Sam grinned. "Here it's nearly a religion. Especially the high school and college games." He turned his attention back to the grill.

Mike leaned against the fence and watched the men. They were all dressed the same, in shorts and T-shirts. They were around his age, at various stages of fitness and hair loss. He'd never thought of himself as middle-aged, but these guys looked it and they were his contemporaries. Maybe he needed a new line of work. He rubbed his thigh and thought that might not be a bad idea, but what else did he know how to do?

Darren turned the ribs over again. Mike's turn at the barbecue had been mercifully brief.

Jack, who was married to Christina—or was it Mary?— sat on one of the lawn chairs. "I've been thinking of getting one of those mowers you ride."

Darren laughed. "Your yard isn't any bigger than this one. Where you gonna ride it?"

"We're thinking of buying some property and building a cabin," Jack said.

Darren shook his head. "Then wait until you get the land. But if you need a chipper, I just got a great one. It would make mulch out of a chain-link fence." He poked at the ribs. "Beth wants to redecorate the living room."

All the men groaned. "Don't talk to me about decorating," Jack said. "I was thinking of doing something in a floral print." His voice was high. "How does this sample make you *feel?*"

Sam, tall and thin, with dark hair, motioned with his beer. "It took Sally three weeks to pick out tile for the guest bathroom. Three weeks!"

"And how much did it cost?" Darren asked.

"Don't remind me. For that price, it should have been installed by naked dancing girls."

Roger, a large man with a belly hanging over the waistband of his shorts, leaned forward and lowered his voice. "I have a new assistant. You should see this girl. Twenty-two, maybe. With big eyes and bigger—" He cupped his hands in front of his chest.

"You working overtime yet?" Jack asked.

Roger winked.

Mike took another swallow of his beer, draining the bottle. The sun had slipped low enough that the backyard was in shade. There was a long deck behind the house. Two tables had been set up, with paper tablecloths and plastic glasses. There were lawn chairs scattered on the grass. From the deck, a stone path led to an oval-shaped swimming pool with a large Jacuzzi at one end. He felt as if he'd traveled to a foreign country. The natives might speak the same language, but he didn't understand the subject matter. He also didn't want to hear about Roger's young assistant. It made him think about Cindy, and how Nelson had betrayed her.

He tilted his empty bottle. "I'm going to get another one," he said to no one in particular.

He limped into the kitchen. The women were gathered around the center island. It was a long counter with a sink in the middle.

Christina—or was it Mary?—was peeling a carrot. "He

works so late, leaving me with the kids all the time, then he gets mad when they don't want to do things with him. Why would they? They're teenagers and have their own lives. He only has himself to blame. I've tried to explain that to him, but he won't listen.''

"I worry about the same thing with Nelson," Cindy said. He didn't think she'd noticed he'd come into the kitchen. "He only sees them every other weekend. He can't have a relationship with them that way. I've told him I wouldn't mind if he saw them more, but he can't be bothered."

Sally shook her blond head. "Men. Do you know what I got for my birthday?"

There was a chorus of no's.

She looked up and grimaced. "A gift certificate for a year's worth of car washes."

Cindy laughed. Beth groaned.

"I know," Sally said. "It's pathetic. I told him I wanted a pair of gold hoop earrings. That's not too difficult. But it would have required him going to the mall on his own, and I'm sure he'd rather face a pack of rabid dogs."

"Darren will shop," Beth said. "I just wish he was more romantic. You know, flowers every now and then for no reason. Or maybe even call me up and say, 'Don't bother cooking, honey, let's go out.'" She straightened and shrugged. "He's a sweetie, really. If I ask him to go out, he always says yes, but sometimes I wish he would offer."

There was a murmur of assent.

Mike limped over to the refrigerator and pulled out a beer. Cindy saw him and walked over.

"How are you doing?" she asked quietly.

He moved toward the back door and she followed. "My

leg aches, but otherwise I'm fine.'' He glanced at the group of women in the kitchen, then out at the men gathered around the grill. ''Is it always like this?'' he asked.

She followed his gaze. ''The separation of the sexes? I suppose so. I hadn't thought about it. I think we all like spending time with our friends. These women see their husbands every day.''

He supposed it made sense, but something felt off to him. The complaining, the being apart. ''Do any of the people in these couples love each other?''

The question seemed to have surprised her. She tilted her head and smiled. ''Of course, Mike. What would you think?''

That they didn't seem very happy to him. ''I'm just observing the situation,'' he said. ''Checking out the local customs.''

''Check out the food,'' she said. ''It's nearly time to eat.''

She was right. The next few minutes were a bustle of activity, with salads and bread being set out on the tables and the men serving the meat.

Mike sat at the end of one of the picnic tables and used a stool to prop up his bad leg. He could feel the aching pain from the workout, not to mention the standing around he'd done earlier. He would pay for this activity tomorrow.

He was pleased when Cindy settled next to him. He didn't want to hear any more about Jack's lawn mower, or Roger's new assistant. But as Cindy asked him his preferences and scooped food onto his plate, he realized the dynamics of the group had changed. The men and women were no longer separate. They sat together, two by two.

Darren sat next to Beth. She was talking to Sally. Without glancing at her husband, she picked up a bottle of hot sauce and passed it to him. When he accepted the bottle, he bent forward and kissed her bare shoulder.

Roger sat on the end of a chaise longue with his wife's bare feet in his lap. In between bites, he massaged her toes and pressed her heels into his thigh. When she glanced at him, he murmured something Mike couldn't hear, and winked. His wife smiled and nodded.

They were all like that. Sitting together, exchanging private, unconscious touches, performing a ritual that somehow bonded them. They leaned against each other, brushed arms, kissed lightly, all the while talking with everyone around them.

He felt as if he'd come into a play during the second act and no one could explain the story. Deep in his chest, in a place he'd forgotten he had, he felt a twinge of regret. Perhaps at one time he could have learned the words and actions of this world, but it was too late now.

He looked over at Cindy. She was next to him, close, but they didn't touch. She didn't give him secret smiles or lean against him.

When the meal was over, the women cleared the table while the men sat around and discussed sports. Mike didn't have an opinion on the Houston Oilers. He'd never followed professional teams much. There wasn't any point in getting excited about a season when his work would force him to miss most of the games.

After a few minutes, Darren stood up and stretched. "All right, guys, are we all going to do it, or do you want to flip for it?"

Jack finished his beer. "We used paper plates. How much can there be? Let's just all do it."

With that, the men trooped into the kitchen and began

cleaning. Mike followed along. He grabbed a dish towel and dried the serving bowls as they were passed to him. Darren collected trash, Roger washed, Sam put the leftovers in the refrigerator, Jack wiped off countertops.

The higher-pitched conversation of the women caught his attention. He peered outside. All six had changed into bathing suits and were sitting on the edge of the pool or slipping into the Jacuzzi. His gaze settled on Cindy. She'd put on a one-piece dark green suit that matched her eyes. A headband held her hair off her face, but his attention didn't stray much above her shoulders.

The suit hugged her curves, outlining her full breasts and emphasizing the shape of her hips. He felt his mouth grow dry. None of the other men seemed to notice their wives. He wondered how long he would have to be with Cindy before he ceased to appreciate her body and the way she moved. He supposed she wasn't anything extraordinary, but she appealed to him on a fundamental level. As if he'd been waiting for her all his life.

Nelson was a fool, he thought, not for the first time. Yet, he couldn't help being pleased by the fact that she was single. Of course, he wasn't going to do anything stupid like try to get involved. It would be crazy for both of them. They had nothing in common.

"I gotta check on the kids," Roger said, walking over to the wall phone by the refrigerator.

The heavyset man who'd implied an interest in his young female assistant spent fifteen minutes on the phone with his two children, who had been left without a sitter for the first time.

Jack and Darren joined their wives in the pool and swam around with them in their arms.

Mike stood in the kitchen and stared out the window, close to but not part of their world. What would it be like to have a family to come home to, to actually celebrate holidays instead of ignoring them? What would it feel like to commit to someone forever? To have children and a mortgage, maybe even a dog. How would his life be different if he had a place to come home to?

"You're limping more than you usually do," Cindy said, moving closer to Mike and fighting the urge to slip an arm around his waist. She doubted he would appreciate the help.

"I know." They closed the gate behind them and started down Beth's driveway. "I did too much at the gym."

"I'm sure standing around at the party didn't help." Even if he had looked mighty fine doing it.

Cindy smiled faintly, knowing he wouldn't be able to see her expression in the darkness. It was nearly eleven. They'd stayed late at the barbecue, swimming, and eating too much dessert. She patted her stomach and knew she would now be fighting six pounds instead of five.

She shifted the plastic bag containing the empty salad bowl and cake plate to her other hand. "Are you going to be able to make it?"

"Sure. As long as we go slow." He held on to the fence until they reached the house, then he started down the driveway. "You can go ahead if you'd like."

"No. I'd be afraid you wouldn't make it across the street. You can lean on me."

He shook his head. "I'm too heavy."

The streetlamp was two doors down and the circle of light didn't reach this far. They'd moved out of the range of Beth's back porch light. Night insects chirped and buzzed around them. It was still hot, but without the intensity of the sun. She could smell tropical flowers and cut grass.

Cindy had pulled a T-shirt over her swimsuit, but the rest of her clothes were in the plastic bag with the serving pieces. She swung the bag back and forth in time with their slow steps.

"Did you have a good time?" she asked.

"It was different."

"Hmm, why do I think that's a no?"

They'd reached the sidewalk. Mike paused. "It's not a no. I've never been to a barbecue before. It was unusual. I'm starting to learn your suburban rituals."

He drew in a deep breath. "If it's not too much trouble, could I put my arm around you?"

"Sure." She moved closer. "Lean as much as you need to. I'm stronger than I look."

His arm settled on her shoulders. She could feel his heat and inhale the scent of him. He smelled masculine. It had been a long time since she'd been this close to the opposite sex. Years, in fact, not counting brotherly hugs from her friends' husbands or the moments she had spent trapped under Mike on the sofa.

She placed her arm around his waist and held on. "You doing okay?"

"Fine. Sorry to be such a problem."

"It's no big deal. I should have noticed you were in pain." She tried not to notice how right it felt to be next to him. It was just because he was a good-looking man, she told herself. But she knew it was more than that, and it scared her to death.

"I'm glad we went tonight," she said, to distract herself. "Having plans on Saturday night helps me forget the kids are gone."

"You really miss them."

"Of course."

"But I heard you say you wanted Nelson to spend more time with them."

They inched their way down the driveway onto the street. She could feel Mike tense with each step. "It's hard for me when they're gone, but I believe children need a mother and a father. I'm doing the best I can, but I still want them to see Nelson. He doesn't want the responsibility, though." She sighed. "There's a father-daughter campout in a few weeks. He swears he's going to go with Allison, but I know him. About a week before they're supposed to go, he'll call and tell me that something's come up. That will break her heart. I think Nelson doesn't want to risk spending time alone with the children. I think he's afraid of them."

"This guy has a lot of problems, Cindy. You have great kids."

She felt a flush of pleasure. "You don't know any other kids, so why should I trust your judgment?"

"I just know." He limped silently for a minute then said, "If Nelson backs out of the campout, I'll go with Allison."

She stopped and stared at him. They were standing a little more than halfway across the street. The streetlight didn't reach here and there weren't any cars on the cul-de-sac.

"Why would you do that?"

"Why not? I like Allison, and I enjoy camping. It was one of the best things about being in the service."

"You're crazy," she told him. "We're talking about a father-daughter campout. There will be seventy or eighty little girls running around and getting into trouble."

"So?"

"You must have hit your head harder than you thought when you fell off that building."

Her tone was teasing. He glanced at her. "It's no big deal. I'm happy to go with her. Really. Why is that so hard to believe?"

Her eyes had adjusted to the darkness and she could make out his features. He was still good-looking enough to make her thighs overheat and her palms sweat. Right now they were standing so close, their hips brushed together. His arm was around her shoulders, hers was around his waist. If she was really foolish, she could pretend this was a romantic moment. That he was holding her because he wanted to and not because his leg was about to give out on him.

"You're very sweet," she said. Without thinking, she raised herself on tiptoe and leaned forward to kiss his cheek. "Thank you," she murmured just before she touched his skin.

But in that second, he turned his head and her lips brushed against his mouth.

Cindy froze. She told herself she should pull back, but the arm around her shoulders tightened. Besides, she didn't want to. She hadn't felt that shiver of anticipation in a long time, although she wasn't sure she remembered exactly how one kissed a stranger.

While she was still debating, Mike took the decision out of her hands. He bent his head closer and pressed his mouth to hers.

His lips were as firm as she'd imagined them to be. He didn't attack or invade; instead, he held the contact, prolonging it until the electricity crackled between them and she had to drop the plastic bag she was holding.

Her eyes were closed. It seemed like too much trouble to open them. He drew back slightly and murmured her name. She smiled at the sound of his voice. "You're so beautiful," he whispered. She knew she wasn't, but at that moment, she didn't care.

He pulled her firmly against him. She went willingly. His chest was broad and hard. Her breasts nestled against him as if they'd been as lonely as the rest of her. She angled her head so when he brought his mouth down on hers again, she could feel all of him.

He kissed with the slow thoroughness of a man who enjoyed the act for its own sake and not just because it was the quickest road to sex. He brushed her mouth back and forth, then touched her lower lip with his tongue.

She parted for him, wanting to taste him and feel him, but he didn't enter. Instead, he traced the shape of her mouth, learning every curve, as if later he might be called upon to describe it in detail. She raised her free hand to his shoulders and melted against him.

There was heat. From the concrete road, from the night air and from their bodies. The temperature between them rose until she felt the flames licking at her most feminine place.

He was rock-hard, the muscles in his back thick ropes that shifted and tightened under her fingers. The arms around her shoulders and waist tightened as if he feared she would want to escape. She thought of telling him that it had never crossed her mind, but she didn't want to interrupt his kiss.

He drew her lower lip into his mouth and suckled gently. He swept his tongue across her dampened skin, sending hot liquid need down her chest and into her breasts. She felt herself swelling, aching, reaching for him. Her hips pressed against his and she cradled the part of him that echoed her desire.

In the back of her mind, some small still-rational part

of her compared him to Nelson. They were the same height so the pose should be familiar. But it wasn't. Mike bent toward her as if kissing her was the most important task of his day. Nelson had always made her stretch up to meet him. Their bodies were different. Nelson had been wider, softer. Mike was all hard planes and steely muscles. She hadn't kissed a man other than her ex-husband in nearly twelve years. She'd forgotten how wonderful kissing could be.

At last he entered her mouth. Instantly, all thought fled as she could only feel the gentle, smooth exploration. He tasted of the brandy they'd had, and deliciously of himself. She wanted to crawl closer, to be inside of him, feeling more. She wanted to touch him everywhere and be touched in return.

She stroked his back, his shoulders, then the short silky strands of his hair. His palms echoed her journey in reverse as he first buried his fingers in her hair, caressed her shoulders and back, then dipped lower to cup her derriere.

She arched her hips against him, bringing her belly into contact with his arousal. His body tensed and he groaned low in his throat.

"Cindy," he said softly, breaking the kiss and speaking into her ear.

She slid her hips back and forth, taunting them both. His breathing was harsh. He punished her with sharp nips on her earlobe, then soothed the spot with moist kisses. The shivers started there and rippled down to her knees.

As first kisses went, it was a pretty exciting one. She giggled.

"Is that a statement about my technique?" he asked.

"No, it's just…" She caught her breath as his hand slid up her hip to her waist. She opened her eyes and stared at him. "Mike?"

His face was taut with need, his mouth damp from their kisses. "What?" he asked.

"That was my first kiss since the divorce," she said quickly, suddenly too shy to look at him. "If I'd known it was going to be this good, I would have done it sooner."

He was silent so long she was forced to glance up at him. His eyes darkened with an emotion she couldn't read. "Mike, I'm sorry. I didn't mean anything by—"

He brought his mouth down on hers, effectively silencing her. She went to him willingly. His hand stayed on her waist, but she willed it to move higher. The ache in her breasts had reached a fever pitch she knew only his touch would soothe.

When he didn't react to her mental message, she tried something more direct. She swept her tongue into his mouth, touching him, tasting him. She rocked her hips against his, reaching her hands down to his rear and holding him in place. At last, his hand began to slide higher.

The sharp metal-against-metal squeak of a garage door being closed caught her attention. She broke the kiss and turned her head to listen. At that moment, she realized they were standing in the middle of the street where virtually anyone could see them.

"Oh, my," she murmured. "What will the neighbors think?"

Mike shifted away from her and straightened. He had to clear his throat before speaking. "That I'm the luckiest guy in town," he said. He cleared his throat again. "I'm going to stay out here for a little bit. Why don't you go on in?"

She wanted to protest. A part of her was willing to continue what they'd been doing—even let it build to its natural conclusion. But the sensible part of her brain screamed that was out of the question. She barely knew the man. They couldn't make love. Correction. There wasn't any love here. They couldn't have sex. She didn't do that with men she didn't know, and Mike, well, she didn't know Mike's thoughts on the subject, but she had a feeling she was the last woman he would choose.

She picked up the plastic bag she'd dropped and glanced at him. "Are you going to be all right?"

"Yeah. Just give me a minute to recover."

She liked that his voice was shaking a little. She walked the rest of the way across the road, stepped up onto the curb and headed for her front door. Her body was still humming from their encounter. But as she moved into the cool foyer and shut the door behind her, she realized how empty the house was, and how very alone she felt. Even when Mike came inside, he wasn't coming home to her.

Chapter Seven

He was in enemy territory without a survival guide, and he had no one else but himself to blame.

The grocery store was huge. Mike was used to small corner markets that carried one brand of only a few kinds of food, while sporting an impressive selection of beer and hard liquor. He limped in through the automatic door and entered a foyer. On one side was a machine that dispensed water, a full-size ice freezer, a popcorn machine that made the area smell like a movie theater and two large containers—one for paper bags, the other for plastic—with signs above them reminding shoppers to recycle.

There was another set of sliding doors, then he entered the store itself. And stopped in his tracks.

He had nothing to compare it to, but he knew he'd stepped into a strange and frightening land. There was merchandise everywhere. Not just food. From where he was standing he could see plants, a video-rental department, a pharmacy, a hot deli, a florist and a salad bar that would put most restaurants to shame.

He swore under his breath.

When he'd moved out of Cindy's that morning, she'd offered to go grocery shopping for him, so he wouldn't have to worry about stocking up on his first day alone. Foolishly, he'd turned her down. He hadn't wanted to be any more trouble. Besides, they'd spent the last forty-eight hours performing an elaborate dance of avoidance and lies. Not only had they tried not to be alone together—a real trick for most of Sunday while her children were gone—they'd both pretended to forget the kiss. Or maybe he'd been the only one pretending. Maybe she'd been able to dismiss it from her mind.

The memory of her soft mouth against his had kept him up all Saturday night. Two cold showers hadn't helped his painful condition, nor had trying to think about something else.

He'd kissed women before. He rarely went more than a few months without a bed partner, although the last year or so had been pretty lean. But it was more than need that made him relive every moment of her in his arms. It was something much more dangerous and he didn't want to know what it was.

Before his line of thought produced its usual and obvious reaction, he limped over to the grocery carts and pulled one loose. It slid out easily. No sticky wheels or wobbly carts out here, he thought as he headed for the produce section.

He needed everything. Grace had planned to be gone for at least three months, so both the refrigerator and pantry were empty. It hadn't taken him long to settle into his sister's place, probably because everything he owned fit into two duffel bags.

His way of life was strange to Cindy. He'd seen it in the look on her face when she'd helped him pack. She kept asking if he didn't have something else to take with him.

As he stared at the rows of perfect peaches and nectarines, he snagged a plastic bag from the roll at the end of the counter and remembered last night. It had been the best time he'd had in months. The kids had arrived home about four. He and Cindy had gone to the video store and rented a couple of movies. They'd ordered pizza, then made root-beer floats.

As he reached for a couple of nectarines, he tried to recall if he'd ever had a root-beer float before in his life. He'd sure never made one at home. The kids had laughed and Cindy had been smiling. Her green eyes had lit up with emotion as she stared at her children. She'd hugged them close, as if having them home was a precious gift, and they'd held on just as tightly. In that moment, he hadn't felt left out as much as envious. He wanted that for himself, too. A place to belong. Someone to belong—

His cart jerked in his hands. He turned his head and saw a petite dark-haired woman smiling at him.

"Oops," she said, and pulled her cart back. "Didn't mean to bump you." She glanced at the nectarines in his bag. "They're on sale this week."

"I hadn't noticed." He looked up at the sign. It was on a chalkboard and illustrated by a cartoonlike figure.

"The grapes are pretty cheap, too. And tasty." She reached into her cart and fumbled with a bag. When she straightened, she had a grape resting in the palm of her hand. "Try one."

"Ah, thanks." He took the grape, feeling vaguely like

Snow White when she'd taken the apple in a movie he'd watched with Allison.

The tiny woman leaned toward him. "You're Mike Blackburne, right?" He must have looked confused because she laughed and placed her hand on his forearm. "I'm in a step aerobics class with your sister Grace. She told us all about you." Her eyebrows arched.

He started backing up. "Ah, it was nice to meet you…"

"Belinda," she said. "I was wondering if you might like to come over to dinner sometime."

He looked at her left hand and saw a diamond band sparkling there. "I'm not sure your husband would be pleased."

"Oh, he's gone a lot." Her smile broadened. "It could be our little secret."

"I'm not very good at keeping secrets," he said. "But thanks for asking."

With that, he turned his cart down the main aisle. He wanted to leave the store, but he needed food and it was unlikely the woman was going to pursue him in this public store.

"I'm in the book. Phone me if you change your mind," she called, then gave her last name.

He nodded and kept on going, slowing long enough to grab a bag of premade salad, and some broccoli. He cruised through the bakery department, searching for his favorite brand of bread. They must not make it in Texas, he decided after a few minutes of fruitless searching.

By the meat counter, two women shopping together tried to engage him in conversation, but he only smiled and kept on moving. He could feel a cold sweat breaking out on his back. It wasn't caused by exertion, he was barely moving at a fast walk. So it was something else. If he was honest with himself, he would admit he didn't like these people knowing who he was. It made him nervous.

He turned down the cereal aisle and picked out a box. At the far end were the paperback books and magazines. He paused there to find something to read. There was an entire section of the romance novels Cindy liked. He thought about picking one up for her, but didn't know which she might already have read.

He liked watching her read. She got lost in the story. Often he'd come into the family room and found her sprawled out on the sofa, one foot dangling over the back of the couch. How many times had he wanted to go to her? He'd known her skin would be soft before he touched it. He'd known she would taste of heaven long before they kissed.

Maybe that's what was bothering him. Usually, realities fell far short of the imaginings, but Cindy was even better than he'd hoped and he wasn't sure why. Of course he'd thought of kissing her, but the real thing had been different. Maybe because in the past kissing had been something he did on the road to going to bed with a woman. With Cindy, he'd enjoyed the act of kissing simply for itself. The process—holding her, feeling her lean against him, tasting her—had been enough. Although he didn't want to think about what could have happened if they'd been inside the house instead of standing in the middle of the street.

He picked up a book and flipped through it. But instead of words, he saw Cindy's face as it had been in the glow of the streetlight. He saw her swollen mouth and the passion in her eyes. Just thinking about it turned him on. But he knew it wasn't right. She was—

Another cart slammed into him. He looked up as a

blond woman with an infant in the cart and a young girl trailing behind smiled at him.

"I'm sorry," she said. "I wasn't watching where I was going." She pointed at the book Mike was holding. "Does that look any good?"

"I don't know." He thrust the paperback at her, then grabbed his cart and hurried down the aisle. His injured leg screamed in protest, but he didn't slow down until he was safely lost in the canned goods.

Once there, he paused to catch his breath. They knew him. He could read it in their faces. They talked about him and when they got home they would call their friends and mention running into him in the grocery store. He'd heard they were interested, and it scared the hell out of him. He would feel safer in a roomful of armed terrorists. At least there he would know the rules.

Moving cautiously, making eye contact with no one and walking as quickly as his injury would allow, he walked to the aisle with soda and grabbed two twelve-packs. Up ahead were chips. He started toward them when a cart turned in at the far end. That sixth sense that told him to duck in time to avoid gunfire screamed for him to turn. He turned. As he whipped around to the center aisle, his peripheral vision registered a familiar form. Beth. He groaned. That was all he needed.

He was standing by the frozen foods. Mike quickly scanned the contents of the freezer, opened one glass door and pulled out five of the same dinner. He couldn't afford to be picky now. Before anyone else could speak to him, he made his way to the checkout counters.

Once there, he was trapped behind a prim woman who seemed to know everything about his wounds. For a moment, he was afraid she was going to ask to see the scar.

Finally she left, helped to her car by an elderly box boy who was nearly twice her age and half her size.

Mike breathed a sigh of relief.

"How's it going?" the checker asked as she unhooked the front of his cart and started scanning groceries.

"You don't want to know," Mike said. He reached in his back pocket and pulled out his wallet.

"I haven't seen you in here before."

"I'm just visiting." He was mesmerized by how quickly she pulled his food across the small glass sensor. It beeped with the regularity of a pager going off.

"You're Mike Blackburne, right?"

His head snapped up and his attention narrowed. The woman was in her late twenties, with curly brown hair and blue eyes. "How did you know?"

She smiled. "Grace shops here all the time. We talk. She showed me your picture. If I'd known bodyguards were so handsome, I would have tried harder to get into trouble."

He swallowed. "It's not as romantic as it sounds."

"I don't know. It sounds pretty romantic to me." She glanced over her shoulder at the big wall clock above the produce section. "I get off work at three. Would you like to go for a cup of coffee?"

He fought the urge to whimper. "Thanks, but I've already got plans."

She took his money. "Too bad." After making change, she handed it to him. "I'm here Monday through Friday. Come by if you change your mind."

"I will. Thanks." He grabbed the two bags of groceries. Before he got outside, he was stopped twice more. The first time, a soft-spoken woman asked him if he would be willing to come to the Christian Women's luncheon to discuss security. He gave her Grace's phone number. The second woman didn't say much. She just looked at him as if he were a side of beef and she'd been starving for weeks. He literally jogged into the parking lot.

His leg was throbbing, he was dripping sweat and he hadn't even been to the gym yet. What the hell was going on here?

All he wanted was to escape. He reached into his shorts pocket and grabbed the keys. Then he scanned the row where he'd left Grace's white Ford Explorer.

"Dammit."

There were five white Ford Explorers sitting next to each other. They were identical. He hadn't thought to memorize Grace's license-plate number. Muttering under his breath, he hit the disarm button on the car alarm and walked past each one. The third vehicle beeped and snapped open the locks. He pulled open the door, shoved the groceries onto the front seat and scrambled up beside them. Barely stopping long enough to fasten his seat belt, he put the car in reverse and backed out of his space.

Once on the main road, he clung to the steering wheel as if it were a life belt and he were adrift at sea. He drove automatically until he reached his sister's subdivision. He pulled into her driveway and jumped out of the car. Without knowing what else to do, he crossed the lawn and went around to the back of Cindy's house. Her blue minivan was parked in front of the garage. He pounded on the back door.

When she pulled it open, she stared up at him. "Mike, what's wrong? You look awful."

He glanced over his shoulder. "They're coming," he said. "You've got to hide me."

* * *

For a moment, Cindy thought Mike had slipped into some delusional state. "Who's coming?"

He shook his head as if to clear it. A single lock of hair fell onto his forehead. "I went to the grocery store. They were everywhere. They kept talking to me and offering to squeeze my melons." He shuddered.

"Who?"

His dark eyes met hers. "Women."

She knew exactly what had happened. It wasn't hard to imagine, especially in a small community like this. Cindy took his hand and drew him into the house. "You're safe now. They won't hurt you here."

His breathing slowed to normal. He glanced down at her and frowned. "You're laughing at me."

She tried to keep the corners of her mouth from turning up, but she could feel herself starting to smile. "Maybe just a little. You were at the market, Mike. You make it sound like you just battled the thundering hordes."

"Yeah, well, you weren't there. They kept bumping into me with their carts. I don't understand how these women manage to drive around without getting into accidents, yet at the grocery store, they can't go two feet without bumping into something."

"Have you ever thought they were doing it on purpose?"

"Oh, God." He dropped his chin to his chest.

"Did you come right over when you got home?"

"Yeah. Why?"

"I was just wondering if you'd bothered to put your groceries away."

He swore. She giggled.

"You could try and be a little more sympathetic," he called over his shoulder as he marched out of her house.

Closing the door behind her, she followed him outside. "I think you're overreacting."

"So I shouldn't run in the opposite direction when I see Beth?" he asked as he fumbled with the passenger door. It was locked.

Before he ripped it off at the hinges, she plucked the keys dangling from his back pocket and hit the disarm button. Instantly all the doors unlocked. Mike jerked open the door and grabbed the two bags. She took one from him and started for Grace's back door.

"Running from Beth isn't necessary," she said as she set the bag on the counter and began to unpack the groceries. "I've told you. She talks a good game, but the truth is, she loves Darren. If she actually saw you naked, she would probably die from embarrassment."

"Let's not test your theory."

She pulled out a frozen dinner. The next one was the same. And the next. When she'd stacked all five together and placed them in the freezer, she glanced at him. "You really like Salisbury steak, don't you?"

He was shoving a bag of salad in the empty produce bin. He straightened and shrugged. "It seemed like a wise idea to get out of there as quickly as possible."

Sunlight streamed through the kitchen windows. Grace's house had a different floor plan from her own. This kitchen was long, with darker hardwood floors and brick accents. Mike leaned against the counter as if the morning's activities had worn him out.

His brown hair had grown out of its military cut. It was almost to his ears. He was still tanned and lean, his red T-shirt emphasizing the width of his shoulders and the muscles in his back. His shorts barely covered the bandage on his leg. He was tall, handsome and single.

"Like catnip to a cat," she said softly.

"What?"

"That's the problem. Look at where we are," she told him. "Nothing exciting ever happens here. Our business is families and raising children. We don't deal in international espionage."

He folded his arms over his chest. "How do you stand it?"

"How do you stand the city?" She emptied the second bag. After rinsing the fruit, she pulled a glass bowl out of Grace's cupboard and put the nectarines in it. Then she set the bowl in the refrigerator.

"The city is great," he said. "You can get anything, anytime you want. Movies, restaurants. Something is always happening. Not like here."

"I don't want anything to happen. Did you eat lunch?"

He shook his head.

"Come on. I'll make you a sandwich."

"Cindy, I moved out of your place this morning so I wouldn't be a bother."

"It's no trouble. I wasn't expecting you to leave so quickly. I've got plenty of food." She smiled. "You've had a harrowing experience. I don't think you should be alone just yet."

"Go ahead and mock me while I'm in a weakened condition." He followed her back to her house.

When he was settled at the table, she pulled deli meat out of the refrigerator, then grabbed some bread. He didn't have to know, but she was grateful for the company. In the last couple of weeks, she'd gotten used to having him around. Today, with him gone and the kids off playing with friends, the house had been too quiet.

"You never answered my question," he said. "Why do you stay here?"

"Because this is what I've always wanted."

"Roots?"

"Exactly. I like that it's boring. If I had my way, the rest of my life would be just as dull. You know, the Chinese have a saying—'May you live an interesting life.' Or is it live in interesting times? Either way, you get the point. I like the sameness, the traditions. My idea of happiness is serving exactly the same thing every year at Christmas. I like teaching the same curriculum each year at school. The kids are different and they learn at different rates. That's the challenge. But the rhythm is the same."

"Doesn't sound very exciting."

"I've had enough excitement to last me a lifetime. I grew up moving every year or two. I never made many friends. By the time I finally got in with some kids, it was time to move on." She remembered those times clearly. What she recalled most was always being lonely. "I never want my children to have to think about not fitting in. I want them to belong."

"I find it hard to believe you didn't always fit in."

"Why? You don't."

"How did you know that?"

His expression of surprise made her laugh out loud. "Mike, it's so obvious. You've never fit in. Look at how you're reacting to the suburbs, and this is about the most normal, most boring place in the world. You live on the fringes. Belonging gets in the way of what you do. Face it, a man comfortable with the rhythm of life doesn't choose to be a bodyguard."

She spread mustard on the bread, then folded several thin slices of roast beef. By now, she knew how he liked his sandwiches. She added extra lettuce without asking, and skipped the tomato.

"To answer the question you're thinking," she said as she set the plate in front of him, "the reason I know so much about you is that you're a lot like my dad. He didn't want to settle down, either. The only difference is that you're smart enough to do it on your own. He got married and dragged us along with him until we got to be too much of a burden. He loved the military and so did you.''

He took a bite of sandwich and chewed slowly. She grabbed two sodas and set one in front of him. After taking the seat across from his, she popped her can and took a swallow.

''The Marine Corps was the first place I fit in,'' he said. ''Sounds pretty sad, huh?''

''It makes perfect sense.'' Grace had told her a little about his childhood. By the time her friend had been born, Mike was nearly ten. He was always on the outside looking in, although he'd really cared about his baby half sister.

''I worked with the Military Police for a while, and I found out I was good at taking care of people. From there, I went to work for the Secret Service before going out on my own.''

''Do you ever think about doing anything else?''

He glanced down at his leg. ''It's been on my mind. I'm nearly forty. Everything's starting to go. The reflexes, timing.''

''Oh, yeah, you're so old. That's why all those women are chasing you.''

He didn't smile. ''It's a game for the young, Cindy. There aren't a lot of old bodyguards.''

''But you love the danger too much to give it up.''

''Maybe.'' He stared over her left shoulder, but she knew he was seeing something other than the kitchen. ''I spent my teenage years in trouble with the law. Now this is all I know. But taking a bullet has a way of making a man reevaluate what he wants to do with his life.''

"I can't see you sitting behind a desk."

He grinned. "Me, neither."

She wondered what kind of man voluntarily faced death every day, then decided she didn't want to know. There was no point in getting emotionally involved. When he was healed, Mike would be moving on. She might see him from time to time when he came to visit Grace, if he ever did, but they could never have a relationship. If she forgot that, she was going to get hurt.

"I bet you did very well on jungle patrol," she said.

"Not bad."

She leaned forward. "Surviving in the jungle is a matter of blending in with the cover and adapting, right?"

"So?"

"I think that's your problem. You need to think of the suburbs as a different kind of jungle. You haven't been blending in and adapting. You need to get familiar with the territory and act like the natives. You need a cover."

He grinned. Her heart flopped over a couple of times in her chest. She ignored the sensation, along with the tingling that started in her toes and worked its way up. It was just a chill from the air conditioner or a rare summer malady she'd picked up somewhere. It wasn't Mike. She refused to be attracted to him. Okay, she wasn't going to lie to herself. She refused to be *more* attracted to him. It was bad enough that she couldn't stop thinking about their kiss. It haunted her and made her hunger for his touch.

She'd hoped it was just a general sort of awakening, a sign that she was finally ready to start dating. But her fantasies were specifically about Mike. Whenever she tried to picture herself in the arms of another man, the fantasy disappeared. Life was not fair.

"A cover," he said slowly, then nodded. "You're absolutely right. I've been doing this all wrong. I need to blend in.'' He drew his eyebrows together. ''I've got the right car. God knows there are plenty of white Explorers here. But I don't have a family. That's a problem.''

''You can borrow my kids.''

His gaze locked with hers. ''But that's not going to be enough, is it? I also need a wife, or at least a woman in my life. So what do you say, Cindy? This was your idea. You willing to see it through?''

''What are you asking?'' Her voice was shaking and she didn't know why. Actually, she did know why—she just couldn't believe it!

''Will you pretend to be my girlfriend?''

Chapter Eight

Cindy parked in front of the mall. The two-story structure was all gleaming glass, with lush plants around the entrance and throughout the parking lot.

Mike eyed the building with distaste. Spending the afternoon shopping wasn't his idea of a good time, but Cindy had convinced him it was the quickest way to get the message out. According to her, everyone eventually ended up at the mall. He hoped those who spread rumors had decided to visit today.

He opened the passenger door and stepped out into the noon heat. It had rained the previous day and the humidity was unbearable. He'd worked in high temperatures before, but nothing like this. It might only be in the low nineties, but with the moisture in the air, he felt as if he were slowly being steamed alive, like a piece of broccoli.

"Can we go to the movies?" Allison asked as she scrambled from the back seat.

Cindy waited until all the doors were closed, then hit the alarm button on her key chain. The minivan chirped twice then was silent. "That's a good idea," she said.

"Not some dopey cartoon," Jonathan said. "Please, Mom, can we see that new action movie?"

Cindy brushed Jonathan's blond hair out of his eyes. "It's rated for adults only, so you know the answer to that, don't you?"

Jonathan turned to Mike. "Mike, you explain it to her. Sometimes it's important for a guy to do stuff, you know, like a man. Women don't understand that."

Mike stared at the kid. He was nine years old. Where did he hear that kind of talk? He grinned at the boy. "Mothers rule the world, kid. The sooner you learn that, the easier life will be."

"Ah, Mike." Jonathan scuffed his toe into the steamy blacktop.

Cindy leaned toward her son and got him in a headlock. "I am your leader," she said, spacing the words out evenly and trying to sound like a machine. "You will obey me, or I will turn you into a toad."

Jonathan laughed up at her. The boy might look like his father, but he had his mother's good humor. "Ribit." They were still giggling when they reached the mall.

Mike held open the door. Allison skipped inside, followed by her brother. Cindy paused and glanced at Mike. "You can change your mind," she said.

"You're the one doing me a favor. If you want to back out, I'll understand."

She shook her head. "I've already agreed. If nothing else, it will be worth it to see the look on everyone's faces." Her green eyes danced with excitement.

A couple of days ago, those same eyes had widened with shock when he'd suggested she pose as his girlfriend to protect him. He'd been sort of shocked himself that he'd even asked. He hadn't planned it, but once he'd said the words, they made perfect sense. He hadn't expected Cindy to go along with it. After all, there wasn't anything in it for her. Much to his surprise, she had quickly agreed to the masquerade.

"You never told me why you're doing it," he said, waiting for her to precede him into the building.

She stepped inside and he followed her. "Number one, I owe Grace," she said, ticking off the reasons on her fingers. "Two, sometimes divorced women are treated as if they are invisible. I want to remind a few people that I'm still alive and well. Three, Nelson might find out and after what he's put me through, he deserves it. And four…" She smiled at him. Her dimple deepened. "I feel sorry for you. If you could have seen the panic in your eyes."

"Oh, gee, thanks. My ego needed a boost." With that, he put his arm around her.

Cindy stiffened. Her smile faded and she stared at him as if she'd never seen him before.

"Cindy?"

He started to lift his arm away. She blinked, then laughed and moved closer to him. "Momentary brain lapse. I forgot what we were doing here."

"But we were just talking about it."

"Talking and doing are not the same thing." A flush of color stained her cheeks. She gave him a tight smile, then glanced around. "Allison, Jonathan, you two stay within sight of us, remember?"

A chorus of "Yes, Mom" drifted back to them. Cindy turned to her right. Mike kept his arm around her and adjusted his limping stride to her shorter steps.

The interior of the mall was bright and open, with lush

plants growing out of huge pots on the floor and hanging from beams in the glass ceiling. Most of the shoppers were women with children. About one out of two had strollers. Children were everywhere. Young kids running to store-window displays, then back to their mothers, teen-agers collecting in groups and talking, babies sleeping or crying. Mike felt as if he were in some zoo specifically designed to study the raising of human young.

They'd gone along the bottom level a ways when he tightened his hold on Cindy's shoulders. "Just a minute. I want to look at the mall map."

"It's not necessary. We know our way around."

"I insist." He paused in front of the color-coded map and quickly got his bearings.

"Mike, I swear to you, we've been in every store. I could find my way around here blindfolded."

He released her and looked at the anchor stores. "I want to minimize our exposure. Tell me where we're go-ing so I can plot our route."

His request was met with silence. He turned toward her. Allison and Jonathan were playing on a bench behind her. Mike didn't know the nature of the game, but it required them to circle the wooden seat, with a quick climb over the back every third or fourth trip.

She tilted her head. "Exposure to what?"

Danger. Undesirable elements. He looked around at the women shopping and their children. Not much danger here. Feeling slightly foolish, he shoved his hands into his shorts pockets. "Sorry. Force of habit."

"You might do better if you pretended to be enjoying yourself," she said. "You know, relax a little. Laugh, shop. You ever spend an hour just window-shopping?"

"Can't say that I have."

"It's an art form," she told him. "I'll try to teach it to

you, but you have to give yourself up to the experience.''
She moved close and slipped her arm through his. Her
skin was smooth and warm. He told himself the gesture
was just part of the act, but she did it so easily, so unconsciously, he wanted to believe it was real.

Not real smart, Blackburne, he told himself. This situation was temporary. Cindy was helping him out of a
rough spot, nothing more.

She leaned closer. Her left breast brushed against his
upper arm. He felt the jolt clear to his groin and had to
bite back a groan. ''It would help if you tried to have a
good time,'' she whispered.

''I'll try,'' he told her, then wondered how long it had
been since he'd had fun just doing nothing. He'd been
working nonstop for about three years. Before that—he
shrugged. It was a lifetime ago. He didn't want to think
about the past or the future. There was only today and the
feel of Cindy so close to him.

They strolled down to the movie theater and had a
lively debate over which show to see. Allison wanted to
see a rerelease of a classic and Cindy agreed. Mike didn't
care, so Jonathan was outvoted. He took it well, grum-
bling for a few minutes, then playing tag with Allison
among the potted plants.

They walked slowly to the far end of the mall.

''How's your leg?'' Cindy asked.

''Not bad. I eased up on the workout yesterday. Grace
has a big Jacuzzi tub in her bathroom, and I've been using
that every night. It helps.''

''Let me know if you need the bandage changed.''

The thought of her hands on his bare skin made him
wish he was still bleeding. ''I don't really need the bandage anymore. I'm just wearing it until the exit wound
heals a little more. I don't want to gross everyone out.''

"It's not that bad."

"You're used to it. I've seen the women around here checking out my leg."

She looked at him and raised her eyebrows. "Mike, they're not looking at your wound."

He didn't know what to say to that. Even worse, he could feel a faint heat on his cheeks. Hell, he hadn't blushed in years. "Yeah, well, I figure I can take off the bandage in a week or so."

"We'll have a coming-out party," she teased.

"Mommy, Mommy, look!" Allison stood in front of The Disney Store pointing to an animated display. The little girl had her nose plastered against the window. "Look, Mickey's waving." She waved back. "Hi, Mickey."

"I didn't know they had stores like this," Mike said.

"Everywhere. It's wonderful. They make buying for birthday parties very simple."

He felt a slight tugging on his free hand. Allison was pulling on him. "Come see, Mike. There's bookends I'm going to ask Santa for."

Cindy released him and he allowed the little girl to lead him into the store. In the front were racks of clothing—T-shirts, sweats, nightgowns, along with hats, ties and some odd-looking slippers. Halfway back, two large glass cases lined the walls. In between them were display shelves. Allison stopped in front of one and pointed.

"There," she said reverently.

The ceramic bookends were in two pieces. The right one showed Winnie the Pooh being pulled out of a hole by Christopher Robin. The left bookend was Pooh's back half, being pushed through the hole by Rabbit and Piglet and all Pooh's friends. The detail in the piece was amazing. Mike half expected the creatures to bounce to life.

"I didn't see them before my birthday," Allison told him, "so I'm going to ask Santa to bring them." She looked at him. "Do you think elves know how to make bookends?" she asked earnestly.

"Of course."

"Good." She smiled and curled her small hand around his. "Come see the stuffed animals." She pulled him to the back of the store and introduced him to all the creatures there. He hugged the ones she instructed him to, then spoke to a couple of others. She giggled when he snarled at the evil wizard doll.

The sound of her laughter was as welcome as desert rain. He liked Allison's being happy. It seemed to him in the last week or so, she'd started letting go of her imaginary friend.

"Where's Shelby?" he asked.

"She wanted to stay home," Allison answered easily. "Look, here's Pumba. He's a warthog."

By the time Cindy rescued him, he was well versed in the different characters. "Ask me anything," he said as they left the store. "I can recite plot lines, name characters and their offspring."

"You're very patient. I really appreciate that, and so do the children."

He shrugged. "It's no big deal. They're fun to be with." You're fun to be with, too, but he didn't say that. It would add a complication neither of them wanted.

"Mom, there's Kaleb and Brett. I want to go talk to them." Jonathan practically danced in place.

"Go," Cindy said. "But don't leave that spot."

She headed toward a bench in the shade of a large tree. When she sat down, Allison settled next to her and Mike took her other side. He put his arm around her. Just for show, he told himself, even as he noticed how well they fit together.

Cindy sighed. "I could live at the mall. Everything is new and clean. There's food so I wouldn't have to cook, movies and video games for the children and all the books I could possibly read."

Her hair brushed against his arm. He fingered a strand, noticing the softness and the way it felt against his skin. Without closing his eyes, he could imagine her straddling him, her head bent low as she—

"Mike, these are my friends, Kaleb and Brett." Jonathan grinned. "This is Mike. He's a bodyguard. He's been staying with us because he was shot, but he's getting better now."

Mike nodded at the two boys gaping at him. "Nice to meet you."

"Yeah," the larger of the two said. "You really a bodyguard?"

"That's right."

"You ever shoot anybody?"

"Yes, but only to protect a client."

"Wow, cool."

"Leave Mike alone," Cindy said. "He's resting." She dug in her purse and pulled out a handful of singles. "Go get an ice-cream cone." She looked at Mike. "You want one?"

He shook his head.

Allison jumped off the bench. "I want strawberry."

"I know, honey. Just tell the man." She indicated an ice-cream cart about fifteen feet away, across the open area. The four children made a mad dash to be first in line. Kaleb won, but he quickly relinquished his spot to Allison.

"Peace at last," she said, leaning her head against his

arm. Her eyes closed. "Tell me if they start to leave the area, please."

"I doubt they will. They're good kids."

"Thanks. I work at it. Although right now, all I want is to take a nap."

"Then I probably shouldn't tell you that Mary and Christina from the barbecue are heading this way."

Cindy straightened and her eyes snapped opened. "Where?" She followed where he pointed and sucked in a breath. The two women were standing in front of a shoe store studying a display. "They haven't seen us yet, but as soon as they do..." She angled toward him. "This is your big chance, Mike. Make it good."

From the tilt of her head, she was expecting a quick kiss on the cheek. He thought he'd cured her of that the last time they'd kissed. He touched his finger to her chin and turned her slightly, then bent forward and brushed his lips against hers.

Even as he reminded himself that they were in the middle of a mall and her children would probably see this, he had to fight the urge to deepen the kiss. Her lips were as warm and yielding as he remembered. He was instantly aroused. The situation wasn't helped by Cindy putting her hand on his upper arm and holding on as if she were in danger of blowing away.

He allowed himself to brush his tongue across her lower lip, then he pulled back. Her eyes were unfocused, her face flushed. "Good enough?"

"Extraordinary." Her voice was breathless.

"Me, too," he mumbled.

"What?" Before he had to answer, she glanced up and winced. "They saw us, that's for sure." She gave a little halfhearted wave.

Mike looked over his shoulder and saw the two women

staring at them. When he smiled a greeting, they whispered to each other, then took off for the far end of the mall.

"It should take about an hour," Cindy said. "Beth is going to have fifteen messages on my phone by the time we get back. And is she going to be mad." She leaned against the bench. "Beth can keep a secret, so if you don't mind, I want to tell her the truth."

"Fine, but if she asks if you saw me naked, be sure and tell her yes."

"Should I tell her I was impressed?"

"You have to ask?"

Her laughter warmed him like summer sunshine. In that moment, he forgot that her children and their friends were eating ice cream not fifteen feet away. He forgot about the people shopping around them and the fact that Cindy wasn't for him. He wanted her. He could handle the need. What scared him was that he also wanted to *be* with her. It wasn't just about sex and he didn't know how to deal with that.

Lucky for both of them, Cindy wasn't the type to have a meaningless affair, because he had the feeling it *would* mean something and then where would he be?

A few minutes later, they made their way to the movies. Jonathan grumbled a few times about the cartoon, but he was soon engrossed in the story. The boy sat between Mike and Cindy, with Allison on Mike's other side. Probably better that way, Mike thought, knowing how the darkness would have tempted him.

When the evil trees closed in on the beautiful princess, Allison whimpered in fear. Without thinking, he gathered her up onto his lap. She buried her head in his shoulder and whispered for him to tell her when the scary part was over.

She was small and slight. As he held the child, he wondered how something so fragile could survive. She smelled of summer and strawberries. Her hands were sticky on his arms, but he didn't mind.

At last the princess made it out of danger. He whispered that it was safe to look. Allison twisted around to face the movie screen but she didn't slide off his lap and Mike found he didn't want to make her.

Further into the film, the princess kissed her prince. Jonathan groaned and covered his eyes. "Yuck," he said quietly. "I hate this part."

Mike chuckled, then looked at Cindy. She was smiling at him. He felt the connection, the circle of family. For the first time in his life, he was inside where it was warm.

Mike pitched the ball. The batter swung and missed. Jonathan called out for him to pay more attention to the ball.

Cindy stepped back from the window and reached for the pitcher of brewed tea. She poured the dark liquid into two glasses full of ice, then carried them both to the table.

Beth poured a package of artificial sweetener into hers, then took a sip. "How long does this game of pretend go on?"

"For as long as he's here. If everyone thinks we're a couple, Mike is safe."

"I understand what Mike gets out of it, but what about you?"

"I'm doing it for Grace," Cindy said, sitting down opposite her friend. "I owe her. And for Mike. He's a nice guy."

"He's a little more than that."

"I don't know what you mean."

"Uh-huh, sure."

Cindy didn't dare glance at Beth. She didn't want to see the knowing expression on her friend's face. Beth had brought up an interesting point. Why *was* Cindy helping Mike out?

She was doing it for the reasons she'd told Beth and for one other. She was doing it because she liked pretending it was real. She liked the closeness they shared, she liked him touching her and being able to touch him back. Being with him made her remember all the good parts about being married. Being with him made her feel alive. It was the safest way to get what she wanted. Mike was leaving. She knew that in advance. She wouldn't be foolish enough to give her heart away, so she wouldn't have to worry about getting it broken.

"So, have you seen him naked?" Beth asked teasingly.

Cindy had known the question was coming. She'd even prepared a witty answer. But instead of saying that, she slapped her hands down on the table. "Dammit, there's more to a relationship than sex."

Beth stared at her, then took a sip of tea. "Honey, you're not falling for him, are you?"

She'd surprised herself with her outburst. "Of course not. That would be crazy. We're just friends. Mike is..."

"Handsome?" Beth offered helpfully.

"Well, yes."

"Funny?"

She smiled. "Very."

"Charming?"

"When he wants to be."

"Single?"

"Obviously." Cindy frowned. "What's your point?"

"I don't have one." Beth folded the empty sweetener packet in half. "As long as you're sure you're not falling for him. It seems to me it would be very easy for this game of pretend to get out of hand.''

"I'm not going to let that happen," Cindy said. "He's not my type."

"In the two years you've been single, you haven't had one date. I don't think you're qualified to know what your type is."

"Maybe not, but whatever my type is, Mike isn't it. The man can fit his belongings into two duffel bags. I want someone who's going to stick around. Someone stable. With roots."

"You had that with Nelson, and he still left you."

"Thanks for reminding me."

Beth leaned forward. Her blue eyes darkened with sympathy. "You know what I'm saying. You thought Nelson would be a sure thing, and he wasn't. You assume Mike is wrong for you. Maybe he is wrong. And just maybe he's Mr. Right. You can handle this any way you like. But like I said, this game of pretending to have a relationship could get out of hand. What if you stop pretending, but he still thinks it's a game? I don't want you getting hurt."

"That won't happen. I'd be crazy to fall for a guy like him."

Beth stood up. "Sounds like you're trying to convince yourself more than me," she said, then left.

Cindy sat at the kitchen table a long time. She thought about what her friend had said. It was a risk. She would be the first to admit that something about Mike got to her. It wasn't just his good looks. It was the way he took the time to be with her kids, and his kindness. Okay, and maybe it was the way he turned her on.

The back door opened. Five sweaty children and one sweaty adult spilled into the kitchen.

"We're thirsty," Jonathan said.

She pulled out a pitcher of lemonade from the fridge as her son set out plastic glasses. Mike limped over to the kitchen table and sat down. "They're thirsty. I'm going to have a heart attack. Do you know how hot it is out there?"

The five boys collected their cups and started to leave. "You coming, Mike?" Jonathan asked.

"No," he gasped, and leaned back in the chair. "I can't keep up."

Jonathan laughed and closed the door behind him.

"You have to be careful in this heat," Cindy told him, eyeing his damp T-shirt.

"I know. I still don't have my endurance. The leg is healing, but it's going to be a while."

He took the glass she offered and downed the lemonade in three big gulps. As he handed it back to her, he grabbed the hem of his T-shirt and raised it to wipe his face. She had a brief glimpse of his hard, muscled belly and chest. His bare skin gleamed from sweat. She'd seen his chest several times while he'd been sick. She'd always admired it, but it was only recently that the sight of it sent her heart into overdrive. She supposed it was because when he was a patient, she'd thought of him as someone she had to take care of and now she thought of him as a man.

She poured him another glass of lemonade. "Did you have fun?"

"Yeah."

"Don't sound so surprised."

"I can't help it. I'm discovering a whole new species of humans. Kids are pretty cool."

"Don't let them fool you," she said. "They can be a real pain sometimes."

"I know that." He took a drink, then set the glass on the table.

"You'd be a good father," she said, putting the now-empty pitcher in the sink.

She glanced at Mike. He raised his eyebrows and shook his head.

"You don't agree?" she asked.

"No. I would be pretty good being a part-time parent, but I doubt if I could be there for the long haul. Besides, I'm just a beat-up, scarred, slightly over-the-hill bodyguard. Who would want me?"

He took another drink and closed his eyes as if not really expecting an answer. Cindy thought about how he made her feel when he held her, and how good he was with the kids. She rinsed out the pitcher and started to make another batch of lemonade, all the while the answer to his question echoing silently inside her head.

Who would want a beat-up, scarred, slightly over-the-hill bodyguard? She might.

Chapter Nine

The crash of thunder echoed through the house. Mike sat upstairs in the game room, watching the bolts of lightning filling the sky. Rain pounded against the windows. According to the weather channel on television, the storm was going to be a bad one, lasting most of the afternoon. He stretched out on the sofa, propped his feet on the coffee table and prepared to enjoy the show.

The wound in this thigh had almost healed. He'd been working out regularly at the country club, but never on weekends. His strength was returning, although his endurance was going to take a little longer to reach one hundred percent. It was a slow process, but he was improving daily. That's what he'd come to Sugar Land to do.

He glanced at the clock above the entertainment center. It was late Saturday afternoon. He'd begun to measure his life in two-week increments. The beginning and ending of each time period was Jonathan and Allison spending the weekend with their father. They'd left that morning.

He didn't see them every day, but he still missed them when they were gone. At least every other day, they came over and invited him to play in the greenbelt or go to lunch or a movie with them. The invitations rarely came from Cindy and he wasn't sure if she liked his tagging along or not. She always seemed pleased to see him. If she'd been one of his usual women, he would have known exactly what she was thinking. If she'd been one of his usual women, he wouldn't have cared as much.

In the last few weeks, he'd begun depending on her less. The grocery store was no longer strange. He'd gotten used to everyone's knowing who he was. Since word had spread that he and Cindy were an item, the illicit invitations had slowed. He was grateful, but he sometimes wondered what would happen to Cindy when he was gone. Would everyone assume she'd been dumped? He hadn't thought that far ahead when he'd asked her to pretend to be involved with him. She hadn't mentioned it, but that didn't mean there weren't ramifications for her.

A bolt of lightning hit the ground close to the house. The instantaneous explosion of thunder shook the windows. He rose to his feet and walked downstairs. His limp was barely noticeable. He crossed the kitchen and stared out the window at Cindy's house. From this side he couldn't see anything but her fence and front yard. For all he knew, she was gone. Or entertaining.

He grimaced, not wanting to think about her being with another man. Why wouldn't she be? She was bright, pretty, sexy as hell. Unless all the single men in the area were blind, someone had to have noticed her.

With her pretending to be involved with him, he knew it was illogical to assume she had a man in her house, but once the thought was planted, he couldn't let it go. He wanted to walk over and find out, but he couldn't think of a good enough excuse.

Besides, it wasn't his business. She was just a friend, nothing more. What she did with her personal life was her business. And even if it were his business, he didn't want to get involved. Bad enough that he was already attached to her kids; he wasn't going to make it worse by becoming attached to the lady herself.

That decided, he opened the refrigerator. It was too early for dinner, but maybe he could figure out what he was going to have. He'd finished his stash of frozen dinners. He could go to the market again. Or maybe a movie. He needed to get out.

The next bolt of lightning didn't hit close to the house, nor was the accompanying thunder particularly loud, but even as the sound rumbled through the afternoon, the lights in the house faded and the air conditioner stopped.

He stood in the center of the kitchen waiting for the electricity to be restored. It often went out for a few seconds during storms. After two minutes, he figured it wasn't going to be coming back on anytime soon. Maybe he should go and make sure Cindy was all right.

It was, he acknowledged as he dashed through the rain, a flimsy excuse. Cindy had been surviving storms long before he arrived in town. But it was the best he could come up with under the circumstances. Admitting that he simply wanted to see her wasn't an option.

He ran across her lawn and down the driveway. Once under the protection of the breezeway, he slowed, then stopped in front of her back door and knocked.

"Come in," she called.

He opened the door and stepped inside.

Her house was cool, dark and silent. There were no

lights, no hum of the air conditioner or ceiling fans. "Where are you?" he asked.

"In the living room."

He crossed the family room floor and entered the large open living area. The ceiling was two stories high, the windows nearly that tall. Outside, bushes and crepe myrtle trees swayed in the wind. Cindy was sitting in one corner of the sofa that faced the window. She'd pulled her knees up to her chest. Her shoulder-length hair was loose around her face.

He stopped in front of her and glared. "You shouldn't leave your back door open and you shouldn't just call 'Come in.' What if I'd been a burglar?"

She glanced up at him. Her eyes were a mossy green in the dark gray of the afternoon light, her face pale and devoid of makeup. She wore a white short-sleeved shirt that buttoned up the front and pull-on shorts.

"Only my friends use the back door," she said. "Burglars don't knock and strangers come to the front."

"You should be more careful."

"Yes, Mike. I'll do my best." She leaned her head back against the sofa and closed her eyes.

"You okay?" he asked.

"Fine."

"The electricity is out. I came by to make sure everything was all right."

"Couldn't be better. I love summer storms." She waved one arm toward the far end of the sofa. "Have a seat. Do you want some wine?"

"Sure."

He moved around the light oak coffee table and sat down. Lightning lit the sky like a strobe light. Thunder was one long continuous boom. Cindy rose to her feet and collected a few fat candles from the mantel. She set them on the coffee table and lit them. The flickering lights added a soft glow to the room.

When she returned from the kitchen, she was carrying a bottle of red wine, a corkscrew and two glasses. Mike took the bottle from her and opened it. She settled on the sofa, staying in the far corner, but angling toward him.

"To summer," she said, taking the glass he offered.

"To summer." Their voices were quiet in the still room, the sound of the clinking glass unnaturally loud.

She sipped the dark liquid, then sighed. "Lovely. I hope the electricity stays out for another hour. Just long enough for us to enjoy the quiet, but not so long that the frozen foods spoil."

Mike grinned. "Ever practical."

"I'm a mother. I have to be."

She took another drink, then leaned forward and set the glass on the table. The front of her blouse gaped slightly. He had a brief impression of pale curves and white lace, then she straightened.

"I haven't seen you in a couple of days," she said. "What have you been doing?"

"Working out. I seem to be collecting a smaller audience each time."

"But you still have that core group of devoted fans."

"Don't remind me." He took a drink of his wine. The taste was smooth with a hint of a bite. Very nice. "I've been catching up on my reading. Trying to avoid television. Do you know what's on during the day?" He shuddered. "I can't believe people go on talk shows and admit all these personal problems to millions of viewers. And the soaps. Thank God for CNN."

"And sports."

"That, too."

The wind shifted so the rain pelted the tall windows.

There were three across the back of the living room. Two slender windows on either side of a wide one in the center. The curtains had been drawn back, the lace sheers pushed aside.

Cindy leaned forward. "Isn't it beautiful?"

"Yes." He watched jagged flashes cut through the gray clouds. "I didn't realize the weather changed so much here in Houston."

"It's never boring, that's for sure." She gave him a quick smile, then turned her attention back to the storm. "Fronts come through quickly. In the winter it can go from sixty-five to below forty degrees in about fifteen minutes. You can run the air conditioner in the morning and the heater that night."

"I can't believe you ever use the heater," he said.

"It is a little warm right now."

"Warm? I've been in saunas that are cooler than this."

"It will be cool right now, in the rain, but as soon as the storm passes, it will get muggy. But it gets hot back East and in Los Angeles in the summer."

"Not like this." He took another sip of wine, then leaned back on the sofa, resting the glass on his belly. "L.A. is a dry heat and it comes and goes in cycles. New York has humidity, but nothing like this. I spent some time in Singapore during the summer. Now *that's* heat."

She turned toward him. "Where else have you been?"

He shrugged. "Everywhere. It all blurs after a while. You traveled a lot, too, when you were a kid."

"Not like that. It was military bases and mostly in the States. We never went anywhere fun. That might have made up for moving all the time. If I had my wish, I would never move again."

He glanced around the room. "It's very nice here."

"Thanks. I like it. When I was growing up, I used to

think about the house I would buy when I was an adult. I used to plan the rooms and how I would decorate them.''

"How close did you come?"

She picked up her wine and chuckled. "Fortunately, I modified my plans as I got older. I can't remember what I would have chosen when I was Allison's age, but I'm sure it would have been awful." She took a sip, then continued, "I always wanted my home to be welcoming. The sort of place someone would want to stay."

"Then you've accomplished your goal." He'd felt welcome in her house from the first moment he regained consciousness. Now, with a storm raging outside, the house felt like a haven.

"Thanks. I'd like to redo this room." She patted the floral-print sofa. "Maybe get rid of those drapes. I don't like the gray. It's a little cold for me, but Nelson liked it. I've changed the bedroom since he left and I'd like to do more, but it has to be slow. I'm still trying to make it on a teacher's salary."

She leaned toward the coffee table and set down her wine. As she shifted back in place, she moved closer. Mike told himself it was a completely unconscious action. Cindy considered him a friend. She was relaxed around him. She wasn't coming on to him.

But his body didn't want to listen to logic. From the moment he'd first seen her, he'd thought she was attractive. If he recalled those first few foggy minutes correctly, he'd thought she was a naked angel sent to him from heaven. Now he knew she was even better than that, she was a flesh-and-blood woman. And he wanted her.

He rested his head on the sofa and sipped his wine, all the while listening to her plans about wallpaper and new carpeting. He enjoyed the sound of her voice. It nearly blocked out the blood roaring through his veins. His skin was hot, his groin hard. Just being with her turned him on. He didn't want to think about what would happen if they actually touched. Or kissed. Or made love.

He had a bad feeling it would be pretty damn good—and a complete disaster. He wasn't into commitments and Cindy didn't know any other way to do it. So they would be friends, and when he left here late this afternoon, he would take a cold shower and think pure thoughts.

"Mike! You're not listening to me."

"Sorry. Men are genetically predisposed not to be able to talk about decorating."

"That's not true." She gave him a mocking glare. "Men very much want to live in a nice house, but many of them don't want to be bothered with doing any of the work required to get it that way."

"That, too," he admitted. He finished his wine and sat up to put the empty glass on the table. When he settled on the sofa again, he turned toward her. They were definitely closer to each other now. Each of them had about eight inches of space behind them, and less than that between them. Cindy was shaking her head. She hadn't noticed. He wondered if she would.

"I don't know how you stand not having a home," she said.

"You get used to it."

"I never did."

"You never wanted to."

She sat on her right hip, with her knee nearly touching his thigh and her body resting against the sofa. "What's so great about having nowhere to belong?"

"I wasn't like you, Cindy. I was a bad kid."

"What makes you think I was a good one?"

He reached out his hand and touched the tip of her nose. "I can see it in your eyes. You sat in the front of the classroom, did your homework every day and got good grades.''

''You were the bad boy in the back of the room. You annoyed the teacher with your smart remarks and tempted the girls with your smoldering eyes.''

Was she tempted? The heat inside him begged him to find out. What kept him in check was the fact that he liked Cindy, and she deserved a hell of a lot better than him.

''I stole cars,'' he said.

She didn't act surprised. ''Did you go to prison?''

''Aren't you shocked?''

''You once mentioned your being on the wrong side of the law when you were a teenager. No one ends up where you are by taking an ordinary path.''

She was smart. He liked that about her. ''I was given the choice between prison and the military. I decided on the military, the judge picked the marines. Looking back, I suppose he figured they'd either straighten me out or kill me.''

''And here you are.''

''I know now that I just wanted attention. My mother had remarried and started a second family. She never cared what I did, anyway, so it was easy to run the streets. But I got caught.'' He drew in a deep breath and let it out.

''Why a bodyguard?'' she asked. ''There are a lot of other kinds of security jobs.''

''I don't have a death wish. That's what some people think. It's not about the dying, it's about being better. When a client hires me, he's usually been threatened. My job is to be smarter and faster than the enemy. Think like him, know him, then beat him. If I do my job right, no one gets hurt. If I don't, someone dies. Those are about the highest stakes around. Every situation is different, but the enemy is constant."

She'd tilted her head in that way that told him she was pondering something. "What are you thinking?" he asked.

"You might not have a death wish, but you are willing to die. What makes you offer that sacrifice?"

"I don't think of it like that. Death is just another way of finding out I didn't do my job right."

She leaned forward. Her hair swung down against her cheek and she brushed it back impatiently. "That's why you don't have a place, isn't it? Caring about something, belonging, makes it too difficult to accept that ultimate price. Or do you think that's what you deserve? Is it a punishment? What are you paying for, Mike?"

Her gaze was intense, all her attention focused on him. He stirred restlessly on the sofa, not knowing how to answer her. She'd strayed dangerously close to the truth he'd always tried to hide, even from himself. The specter of not being good enough had haunted him from childhood. He'd always believed the reason he'd been emotionally abandoned by his mother was that there was a problem with him. His stepfather's ambivalence had reinforced that idea. Women came and went in his life with a regularity that convinced him they could all see the truth. It wasn't them, it was him. A flaw he couldn't hide or fix. Once he realized he lacked whatever made a person lovable, he made sure he was in a situation where love was impractical. It was easier than facing the reality of his own shortcomings. So much for hiding behind a facade of confidence. Cindy had seen right through him.

"I'm sorry," she said, and touched his forearm. "I've had just enough psychology to spout nonsense. I didn't mean to offend you."

"I'm not offended," he said, wondering how she'd seen the truth so quickly. He felt exposed, as if he'd walked into a formal event completely naked.

"How long can you keep on doing it?" she asked. "Where do old bodyguards go?"

"I don't ask that question. This is all I know."

"Are there security jobs available?"

"Sure. Some companies hire bodyguards to train executives to protect themselves, especially when they travel overseas."

"You'd be good at that."

"Why?"

She smiled. "You're very patient with the children. That's the mark of a good teacher. Trust me on this, I'm an expert."

Her fingers still rested on his arm. Her casual exposure of his greatest weakness had destroyed his desire as effectively as sunlight burns a worm. But her equally casual acceptance of the flaw allowed him to breathe normally and stay in his seat. Gradually, her touch soothed him.

She drew her hand back to her lap. "Of course, if you took a different kind of job, you wouldn't be able to seduce women so easily."

He laughed out loud. "Is that what you think I do?"

"Don't expect me to believe that you haven't used your job to get sex. I've seen what's happened here. The bodyguard thing really pushes some female buttons. I think it's because we assume you can take care of us."

He wondered if she really meant "us," as in she was attracted to him, too.

"So, have you?" She blushed.

"Now you sound like Beth."

"And you're avoiding the question."

"Yes, I've used my job to get women, but not often."

She scrambled into a kneeling position, then sank back until she was sitting on her ankles. "Really? What's it like?"

"For one thing, most women don't ask so many questions."

"But you're not interested in having sex with me," she said with a dismissive wave of her hand. "Come on. Tell me what they ask or say."

"They want to know about the glamour, the celebrities."

She wrinkled her nose. "That's boring."

He shook his head. "You're not like those women. Maybe that's why I'm having such a hard time fitting in here. My job is based on predicting other people's actions before even they know what they're going to do. Here I'm completely at a loss."

"You don't understand our world, so how can you predict us?"

"Excellent point. For a girl."

"Now *you* sound like Jonathan."

He smiled, then he leaned against the sofa back and studied her. "I understand criminals better than suburban women and children."

"Isn't that an interesting comment on the 'burbs? And here I thought we were so normal."

She laughed. The corners of her eyes crinkled. The lightning had passed, but rain continued to splatter against the windows. The electricity hadn't come back on. The afternoon was still gray and dark, with the only light coming from the candles flickering on the coffee table.

"You're very beautiful," he said without thinking.

Her laughter faded into a rueful smile. "I wish that were true."

"Why would I lie?"

"Because you're a nice guy."

"No one's ever accused me of that before."

"You're nice to my kids and to me. You make me feel good about myself." She tugged on her shorts. "Look at me. I didn't even put on makeup or get dressed up this morning, and Nelson actually came to the door. For the first time, I didn't care what he thought of me. I didn't mind that Hilari is four inches taller and twenty pounds lighter than I am. You're right. Nelson was a fool for leaving me. I probably should have figured that out a while ago, but I didn't until you mentioned it. I'm really grateful for that."

"Funny, I don't want your gratitude." She saw him as some damn do-gooder.

She straightened. "Did I say something wrong?"

"No. It's not you. It's just—hell…"

He reached forward and grabbed her upper arms. If she'd protested or resisted in the slightest, he would have let her go. But she watched mutely as he drew her closer. He lowered his mouth to hers. Her eyes fluttered closed and she breathed his name.

Even as he touched her lips, he told himself it was a mistake. He couldn't get involved with her or make promises. He didn't know how, and he refused to lie to her or lead her on. Which made kissing her a mistake. But when her arms came around the back of his neck, he knew he would pay whatever price this moment cost. She was worth it all.

Her mouth was soft and yielding. She tasted sweet. Still holding her arms, he shifted and lowered them both to the sofa. They pressed together from shoulder to knees, their legs tangled, their torsos brushing. Her arms held him close as if she feared he would escape. If he hadn't been so busy relearning every millimeter of her delicious mouth, he would have told her there was nowhere else he would rather be...except possibly in her bed.

Her fingers combed through his hair, sending shivers down his spine. He'd mentioned getting it cut, but she'd teased him about being afraid of looking normal. He loved the feel of her nails stroking his scalp and her palms massaging his neck. In that moment, he resolved to never cut his hair again.

As his mouth pressed against hers, he slipped his hands down her spine. He could feel her warm skin and the tempting fastener of her bra. He lingered there as if he could unhook it by will alone. She felt delicate and fragile against him. He could nearly span her back with a splayed hand. She was soft where he was hard, as if their bodies had been specifically designed for this moment.

She moaned impatiently, then squirmed against him. Her mouth parted. He tried to resist the temptation, touching his tongue to her lower lip before slipping inside. But her heat beckoned and he didn't have the strength to deny her or himself. He moved into her mouth.

The contrast of textures delighted him, her quivering response, the brush of her tongue against his, sent blood surging through his body before pooling in his groin. His erection flexed inside his shorts. She arched her hips toward him as if she'd felt it and wanted more.

He angled his head, seeking all of her mouth. They touched, moist heat to moist heat. Over and around, again and again, until his breathing was rapid and his body hot with longing. She moved her legs against his. Her smooth skin taunted him with images of her naked beneath him, her long legs wrapped around his hips as she drew him in fully. The picture was so real, the feeling so intense, he had to fight the need to explode right then.

He grabbed her hips and shifted, drawing her on top of

him. She straddled him. Instantly, her feminine heat surrounded his groin. He caught his breath.

"That might have been a mistake," he murmured against her mouth.

She laughed. "What *are* you hiding in your pocket?"

He kept his hands on her hips, urging her to rock against him. It was the sweet kind of torture. He grimaced, then stilled her.

"If you knew what you did to me," he said.

She rocked once more. He sucked in a breath. "I have a fair idea," she told him. Her smile faded. "You do the same. Every part of me is on fire."

Her confession was nearly as arousing as her actions had been. He wrapped his arms around her back and drew her down until her breasts pressed against his chest. His mouth opened and she plunged inside, taking him as he'd taken her.

He moved his hands lower, down her back to the curve of her hips. Sliding up, he slipped his fingers under the hem of her shorts and touched the backs of her legs. The skin was silky smooth. She whimpered.

Closing his lips around her tongue, he suckled gently. Her thighs tightened. He moved his hands back up her hips and her waist, to her ribs. Still he held her captive in his mouth. Her pelvis began to move against his. He forced himself not to notice, then cupped her breasts.

She froze in place as if every part of her focused on his touch. She filled his hands. He could feel the tautness of her nipples through her shirt and bra. He circled his palms against the tight buds and made her shudder.

Even as his fingers learned her curves, he moved his head and kissed her jaw, her ear, then nibbled on her neck. Her breathing was rapid pants, but then so was his. His blood bubbled and boiled, his groin throbbed in time with the rapid cadence of his heart. It would have been easy to pull her shorts off and push his down. Too damn easy.

He moved her next to him, then turned on his side. One by one he unfastened the buttons on her shirt. She made it difficult by kissing his face and sticking her tongue in his ear. He laughed softly.

"I like to hear you laugh," she murmured. "You don't do it enough."

"You wear too many clothes." He pulled her shirt free of her shorts and stared down at her lacy bra. Her full breasts strained against their confinement. He could see her pale skin and the deep rose of her nipples.

"Touch me," she whispered.

Her green eyes were dark with desire, her mouth swollen from his kisses. He'd never seen anything so lovely in his life. He'd never wanted a woman as much. They were both adults. They knew what they were doing.

Even as his fingers touched her breast and his thumb traced her nipple, he knew he was lying. Cindy was reacting, not thinking. He would be willing to bet his next job that she hadn't been with a man since Nelson left. Mike wasn't sure he wanted that kind of responsibility.

"Yes," she breathed as he rubbed the sensitive tip.

He also wasn't sure he could resist her. He wasn't anybody's idea of a hero. Why couldn't he just take what she offered and forget about the consequences? They'd never bothered him before.

"I want you," he said.

Her eyes fluttered closed, and she arched her breasts toward him.

He reached behind her for the hook to her bra. As his fingers fumbled with the fastener, the electricity came back on.

Instantly, light flooded the room. The refrigerator began to hum and the air conditioner kicked in.

"Talk about getting a sign from above," he said and drew his hand away.

She stared at him. "You're not stopping?"

"We both know I'm the wrong guy for you."

"Of course, but..." She drew in a deep breath and let it go slowly. "I can't believe you're being sensible about this."

He smiled regretfully and pushed up off the sofa. "I can't believe I am, either." He held out his hand. She placed her fingers against his and he helped her to her feet.

Her hair was tousled, her face flushed. Worse, her shirt was open and he could see her perfect breasts. The painful throbbing in his groin reminded him he was going to regret this act of nobility for a long time.

"I'm sorry," he said. "I had no right to start anything."

"I don't know if you did or not. Isn't that interesting? I do know you're all wrong for me, so it really is best that we stopped." She pulled the ends of her shirt together and started fastening the buttons. "I have a favor to ask. Could you please be a little less attractive next time? Maybe even act surly around me or the kids."

"I'll do my best."

She tucked her shirt into her shorts and glanced at him. "Still friends?"

The desire had faded from her eyes, leaving behind embarrassment. She was bluffing her way through. He hated that he'd made her self-conscious. "Always," he promised. "Cindy, I'm really sorry."

She held up a hand. "You have nothing to apologize for. It was bound to happen. We spend a lot of time together, we like each other. No big deal. I can handle this. Really.''

"Then I'll see you soon," he said, walking toward the back door.

Her smile was tight. He wanted to say something, anything, to make her feel better, but he couldn't find the words. Soon he would be gone and she would forget him.

He wouldn't forget her, though. She was the first time he'd ever thought about staying.

Chapter Ten

Cindy sat at the kitchen table staring at her piles of coupons. Tomorrow was double-coupon day at the market, and she wanted to take advantage of the savings. But figuring out what on earth she could make with a half-price can of olives even though none of them really liked olives wasn't the challenge it used to be. She was distracted.

She leaned back in her chair and glanced out the kitchen window. She could see the greenbelt and her children playing. One of the fathers had built a playhouse. They couldn't leave it out all the time, but the family dragged it out on weekends. A herd of children was playing some elaborate game. The summer heat didn't seem to bother the kids. Cindy admired their endurance and their enthusiasm. She was barely getting by.

It was all Mike's fault.

She'd been doing fine until a week ago. Until a summer storm had brought him to her door. She'd been able to deal with her own ridiculous fantasies about him because she knew they were just daydreams without a chance of coming true. She'd had a crush on him, had even imagined what it would be like to make love with him. The fantasy had been wonderful. Unfortunately, the reality was even better.

Even thinking about his kisses or the feel of his hands on her skin made her tremble. She tried to tell herself she was reacting to the fact that she hadn't been with a man since before Nelson had left. And the last year of their marriage hadn't been very physical. So naturally she'd responded to the sexual advances of an attractive man she admired. But in her heart she knew it was more than that. When she and Nelson had made love, she'd been satisfied. Okay, maybe the earth didn't move, but she understood the workings of her body and she knew she'd achieved physical release. She enjoyed the process, but it hadn't haunted her.

She couldn't put those moments with Mike out of her mind. When she least expected them or wanted them to appear, the memories were there. Talking to friends, reading bedtime stories to her children, doing laundry. She would blink, and suddenly she could feel his strong hands on her body. Her breasts grew heavy, her thighs trembled and she was ready for him. Only he wasn't anywhere around.

What made it worse was that Mike was able to put the situation out of *his* mind. Not by a word or a look did he even hint at how close they'd come to crossing the line. After his initial apology, he hadn't said a word on the subject. Nor did he avoid her. He was friendly, considerate, great with her kids and exactly like a big brother to her. She couldn't ask for a better neighbor. She was getting everything she wanted; she should be thrilled.

So why couldn't she concentrate on her coupons? Why did she continually glance out the window hoping to catch a glimpse of Mike? He'd left on a jog just a few minutes ago. He wouldn't return for an hour. But she kept checking, hoping he would come back with a skinned knee or something that would require her services. What kind of person hoped someone would get injured just so she could be close to him and touch him for a few minutes? She was definitely messed up.

"Stop thinking about him," she commanded herself.

It was good advice. Mike was going to get better and leave. As they'd both agreed, he was completely wrong for her. Bodyguards don't get off work every day at five. That's what she wanted. Someone stable, someone she could count on. There were no promises in life, but she wanted the next best alternative—she wanted a sure thing. Mike Blackburne was a wonderful man, but he didn't come with guarantees.

Before she could scold herself for continuing to think about him, the phone rang. She gratefully abandoned her coupons and picked up the receiver.

"Hello?"

"Cindy, it's Grace. Where's my big brother? He's not picking up at the house." Like the last time Grace had called, the connection from Hong Kong was amazingly clear.

Cindy laughed and took the cordless receiver back to her seat at the table. "Mike is fine. He's out jogging."

"Jogging? Is he nuts? It's got to be a million degrees there, now. It's July, for heaven's sake."

"A million and ten degrees. He swears he's acclimating." She glanced at the clock over the oven. "He just left, so he won't be back for about an hour."

"Oh, no, he's trying to kill himself."

"Grace, he's doing great. The reason he's gone so long is that he jogs really slow. I mean, Allison can run faster than him. The bullet wound is healing well, he's been working out, he's getting stronger. Your brother is fine."

"Oh?" Grace's voice was questioning. "Fine as in healthy, or fine as in 'what a fine specimen of a man'?"

"Healthy. He's perfectly healthy."

"You have to admit he's very handsome."

He was handsome. So handsome it drove her nuts, but no, she didn't have to admit it. "How's Hong Kong?"

"Wonderful. Don't try to change the subject." Grace paused for a moment. "I've heard you two are an item."

Cindy propped her elbows on the table and rested her forehead in her hands. "We're pretending to be an item. Women here were coming on to him. You know how it is. He didn't know what to do, so we decided to throw everyone off the trail by getting word out that we were dating. I'm just trying to be a good neighbor."

"Uh-huh. So that's why he kissed you when you were at the mall?"

Cindy didn't swear much, but she was sure thinking about starting. "I can't believe you heard about that."

"I received two letters and one phone call on the subject. So it's true?"

"Yes, he kissed me, but it was just because we wanted people to think we were a couple. If you heard about it, it obviously worked."

"So there's nothing romantic between you?"

"I swear." Cindy made an X over her heart. There wasn't anything romantic between Mike and her. That didn't mean she wasn't tempted, or didn't have her daydreams.

"And you've never kissed any other time?"

That she wasn't willing to swear to. "Grace, you're

looking for something that doesn't exist. Mike is a great guy. I like him, the kids think the world of him and I'm thrilled to be able to pay you back for all that you've done for me. But I'm not having a relationship with your brother. We aren't right for each other.''

Grace sighed. "I know. I was just hoping for a miracle. Mike's nearly forty. He can't run around after bad guys forever. I just want him to be happy, and I thought maybe you would be the one to help him see it was time to settle down. You guys would be great together.''

Cindy didn't want to think about that. Being great with Mike was a guaranteed ticket to heartbreak. She didn't need the problem, despite the temptation.

"Can we please talk about something else?" Cindy asked.

"Sure." Grace chattered about her travels in Hong Kong and all the wonderful silks she'd bought. Cindy brought her up-to-date on the happenings in the neighborhood.

After a few minutes, Grace sighed. "I've got to go. I've limited my phone-call time to two hours a month and I've just used up nearly a quarter of that. Give Mike a kiss for me.''

"Grace!"

"On the cheek. You're so suspicious. Take care of yourself, too. I miss you.''

"I miss you, too. Bye.''

She hit the off button and set the portable receiver on the table. She wanted her friend back, but before Grace returned, Mike would leave. It was an interesting dilemma.

The phone rang again. Cindy grinned. No doubt Grace had just one more thing to tell her.

"Hello?''

"Cindy, I need to talk about Allison."

Her smile faded and with it, her good humor. The voice was familiar. A few months ago, just hearing it would put her stomach in knots, but that had passed. Now she felt nothing but mild annoyance at the interruption. She glanced out the window and saw her daughter laughing with her friends.

"What's the problem, Nelson?" she asked coolly, knowing exactly why her ex-husband had called. She'd been expecting it for a while now, but had hoped she was wrong.

"She's got that campout in a couple of weeks. I'd told her I would go with her."

"But you've changed your mind." It wasn't a question.

"I hadn't realized it wasn't on our regular weekend. I've made other plans."

She gripped the receiver tightly. "This campout is very important to Allison. It's a father-daughter event. You've never done anything with her alone. She needs that, Nelson. She needs to know you care about her."

"Of course I care. What have you been telling her?"

He sounded outraged. If the situation wasn't so serious, she would have laughed. "I don't have to tell her anything. You're doing this all by yourself. You see the children every other weekend and no other time. You don't come to their school programs, you don't see them on holidays."

"I have a life. I have responsibilities."

She felt the first stirrings of temper. "You have two children. What is more important than that? They need more than visits every other weekend. They need to think you're a part of their lives and not some distant relative they see occasionally."

"We've had this conversation before, Cindy. If you're

upset about having to take care of the children, you should have thought about that before you insisted on getting pregnant. If you'll remember, I wanted to wait. I'm not getting into this with you again."

He paused. She gritted her teeth. Now when they had these talks, she wondered what she'd been thinking when she'd married this man. With the hindsight of time, she realized she'd only seen Nelson's exterior package. She'd been blinded by the stable family and his career choice. She hadn't looked closely enough at the man behind the facade.

The mistake had been hers. She could live with that. What hurt the most was how her children had to suffer, too. It wasn't right. They deserved a father who loved them, not one who did what the court mandated and nothing else.

"Cindy, are you still there?" he asked, his voice laced with irritation.

She sighed. "What's your point, Nelson?"

"I'm not going on the campout. I have plans with Hilari, and I'm not breaking them. I would like you to explain that to Allison, please."

"Why should I do your dirty work for you?"

"If you don't want to tell her, then put her on the phone, and I'll do it myself."

Cindy suspected Nelson wouldn't be kind to his daughter. "She's letting go of Shelby," she said softly. "After all this time, she goes hours, sometimes days without mentioning her. Doesn't that mean anything to you?"

"Who's Shelby?"

Cindy shook her head. Her ex-husband was hopeless. "I'll tell her myself," she said. "Goodbye, Nelson."

She hung up without waiting for his reply. She'd tried, but it had been too late for years. Nelson was right—he hadn't wanted children as much as she had. He'd wanted to wait. But she'd insisted. It was all part of her plan to be normal. It hadn't worked, of course, and she had a lot of regrets. But having children wasn't one of them. Her kids were the best part of her life. If she had a chance to do it all again, she would willingly marry Nelson, put up with him and his leaving simply because she couldn't imagine life without Allison and Jonathan.

She walked to the back door and called her daughter. The smiling child raced toward the house. Laughter lit up her eyes. Her children deserved better than Nelson. So she would lie for him. Make up a business meeting he'd tried hard to break. She wondered how long the lies would work. At some point in his life, Nelson was going to realize what he'd lost with his children. She liked to think she was a decent person, but chances were she was going to be right there telling him he only had himself to blame.

Mike left the jogging path and angled up toward the cul-de-sac. His breath came in pants and sweat dripped from him. He supposed he deserved it for running in the late afternoon. The temperature was only in the upper eighties, but the humidity was almost that high. He slowed to a walk and pulled off his T-shirt. He used the damp cloth to wipe his face.

As he walked in front of Cindy's house, he resisted the urge to glance over and see if she was home. He was doing his best to stay out of her way. The less contact they had, the better.

By the time he reached Grace's back door, his breathing had slowed to normal. He stepped into the cool kitchen and headed for the refrigerator. He'd left a half-gallon bottle of water on the top shelf. In the time he was running, the water had cooled some but wasn't really cold.

He could down the whole thing without worrying about stomach cramps.

He tossed his T-shirt over one of the kitchen chairs and grabbed the bottle. Tilting his head back, he began to drink.

He was getting stronger every day. His workouts at the country-club gym were starting to pay off, although he was damn tired of his audience. Most of the men stayed away, but the number of women using the treadmills and other pieces of equipment had been constant.

He set the bottle on the counter and drew in a couple of breaths. Before he could pick it up again, the back door flew open and Allison raced toward him.

There were tears in her eyes and on her cheeks. Her face scrunched up in pain. Instinctively, he crouched and held out his arms. She barreled into him, crying as if her heart were broken.

"What's wrong?" he asked, running his hands down her back and legs, checking for an injury. "Did you fall down?"

"No," she said, clinging to him.

She buried her head in his shoulder. He could feel her hot breath and tears against his bare skin. "Are you hurt?"

"No…" This time the word was broken by a sob.

He shifted until he was kneeling on the floor and rocked her back and forth. Her crying continued, loud sobs punctuated by hiccuping breaths and shaking.

Finally, she raised her head and stared at him. Her green eyes were dark with tears. Her nose was red, her cheeks flushed. "I'm running away," she said. "I want you to drive me."

"Where do you want to go?"

She thought for a minute, then brushed her hand across her cheeks and sniffed. "Far away."

"Why?"

Fresh tears filled her eyes. "My daddy isn't going on the campout. I'm going to be the onliest girl there without a daddy."

Mike grimaced. Cindy had mentioned the campout a while ago, voicing her concerns that Nelson wouldn't bother to attend. Allison had also talked about the event. He knew it was important to her. For a moment, he thought about finding Nelson and explaining the facts of life to the man. Nelson couldn't continue to ignore his children. Then Mike figured Nelson wouldn't listen. Instead of talking, Mike decided he should just beat the hell out of him.

He had a feeling Cindy wouldn't approve of his actions. Besides, beating up Nelson would only make *him* feel good. Allison was the one who was hurting.

"Are you mad at your mother?" he asked.

She shook her head. "Mommy says she's coming with me in his place. I want Mommy to go, but it's not the same."

"I know, darling." He pulled her close and kissed the top of her head. "Running away is going to hurt your mother though, and she's not the one you're mad at. Have you thought of that?"

"No…" The sobs were back.

He held her as she cried. She smelled of grass and little girl. She felt so fragile in his arms, so easily bruised by the world and by her own father. He knew all about a parent hurting a kid. He'd lived it. If there was any justice, Nelson would hook up with someone as self-centered as himself.

"Your mother would be frightened if you ran away.

She'd think that you didn't love her anymore. Do you want her to think that?''

"I love Mommy." The voice was muffled against his skin. He could feel the hot breaths of air. "But Daddy doesn't love me."

It was as if someone had jerked his heart out of his chest. He fought against the physical pain. Damn. He wasn't the right person to be having this conversation with Allison. He didn't know the first thing about raising kids. He was probably going to scar her for life, but he had to try to make her understand the truth.

"You are a wonderful girl," he said slowly. "You're bright and kind. You're good to your friends and very sweet. You also have the prettiest face I've ever seen. Your parents love you very much." He had his doubts about Nelson, but Allison didn't need to know that. "Grown-ups sometimes get so caught up in their own lives. Your father has forgotten how much fun it is to be with you. Until he remembers, he's going to do silly things, like canceling your campout. But just because he forgets, it doesn't mean he doesn't love you. It's not your fault. It's his."

She raised her gaze to his. He could see the confusion there. These were pretty complex thoughts for a seven-year-old. But even if she didn't understand everything he was saying, he wanted her to get the gist. Nelson was the jerk, not her.

"I like you very much," he said. "If I had a little girl of my own, I would want her to be just like you."

Her smile blossomed like a flower opening in sunlight. He touched the dimple in her cheek. He'd spoken the words to make her feel better, but at that moment, he knew they were true.

"I like you, too," she whispered.

The wound in his chest began to heal.

Fighting a sudden burst of emotion, he rose to his feet and held out his hand. "Your mom is probably worried about you. Let's head over there and tell her you're okay."

Allison came with him willingly. As he walked around the front of Cindy's house, he saw her in the garage, going through boxes. He sent Allison inside and continued down the driveway.

The three-car garage had a workbench running along the back. There were a few tools hanging from a Peg-Board. The minivan filled the space on the right. Several boxes marked Christmas Decorations stood against the left wall. Three bikes took the place of the second car. Next to them was the pile of boxes Cindy was going through. She'd pulled out sleeping bags and a lantern.

"What are you doing?" he asked.

She glanced up at him and grimaced. "Nelson punked out of the camping trip. Allison is heartbroken."

"I know. She came to my house. She wanted to run away and needed me to drive her."

Cindy paled. "Is she—"

"She's fine. I brought her home. We had a talk." He shifted his feet. "I don't know if I said the right thing or not, so you might want to talk to her." He hesitated, not sure how much he should tell her. "She knows it's not your fault."

"Oh, but it is. I married the jerk."

A headband held her hair off her face. A single strand drifted over her eyes and she brushed it away. Her expression was defeated. He wanted to comfort her, but somehow doing that had been easier with Allison. Maybe because his relationship with the child was less complicated.

She reached into the box and pulled out several flashlights. "This isn't the first time Nelson has done this to her. But it's never been with something this big. I thought—" She shook her head. "This is her first campout. I'd had such hopes for her. What is she going to remember when she looks back on this?" She drew in a deep breath. "It doesn't matter. I swear, that little girl is going to have the time of her life. I'm going to make sure of it. I've already arranged for Jonathan to stay with a friend."

"You're going in Nelson's place?"

She nodded. "They need some mothers to come along, anyway. I wasn't going to go because I didn't want to be in such close quarters with Nelson. Now that's not a problem. My only concern is that Allison is going to be the only girl there without an adult male along. Some of the girls don't have fathers, but they all have uncles or big brothers or something."

"We've already talked about this, Cindy. I'm happy to go."

She gave him a weary smile. "That's really nice but not necessary."

"I don't mind." He didn't. Allison was a sweet kid. He enjoyed her company. The idea of spending four days with Cindy was torture, but not the unpleasant kind. Besides, fifty or so little girls would be great chaperons.

"You're crazy."

"Maybe," he admitted. "I've never been around children. I just assumed I didn't like them, but that's not true. I like yours. I like the kids in the neighborhood." Selfishly, when Allison remembered her first campout, he wanted her to remember him. It was as close as he could come to belonging.

She tilted her head. "What do you know about camping?"

He grinned. "Everything. I used to be a marine."

"So if enemy forces attack the beach, you'll know just what to do?"

"Exactly." He folded his arms over his chest. "I'm great with camp food."

"Do you know how often little girls have to go to the bathroom in the night? They always wake up an adult. They aren't allowed to do anything by themselves. Everything is the buddy system. Are you prepared for that?"

"This isn't about me, it's about Allison. If I went, she would fit in with the other girls. She wouldn't be the only one without a guy. I might not be her father, but I'm a pretty good substitute."

Cindy blinked several times. It took him a moment to figure out she was fighting tears. "You've only known my children six weeks, but you're already a better father than Nelson ever was." She sniffed. "Thanks, Mike. I really appreciate your offer and I hope the campout isn't too horrible for you."

"It'll be fun."

She moved close to him. "Let's go tell Allison. She'll be thrilled."

Her gaze met his. He could see the tears darkening her irises to the color of emeralds. Her mouth trembled. He wanted to claim it with his own. Not because he wanted her—although he did—but to comfort her. Because he cared.

Caring scared him more than a psycho with a .45. It scared him more than dying.

Chapter Eleven

"Is everybody ready?" Cindy asked.

Six little girls looked at her and nodded earnestly. She raised her hands to cover her ears and yelled, "Go!"

Instantly, the loud, high-pitched scream of whistles filled the air. The seven-year-olds kept blowing until Cindy could feel the pounding start high in her temples. She forced herself to keep smiling. She'd learned a lot of tricks on camping trips with Jonathan and this was one of them.

"What are you doing?" Mike yelled over the sounds of the whistles.

She couldn't hear what he was saying, but she read his lips. "Getting it out of their systems. They have to wear their whistles at all times and blow them if there's an emergency. It's just too much temptation for most kids. This way—" The sound stopped. Cindy lowered her hands to her sides and glanced at the girls. They giggled together. After one or two short peeps, there was blissful silence.

"This way," she continued in a normal voice, "they've had their fun. Now they can ignore the whistles unless there's a problem."

He shook his head. "It's not like the marines."

"I'll bet."

She followed his gaze and saw about sixty little girls and their fathers milling through the camp. The kids were sleeping in platform tents. Most of the tents had yet to be erected. Fathers, some experienced campers, most not, argued with one another and their children over the best way to put up the tents.

The adults slept on the ground. Mike had already taken care of putting up their two small tents and Cindy was grateful. Camping wasn't her favorite activity, but she was willing to be here for Allison. Helping her daughter have a good time was all that mattered.

The crowd had no order, no leadership. Loud voices rose. Some of the girls were already crying. "You want to take over as drill sergeant?" she asked.

"Don't tempt me."

Cindy returned her attention to the six girls. Each small group had a woman assigned to them. It meant the fathers didn't have to deal with personal business such as supervising showers. Not that the girls were going to bathe very much over the next four days.

Most of the men were talking to one another and not their children. Cindy supposed they didn't know what was expected of them. There was going to be a general meeting in about a half hour, then dinner. At the meeting, the camp director, Mrs. Stewart, would explain the rules of the camp.

"We should probably get the cook fire started now,"

Cindy said. "That way the coals will be ready when the meeting is over."

"Coals?" He raised his eyebrows. "You guys really rough it, huh?"

"They are just little girls." She smiled. "Wait until you see dinner."

"Fast food?"

"No, prepared plates. I made one for you. Everything is cooked. We just heat it over the fire. Sort of like an open-air microwave."

"You're kidding?"

She leaned close. "Did you expect them to hunt for their meals? Maybe eat grubs and berries?"

His dark eyes crinkled at the corners as he smiled. "At least they'd learn something that way."

"Yeah, they'd learn they didn't like camping."

They exchanged a look of understanding and connection. Cindy felt the pull clear to her belly. She tried to resist it as much as she could. There was no reason for them to impress anyone here with their supposed relationship. They could drop the act and go back to being friends. But she found she didn't want to. She liked Mike putting his arm around her and holding her close. She liked the way he looked at her as if he thought she was pretty. She liked pretending it was real.

A very dangerous line of thought, she told herself.

Before she could say or do something, she was rescued by a pretty woman holding a can of bug repellent.

"Hi, Cindy. I don't know if you remember me. I'm Pam," the woman said. Her thick brown hair was cut short. Green eyes danced with humor.

"Of course I do." Cindy grinned. "You were at the last campout I came on. It was all boys then."

Pam nodded. "Girls should be a lot easier. At least we won't have that snake-catching contest."

Both women shuddered.

"Is your husband with you?" Cindy asked.

Pam laughed. "Are you kidding? Pass up an opportunity to sleep in dirt and fight with fire ants? He wouldn't miss it." She glanced at Mike. "And this is…?"

"Oh, I'm sorry. Mike Blackburne, this is Pam East. Mike is a friend of the family. He's my daughter's substitute father for the weekend."

They shook hands. "Nice of you to come along," Pam said.

"I wanted to," Mike told her.

Pam held up the can of spray. "I'm responsible for insect dieting. If you haven't sprayed up, you need to. The girls, too. Any of you need an extra dose?"

"No, thanks. We coated the girls before we let them out of the car."

"See you," Pam said and walked to the next group of children.

Cindy watched her go. "It's not fair," she said when the other woman was out of earshot.

"What isn't fair?"

"Pam and Steve. They're a great couple. I met them the last time I came camping. They accompany several campouts each summer, giving up their vacation time." She looked at Mike and grimaced. "They don't have any kids of their own. They've been trying for years, but nothing. They're hoping for a private adoption. Who knows how long that's going to take." She drew in a deep breath. "Last I heard, they'd about given up. It's a shame. There are parents like Nelson who don't even care about their kids, then there are people like Pam and Steve who can't have them."

"You mean, they come on the campouts just because they want to help?"

He sounded so startled, she laughed. "Yes, Mike. Some people like children."

"I don't dislike them. I'm just surprised."

"That there are good people in the world?"

"Maybe. I don't see a lot of them in my line of work."

She wanted to go to him and hold him. Before she could give in to the impulse, a call came for the camp meeting. Cindy and Mike collected the girls and walked slowly toward the open meeting area.

A small platform had been built at one end. Everyone settled on the ground. Cindy sat down cross-legged and realized her butt was too old to be comfortable without a real chair. Mike struggled to find a comfortable position. If the look on his face was anything to go by, the healing muscles in his thigh weren't happy about being stretched out. Allison shimmied between them and plopped onto the ground.

She grinned. "I like camping."

Cindy brushed Allison's bangs out of her face. "You haven't actually done any yet."

"But I still like it."

"I'm glad." She kissed her daughter's forehead.

The camp director, Mrs. Stewart, stepped up onto the platform. She welcomed everyone to the father-daughter camp, then proceeded to read from a list of rules. Cindy knew most of them by heart. The most important one was the buddy system. No child was to go off by herself. Anywhere. Not even to the rest room. The talk went on.

Cindy glanced around the open area. It had been cleared of brush and trees. There were patches of grass, but by late July, hundreds of campers' feet had worn most of it away. Tall trees ringed the camp. In another half hour or so they would provide shade from the sun. Cindy wiped her forehead. It wasn't too bad, only in the eighties. For a Houston summer, that was practically chilly. The humidity was low, too, which was a pleasant change.

"The beach is off-limits tonight," Mrs. Stewart was saying. "The alligators are out."

"Alligators?" Mike asked quietly.

"Sure. They're in the river." She smiled. "This is swampland, what did you expect?"

"You camp near alligators?"

"It's a great punishment if the kids get out of hand. We just hold them by their ankles and dangle them over the water." She could feel a smile tugging at the corners of her mouth, but she kept her face serious.

Allison looked at her. "Really?" she asked, her eyes big.

Cindy nodded.

"I'll be good, Mommy."

"I know you will."

"So that's how it is," Mike said and winked.

It was a silly meaningless gesture that made her tingle all the way to her toes.

When the meeting was over, Allison and her friends scrambled to their feet. The parents rose more slowly. Mike stood up and held out his hand. Cindy placed her fingers against his and allowed him to pull her up. She brushed off her shorts, then grimaced.

"We forgot to start the fire for dinner. The girls are going to be hungry and cranky."

"No problem," he said. "I saw starter cans in with the cooking supplies."

When they got back to their section of the camp, three men had collected around the fire pit. They were arguing over the best way to start the fire. One little girl stood nearby, her expression mutinous.

"But, Daddy, we *can't* use starter fluid. It's against the rules."

"Do you want to follow the rules, or do you want to eat?" the man asked, obviously annoyed.

"Try these," Mike said, handing him a starter can. He then showed the man how to stuff newspaper into the can, followed by charcoal briquettes. Mike lit the paper on fire. After a few minutes, he used tongs to pull away the can.

Allison laughed and clapped her hands together. "They're already red."

Cindy smiled. "I'm impressed, Blackburne."

The children got out their prepared dinners and set them on the grill. One girl had a whole yam. Mike looked at it, then at her. "Honey, this isn't going to cook until morning."

"Mommy said it would be good for me. Lots of vitamins. I don't have anything else." Her voice trembled.

Allison spoke up. "I'll share my dinner," she said. "I have lots."

The two girls sat next to each other on a log. Mike stepped around it and moved next to Cindy. "Don't ever question your abilities as a parent."

She stared at her youngest, then shook her head. "I'd like to take credit for that, but I think it's just her. She's a sweet kid."

Slowly, all the meals were heated and everyone sat down to eat. Several of the men jockeyed for position, as if one's status at a campout was as important as the hierarchy in a boardroom. A few fathers ignored the posturing and settled beside their daughters, clearly enjoying the time with them.

Mike stayed near Allison and her new friend. He made

sure they had enough to drink, then brought Cindy her meal. When everyone had eaten and the plates had been cleared away, he and Steve started the marshmallow detail so everyone could have S'mores.

Mrs. Stewart came by and began singing camp songs.

"Something tells me this isn't how the marines do it," Cindy said, leaning close to Mike. He was helping a girl fit a marshmallow over the end of a green stick. When the sticky treat caught fire, he blew it out and gently directed her to hold it over some smoldering coals.

"We didn't roast a lot of marshmallows," he admitted, leaning back against the log. "But we did sit around fires at night."

"Telling lies about women?"

"Mostly."

It was nearly dark, but she saw the flash of white teeth as he smiled. "What were your lies?"

"That I knew any woman. I was very skinny when I was eighteen."

She almost mentioned the fact that he'd definitely filled out some since then, but managed to hold back the words. Mike had enough trouble with women falling all over him without her starting to do it, too.

When all the girls had their fill of dessert, he roasted a couple of marshmallows for her. The off-key singing continued. Songs about stars and animals and old folk tunes. The children laughed when they didn't know the words, or made up new ones. Cindy liked the closeness of the moment, and the feel of Mike next to her. When he put his arm around her, she leaned against his shoulder.

"I like Pam," he said.

Cindy glanced through the smoldering fire and saw Pam and Steve sitting across from them. They were feeding each other marshmallows and smiling in that special way lovers do.

"Why?" she asked.

"She barely noticed I was alive."

Cindy laughed. "You're right. She wasn't the least bit impressed by you." Her laughter faded as she studied the couple. "They're so happy together. I envy them. They have everything I always wanted."

"I'm tired, Mommy," Allison said and crawled into her lap. The child shifted so she was half on Mike, as well, then rested her head on his chest.

Mike touched her daughter's hair. "You have what they want," he said quietly.

He was right, Cindy thought. Life wasn't fair. But sometimes, like now, it was very close to perfect.

"Cindy, wake up."

Someone was shaking her arm. She pulled the sleeping bag up over her head. "Go away."

"I'm going to stay right here until you wake up."

That voice. She recognized it. What was Mike doing in her bedroom? What was she doing sleeping on the ground?

"Oh, we're camping," she muttered and raised her head. "What do you want?" She squinted. "It's still dark. Go away. Do you know how many times I had to take little girls to the bathroom last night? Fifty-seven. Or was it twenty? I can't remember. I just know I barely got any sleep."

"You have to get up."

She pushed the hair from her eyes. "You're disgusting," she said, glaring at his smiling face. "No one should look that good in the morning. I feel as puffy and attractive as a blowfish. Go away."

Mike glanced over his shoulder, then reached into her sleeping bag and grabbed her arms. Before she could protest, he pulled her out and set her on the covers. "You've got three minutes to get dressed, Cindy. If you're not ready, you're coming with us the way you are."

"Who is us and where are we going?"

"It's a surprise."

"I hate surprises," she muttered, but he was already gone.

At that moment, she happened to glance down at herself. She bit back a moan. She'd known the girls would come to her to escort them to the rest rooms in the night so she'd gone to bed wearing shorts under her nightshirt. However, in her fitful sleep, it had twisted off one shoulder, exposing plenty of flesh. Mike hadn't even noticed. So much for dazzling the man with her feminine charms. She probably looked so old and haggard, he couldn't register anything else.

She drew the tent flaps together and quickly put on a bra and shirt. After spraying again with bug repellent, she slipped on socks and shoes, grabbed a flashlight, then made a mad dash for the rest room. A quick combing restored her hair to almost normal. She splashed water on her face and brushed her teeth. She was back at her tent in less than five minutes.

The western horizon was still dark, but dawn was breaking to the east. Mike was waiting for her with Allison and two of the little girl's friends.

"Where are we going?" Cindy asked again.

Mike put a finger to his lips and started walking away from the camp.

Cindy and the girls followed silently. After about fifteen minutes, they came to a clearing. A small house belonging to the park ranger stood at one end. There was a fenced garden and green grass. Mike paused by the edge of the lawn.

As if their presence had triggered a prearranged signal, a doe and two fawns stepped out of the bushes. The girls gasped.

The creatures moved with long-legged grace. Their smooth coats were almost gray in the predawn light. The back door of the house opened and the park ranger put out a large dish of food.

"They're beautiful," Allison breathed. Her friends agreed.

The silence stretched on as the animals ate. The babies finished first, then began a game of tag in the clearing. They chased each other, jumping playfully over imaginary barriers.

The girls stared raptly. Cindy felt her throat tighten with emotion as Allison shyly took hold of Mike's hand. He squeezed her fingers and smiled down at her. Allison smiled back.

Cindy knew her daughter would remember this moment forever. She would share it with her children, telling them about the first time she'd watched fawns frolic in the early morning.

Cindy knew she would remember this moment, too. It marked the exact second her daughter fell in love with Mike. Allison had handed over her heart with a child's trust that the affection would be returned. Cindy wondered if her own heart was far behind.

Mike glanced at her. "What do you think?" he asked softly.

"They're wonderful," she said, motioning to the fawns. The mother had finished eating but seemed content to let her children play.

Mike knelt in the damp grass and pointed out the different markings on the fawns. The girls listened intently. Again she marveled at how much better Mike was with the children than Nelson had ever been. Maybe some fathers were born, not made. She wondered what Mike would be like with his own children.

The thought was as tempting as chocolate to someone on a diet. She didn't want to dwell on it, but once it was in her mind, she couldn't get rid of it.

She reminded herself that men like Mike didn't stay. But that didn't erase her desire to see him holding a baby of his own. Her baby.

"When you have enough beads to fit around your wrist, add a couple extra so the bracelet will dangle," Cindy said. "We don't want it so tight, it cuts off your circulation."

Several of the girls looked up at her and giggled. Mike smiled as he patrolled the tables, making sure everyone concentrated on her craft. "Stay two arm's-lengths apart," he cautioned, trying to avoid the inevitable stabbing with the dull needles used to string the beads.

"Bet they didn't do much of this in the marines," Cindy whispered as he circled behind her.

"You're right." He gave her short ponytail a playful tug, then returned his attention to the girls.

Most of the fathers were over with the knot-tying group. He was willing to admit it was more macho to tie knots than make bead bracelets, but he wasn't on the trip to affirm his masculinity. He was here to be with Allison and this was the craft she'd chosen.

"My cord's got a kink in it," one of the little girls wailed.

Mike was instantly at her side. He slipped off a couple of beads, smoothed the cord until it was straight, then handed it to the now-smiling child. "Better than new," he said.

Pam walked over to him and placed her hands on her hips. "You're very good at this. Cindy has been telling us you don't have kids, but I'm starting to wonder."

"I've spent the summer practicing," he said. "Allison and her brother live right next door."

"You've learned well." Pam glanced from him to Cindy. "Maybe you should think of having a few of your own."

"No way." He raised his hands in a gesture of surrender. "I move around a lot."

Her smile faded and her green eyes darkened with sadness. "It's a waste, if you ask me."

Before they could continue the conversation, Pam stepped away to help another child. Mike watched her go. As he'd told Cindy, he liked Pam; she didn't treat him any differently than she treated any of the other men. She knew he was a single guy, a bodyguard, and she couldn't care less. It was refreshing. Cindy had teased him about being disappointed not to add one more member to his fan club, but in truth he was relieved. There was only one woman he wanted fawning on him and that was Cindy.

His gaze drifted over to his next-door neighbor and ersatz girlfriend. Cindy was bending over the table helping one of the girls. Her shorts pulled tight around her rear and he wished he were standing behind her so he could admire the view.

Down, boy, he told himself silently. This wasn't the time or the place. Although she was awfully tempting with her sunburned nose and no makeup. She wasn't the glamorous type he usually dated. She was genuine and caring. She didn't play games and when she gave her heart, it was forever. He wished he were a different kind of man.

Someone who would be able to give her what she needed and deserved.

Cindy finished with the girl and strolled over to him. "How's it going? You want to make some jewelry for Grace?"

"I think she'll be buying all she needs in Hong Kong."

"But a necklace or bracelet from you would be very special."

He made a fist and pretended to clip her jaw. He brushed against her soft skin. Longing swept through him. "You think you're very funny."

"I don't just think it, I know it for a fact." She smiled, then pointed at Pam. "I saw you two talking."

"I'm still surprised that she and Steve come on these trips, and they don't have any kids of their own."

"Some people believe in giving something back."

Interesting concept, he thought. What did he ever give back?

Before he could answer that question, a messenger van pulled up to the edge of camp. A young man stepped out. "I'm looking for Steve and Pam East," he said loudly.

Pam heard him. She turned and paled. Mike understood her concern. The envelope in the messenger's hand looked ominous.

"I wonder what's wrong," Cindy said. Most of the girls stopped what they were doing and watched.

Steve raced over to his wife and put his arm around her. Together they approached the messenger. The man handed them the envelope. The normally noisy camp grew silent; even the insects seemed to have stopped buzzing. Cindy clutched Mike's arm.

"I hope nobody died," she whispered.

Steve and Pam read the message. Pam threw herself into her husband's arms and started to cry. Cindy jogged toward her. Mike followed. Then he realized the couple wasn't sad. They were laughing. Steve swung his wife around.

Pam glanced up at Cindy. "We're going to have a baby. A birth mother has chosen us. We met with her last week, and we almost decided not to come on the campout so we could wait by the phone for her answer, but she was taking her school exams and said she wouldn't decide until Monday. I guess she changed her mind." She smiled through her tears. "Next to falling in love with Steve, this is the most wonderful thing that has ever happened to me."

Cindy hugged her friend. The other women in the camp approached and embraced as the men shook hands.

"We're going to have to leave right away," Pam said, wiping her face. "The baby is due in less than two weeks. There are a million things to prepare. A baby."

Her happiness was so bright it nearly blinded him. As she moved toward her tent to collect her belongings, she paused in front of Mike.

"Are you sure this is what you want?" she asked.

He didn't have an answer so he hugged her.

"I'm so happy," she said. Steve came over and the two men shook hands.

Mike watched as everyone helped them pack. In less than fifteen minutes, the couple was heading back to Houston. He stood on the edge of the crowd, strangely detached from their joy. He was happy Pam and Steve were finally going to have their child, but he didn't understand why they'd wanted one so much in the first place. At times, he didn't feel completely human. It was as if some of his emotions had atrophied from disuse.

Cindy picked up Allison and held her close. Mother and daughter clung to each other, their love visible to him.

The pain in his chest told him that his heart was working. He still felt the pain of being on the outside, looking in.

"I want to call Daddy and tell him I had a good time," Allison said as Cindy pulled into the driveway. The girl had unfastened her seat belt and had the side door open before Cindy had set the parking brake.

"He might not be home," Cindy called after her. "And you can't get inside until I unlock the door."

Allison danced impatiently. Cindy rolled her eyes at Mike. "I think her first campout was a success."

"Seems that way."

Cindy wondered what was bothering him. He'd been quiet for a couple of days now. The nearest she could pinpoint it, he'd started acting withdrawn right after Pam and Steve had left. She wasn't sure why that would have upset him.

She heard a call from across the greenbelt. Jonathan burst out of his friend's house and ran toward home.

"You guys are finally back," he yelled.

Cindy gave her keys to an impatient Allison, then turned to greet her son. He hugged her tight then frowned. "Next time, I want to go camping with you guys. You had all the fun, and I was just stuck here with nothing to do."

"Interesting. I could have sworn Brett's mother said you guys were going to Astro World, to the movies and ice skating. Didn't you do any of that?"

"Sure, but it wasn't camping with Mike." He turned to the man. "How was it? Were the girls all real dumb?"

Mike pulled camping gear out of the rear of the minivan. "We had fun."

"I want to go on a camping trip, too," Jonathan said. "Mike, will you take me?"

Mike straightened, a sleeping bag under each arm. He drew his eyebrows together, obviously surprised. "You want to go camping with me?"

"Sure. It would be great. Just us guys. You know, roughing it."

"We'll talk about this later," Cindy said, rescuing Mike. The poor man didn't know what to say. "Go inside and see if your sister has gotten hold of her father. You can talk to him, too."

When Jonathan slammed the back door shut behind him, she turned to Mike. "Sorry about that. I didn't know he was going to put you on the spot. There's really no time between now and when school starts, and it's unlikely you'll be coming back later in the fall. I'll explain it to him."

"I wouldn't mind going. Maybe around Thanksgiving."

That sounded suspiciously like a long-term commitment. "Why would you want to?"

"I like Jonathan."

"I know, but—" She didn't know how to explain it without sounding like a fool. "Thanks."

She grabbed a cooler and headed for the house. Inside her stomach she felt a flicker of hope. She doused it with a large dose of reality. Agreeing to go camping with a nine-year-old boy wasn't the same as making an emotional commitment to her. This was all temporary. When he was healed and the time was up, Mike would be moving on. Occasional visits wouldn't be enough for her.

She was still looking for a sure thing.

Chapter Twelve

Cindy closed the door to Jonathan's room and sighed. It had taken the better part of an hour to get them both calm enough to sleep. Allison had to be exhausted from the camping trip and, according to Brett's mother, Jonathan and Brett had been staying up late playing video games, so getting them to bed shouldn't have been a problem. But nothing was as it was supposed to be with children. There were always surprises.

Like Jonathan wanting to go camping with Mike. She probably shouldn't be all that shocked. Her son liked and respected Mike. It made sense he would want to spend time with the man. It wasn't as if Nelson ever did anything with the children aside from taking them every other weekend.

She walked along the hallway, then down the stairs and into the kitchen.

"They're finally asleep," she said. "I know they were

exhausted, but they kept fighting it." Mike had already started the dishwasher and was finishing up with the pots. "You didn't have to do that," she said.

"You didn't have to invite me to stay for dinner," he answered easily. "I get tired of frozen meals."

"You could cook something yourself."

He glanced at her over his shoulder and grinned. "It's easier to wash your dishes."

She'd thought Mike would have had enough of her and children for one weekend, but when she'd invited him to stay and eat with them, he'd accepted. Jonathan had wanted to hear every detail of the camping trip and Allison had been in heaven, at last having something to hold over her older brother. Mike had kept both children entertained, reenacting the events of the campout.

She'd taken the opportunity to wash away the dust and grime. There had been showers at the campsite, but none she wanted to use. It was wonderful to finally have clean hair again. Mike had also showered and shaved, although if she were honest with herself, she would have to admit that she missed the stubble. It gave him a dark and dangerous look. As if he were a renegade, or an outlaw of some kind. As if his career wasn't romantic enough already.

"What are you smiling at?" he asked, picking up a dishcloth and drying the largest pot.

"Nothing. I'm just happy to be home with running water and electricity."

"That campground is hardly roughing it."

"It's wild enough for the likes of me. I've never seen the appeal of living with creepy-crawly things or sleeping in the dirt."

"It's getting back to nature."

"This from a man who lives in the city."

He winked. "Can't make a living from a tent."

"Probably not."

The sun had barely set in the western sky. There were still hints of pink in the clouds. Outside, fireflies danced through the greenbelt. Other invisible creatures had taken up their nightly chorus. She and Mike were standing in her kitchen. He was drying pots, for heaven's sake, and her kids were sleeping upstairs. It wasn't a magical moment. And yet she felt very strange inside. Her stomach was filled with nervous fluttering. Her arms and legs felt both heavy and light. Her skin tingled.

Maybe it was because Mike's dark gaze never left hers. Maybe it was because they'd just spent four days together and neither of them seemed to want the time to be over. Maybe it was because she could remember what it felt like to be in his arms and right now there was nothing she wanted more.

She was barefoot. After her shower, she hadn't bothered putting on makeup. Her hair was straight, her clothing a simple T-shirt and shorts. Yet the way Mike was looking at her, she could have been dressed in black silk and pearls. She was drawn to him, drawn to the man who had taken the time to make her children feel special and herself feel desired. Except that he would leave her, he was everything she'd ever wanted.

Before she could step closer to him and perhaps make an incredible fool of herself, a car turned into the driveway. She glanced out the kitchen window and frowned. The red convertible looked familiar.

"That's Nelson's car. What's he doing here?"

Mike shrugged and went back to drying the pots. She started toward the back door, but before she got there, it flew open. Her ex-husband stomped inside.

He glanced from her to Mike, then frowned. "What the hell is going on here?"

His rudeness annoyed her almost as much as his question. "That's what I'd like to know," she said, marching past him and closing the door. She glared at him. "This is my house, Nelson. I bought you out. The deed is in *my* name. You no longer have the right to do as you please here. If you want to come inside, you knock."

"I told you to keep the door locked," Mike said.

"I should have listened."

Nelson stared at Mike. His gaze narrowed. "So you're the bodyguard."

Mike put down the pot he'd been drying and smiled. "You're the ex-husband."

The men were about the same height, with the same coloring. But there the similarity ended. Mike was lean and dangerous, trained to kill. Nelson sold insurance and had never done anything about the extra twenty pounds he'd gained.

Nelson turned back to her. "You had no right to take this paramilitary type camping with my daughter. Don't do it again."

"Are you crazy? You're telling me who can and can't see Allison? Is that right?"

"Yes. She's my daughter."

"Only when it's convenient for you. Mike did me a favor by coming with me. Allison was crushed when you backed out of the camping trip. She was in tears. Mike stepped in and made her feel better. He did your job for you."

She moved closer and stuck out her index finger. "While we're on the subject, don't you ever tell me who I can and can't see."

"I'll do what I damn well please," her ex-husband said,

his brown eyes bright with anger. "You're their mother. You have to set an example."

His temper didn't frighten her. She was just as furious. "And you don't?" She didn't give him a chance to answer. "You're the one who dumped me, then lived with a woman before marrying her. Now you've dumped wife number two for Hilari. Yet you come in here and want to judge me? I'm a damn good mother to those children. It doesn't have anything to do with whom I do or don't see, it's about something else. Something you can't understand. It's about caring for them. It's about being with them when they need me. They count on me, Nelson. They know you only care when it's your weekend. But I'm *always* there for them."

"You've turned my children against me."

"No. You did that yourself."

"I won't let you live with this guy."

She didn't bother reminding him that Mike didn't live with her. That wasn't the point. "You don't have any say here. I'll do what I want."

Nelson flushed with anger. "You'd better listen to me."

"Or you'll what? Sue me for custody?" She smiled. "I don't think so. You couldn't be bothered."

Nelson took a step toward her. Cindy was startled by the physical threat, but she didn't budge. In the back of her mind, she wondered if Nelson was trying to act macho because Mike was here. That made her dislike her ex-husband even more.

"I wouldn't try that if I were you," Mike said softly.

Sometime while she and Nelson had been arguing, he'd put the dish towel and pot down and had approached. He stood balanced on the balls of his feet. Like a wildcat ready to pounce, he was pure coiled strength.

"On second thought, do it," Mike said, his voice still quiet. "Raise your hand to her, buddy, but make it good the first time because when I'm done with you, you'll never threaten a woman again."

Nelson drew himself up to his full height. "I've never hit a woman in my life. Is this what you've been doing, Cindy? Telling lies about me?"

"You've never hit any of us," she said. "I didn't tell anyone you had. That's not your style, Nelson. You prefer to walk out on your family."

The muscles in his jaw tightened. "Call off your trained attack dog so we can talk about this civilly."

"There's nothing to talk about," Mike said. "You're not married to Cindy anymore. You have no rights here."

"And you do?" Nelson asked.

"No. Cindy's in charge." Mike turned his gaze on her. "You want me to beat him up for you?"

Cindy held Mike's gaze. He wasn't angry. His offer came from a desire to protect her. There was a part of her that wanted to see Nelson broken and whimpering. He'd been pretty cruel when he'd left, making her feel as if the failure of the marriage was all her fault. For a long time, she'd thought she was too old and too unattractive to be of interest to any man. Mike had helped change that.

But punishing Nelson wouldn't accomplish anything. Still, she waited until a bead of sweat formed on her ex-husband's upper lip before slowly shaking her head no.

"No matter what I think of him personally, he's still the father of my children. It's better if we all behave like adults."

Nelson exhaled audibly, then reached for the door handle. "I'm outta here," he muttered. "You guys are crazy."

"You have the children next weekend," Cindy reminded him as he ran for his car. "Be sure to be nice to them."

She closed the door and leaned against it.

Mike came up behind her. "You mad at me?"

She smiled. "No one has ever defended my honor before. I'm not mad. I'm a little ashamed of myself, though. I kept picturing Nelson beat up and writhing on the floor. It was a lovely image."

"Guys like him need a little humbling every now and then." He returned to the kitchen and continued drying the pots.

She straightened and walked to the counter separating the kitchen from the family room. "He seemed so stable once. So normal. What a mistake to have married him," she mused aloud.

"Obviously. The guy's a fool."

"And a jerk."

"A wimp." He tossed her the towel. "Finish drying. It's my turn to pick the video we're watching." With that, he walked to the built-in bookcases on both sides of the TV and began scanning the titles.

Cindy stared at him. She'd already made one big mistake in her life by marrying Nelson. She didn't want to make another. Which, of course, meant her not getting involved with Mike.

Or was the mistake letting him go?

Mike had strung a hammock between the two pecan trees in Grace's backyard. He lay stretched out in the shade provided by the leafy trees. A paperback spy thriller was open on his chest, but he didn't feel like reading. It was enough just to relax, sip his beer and think about nothing. He could get used to this kind of life.

The neighborhood was quiet. Cindy's kids had left for

their swim-team practice a couple of hours ago. He didn't know where the other neighborhood children were. It seemed like the perfect time to take a nap.

He closed his eyes. Immediately, he pictured Cindy. Her long curvy legs. The thrust of her breasts. The way she'd tasted and felt next to him. Her mouth had been—

The ringing of the phone cut through his thoughts. He reached for the cordless and pushed the on button.

"Yeah," he said into the receiver.

"Mr. Blackburne, this is Alicia from your answering service. You've had a call."

He took the information, then punched the off button. A call. The world was knocking on his door again. He flexed his leg. It had been two months. It was already August. He was about as close to fit as he was going to be. In another couple of weeks, he would be at a hundred percent. There was no reason not to return to work.

But it was several minutes before he picked up the phone again and punched in the numbers. Even as it rang somewhere in Washington, he thought about hanging up. But he didn't.

"Hello?"

"This is Mike Blackburne. Mr. Anthony called me about a job."

"Ah, yes, you're the bodyguard. Thank you for calling so promptly, Mr. Blackburne. You come very highly recommended. Let me tell you a little about our problem."

Fifteen minutes later, Mike stretched out on the hammock and wondered if he'd made the right decision. The fact that he was even bothering to question it told him how far gone he was. He should be itching to get back to work. Usually, two weeks away from the game was all he could stand. It had been two months.

He tried to remember the thrill of the chase, the excitement of pitting his skills against those of the enemy. Suddenly, he felt nothing but tired and old. He didn't want to go.

The job started in three weeks. What was he going to tell Cindy? He grimaced. Would she even miss him? She'd known from the start that his visit was temporary. They'd both agreed they couldn't be more wrong for each other. So it shouldn't matter that he was finally moving on. Yet it did matter. He wondered how he was going to get through the day without her.

The gate latch clicked and Jonathan stepped into the backyard. "Hey, Mike," he called. "You wanna play ball?"

"Sure," Mike answered, pushing into a sitting position.

Jonathan's hair was shaggy, his body tanned from his hours in the sun. He looked like a typical kid. Mike was going to miss both him and Allison.

"How was swim practice?" he asked.

"Okay, I guess. We don't have any more meets or anything. It's almost time for school to start."

"Already?"

"Yeah. We get out at the beginning of June and go back in August. I wish we never had to go back." Jonathan's smile faded. "Are we going camping over Thanksgiving?"

It still surprised him that Jonathan wanted to. Cindy had tried to explain it to him several times. He could believe that the kids liked him—after all, he liked them, too. But the concept of making personal plans for the future was foreign.

"I don't know," Mike said truthfully. "I've got a new job, and I don't know how long I'll be on it."

Jonathan stared at him. His brown eyes widened. "What do you mean? Are you leaving?"

"I don't really live here," he said, motioning to the house. "Grace does. You knew I was just staying here for the summer."

"Yeah, but—" Jonathan turned away and his shoulders slumped. "I thought it was different."

"How?"

The boy didn't answer.

When the silence grew awkward, Mike cleared his throat. "Listen, I'll come back. Grace is here and she's my sister. I'll visit."

"You never visited before. I thought you liked us."

"I do."

"Then how can you leave?"

He stared at Jonathan's slender back. The kid was only nine. How could any of this make sense? "I've got a job. When it's done, I'll come back. I promise."

"But you'll leave a-again."

It took Mike a minute to figure out the break in Jonathan's voice meant he was crying. He didn't know what to do. Before he could offer comfort, the boy started walking away.

When he reached the gate, he pulled it open and stepped through onto the driveway. He glanced back at Mike. Tears filled his eyes and trickled down his cheeks. He brushed them away impatiently. "You're leaving," he repeated. "Just like my dad."

As the boy walked away, Mike realized Jonathan had already learned his mother's lesson. Men leave.

The two kids scrambled out of the car and dashed across the greenbelt. "Be sure to say thank-you for being invited," Cindy called after them.

She got a vague wave in response. Brett had invited Jonathan to a movie and early dinner and had agreed to let Allison tag along. After a day spent shopping for school clothes, the silence was going to be a welcome relief.

She opened the back of the minivan and pulled out several bags. The kids had sprouted during the summer and they needed almost everything new. She'd been saving Nelson's child support for the last three months and had used up most of it in a single shopping trip. The price of the shoes alone had nearly sent her into cardiac arrest.

She clutched the bags in one hand and fumbled with her keys with the other. After opening the back door, she tossed the bags on the sofa, then walked into the kitchen to pour herself a glass of iced tea. She was taking a sip when she saw someone prowling in her backyard.

Her first instinct was to scream for Mike, but she didn't know if he was even home. She hadn't seen much of him in the last couple of days. Her second thought was to dial 911. She'd just reached for the phone when the man moved closer to the family room windows.

The receiver fell to the floor. A sharp pain cut through her midsection. She fought against the need to double over. Her breathing was labored, her mouth dry. Then the sensations passed and she was left with a giant hole where her heart used to be.

The prowler wasn't a stranger. It was Mike. She hadn't recognized him because he'd cut his hair. Once again, the short, military style exposed his ears and the back of his neck. She knew what that meant...he was leaving.

She replaced the receiver then walked to the back door and opened it. "You want some tea?" she asked, trying to sound calm.

He glanced at her. "Sure." He came inside and pointed to the windows. "I was checking your security. You've got one or two broken latches. I'll fix them. Have you thought about getting an alarm put in?''

"No.'' She could barely get the word out.

After pouring his tea, she added the correct amount of sugar. He took the glass, then glanced at the packages on the sofa. ''You've been busy.''

"School starts in two weeks. The kids needed new clothes. I got some things, too. It looks like we'll all be back to work. Including you,'' she said as nonchalantly as she could.

He leaned against the counter. ''Jonathan told you.''

"No, I figured it out all by myself.''

"How?''

"The haircut.''

"Oh.'' He reached up and touched his bare neck. ''I guess it doesn't exactly fit in around here.''

The hole in her chest wasn't getting any smaller and she was finding it difficult to keep breathing. ''You told Jonathan?''

"A couple of days ago. He was asking me about the camping trip. I said I would come back, but I can't know exactly when.'' His eyes darkened. ''I mean to keep my word, Cindy. Maybe you could tell him that.''

"I will. You're not Nelson. You'll take him camping. But Jonathan won't believe you until you actually show up. He's been disappointed too many times by his dad.''

"I'm sorry for that.''

"It's not your fault.''

She couldn't believe they were having this very normal, very rational conversation when all she wanted to do was scream at him. How could he just walk out of her life? It wasn't supposed to happen this way. She wasn't supposed to care.

She set her drink on the center island and forced herself to smile. "When do you leave?"

"The job starts in three weeks. I'll need a few days to get my things in order. I've got to pick up my business suits from the dry cleaners in L.A. I probably have a few papers to go through. That sort of thing. I was planning on leaving a week from Friday."

She didn't want to ask but she couldn't help herself. "Were you going to tell me or were you just going to disappear?" She hated that her voice was shaking.

"Cindy." He put his drink down and moved close to her. "I was going to say something today. That's why I was looking at the house. I want things to be okay after I'm gone."

"I've managed to survive all these years without you. I think I'll continue to make it."

"That's not what I meant."

Emotions swirled around her, through her. She didn't understand them. Mike wasn't breaking the rules, she was. She'd known from the first minute they'd met that he was leaving. He'd never once tried to convince her otherwise. So what was her problem? Why did she want to break down and cry? Why did she want him to hold her and promise to never go away? Nothing made sense.

It wasn't fair.

He touched her chin, forcing her to look at him. The handsome lines of his face made her heart ache. He'd been so good to her and to her kids. He'd made her remember what it was like to be a woman, and to be alive. She was going to miss that.

"Indulge me," he murmured. "Let me pretend you'll miss me and not do well without me. And get those damn window locks fixed."

She smiled. "You can do it yourself if you want."

"Thanks." His fingers stroked her cheek. For a minute, she thought he was going to kiss her, but he didn't.

"I'll miss you," he said. "You've been a good friend to me. You helped me fit in here."

"No problem," she said airily as she moved away from him. She clutched the tea glass as if it were a lifeline. "I was just doing Grace a favor." She sounded fine. It was good that he didn't know how much that cost her.

"You didn't have to pretend to be involved with me. Is that going to be okay?"

"What do you mean?"

He shrugged. "I don't want people thinking you got dumped. Why don't you tell everyone I turned out to be a jerk."

"I'll be fine, Mike. People will think what they like and there's nothing we can do about it. Beth knows the truth. She'll tell the rest of our friends. No one else matters."

They stared at each other. It was as if they both had so much to say, but it was all too dangerous. She wasn't going to ask him to stay and he wasn't going to offer. It was better this way. The leaving would be swift and painful, like a burn. In time, she would heal and only she would be able to see the scar.

Chapter Thirteen

"Mike's leaving," Cindy said, slouching in her chair at the kitchen table.

"When?" Beth asked.

"In a week and a half." She resisted the urge to sigh. She was acting like a melodramatic teenager. The only problem was she didn't know how to stop.

"You seem surprised. His visit here has always been temporary."

"I know that," Cindy snapped. "That doesn't mean I have to like it."

Beth stared at her wide-eyed, then straightened in her chair and took a sip of tea. "I guess you told me," she said softly.

Cindy leaned forward and touched her friend's hand. "I'm so sorry. I'm behaving horribly. Really, I apologize. I shouldn't take out my frustration on you."

"Hey, I'm your best friend. Who better?" Beth grinned. "Why don't you tell me what's really wrong?"

"I can't explain it. You're right, I *did* know he was leaving. It shouldn't be a surprise, but it is. Maybe because I didn't see it coming. Maybe I secretly hoped he would change his mind. I'm not in love with him, he's not in love with me, but I don't want him to go. Does that make sense?"

"No."

Cindy smiled and rested her elbows on the round table. As usual, her kids were playing in the greenbelt. She could see them taking turns on a swing made from an old tire. A larger, older boy tried to push Allison out of the way. Her daughter pushed him right back and stood her ground. The boy slunk to the rear of the line.

"Allison hasn't mentioned Shelby in nearly two weeks," she said. "I finally asked about her. Allison told me that Shelby went back to her real family. I'm thrilled that Allison is doing so much better. My head tells me she would have grown up enough to let go of her imaginary friend on her own. My heart tells me it was Mike."

"What happens to Allison when Mike leaves?"

"I think she's going to miss him. We all are. I also think she's going to be fine."

Beth studied her. "So it's not Allison you're worried about."

She shook her head. "No. It's me."

"I thought it wasn't serious," her friend said. "You were supposed to be pretending."

"We were pretending. It's not real." Cindy resisted the urge to lay her head on the table. She was cranky and out of sorts and she didn't know why. Yes, of course she knew why. Mike was leaving. But why did that change anything? He'd been leaving from the moment they'd met.

"We're just friends," she said, as much for her benefit as for Beth's.

They *were* just friends. They talked and laughed and had fun. She knew she wasn't in love with him. So why was she taking this so badly? Why did she still feel that hole in her chest? It hadn't closed at all. If anything, the edges were more ragged and raw.

"That's the problem," Beth said softly. "You want to be more than friends."

Cindy opened her mouth, then closed it. She opened it again. "That's not true."

But even as she said the words, she wondered.

"Of course it is." Beth smiled. "Mike is a very good-looking man."

"You've noticed."

"Along with half the county. He's been living right next door for weeks. You've pretended to be an item. I know you've kissed him, I have witnesses."

A guilty flush stained Cindy's cheeks. Beth knew about the brief kiss witnessed in the mall. She didn't know about the half hour or so Cindy and Mike had spent on the sofa during that thunderstorm. Of course, Beth was pretty smart. She might have guessed.

"What's your point?" Cindy asked.

"You've been about as close as a man and woman can be without being lovers. Now that he's leaving, you're having regrets about not taking that final step. Considering the options, Mike is your safest bet to test yourself as a single woman."

"You're saying this is all about sex."

"Isn't everything?"

Cindy grimaced. "Not in my life. Not for a long time."

"Then you'd better do it, so you don't forget how."

"Gee, thanks for the vote of confidence."

Cindy sipped her tea. Was Beth right? Was she feeling regret for not having taken their relationship to its next level? But she and Mike didn't have a relationship. They were friends. And friends don't have sex. She'd never really even thought about it.

Liar, the voice in her head whispered. Of course she'd thought about it. There were nights she couldn't sleep for thinking about being with him, touching him and being touched. Her body had been on fire, aching, needing.

"He's not interested in me that way," she said glumly. "I don't think I turn him on."

Beth didn't say anything. Finally, Cindy looked at her friend. Beth arched her eyebrows until they nearly touched her fringed bangs. "Oh, stop it," Beth said simply. "I've seen the smoldering looks that pass between the two of you. I've seen the little knowing glances and the touches. Don't tell me you haven't played footsie a time or two."

The blush burned hotter. "We haven't really done very much."

"But you've done something."

"We've, ah, kissed."

"Did he want to do more?"

"I don't know. He didn't say anything."

Beth rolled her eyes. "Cindy Jones, you're the most unaware woman on the planet. If I didn't know for a fact that you had children, I would swear you'd never been with a man. He doesn't have to *say* anything. As for his wanting more, you know exactly what I'm talking about."

"Ah, yes, well, maybe he was a little interested."

"It's little?"

"Beth!"

Her friend grinned. "Then you have your answer."

"But he's never made a move or anything. What if it was just a normal male reaction to the situation? What if it wasn't about me specifically?"

"Then make it about you. Mike likes you. Why wouldn't he want to make love? All you have to do is let him know that *you* want to, too."

Cindy winced. "I can't do that. What on earth would I say? 'Gee, Mike, how about a roll in the hay?' What if he's not interested? Besides, it's so complicated. Where? When? And what about birth control? I haven't been on the Pill since Nelson left."

"Condoms," Beth said firmly. She took a sip of her tea and leaned forward. "This is the nineties, and you have to be sensible. Something else over-the-counter, too. Maybe that sponge thing."

"I can't do this," Cindy moaned.

"Of course you can. Besides, if you don't take care of birth control and he's not expecting the invitation, he might not be prepared. Then where would you be?"

"Don't you think it would be easier to just forget the whole thing?"

"Yes, but is that what you want?"

Cindy didn't know anymore. Part of her wanted to be with Mike. She liked him, he made her feel alive and attractive. He made her believe that her dreams were still possible. Part of her wanted to run in the opposite direction. She'd never done anything like this in her life.

"I've only ever been with Nelson," she said. "What if we've been doing it wrong?"

"Then you might as well find out now." Beth stared at her. "I don't understand. One minute you act as if you really want to do this with Mike, and the next you make me feel as if I'm pushing you into prostitution. What's going on?''

"I'm scared," Cindy admitted. "I'm afraid of what will happen if we do this, and I'm afraid of regretting it for the rest of my life if we don't. I keep telling myself that you're right. I've got to get back into circulation. I want to focus most of my attention on the children, but I have to take care of myself, too. Otherwise, when they're grown and gone, I won't have anything. It's just so hard to find the balance. And I'm terrified. What if he doesn't want me?''

Beth shook her head. "You're crazy to worry about that. You're a wonderful woman. I've seen the way Mike looks at you. Of course he wants you. What man in his right mind wouldn't?''

"Nelson didn't.''

"He's dating bimbos and is hardly in his right mind. All you have to do is prepare a nice dinner. A few flowers, a tablecloth, wear a dress. He'll get the idea.''

"You make it sound so simple. What if he doesn't?''

"Then take his gun and shoot him.''

In spite of her concerns, Cindy laughed out loud. "A great idea, only he doesn't have a gun.''

"Not to worry. You can borrow one of Darren's.''

"Great. Then I'd be in prison, and I still wouldn't have been with a man.''

Beth smiled. "Are the kids with Nelson this weekend?''

Cindy nodded.

"Then that's when you make your move. You won't have to worry about being disturbed. I promise not to call.''

The weekend was only two days away. Could she do it? Did she want to? It seemed so calculated.

Beth rose to her feet. "I've got to get home and phone Darren."

Cindy followed her friend to the door. "You can call him from here if you want."

"No, thanks. It's going to be a very personal conversation. I'm going to tell him that I'm grateful that we're married and beg him to never leave me. I wouldn't do the single thing well."

"Tell me about it."

Beth stepped onto the front porch and paused. "You deserve this, Cindy. You've spent most of your life thinking about everyone but yourself. Take a chance. Have some fun. Mike is a good guy. He won't let you down. You don't have to fall in love. In fact, it would be easier if you didn't. Just enjoy the moment and keep it to remember later."

"That's good advice. Thanks."

She watched Beth cross the street, then circle around to her back door. She envied her friend's married state. There were negatives in all relationships, but the good often outweighed the bad. Sometimes it was boring, but right now boring sounded wonderful. She wished it could have been different.

Cindy walked back to the kitchen and carried the tea glasses to the sink. She couldn't change the past, but she could affect the future. She could make choices for the right reasons, not just because she was reacting to a situation. So what did she really want?

Mike.

The answer came swiftly and without warning. She wanted to be with him and know what it was like. Beth had been right. She needed the memories to carry with her. She liked him, she admired him. She was going to miss him when he was gone, but she wasn't in love with him. At least she'd been sensible enough to hold on to her heart.

She prayed he was interested in her that way. She was reasonably sure he wouldn't turn her down flat. After all, the few times they kissed, it had been wonderful. It would have been easy for things to get out of hand. She thought he liked her, too. It would be as simple as friends becoming lovers. Nothing more.

So she would do as Beth suggested. She would invite Mike over for dinner on Saturday night when the children were gone and she would seduce him.

Cindy had said to arrive at six, so Mike knocked on her door at 5:59. He'd brought over a bottle of wine. When a finger of guilt tickled his spine, he reminded himself he was just being neighborly and thanking Cindy for the invitation. He wasn't trying to get her drunk.

He was still smiling at the thought when she opened the back door. His mouth dropped open. He closed it quickly and stared.

"Hi," she said shyly, then stepped back to let him inside.

"Hi, yourself," he managed to say, and handed her the bottle of white wine. As she took it and moved into the kitchen, he found himself unable to look away from her long, bare legs.

He'd seen them countless times before. She wore shorts every day. So that wasn't different. But the dress was.

He found it odd that her shorts exposed more of her legs than the dress did, yet somehow a narrow skirt falling to midthigh was about a hundred times more seductive. And she'd been damned impressive in shorts.

He swallowed hard and raised his gaze. The pale peach fabric skimmed over her hips, hugged her slender waist before molding her back to her shoulders. There was a long, slim zipper from the nape of her neck down to the swell of her buttocks. His fingers itched to pull it. When she turned, he saw the sleeveless dress didn't dip especially low, but it outlined her full breasts. Wide straps left her shoulders bare.

It was a simple dress. Nothing about it screamed sex, or even seduction. But he'd never seen Cindy in a dress before. Desire burst to life, filling him with a nearly uncontrollable need and sending blood to his groin. In less than five seconds, he was obviously and painfully aroused.

"You look great," he said.

"Oh. Thanks." She touched her hair self-consciously. She'd curled it.

He moved closer. She was wearing more makeup than usual. Her eyes were dark and mysterious, her mouth full and kissable.

Slow down, Blackburne, he ordered himself. This was Cindy, his neighbor and friend. Nothing more. The dress was probably just a whim. It was Saturday night, the kids were gone and she wanted to make herself pretty. It didn't mean a thing and he would be a fool to think otherwise.

"Do you want some wine?" she asked.

"Sure." He took the corkscrew she offered and opened the bottle. While she was pouring, he noticed the kitchen table was bare. He peeked into the dining room. The large table had been set with a tablecloth and fresh flowers. There were two place settings at the far end. The dimmer switch was turned to low and there were candles waiting to be lit.

"Here." She handed him the wine.

"Thanks." He took a large swallow and nearly choked. He recovered, then coughed a couple of times.

"Are you all right?" she asked.

He cleared his throat. "Fine."

He tugged at his T-shirt. It didn't have a collar but he felt something tightening around his throat. Nerves maybe.

She sipped her wine. The kitchen was silent except for the ticking of the wall clock. The oven was on. He could smell something delicious.

"What's for dinner?" he asked.

"Beef Burgundy."

"Then I should have brought red wine."

"Oh, I have some for dinner. I thought we could have this first."

"Are you trying to get me drunk?" he teased.

Instead of laughing, Cindy looked away nervously. "Would you like to go into the living room?"

The living room? Not the family room? "Sure."

He followed her. She stopped to flip on the stereo system in the corner. The CD player had already been set. At the push of the button, soft music filled the room. He sat on the sofa, wondering if she would sit next to him. Instead, she perched nervously on the edge of the wing chair opposite. Silence stretched between them.

"It doesn't seem as hot today," she said at last. Her gaze met his, then slid away.

"I noticed. Are the kids with their dad?"

She nodded. "Nelson promised to buy them a few more things for school. Jonathan needs a jacket for when it gets colder. His is too small."

Silence again.

Mike leaned back in the couch and rested his right ankle on his opposite knee. Something was wrong. This was Cindy and they'd never had a problem talking to each other before. She was bright, funny and he enjoyed her company. Only the stranger sitting in front of him wasn't the Cindy he knew. Something had happened to her. Fear mixed with an instant need to fix whatever the problem was.

"Your hands are shaking," he said quietly. "What's wrong?"

She closed her eyes briefly and swallowed. "Nothing. Everything. Maybe you should just leave."

He lowered his foot to the ground and leaned toward her. "What? Leave? What's going on here? I thought you invited me to dinner."

"I did. I just—" She raised her gaze to his. Her irises were dark with an emotion he couldn't read. "I thought it would be easier than this. I thought—"

"What?" He set his wine on the coffee table in front of him and crossed the room. He knelt beside her and took her free hand in his. "Cindy, it's Mike. You can tell me anything. Did Nelson say something to you?"

"Of course not. We're back to him honking for the children. Everything's fine with Nelson.... It's you."

She spoke the last two words so softly, he wasn't sure he'd heard them. "Me?"

"I'm..." She snatched her hand away and glared at him. "Dammit, Mike, I'm trying to seduce you. Okay? Are you happy? You can laugh now." She set her glass on the small table to her right and clutched her fingers together.

He couldn't have been more stunned if she'd slapped him across the face. "You're trying to seduce me?"

"Stop repeating everything I say." She looked at him as if he had the IQ of a snail. "What did you think all this was?" she asked, pointing at her wineglass, then plucking at the hem of her dress. "There are candles and fresh flowers on the table."

"I noticed."

"You did? Then why didn't you say something, or better yet, do something?"

"Like rip off your clothes?"

"At least then I would have known you were interested." She rose to her feet and walked into the kitchen. Once there, she stood at the sink, with her back to the room.

"What makes you think I'm not?" he asked as he followed her.

She trembled slightly but didn't answer his question. He didn't know whether to laugh or tell her how foolish she was being. Why did she think she had to seduce him? Didn't she know how much he wanted her?

The obvious response was no. She was terrified of doing the wrong thing. Judging from the way she was acting, his suspicions that she hadn't been with anyone since her divorce had to be true. He would also guess that she hadn't been with a lot of men before her marriage. Which meant she was practically an innocent. The thought should have scared him to death. But for some macho, perverse reason, he was pleased.

"Other women have it easy," she said. "Other women seem to find men to have sex with. But not me. No, that would be too simple."

"How many men have turned you down?"

"Just you." She sighed. "Look, I'm really sorry. I shouldn't have changed the rules without checking with you first. It's not fair. I guess I just sort of hoped it would all happen naturally. If you only knew how awful all of this was."

"What's awful? The thought of making love with me?" He leaned against the doorframe.

"No, of course not. That's what I wanted. But there have been so many details to work out. I've been overwhelmed. Finding the right dress. I must have changed about fifteen times. Then I had to plan the right dinner. Something elegant, but easy to eat and prepare. And something that didn't need perfect timing. I mean, what if you'd instantly swept me off my feet? I wanted to be able to turn off the oven and not have dinner ruined.''

"What else?"

She shook her head. "I didn't know which tablecloth to use. Red was too Christmassy and white was too, I don't know, weird, I guess. Like it was a wedding or something. And then there was the whole issue of birth control."

"You planned ahead?"

"Of course. I mean, what if you weren't prepared? I didn't think of that, by the way, Beth did."

"You've talked this over with her?"

"In detail." She clutched the edge of the counter so hard, her knuckles turned white. He could see the muscles in her arms tightening. "She told me to go for it."

"I always liked Beth," he murmured, more and more intrigued by this side of Cindy. She'd really thought this through. She wanted to be with him and had made it happen. He wondered if any other woman in his life had ever cared so much. He wondered if he ever had.

"What did you say?" she asked.

"Nothing. You were explaining about the birth control."

"I didn't know what to get. I haven't been on the Pill since the divorce so I needed something for me, and Beth reminded me to buy condoms. This is the nineties, and I do want to be sensible. Do you know how many kinds of condoms there are?" She spun to face him and grimaced. "About a dozen brands, all these different types, with strange descriptions. What does it all mean? I was so con-

fused. I had to stand there reading packages, like some
pervert. Plus, I had to drive clear into the city so I could
find a drugstore where no one would know me.''

"I hope you bought large ones.''

"What?'' The color drained from her face. "What did
you say?''

"What size box?''

"Oh.'' Some of the color returned, although most of it
centered in a bright spot on her cheeks. "I don't know.
The little one. I think it has three inside.''

He pushed off the doorframe and started toward her.
On the way, he paused long enough to turn off the oven.

"Mike?'' She glanced around as if trying to back up.
Only the kitchen sink was behind her. She was trapped.

"Only three,'' he said, stopping in front of her and
lowering his mouth to hers. "That won't be nearly
enough.''

Chapter Fourteen

His lips were firm. The kiss didn't last but a moment, still she felt it all the way to her toes...and her soul. Her arms hung at her sides and she curled her fingers into her palms. She wanted to touch him, she wanted to hold him and be held, only it wasn't that simple.

She broke free of the kiss, then sidestepped, slipping past him and the island, heading for the dining room. Once there, she stared at the perfectly set table and sighed. It had been a mistake from the beginning. She wasn't the seducing kind.

"You can leave now," she said.

Mike followed her. He placed his hands on her shoulders. "You can't believe that's what I want."

It was a lot easier to have this conversation without looking at him, so she continued to study the flowers she'd purchased that afternoon. "I know you wouldn't want to hurt me. We're friends, and you care about me.

That caring might make you do something you'd otherwise rather not do. I'm not saying you'd have to grit your teeth and think of England, but maybe you're being pushed in a direction you don't want to go. I don't want that.''

"I'm a grown man, Cindy. I know how to say no. Right now, there's nowhere else I'd rather be. There's no one else I'd rather be with. This isn't about you seducing me, it's about me finally giving in to what I've wanted from the moment we met. Do you know what my first thought was when I was lying on my sister's sofa, more dead than alive?''

She could barely remember their meeting. Probably because he was rubbing his palms up and down her bare arms. The combination of heat and friction made it difficult to think about anything but what she was feeling. She wanted to lean back against him, against his hard, lean strength. Instead, she forced herself to murmur, "No."

"I couldn't lift my head, so all I saw were these beautiful, honey-colored thighs. I remember thinking it was very nice of God to insist angels walk around naked.''

In spite of feeling incredibly stupid and exposed, Cindy smiled. "I'm hardly an angel."

"You're right about that." He turned her until she was facing him. "You're a woman, and I want to make love with you.''

His brown eyes blazed with passion. He might be able to fake the affection in his voice or the gentleness of his touch, but she doubted he would be able to invent a fire that bright without some passion to fuel it.

She wanted to believe, she needed to more than anything. Of its own accord, her hand came up and touched his jawline. The skin was smooth; he'd shaved before coming over.

She wanted to ask if he was sure. She wanted to believe it didn't matter if he wasn't. She wanted him to sweep her off her feet so she could stop thinking so much. Instead, she said, "I haven't been with anyone but Nelson. For all I know, I'm doing something terribly wrong. Promise you won't laugh?"

He smiled. "Don't you know I don't care what you do or don't do? I just want to be with you and touch you. I want to taste every part of you. I want to listen to your breathing as the promise of ecstasy makes you gasp for air. I want you to scream my name and beg for more. I want to be in you, hard and deep until you can't do anything but feel."

She stared at him, then blinked. "I'm not much of a screamer."

"That's all you got from that?"

"Well, my knees are shaking a little."

"Let's make them shake a lot."

He leaned over the table and grabbed a single white rose. After handing it to her, he bent down and picked her up in his arms. She shrieked and wrapped her arms around his neck.

"What are you doing?"

"I would have thought it was obvious."

He was strong, his hold on her secure, but she didn't like the feeling of being so out of control. "The bedroom is less than twenty feet away. I could have walked."

"That's romantic," he said, stepping into the bedroom and kicking the door closed behind him. He walked to the bed and set her down next to it. He took the rose and put it on the nightstand.

Cindy glanced around the room and winced. She'd removed the comforter and drawn back the sheets. Small unlit candles covered her dresser. There was something sheer and lacy on the counter in the bathroom, just in case.

"Call me subtle," she said miserably.

Mike didn't answer. He sat on the edge of the high mattress and grabbed her wrist. He tugged until she was forced to step between his parted thighs.

This had all been a mistake, she thought grimly. She should never have tried the seduction thing. She just didn't have the experience to be good at it. Now, glancing around at her preparations, she felt like a foolish child wishing after the moon. Or a teenager worshiping a rock star. All she needed was Mike's picture on the wall.

When the front of her thighs bumped the insides of his, Cindy returned her attention to what was going on. Mike's hands rested on her waist and he was urging her closer. The fire inside of him burned so hot she could feel the flames. They lit an answering spark within her. The spark flared to life, growing until it threatened to consume her. It burned away her doubts and questions until only need was left behind.

"Kiss me," he commanded.

She complied willingly.

His position on the bed put him slightly below eye level. She bent her head until their lips touched. She wasn't sure what she expected, maybe a wild assault, maybe cool disinterest. Instead, his lips clung to hers, touching, sharing, but not taking. She could feel the soft pressure as he moved his head slightly, fitting them together. She raised her arms and placed them around his neck. His hands settled on her back. As she moved closer, he pulled her next to him. From chest to thigh they touched.

His heat was like a sensual blanket. It swept over her shoulders wrapping her in a thick cloak of need. A tremor raced through her, then another. Yet they were only kissing, as chastely as virgin lovers who might yet be separated.

She stroked the back of his neck. His haircut was still painfully new. She could feel the first hints of stubble, then the military-short strands. She traced the shape of his ears, his jaw. Smoother skin there, but different from her own.

He shifted, splaying his legs more until her thighs settled against his groin. She could feel the hardness of him, straining against his shorts. He couldn't fake that, either. She relaxed, giving herself up to the sensual experience.

He chose the moment of her surrender to test the seam of her mouth. She parted for him instantly, anticipating the sweet taste of him and the pleasure he would bring. He didn't disappoint her. His tongue swept across hers. Shivers raced down her arms and chest, settling in her breasts. She drew in a deep breath, to bring her more in contact with him. The action didn't ease the aching she felt there, or between her legs. Even her lacy, silk bra felt scratchy and thick.

He broke the kiss, only to trail kisses across her jaw and down her neck. He licked the hollow of her throat, traced a moist path to the neckline of her dress, then moved lower still and gently bit the puckered tip of her breast.

She sucked in her breath. Through the layers of clothing, she felt the pressure of his teeth. Involuntarily, her hips arched toward him, her head arched back. Breath caught in her throat. She squeezed his shoulders, silently begging for more.

Over and over he raked his teeth against the sensitive nub. The hands at her waist held her in place. If she'd had the strength, she would have laughed. She had no plans to leave. But as she swayed slightly, unable to keep her balance under his sensual assault, she thought he might not be holding her still as much as holding her up.

She clung to him. Her fingers weaved through his silky, short hair. She cupped his head, finally urging him to taunt her other breast the same way.

His ministrations there were twice as sweet. Her legs trembled violently. Her breathing was rapid gasps. She could feel the moist heat between her thighs. She was shaken and ready for him, and they both still had their clothes on.

"Sweet Cindy," he murmured against her chest. "Tell me you like this."

"Are you kidding?" she gasped.

He raised his head and looked at her. A slow, satisfied, very male sort of smile stretched across his face. She wondered if she should be offended or at least protest the power he had over her. Before she could decide, he began pulling her zipper down and she found she didn't really care what he did, as long as he didn't ever stop.

He slipped the dress over her shoulders. It slid down easily, falling into a pool at her feet. His gaze moved from her face to her breasts, then lower. She felt it as tangibly as a touch. Her skin was both hot and cold, and she held on to his shoulders as the only solid thing in her spinning world.

"I knew you'd be this beautiful," he whispered, then kissed her collarbone.

She wanted to protest she wasn't beautiful. She was slightly over thirty, she'd had two children and she hadn't won the battle with those last couple of pounds. But he didn't seem to care and she decided not to point those facts out to him.

His fingers moved up and down her spine, creating spirals of need and anticipation. His hands slipped over her hips, then cupped her buttocks tightly. Finally, he moved down her legs to the backs of her knees, then up, repeating the journey in reverse.

Every muscle, every inch of skin longed for the brush of his fingers. As he touched her, heat flared to life, leaving tiny points of flame lit all over. He again trailed kisses down her chest, to her breasts, but this time he dipped lower. He licked the sensitive valley between her breasts, then bent his head and bit the skin over her ribs.

His breath tickled her, his hands taunted her, his mouth left her trembling and weak. It had never been like this before. Mike loved all of her, touching her everywhere, bringing her to the highest pitch of arousal she'd ever known. He didn't just stroke her breasts for a few minutes, then move his hand lower to bring her to the point of completion. He seemed to have forgotten there was a destination and was instead enjoying the journey for its own sake.

His hands moved back up her spine. Before he could taunt her again with a nibble on her side, she placed her hand under his jaw and forced him to look at her.

"Kiss me," she commanded.

"Yes, ma'am." He puckered his lips obligingly.

She smiled. "I didn't expect to laugh."

"What did you expect?"

"To feel awkward and out of place. I was afraid I was going to lie on the bed like a piece of wood, wondering how I was going to explain my lack of response."

"That doesn't say much about my technique."

"This was just a little more about my fears than your ability."

"And now?" he asked.

"I'm on fire."

She lowered her mouth to his. This time she was the one to brush his lips with hers. She learned the shape of him, then used her tongue to discover his taste. She swept over his lower lip and dipped inside, savoring the tightening of his muscles and the half-swallowed groan.

Still kissing him, she moved out of the V of his thighs, and nudged his knees together. She straddled him, bringing her waiting moistness in contact with his male need. Wiggling closer, making him writhe, she deepened the kiss, exploring all of him, learning what made him quake, what made him go still and what made that hardness flex against her.

He broke away and swore. "You're trying to make me lose control."

"Is that possible?"

"Oh, yeah. If you don't stop moving like that, you'll make me prove it."

"Thank you," she murmured. She didn't believe he was all that close to being swept over the edge, but it was wonderful to hear the words. She liked knowing she brought this strong man to the point of breaking. She wanted him to shatter, then together they would put the pieces back in place.

She kissed his jaw, tasting the faintly bitter flavor of his after-shave, then moved to his ear. She nibbled on the lobe and suckled the sensitive skin underneath. His breathing grew more rapid.

His fingers found the fastener of her bra. With practiced ease, he slipped the hooks free. She straightened slightly so the garment slid down her arms. She grabbed it and tossed it aside.

Mike stared at her breasts as if he'd never seen a naked woman before. Slowly, reverently, he cupped her. She was pale against his tanned skin. His fingers moved back and forth creating exquisite electrical sensations that arced down to her most feminine place. He lowered his head between her breasts, as if to bury himself within her. He was warm, with only the faintest hint of stubble to create delicious friction.

Her own breathing increased to match the rapid cadence of his. When his mouth closed on her nipple, she caught her breath, wondering if she'd ever felt anything so incredible in her life. His warm, damp tongue circled her, teasing her tightness until her hips began to rock against him. She gasped his name, clutching at him, begging him to never stop.

Back and forth he moved, caressing first one then the other breast. His fingers supported her, stroking her pale flesh, pushing her toward the edge of sanity.

When she thought she might slip over into madness, he wrapped his arms around her waist and gently lowered her to the bed. He rolled until he knelt between her thighs. She was stretched across the width of the mattress, her feet dangling off the side. The sheets were smooth and cool against her heated skin.

He shifted so he was lying next to her, then reached behind him for something on the nightstand. When she was able to bring her gaze into focus, she saw he was holding the rose.

"Lovely," he said, first staring at, then sniffing the pale flower. He held it close to her nose. She inhaled the sweet fragrance. Roses would forever remind her of him.

It was probably close to seven o'clock, but the sun was still bright in the sky. The pulled drapes couldn't keep out all the light. She could see him clearly, and the furniture in the room. Her nearly naked body was his to view, yet he seemed preoccupied by the rose.

"They've taken off the thorns," he said, turning the

stem and studying it. "Just as well, I wouldn't want to hurt you."

With that, he brushed the flower against her throat. The petals were soft. She could smell the sweet scent and feel the faint caress against her heated skin. She arched her neck. He traced the line of her jaw, her ears, then moved down her chest to her breastbone.

The delicate petals tickled and aroused. Goose bumps dotted her skin. Mike stretched out beside her, supporting his head on one hand. With the other, he held the rose and circled her breasts. First one, around and around, moving higher to her nipple, but not touching it, then the other. Back and forth, he taunted her.

Her breathing came in gasps, then she forgot to breathe at all. At last he brushed the tip with the head of the flower. At the same moment, he brought his mouth down on her other breast. Her hips tilted, her fingers clawed at the sheet. She didn't know she could feel so much pleasure and still live.

He continued to stroke her body, dragging the rose across her belly. Every muscle quivered in anticipation. He paused to remove her panties, then trailed the flower down her legs. He tickled the soles of her feet, then moved higher, sweeping the petals across the insides of her knees and up her thighs.

She parted for him. She was damp and swollen, her woman's place aching for his touch. If she'd been able to speak, she would have begged. As it was, she could only try to survive this sensual assault, waiting for the culmination that would surely shatter her being.

He touched the rose to the damp curls. He rose and knelt between her legs. Again and again he touched her with the flower. The petals merely teased her, without bringing her the promise of release. She moved her hips up and down, silently urging him to touch her, take her. Anything.

He laughed softly. "Impatient little thing, aren't you?"

"Yes," she gasped.

He leaned forward and placed the rose on her belly. With one graceful movement, he drew his T-shirt over his head and tossed it aside. His torso was smooth and tanned, gleaming in the diffused light. She reached for him.

"Not yet," he said, lowering himself to the mattress and dropping a quick kiss on her right thigh.

His hands slipped under her legs as he grasped her buttocks, then bent closer. She screamed when he stroked his tongue against her. From the place that would bring them both release, to the tiny but engorged center of her pleasure, he tasted her. His breath was hot, his tongue sure.

She'd heard of such things, her ex-husband had even tried it once or twice, but she'd felt so awkward and exposed, she'd asked him to stop. Now the thought of Mike stopping was enough to make her sob. She could feel her body collecting itself, already prepared to explode. Her scalp tingled, the soles of her feet burned. Every point in between was alive and taut with need. Her muscles contracted and tightened, making her legs jerk and her hands clutch and release the sheet.

His tongue continued its magical ministrations, circling around, moving up and down, dipping inside, as if her flavor was a treat to be savored. He moved closer, shifting her legs over his shoulders, as if *he* needed more. She was off-balance and falling, exposed and out of control and she didn't want it to end.

But the pleasure could not be denied. Like the glory of a sunrise, it began with only a hint of light. Her muscles started to clench in a secret rhythm. Her hips rose against his mouth, her fingers clawed for support as she moaned her need.

She spoke his name, at least she tried to form the words. She tossed her head from side to side. The insistent stroking of his tongue forced her to his pace, not hers, so she hung suspended, until the last rapid flick sent her exploding into the light. She soared in a storm of ultimate pleasure as her muscles trembled in a cascade of satisfaction.

When the world had stopped spinning, she found herself cradled in Mike's arms. He stared at her intensely.

She touched his face, his cheeks, then traced his mouth.

"That was wonderful," she murmured.

"I'm glad."

"How did you do that?"

"I had great material to work with. You're very responsive."

She could feel the blush climbing, but she didn't bother to look away. After what they'd just shared, how could there be any secrets?

"I've never been that responsive before," she admitted.

"Then you *have* been doing it wrong."

She giggled. "I guess so. Thanks for showing me the right way."

"My pleasure. Anytime. And I mean that."

His eyes were dark and smoky, his expression caring. But she could feel the tension in his body. His erection pressed against her bare hip.

As she raised her head toward him, she ran her hands down his back. Even as their mouths met and tongues tangled, she stroked his coiled muscles. His skin was sleek and smooth, his strength overwhelming. Except for the scar on his leg, he was back to normal.

Even so, a slight pressure on his shoulder was all she needed to roll him onto his back. She knelt next to him and studied the breadth of him. His belly was flat, his hips narrow. The male part of him thrust up against the fabric of his shorts.

She bent over his chest and touched her tongue to his nipple. At the same moment, she placed her palm over his hardness. His response was an instant guttural cry. He cupped her face.

"You're killing me," he murmured.

"What a way to go."

His smile was slightly pained.

He sat up and kissed her. While his mouth kept hers busy, he drew off his shorts and briefs. He reached for her hand and brought it back to him. This time, instead of strained fabric, she touched bare skin. Her fingers closed around him. He drew her tongue into his mouth and sucked, matching the speed of her strokes between his thighs.

Soft skin encased the hard ridge of his desire. She explored his impressive length, then moved lower. He spread his legs, allowing her to touch him there. Flesh yielded. She cupped him gently, rubbing her fingers until he writhed against her caress and hoarsely called her name.

She lowered her mouth to his shoulder, nibbling his hot skin. He tasted salty.

"Where are they?" he asked, his breath ticking her ear.

"What?"

"The condoms."

"Oh." She raised her head and glanced at him, suddenly embarrassed. "Under the pillow."

He slid his right hand along the sheet, searched for a moment, then pulled out the small, square box.

"Did I get the right kind?" she asked, suddenly anxious. "There were so many and I didn't really know what you would want and—"

He touched his finger to her mouth. "You did great. They're fine."

She gave him one final, parting stroke, then sat back and watched him draw on the protection. She'd been afraid that moment might be awkward, but it was a caring gesture. He didn't try to persuade her otherwise, or make her feel foolish. He simply did what he had to in order to take care of her.

When he was done, she lay down next to him. He moved over her, settling between her legs. At the first touch of him against her sensitive center, her body began to clench in anticipation. She hadn't thought to experience release again, but suddenly she wanted to. Desperately.

She drew back her knees and arched her hips toward him. He pressed against her. She was so damp, he slid in easily, parting her tight flesh, sending shivers of pleasure radiating outward, like a pebble dropped in a pond. She wiggled closer. Her breasts bounced with the motion and his breath caught. She smiled slowly. She liked knowing he found her exciting.

She moved her hand and touched the trimmed stem of the rose. A few of the petals had fallen off, but most of the flower was still whole. His dark eyes met hers. She saw the need raging there, matched only by the throbbing between her legs.

She brought the flower up to his chest and stroked his skin. His muscles tensed. She did it again, this time searching out his flat nipples.

"Cindy, don't," he said tightly.

"Why not?"

"Because I won't be able to hold back."

"Maybe I don't want you to."

She brought the rose lower, dipping it into his dark curls, stroking it against the base of his organ as he withdrew, only to plunge in again.

"Two can play at this," he said, then grabbed the rose from her. He touched the head of the flower to her breasts, teasing her with a quick back and forth motion.

Now it was her turn to moan. She couldn't focus on anything but what he was doing on her chest and between her legs. Her vision blurred. She felt his muscles tense for one final assault. He groaned his denial.

"Yes," she said loudly, drawing her knees all the way to her chest and thrusting her hips toward him.

He drove deeply into her, triggering massive contractions of ecstasy. His body shook as he, too, fell into the bliss. They clung to each other until the shaking stopped and their breathing returned to normal.

Cindy lay curled next to Mike. She couldn't see the clock, but she guessed it was around ten Sunday morning. On the floor was the wooden tray she'd used to feed him while he was sick. Instead of the remains of weak soup and toast, there was an empty bottle of wine, bowls used for the beef Burgundy, and an empty pint of gourmet strawberry ice cream. She smiled when she remembered what Mike had done with that. It had been very sticky and they'd both needed a shower afterward.

He'd been right about the condoms. They used the last one just a couple of hours before. Which meant, as much as she wanted to, she really shouldn't wake him up. Although there were other ways of bringing pleasure. He had certainly proved that to her.

She turned her head so she could study his profile. His nose was straight, his mouth well formed. There was a tiny scar by his left eyebrow, probably from a childhood accident. She'd never noticed before. Probably because she'd never been this close to him before.

A lock of hair fell onto his forehead. She wanted to brush it away, but she didn't want to wake him. Instead, she scooted closer, tangling her bare legs with his.

He breathed rhythmically, sleeping without dreaming. She was too aware of herself to sleep. She could hear her heart beating, feel her skin, the tingling between her legs.

She'd expected to enjoy making love with Mike. They liked each other, they had fun together, they shared a mutual attraction. Why wouldn't it have been wonderful? So the fact that he left her breathless and trembling wasn't a surprise.

She hadn't expected to fall in love.

Cindy closed her eyes for a moment. The rush of emotions had caught her off guard. She tried to tell herself it was just a chemical reaction to the moment. Once the glow wore off, so would her feelings. But she knew the truth. Somehow in the tangle of sheets and bodies, she'd exposed her heart. She suspected she'd fallen in love with him a long time ago. Their intimacy had only forced her to acknowledge it.

She'd thought she might want to rage against the truth. But she felt calm. Knowing what she knew now, even knowing Mike was leaving, she wouldn't change anything. With him, she was alive. He reminded her she was a woman, he'd shown her she could love again. If the price of that was a broken heart, she would pay it and survive. For in time her heart would heal. The crack would always be visible, and she would never love anyone exactly as she loved Mike, but it was far better to feel the pain of loss and be among the living, than exist the way she had for the last couple of years—protecting herself from the world, merely surviving in a cocoon of fear.

Some risks were worth taking. She wouldn't try to change him. She knew the lesson well. Men leave; men like him, especially. She couldn't trap him, nor did she want to. He couldn't separate what he was from what he did and she didn't have the right to ask him to. So she would love him, and when his time was up, she would let him go.

Mike stirred against her. "Why aren't you asleep?" he asked, his voice thick with sleep.

"I was just thinking."

"'Bout what?" He pulled her closer until her head rested on his shoulder. His arm encircled her waist as her bare breasts nestled against his side.

"I was wondering if you would stay here with me until it's time for you to go back to L.A."

He opened his eyes and stared at her. His smile was slow and sexy. She felt it all the way to her toes.

"I was hoping you'd ask me. There's nothing I'd like more."

Chapter Fifteen

"You can stay just one more day," Allison said as she stared at him.

Mike dropped the T-shirt he'd been folding and gathered her close. The little girl snuggled against him. The feel of her, her scent, the trusting way she expected him to keep her safe, were all familiar to him. Too familiar. He wasn't going to be able to forget her, or any of them.

"My plane is leaving in a couple of hours."

"You can change your flight," Jonathan said.

The boy stood at the end of the bed, clutching the bedpost. He kept looking away and brushing his hand across his face.

"I've got a job to get to," Mike reminded them, releasing Allison and wondering why his chest felt so tight. "I've already delayed twice. As it is, I'm going to have to fly to Los Angeles, take care of business, then fly directly to Washington."

Cindy came into the room. She shook her head. "I told you two not to bother Mike this morning. He's on a schedule. He's already stayed as long as he can. Come on. Say goodbye, then go outside and play. All your friends are there."

Allison ran from the room. Mike stared after her for a moment. He never thought he would come to care about children, but these two had really found their way inside. School was going to be starting soon. When he was gone, he would wonder if they liked their teachers and how their classes were going. He would think about Jonathan at football games and hope Allison hadn't brought Shelby back to life.

Jonathan cleared his throat several times, then gave in to the tears. They flowed down his cheeks. Mike knelt and held out his arms. The boy flung himself into his embrace.

"I'll miss you," Mike said, his voice strangely hoarse.

"Yeah, me, too. We're still going camping, right?"

"I'll be back. I don't know when yet, but I'll call. No matter what, we're going camping."

Jonathan pushed away, then ran from the room. Before Mike could rise to his feet, Allison returned. She was carrying several large sheets of paper, the thick kind kids use for crafts. Holes had been punched along one side and yarn woven through, holding the sheets together. A strand of blond hair drifted across her cheek and she brushed it away impatiently.

"I made this," she said importantly, handing him the bundle. "It's a story about you."

She smiled and her dimples about did him in. He took the papers. On the cover, printed in fairly uneven script were the words *My Summer With Mike*. There was a drawing, done in crayon, of a man, a woman and two children.

He noticed the man and the little girl were holding hands. As he turned the pages, Allison pointed out the various events to him. His arrival—she'd drawn little hearts on the bandage around his stick-figure leg—playing in the greenbelt, their trip to the mall. Other times he'd nearly forgotten about. There were two pages devoted to the campout.

On the last page, the little girl stood alone. There were x's and o's underneath her figure. "Those are hugs and kisses," she said, pointing.

Cindy stepped forward. "She made it herself. Allison even thought up the idea. She's been working on it since we found out you were leaving."

"It's beautiful," he said, touching the handmade book. "The most beautiful gift anyone has ever given me."

Allison beamed with pleasure. "Now you won't forget me."

"I could never forget you." He touched her hair, then her cheek. "I'll remember you always. I promise."

"Bye, Mike." She leaned forward and kissed his cheek, then ran from the room. A few seconds later, the back door opened and slammed shut.

He stared at the book. "I wasn't expecting anything like this. It must have taken hours."

"She really cares about you." Cindy moved close and pointed to the cover. "The best part is, she didn't put Shelby anywhere in the story. I hope that means her imaginary friend is gone for good."

He rose to his feet and laid Allison's gift on the bed. "I don't want to be responsible for her return. That concerns me."

"We'll be okay. We survived before you, we'll survive after you're gone." Her gentle smile took the sting out of her words. "Trust me, Mike. Just worry about yourself and your next job. We don't want you shot up again. You want some coffee?"

"Yeah, sure. Thanks."

She left the bedroom. He finished packing. Everything he'd brought with him, practically everything he owned could fit into two bags. There was a time he'd been proud of that. Now he wasn't so sure. He would have to carry Allison's book in his hand. He couldn't fit it into his bags without folding it and he didn't want to damage the pages. He would have to get a larger suitcase. Or leave the gift somewhere safe.

He could smell the scent of coffee, but instead of walking to the kitchen, he moved to the bedroom window. He'd spent the last week and a half with Cindy. The children had acknowledged his presence with the casual acceptance of the young. Several mornings, they'd come in early and thrown themselves on the bed. Once the children returned from their father's, he and Cindy had been careful about dressing after making love, so when Jonathan and Allison had joined them, it had been a free-for-all of tickling, jokes and laughter. He'd been part of a family.

He stared out the window at the grassy lawn beyond. The crepe myrtle was in full bloom. Come winter it would stand bare. Cindy would cut it back and then it would grow and bloom again. He would miss the blossoms. He would miss the play on the greenbelt and the awful TV cartoons. He would miss the games, the fights, the laughter and even the tears. He would miss holding Cindy and loving her. He would miss watching her shower, then making love with her quickly in the large walk-in closet, her hair still dripping down her back as she buried her face in his shoulder to muffle her moans of pleasure.

He would miss this house, and the city itself. He'd

come to enjoy Sugar Land and all the suburbs had to offer. He would even miss Beth.

There was a time when the thought of his new job would have consumed him, but not today. All he could do was wish he wasn't leaving. The thought of pitting his intellect and skills against the enemy wasn't exciting. The thought of taking another bullet made him grimace. He didn't want to die. Not yet. Not when he'd found what he was looking for all his life.

If only… If only he was the right man for Cindy. If only he knew how to love and be loved. If only he had the right to stay.

"Coffee's ready," Cindy called.

Mike moved across the room. He tucked Allison's book under his arm, then collected his luggage and set it in the foyer. He'd arranged for a service to drive him to the airport. Cindy had offered, but he didn't think he could stand the goodbyes. He would rather remember her here, where she belonged.

He walked into the kitchen. Cindy was sitting at the round table. He took the chair across from her and picked up the mug she'd left there.

"When does school start?" he asked.

"In a week and a half. I go back Monday. Lesson plans and all that."

She was wearing white shorts and a green T-shirt that matched her eyes. A headband held her hair off her face. He studied her features, memorizing them for the long days ahead. He wanted to believe she would mourn him, but he knew better.

"Now that you've gotten your feet wet, you can start dating," he said.

She'd brought her cup to her lips, but she set it down untasted. "I don't think it's going to be that simple."

"You can't let Nelson win forever."

"He's not winning anymore. I don't care about him. I haven't been dressing up on the mornings he picks up the kids."

"I noticed."

She smiled sadly. "I gave him too much power. I see that now. I wanted my perfect dream, my sure thing, and I figured he was the way to get it. I've learned there are no sure things in life. We just have to take what we're given and make the best of it. My kids are happy, I'm learning to be happy. I suppose I could date if I wanted to, but not right now."

She glanced down, then quickly up again. Her eyes darkened with emotion. "I love you, Mike." She held up her hand to stop him from speaking. "Before you get all worried, I don't expect you to say anything back to me. I'm not asking for something, I just wanted you to know. At first I wasn't going to tell you, but then I realized I couldn't let you go off without saying the words. I suppose they're more for me than you. Maybe that's not fair, I don't know. But it's true. I love you." She paused. "You okay?"

"Yeah, sure." But he wasn't. He was reeling inside. Cindy had done this once before. She'd managed to bring him to his knees with just a few words. She'd learned his biggest secret, that he wasn't enough, then had blithely changed the subject.

Now she spoke of loving him. He wanted to grab her by the shoulders and shake her until she said the words again and again. At the same time, he wanted to demand she take them back. She couldn't love him. No one ever loved him. He came and went from people's lives, a brief encounter, a fond memory, but he never inspired real feelings. He couldn't.

She reached out her hand and squeezed his fingers. "I never thought I'd be willing to take that kind of risk again," she said. "You showed me that some risks are worth taking. Loving you is worth all of it. You'll be gone, and I'll miss you, but that's okay. We've had some wonderful times together. I'll always treasure them. And that's what loving is about, I think. Finding the magic in a world gone mad." She sighed. "I would love to come with you, but I can't. My life is here, with my children. Yours is somewhere else. But for this summer, we had something wonderful."

Tears glistened in her eyes. She blinked them away. "Damn. I promised myself I wouldn't cry."

"You almost never swear."

"I know. I guess I'm more upset than I thought. But I'll be fine. I promise."

He didn't want her to be fine. He wanted her to scream at him, demand that he stay. Instead, she smiled bravely.

The pain in his chest deepened. She would remain here in her world, a world full of light and love. He would return to the shadows, to his temporary jobs and a life that fit in two duffel bags.

"Cindy, I—"

Outside, a car honked.

She rose to her feet. "Your car is here. It's time to leave."

The next few minutes were a blur of hugs and goodbyes. The children ran to be with him one last time. Cindy clung to him, and kissed him feverishly. He wanted to tell her he'd changed his mind, but she was so determined to go on without him. She'd made all her plans, accepted the consequences of it all. She would be fine without him.

As the car drove away, he looked back one last time.

Cindy stood with her children on either side of her. They waved. He could tell they were crying.

"Where you heading?" the driver asked.

Mike leaned back against the seat. "L.A.," he answered. "Home."

But as he spoke the word, he knew it was a lie. All he'd ever wanted, all he'd ever longed for in his life was behind him. He wondered if he would ever find his way back.

Washington, D.C., was not the place to spend August. The heat, the humidity and the tourists all conspired to make his life hell. Mike paced to the window of his small bedroom and opened it. The air conditioner clicked on in angry protest, but he ignored it. He breathed in the muggy air and closed his eyes. If he ignored the sounds, he could pretend he was in Houston again.

But he wasn't. Instead of shorts and a T-shirt, he was wearing a suit and tie. The holster strapped under his arm held a pistol. He was once again the highly trained, highly paid bodyguard.

He closed the window, but he couldn't block out the memories. He'd only been gone two weeks, but he'd already broken down and called. He'd chatted casually with Allison and Jonathan, but his conversation with Cindy had been strained. She'd started crying and told him he was making it hard to be brave. Maybe he should give them time to recover.

He'd agreed not to call again for at least a month and then only to set up a camping trip with Jonathan. That decision made, life should have been easier. But it wasn't.

He couldn't stop thinking about her. About what she'd said to him. He couldn't stop hearing her say she loved him.

He'd seen Cindy with her children. He knew how strong and constant her love was. He knew she gave unselfishly, in a way he could never have imagined. As he lay awake at night, he explored his own long-buried feelings. Since he was a child, he'd tried not to care. That was the main reason he'd left Houston. He couldn't stay with Cindy and just take. He had to be able to give something back. But he wasn't sure.

He wanted to do it right. To be the perfect husband and father. Allison and Jonathan didn't need another man walking out on them. He had to be willing to stay, no matter what. But he didn't know how to be a parent. He didn't know how to be a husband. He could barely commit long enough to be a lover.

So he honored Cindy's wish and didn't call.

But his heart ached, and the wound inside of him bled as if it would never heal. He stood by the window watching people walk by. There weren't many in this exclusive section of Georgetown. Occasionally, a mother and her children strolled by. Or maybe it was the nanny.

Allison's book lay open on his bed. He looked through it every night, studying the pictures, the wobbly lines, the misspelled words. Some people would probably laugh at her efforts and only notice the mistakes. He only saw the love.

Cindy slammed down her pen and shoved back her chair. She couldn't concentrate on anything. She walked into the kitchen and paced back and forth on the wooden floor. The house was too quiet. Allison and Jonathan were with their father. Beth and Darren had taken their children to Galveston for the weekend. The neighborhood was strangely silent. She felt as if she were the only person left alive.

She wanted to jump out of her skin.

Cindy rubbed her hands up and down her arms. She was hot and cold at the same time. If she'd been able to delude herself, she would have tried to explain away her symptoms as some kind of flu. But it was simpler than that—and more deadly. She missed Mike.

It had seemed so easy when he was leaving. Loving him had been the right thing to do. It was worth the price she would pay later. Cheap talk while she was still able to see him and hold him and make love to him. Now that she was alone, all she could feel was empty. It was worse than when Nelson left. At least then she'd had her anger to give her energy.

She wanted Mike back. She wanted him to stay with her and be a part of her life. She wanted to wake up next to him and grow old with him. She wanted him to love her back.

She paused by the sink and clutched the cool tiles. That was the killer. He didn't love her. Oh, he probably cared a lot, maybe more than he'd ever cared for anyone. But she knew men like him. Men who came and went on a whim. It wasn't possible for them to put down roots. And even if Mike wanted to, he didn't believe he could. Somehow, somewhere, someone had convinced him he wasn't worth it. So he would never saddle her with what he would consider a flawed man.

She'd let him go because it was the right thing to do. Letting him go had been—

She raised her head and stared out the window. Okay. She was alone. It was time to be completely honest with herself. Letting him go had been stupid. About the stupidest thing she'd ever done. If she lived to be a thousand, she would never find a man as wonderful, as caring, as loving as Mike. And she'd let him walk out of her life. Why?

Cindy drew in a deep breath. The answer to the question floated in her brain for several moments before all the parts connected into a thought she could understand. She'd let him go because the pain of leaving was something she understood. That rejection had happened to her many times before. Demanding what she wanted, what was right for him and for her kids was so much harder. It was uncharted ground. She'd retreated to the familiar and in doing so, had lost him.

She loved him with all her heart, and if she was honest with herself, she believed he loved her back. Look at all he'd done for her. Every action had spoken of caring. Mike was a man who showed his feelings by what he did, not what he said. In time, he would have found the words. But instead of being brave enough to fight for him, she'd passively let him walk out of her life.

She crossed the kitchen in three quick steps. After fumbling through her small personal phone directory, she punched in several numbers, pausing to double-check and get them right. The connection took a few seconds. There was a bit of static, then a sleepy, "'Llo?"

"Grace?"

"Cindy? Is that you?" She heard rustling bedclothes. "What's wrong?"

"Nothing." She glanced at the clock, then added on the extra hours. "Sorry, it's the middle of the night there, isn't it? I didn't mean to wake you."

"It's okay. Are you all right?"

"Yes. No. I need to know how to get hold of Mike. He's gone and I don't have the number."

"You want to phone Mike? Why?"

"I just have to find him." She drew in a deep breath

and clutched the receiver tightly. "If you must know, I love him. I let him walk out of my life because I'm a fool. I know he cares about me and the children, but he's afraid to take that last step. I've got to find him and tell him to come home to us before something terrible happens. He's on a job. What if he gets shot again? Oh, Grace, I was so brave when he left. I made him think I was going to be fine. I'm not fine. I'm a wreck. I have to tell him how much I need him."

"Oh, Cindy, this is wonderful." Grace sniffed as if she was crying, too. "I don't know where he is, but I'll find him for you. I swear I will."

Donovan raised one dark eyebrow. "You're walking away from a great job."

"Maybe," Mike said. "I'll admit the pay is good, but I don't need to go up against a bullet again."

His replacement smiled. "Don't worry. I'll get the bastard."

"You do that."

The younger man strolled out of the room. Mike watched him go, then shook his head. He'd been like that once. Eager, willing to risk it all. But it wasn't that simple anymore. He had something to live for. Three somethings. Four, if he could convince Cindy to have a baby.

He glanced around the room one last time, then picked up his luggage. He'd replaced one of his duffel bags with a large hard-sided suitcase. Allison's book fit neatly in the bottom. It meant he would have to check his luggage. He wouldn't be able to just walk away when he reached his destination. It was going to be a change, but that's what he wanted.

He was nearly out the door when the phone rang. He paused, not wanting to answer it, but what if it was

Cindy? Even as he crossed to the instrument, he reminded himself she didn't have his number.

"Hello?"

"You haven't been all that easy to track down, mister."

"Grace, how'd you find me?"

"I have my ways."

"How are you?"

"Don't change the subject or try to sweet-talk me. Cindy misses you terribly. I want to know what you've done to my best friend."

"I fell in love with her."

There was a pause, then Grace laughed. "About time, big brother."

He stopped long enough to buy a four-door sedan, in dark blue. The rich, leather interior would take a beating from the kids' toys and sports equipment, but he didn't care. He was back.

He exited the highway and turned left into Sugar Land. The streets and stores were familiar to him. A week from Monday he would join the commuters making their way into the city. He would only have to go halfway there. His new job, training oil executives to ward off terrorist attacks and kidnappings, was about five miles from Cindy's house. The pay was good, the hours better. He got off every day at five.

He turned left, finally pulling to a stop in front of the middle school. The two-story brick building was exactly as he remembered it from the times he'd driven past. Up the road was the grocery store, and back the other way, the country club. He knew this small community and the residents. He wondered how disappointed the women would be now that he wasn't a bodyguard anymore. If he had his way, he wasn't going to be single much longer, either.

He found the administration office and got directions to Cindy's classroom. The door was solid wood, except for a window in the top half. He stood there looking at her.

She was wearing a skirt and blouse. Low heels made her perfect legs look even more curvy. As he watched her explaining an equation on the blackboard, he felt the wound in his chest begin to heal. How could he have ever thought of leaving her? This was where he belonged.

After a few minutes, she glanced up and noticed him. Her face paled. She said something to her class, then crossed the floor and stepped into the hall. The door closed behind her.

"Mike?" she said as if she couldn't believe it was him.

"Oh, God, I've missed you." He wrapped his arms around her. They clung to each other. Her body melted against his.

"What are you doing here?" she asked, her voice thick with emotion. "I never thought I'd see you again."

"I said I'd come back to take Jonathan camping."

"Oh. Is that why you're here?"

"No." He released her. She ducked her head, but he touched his finger to her chin, forcing her to look at him. Tears swam in her green eyes. "I came back for you, Cindy Jones. I couldn't think about anything but you. I did a lousy job, and I couldn't see myself getting any better, so I quit." He stared at her intently. "I'm not very good at relationships. I've never had one before. Not like this. So you'll have to tell me when I do something wrong. I'll try my damnedest to be the kind of man you and the kids need. I just want to be with the three of you forever. I love you."

She was staring at him, openmouthed. He swallowed. "That is, if you want me."

"Want you? I love you. I shouldn't have let you go." She leaned against him and sighed. "Are you really here? Is this happening?"

"Yes. All of it." He touched her hair. "I bought a car."

"What?"

"It's kind of big, but it will hold all the kids. There's even room for a car seat if we, ah, you know." He had to clear his throat. "I got another job. Here in town. I've got four weeks' paid vacation, benefits and I get off work at five every day."

"You want a baby, too? I'd love another child." The joy in her smile nearly blinded him. "I can't believe this is happening. You have a job here?"

"Believe it." He took her hands in his. "Cindy, will you marry me?"

Her green eyes burned bright with love. She squeezed his fingers. "You don't have to do all this for me. Just having you back is enough."

"I want to do it right. I want to get a barbecue and learn how to cook ribs. I want to mow the lawn, go to swim meets and make love with my wife every Saturday morning."

"I hope we make love more than that," she teased.

"You have to ask?"

She touched his face. "These are big changes for you. We don't have to do them all at once. Maybe we should have a trial run and see if you can stand living in the suburbs."

He shook his head. "I'm going to marry you. I've been in the suburbs, and I think they might grow on me. Besides, I can't just move in with you."

"Why not?"

He turned her slowly in a circle. Her class was plastered against the door window, staring at them. Administration office personnel stood at the end of the hall. Several teachers had come out of their rooms and were also watching them. "That's why."

"Oh, my."

"Yeah. I have your reputation to think of. What would the neighbors think if we lived together? It would cause a scandal. Besides, you're not getting away from me again. So we're getting married."

"If you insist," she said, reaching up and pressing her mouth against his. She pulled back slightly and grinned. "I can't wait to tell the kids and everyone. They're going to think it's wonderful."

"So do I," Mike said, wrapping his arms around her. "So do I."

*   *   *   *   *

Don't miss these next unforgettable novels
from Susan Mallery, both part of her
LONE STAR CANYON *series:*

Unexpectedly Expecting, Special Edition
#1370, on sale January 2001

Wife in Disguise, Special Edition #1383,
on sale March 2001

Dear Reader,

Once upon a time, back before I developed an idea to write a miniseries about U.S. Navy SEALs, back before that miniseries became a top-selling favorite of romance readers, I wrote a romantic suspense novel called *Hero Under Cover.* This was the very first book I wrote for Silhouette Intimate Moments—and there's not a Navy SEAL in sight!

I love writing series romance, and I've since found a real niche writing my TALL, DARK & DANGEROUS books about SEAL Team Ten's Alpha Squad.

But it all started with *Hero Under Cover....*

Enjoy!

Suzanne Brockmann

HERO UNDER COVER
by Suzanne Brockmann

For those fabulous Kuhlmans—
Bill, who's been trying to teach
me simply to be happy, and Jodie,
who's been showing us all how
to be happy for years

Chapter 1

"**Y**ou're going to do *what!*"

"A strip search," the FBI agent said, heading for the door. "Please follow me."

Dr. Annie Morrow crossed her arms and planted herself firmly. She wasn't going anywhere, that was for damn sure. "You've gone through my luggage with a fine-tooth comb, you've X-rayed the hell out of my purse, and now you want to do a *strip* search? This is harassment, plain and simple. You've held me here for nearly five hours without letting me contact an attorney. My civil rights are being violated, pal, and I've had damn near enough."

On the other side of the one-way mirror, CIA operative Kendall "Pete" Peterson stood silently, watching Dr. Anne—nickname Annie—Morrow, renowned archaeologist and art historian, professional artifact authenticator. According to her file, she was thirty-two years old, and one of the world's foremost experts on ancient metalworkings—coins, statues, works of art, jewelry. The daughter of two archaeologists, she'd been born on a dig in Egypt. She'd lived in thirteen different countries and participated in nineteen different excavations, and that was *before* she'd even attended college.

What the file *didn't* tell him was that she was filled with a seemingly limitless supply of energy. During the course of the five hours he'd been watching her, she had sat still for only a very short time. Mostly she paced; sometimes she stood, she leaned, she tapped her foot, but generally she moved around the small interrogation room like a caged animal.

The file also didn't describe the stubborn tilt to her chin, or the way her blue eyes blazed when she was angry. In fact, the photo included hadn't managed to capture much of anything out of the ordinary, except maybe her long, shining brown hair, and her almost too-sensuous lips.

But in person, in motion, she was beautiful....

"So that's our little Dr. Morrow," came a voice at his shoulder.

Peterson turned to look at Whitley Scott, the man in charge of the FBI side of the investigation. Scott smiled at him, his eyes crinkling behind his thick glasses. "Sorry I'm late, Captain," he said. "My flight was delayed."

Peterson didn't smile back. "We've been holding her for hours," he said. "She's pretty steamed."

Through the speaker system, he could hear Dr. Morrow still arguing with FBI agent Richard Collins.

"I've told you nine million times, or is it ten million now? I was in England to pick up an artifact—a gold-cast death mask from the nineteenth century—for a client. I wasn't out of the U.S. long enough to do whatever illicit crimes you're trying to accuse me of. The shipping papers for the death mask are all in order—you've admitted that much," she said. "What *I'd* like to know is when you intend to let me leave."

"After the strip search," Collins said. He was a good man for this job, Peterson thought. Collins could outargue anyone. He was solid, steady and extremely patient. And he was absolutely never fazed.

"She's just your type, Pete," Whitley said, with a sideways glance at the taller man. "Something tells me you're going to enjoy this job."

Peterson didn't smile, but his dark brown eyes flashed in Scott's direction for a microsecond. "She's too skinny," he said.

In the interrogation room, Annie Morrow had had enough. She slammed her hand down on the table, pulling herself up and out of the chair she'd recently thrown herself into. "You want to strip-search me?" she said. "Fine. Strip-search me and let me get the hell out of here."

She shrugged out of her baggy linen jacket, tossing it onto a chair as she kicked her sneakers off. A quick yank pulled her loose red shirt over her head, and she quickly unbuttoned her pants.

"Umm…" Collins said, rattled. "Not *here*…."

"Why not?" Annie asked much too sweetly, her eyes bright with anger as she stood in the middle of the room in her underwear. "Oh, relax. I have bathing suits that are more revealing than this."

A slow grin spread across Peterson's face. Man, she'd managed to faze Collins. She knew darn well he had wanted her to follow him to a private room where she'd be searched by a female agent. Yet she'd undressed in front of him, simply to upset him. He felt a flash of something, and realized that he liked her—he liked her spirit, her energy, her nerve. He frowned. She was a suspect, under investigation. He wasn't supposed to like her. Respect, admire even, but not like. But, man, standing there, looking at her, he found an awful lot to like.

Annie turned and gestured toward the mirror, hands on her hips. "Don't you think the rest of the boys want to get in on the fun?"

She knew they were watching her. She was really something, really sharp. Her file said she'd had a 4.0 average throughout college, graduating with a Ph.D. in half the time it normally took. He liked smart women, particularly when they came wrapped in a package like this one.

Her bra and panties were both black and lacy, contrasting the smooth paleness of her fair skin. Her breasts were full, her waist narrow, flaring out to slender hips and long, beautiful legs. "I take it back," Pete said to Whitley Scott. "She's *not* too skinny."

She seemed to be looking directly at him. He could see the pulse beating in her neck. Each ragged, angry breath she took made her breasts rise and fall.

"Do you intend to harass me every time I leave and reenter the country?" she said.

Pete glanced at Whitley. The older man shrugged. "She's looking right at you," Whitley said.

"You know she can't see me," Pete said, but he motioned for the mike to be turned on. "The Athens investigation," he said, raising his voice so the mike would pick him up, "hasn't been closed."

Annie threw up her hands and began to pace. "Well, there we go," she said. "We're finally getting somewhere. You *are* trying to harass me. You don't give a damn about this death mask. You still think I have something to do with the jerks that bombed and robbed that museum.''

Pete tried to keep his attention on her words instead of her body. But it wasn't easy. She moved like a cat, the muscles in her legs rippling....

"How many times do I have to tell you that I am *not* a thief?" she continued. "Shoot, I wish I were. It would make this a whole hell of a lot easier. But I'm not about to confess to crimes I didn't commit."

She stopped pacing, coming back to stare directly up at him again. It was eerie, as if she really could see him through the glass.

"There was an explosion and a robbery at the gallery in England two hours after you left it," Peterson said, his voice distorted over the cheap speakers. "This time, people died."

Peterson watched Annie's face carefully as a range of emotions battled through her. Anger finally won.

"So, naturally, you believe *I* was involved. That's great, that's really great. Innocent people die, and the best you guys can do is to give me a hard time as I get on and off planes. You should be over there chasing the creeps that did the bombing, not playing peekaboo with somebody who gets queasy when she cuts her finger, pal."

"Doesn't it seem a little strange that you should go to European art galleries twice in five months, and within hours after you leave, each of them is hit by a bomb and a robbery?" Peterson had been in this business long enough to know that when there was smoke, somebody was trying to hide a fire. He wasn't buying the indignant act. "How do you explain the fact that you left the Athens convention hours before anyone else?"

"I don't!" Annie countered, eyes aflame. "I've already told the FBI, *and* the CIA, and everyone else who's asked, that I left because I'd seen everything at the exhibit and I wanted to catch an early flight home.'' She was pacing the floor now, clearly upset. ''What ever happened to innocent until proven guilty? Huh? Just what the hell is going on here?'' she shouted, right through the glass at Peterson.

There was silence. Big fat silence. It disarmed her as Pete knew it would. Dr. Anne Morrow was low on patience, and impatient people didn't like being made to wait. She turned, gathering her clothes. ''If we're through…'' she said pointedly.

''But we're not,'' Pete said. ''It's called a strip search for a reason.''

What little remained of her patience snapped. ''Oh, give me a break,'' she said, throwing down her clothes and striding over to the mirror. She came up really close—close enough for Pete to see the details of her thick, dark lashes and the streaks of lighter color in the deep blue of her eyes. Close enough for him to see that her skin was as smooth and soft as it looked. If the glass of the window hadn't been between them, he could have lifted his hand and touched her.

Peterson felt Whitley watching him, and somehow he managed to remain expressionless. But, man, it had been a long time since he'd looked at a woman and wanted her this badly. It had been a real long time.

''I assure you that everything I'm hiding in my underwear is attached, pal,'' she said. ''No removable parts.''

''Sorry,'' he said. ''I'm being paid a lot of money not to trust you.''

''What exactly are you looking for?'' she asked.

"Maybe if you tell me, I can check and see if I've got it on me somewhere."

"You ever hear of mules?" Pete asked.

She froze.

He'd managed to shock her, but somehow he didn't feel triumphant about it. "Mules are people who smuggle illegal substances into the country inside their bodies," he said.

"I *know* what a mule is," she said. "Tell me honestly, do you really think I've swallowed the crown jewels? Whole?"

"Not swallowed," he said, and then was silent, letting her figure it out for herself.

"Oh, Christmas," she said. Her face paled slightly beneath her tan, and her freckles stood out. "We're really trying to go for total humiliation here, aren't we?"

"Just going by the book," Pete said. "And the book says that you'll be searched—completely. We have a physician waiting in another room."

"Oh, you mean you don't want to do it right here?" Annie said. She was furious. He could almost see her pulse accelerating as he watched the vein in her neck. "You sure you trust this doctor to do it right, pal? I would've thought you'd want to watch."

"I'd love to watch," he said, his voice coming out low and intimate, even through the tinny speakers. "And by the way, the name's not *pal*."

"I prefer to personalize the disembodied voices that talk to me," she said. "It helps me feel more human. But you wouldn't know about that, would you?"

She turned away from the window suddenly, but not before he saw the glint of tears in her eyes.

Pete felt ashamed of himself. What was wrong with him? Why did he have to be so rough on her?

He was rough on her because he felt for her, because he found himself believing her. And he had absolutely no facts to back him up, just gut instinct. *Gut,* thought Pete, *yeah, right. Aim a little lower....* He couldn't let himself forget that Dr. Anne Morrow was a suspect, quite possibly a thief, connected to people who wouldn't think twice about killing to satisfy their greed.

He watched her pull on her pants and then her shirt as the female agent led her from the room. With a nod, he ordered the microphone connection cut.

Whitley Scott was watching him.

"She's gutsy," Pete said to him. "You've got to give her that much."

"I think she's hiding something," Scott said. "We've got to find a way to get closer to her. But how?"

"Good question." Pete leaned against the back wall of the room, crossing his arms in front of him. "I'm not exactly qualified to work in her laboratory. Or even on one of her digs."

"Client?" Whitley asked. "You could bring her some rare artifact to authenticate. One thing leads to another— a little dinner, a little who knows what, and she's telling you her deepest, darkest secrets."

"Perfect," Pete said expressionlessly. "Except she never dates her clients as a rule. No exception."

"Next-door neighbor?"

"She lives over her lab in a restored Victorian house up in Westchester County," Pete said. "Expensive neighborhood. Way out of our budget. It would cost us close to half a million to buy one of the houses next door—provided someone was even willing to sell. And I've already checked—no one wants to rent."

Whitley nodded, turning toward the door. "Well, keep thinking," he said. "We'll come up with something sooner or later."

Chapter 2

Annie pulled her little Honda into the driveway and turned the engine off. Damn, she was tired. Damn the CIA and damn the FBI and damn everyone who was working so hard to make her life so miserable.

Five months. The harassment had been going on almost nonstop for five months. And now, after the bombing in England, it was only going to get worse. Already everyone in town knew that she was the subject of an FBI investigation. The agents had talked with everyone she knew, and probably a lot of people she didn't know. Her college roommate had called last month to say that even she'd been questioned about Annie. And it had been five years since they'd last gotten together....

Damn, damn, damn, she thought. And particularly damn that horrible man who'd spoken to her from behind the one-way window. Somebody had referred to him as Captain Peterson. If she ever ran into him, she'd let him have a good swift kick where it counted. Except she didn't have a clue what he looked like. She wouldn't even be able to recognize him from his voice, not from hearing it over those awful interrogation room speakers.

She stepped out of the car and went around to the other side to pull the package from England from the passenger seat. *Damn these gold artifacts, too,* she thought, as she barely lifted the crate. *They always weigh a ton.*

Her assistant's car was still in the driveway, so instead of going up to her apartment on the top floors of the house, Annie went into the lab. She could hear the sound of the computer keyboard clacking and followed it to the back room, where the office was set up.

Cara MacLeish was inputting data at her usual break-neck speed. She didn't even stop as she looked up and grinned.

"Welcome back," she said. Her short brown curls stood straight up in their usual tangle, and her eyes were warm behind her horn-rimmed glasses. "I thought you'd be here sooner. Like six hours ago."

Annie lowered the crate holding the gold death mask onto her desk top, then brushed some strands of hair back from her face. "I was detained," she said simply.

Cara stopped typing, giving her boss her full, sympathetic attention, swearing imaginatively.

"Took the words right out of my mouth," Annie said, smiling ruefully.

"FBI again?" Cara asked.

"FBI, CIA." Annie shrugged. "They all want a piece of me."

"Well, look on the bright side," Cara suggested.

They both fell silent, trying to find one.

"They haven't been able to make any charges stick," Cara finally said.

Annie pulled a rocking chair closer to the computer console and sat down.

"And you haven't lost any business because of this," Cara said, warming up to it now. She stretched her thin arms over her head, then yawned, standing up to get the kinks out of her long legs. "In fact, I think business has picked up. We had a ton of calls while you were away."

Annie watched her assistant cross to the telephone answering machine. Next to it, a stack of little pink message slips were held by a bright red wooden duck with a clothespin for a mouth.

"Jerry Tillit called," Cara said. "He's back from South America, and he's got some Mayan stuff for you to look at."

"Did you talk to him, or get the message off the machine?" Annie asked.

Cara blushed. "I spoke to him."

"Did he ask you out again?" Annie grinned.

"Yes."

"And...?"

"We don't date clients, remember?" Cara said.

Annie corrected her. "Jerry's not a client, he's a *friend.*"

"He's also a client."

"So he's also a client," Annie admitted. "But just because *I* don't want to date clients doesn't mean *you* can't, MacLeish. Will you please give the man a break?"

"I did."

"You... What?"

The taller woman grinned, pushing her hair back from her face and sitting down on top of the desk. "I told him I'd go out with him. He's coming up to drop his finds off this Saturday. We're going out after that."

Annie glanced around the cozy office. The room was

really quite large, but with two desks, two computers, a fax machine, a copier and all sorts of chairs and bookshelves, there wasn't much room even to walk. But Cara MacLeish was an essential fixture here. "Don't you be going and getting married, MacLeish," she said sternly. "No running off to South America with Jerry Tillit."

Cara grinned. "I'm only going to the movies with him," she said. "The next logical step might be a dinner date. Not marriage."

"You don't know Tillet as well as I do," Annie muttered. "And that man has a definite thing for you...."

"Speaking of marriage," Cara said, flipping through the phone message slips. "Nick York called—five different times. Something about a party down at the Museum of Modern Art sometime this month."

Annie released her hair from its ponytail, letting it swing free in a gleaming brown sheet. She leaned back in the rocking chair, resting her feet on top of the computer desk. "Shame on you, MacLeish. You know the words *marriage* and *York* cannot be uttered in the same sentence," she said. "York wants only two things from me. One of them is free lab work. And the other has nothing to do with marriage. Who else called?"

"The freight guy at Westchester Airport said a package from France will be in Saturday."

"Great." Annie sighed. "Like I've got any chance of getting to work on it in the next decade." She closed her eyes. "Okay, so I pick it up on Saturday. What else?"

"A guy name of Benjamin Sullivan called," Cara said. "Ring any bells?"

Annie's eyes popped open. "Yeah, of course. He's the owner of the piece I just picked up. What did he want?"

"He left a message on the machine, saying that we should ignore Alistair Golden if he calls," Cara said. She laughed. "I didn't recognize Sullivan's name, but it seemed kind of mystically, cosmically correct to get a message from a stranger telling us to ignore Golden. I always ig   ~ Alistair Golden. Ignoring Golden is one of the things ı do best."

Golden was Annie's chief competitor, and he usually handled all the U.S.-bound artworks and artifacts from the English Gallery.

"And sure enough," Cara said, snickering, "the little weasel called. He was in a real snit, whining about something—I'm not sure exactly what, because I was working very hard to ignore him."

Annie laughed. "I think I know what the bug up his pants was," she said. "When I got to the gallery, Sullivan's package was already crated and sealed. Golden had assumed he'd be doing the authentication job, so he'd already done the packing work."

"Golden packed the crate for you?" Cara said with great pleasure. "No wondering his whine was set on stun. He wanted you to call him back, but unless you want to subject yourself to a solid forty-five minutes of complaining, I wouldn't. I give you my permission to use the 'scatterbrained employee didn't give me the message' excuse for the next time he catches up with you."

Annie smiled. "Thanks. Did Ben Sullivan want me to call him back?"

"He said something about going out of town," Cara said, glancing back at the phone message slip. "Who is he? How do you know him? Come on, fill me in. Height, weight, marital status?"

"As far as I know, he's single," Annie said, then smiled. "But he's also seventy-five years old, so get that matchmaking gleam out of your eyes."

Cara made a face in disappointment.

"Ben's an old friend of my parents." Annie leaned back in her chair, breathing deeply. "I don't think I've seen him since, wow, since I was about fifteen. Apparently, he was talking to Mom and Dad recently, and they told him about me—you know, that I opened this lab a few years ago. When the offer to buy came in on this death mask, he requested that I do the necessary authentication."

"Instead of Golden," Cara said.

Annie grinned. "Instead of Golden." She sat forward, stretching her arms over her head. "Anyone else call?"

Cara nodded. "Yeah. I saved the best message for last. It came in on the answering machine. Let me play it for you."

Cara slid off the table, handing Annie the message slips, then pushed the message button on the machine. The tape rewound quickly, then a voice spoke.

It was odd, all whispery and strange, as if the caller had deliberately tried to disguise his voice. "The mask you have gained possession of does not belong to the world of the living. It is the property of Stands Against the Storm. Deliver it at once to his people, or be prepared to face his evil spirit's rage. The doors to the twilight world are opened wide, and Stands Against the Storm will take you back with him."

There was a click as the line was disconnected. Cara punched one of the buttons on the machine and the tape stopped running. "So, okay." She grinned. "Which one of your weirdo friends left *that* message? And who the heck is Stands Against the Storm?"

But Annie wasn't laughing. Swearing softly under her breath, she stood up, hoisted the crate containing the death mask off her desk and went down the hall toward the lab. Cara followed, her grin fading.

"What?" Cara asked, watching as Annie locked the front door. "What's the matter?"

"We've got to put this in the safe," Annie said, gesturing to the package in her arms.

"Annie, who *was* that on the tape?" Cara asked, eyes narrowing.

"Some crackpot," Annie said, heading back to the sturdy vault that sat directly in the middle of the house, surrounded by the lab in the front and the office in the rear. It was secure, impenetrable. She would feel a lot better after she locked the gold death mask inside.

"If it was just some crackpot," Cara demanded, "why did you rush across the room and lock the door?"

Annie opened the innocuous-looking closet door to reveal the combination lock of the big safe. She spun the red dial several times before entering the numbers. "Because it would be foolish not to take precautions, crackpot or not." She looked up at her assistant. "You must not have had a chance to read the background info I left you on this project."

Cara shrugged expansively. "I cannot tell a lie. I had about an hour of free time last night, and I spent it watching 'Quantum Leap' instead of reading about nineteenth-century Indian chiefs."

Setting the package on the top shelf of the vault, Annie swung the door shut, locking it securely. "Native Americans, not Indians," she corrected Cara. "In a nutshell, the artifact we're testing for authenticity is supposedly a gold casting of a death mask of a Navaho named Stands Against the Storm. He was one of the greatest Native American leaders. He was a brilliant man who truly understood Western culture. He tried to help the white leaders understand his own people as thoroughly."

Cara followed her back into the office. "How come

I've never heard of him?'' she asked. "I mean, everyone knows Sitting Bull and Geronimo. Why not this guy?"

Annie sat down behind her desk, frowning at the chaos on its surface. Why was it that paperwork seemed to multiply whenever she went away for a few days? "Sitting Bull and Geronimo were warriors," she said. "Stands Against the Storm was a man of peace. He didn't get as much press as the war party leaders, but not from lack of trying. In fact, he was in England, trying to drum up support for his people among the British, when he died." She shook her head. "His death was a major blow to the Navaho cause."

"If Stands Against the Storm was such a peaceful guy," Cara said, "then why would he have an evil spirit?"

"The Navaho believe that when people die, they become ghosts or spirits," Annie said. "It doesn't matter how nice or kind a person was during his life. When he dies, he becomes malevolent and he gets back at all the people who did him wrong during his lifetime. Chances are, the nicer the guy was, the more evil his spirit would be—the more he'd have to avenge. You know, nice guys finish last and all that."

"But if Stands Against the Storm died in England," Cara said, "then how could his spirit come after you? Assuming for the sake of this discussion that the Navaho are right about this spirit stuff," she added.

"Death is a major problem for the Navaho," Annie said. She smiled. "Actually, I can't think of too many cultures that look forward to death, but the Navaho *really* don't like it. In fact, if someone dies inside a house, even today, that house will sometimes be abandoned. See, the Navaho believe that the place a person dies in, and the things he touches before dying or even after he's dead, can contain his bad spirit. Making a death mask would be a real invitation to disaster. The Navaho would *never* make something like a death mask. But it was the custom at the time in England, you know, to make a mold of the dead person's face and then cast a mask from it to get a likeness. I guess Stands Against the Storm was something of a celebrity—and certainly a curiosity, a Red Indian from the Wild West—so when he died, they made a death mask.''

Annie looked over at the answering machine. What she couldn't figure out was how it had become public knowledge that she was working on authenticating Stands Against the Storm's death mask. Unless Ben Sullivan, or Steven Marshall, the purchaser, had leaked something....

''Hey, Annie?''

She met Cara's worried brown eyes. ''It just occurred to me,'' the taller woman said. ''That message on the answering machine is basically a... Well, it's a death threat.''

''It was just some nut.'' Annie shrugged it off. ''Besides, I don't believe in ghosts.''

''You gotta admit, it's creepy,'' Cara said. ''Maybe we should, I don't know... Call the police?''

Annie groaned, dropping her head onto her arms on the desk top. ''No more police, no more FBI, no way. I'd much rather be haunted by the spirit of Stands Against the Storm.''

Annie sat up in bed, wide-eyed in the darkness as the burglar alarm shrieked.

Her heart pounded from being awakened so suddenly. She clicked on the light and grabbed her robe. Oh, Christmas! This damned alarm was going to raise the entire neighborhood.

She ran down the stairs two at a time and turned on the lights in the foyer as she crossed toward the alarm-system control panel.

Oh my God, thought Annie. It wasn't a malfunction! The alarm schematic showed a breach in the system on the first floor. A window in the lab was marked as the intruder's point of entry.

Suddenly she was very glad for the shrieking alarm. Across the street, she could see the neighbors' lights go on, and she knew they'd call the police—they always did. She ran back up to her room and opened the drawer on her bedside table. Oh, damn, damn, damn, where *was* it?

She pulled the drawer out of the table and emptied it onto her bed. *There* it was.

She grabbed the toy gun, unwinding a stray piece of string from the barrel, and headed toward the stairs. She ran down and kicked open the door to the lab. She flicked on the light switch with her elbow and the bright fluorescent bulbs illuminated the room.

No one was there—either human or inhuman.

But the window had been broken.

Feeling just a little silly, she put the plastic gun down on the lab counter and stepped carefully toward the large rock that had been thrown through the window. There was a piece of paper attached to it with a rubber band.

Spinning lights from two police cars caught her eye as they pulled into her driveway. She went to the front door and keyed into the control panel the code to cancel the alarm. The shrill noise stopped instantly. Taking a deep breath, she opened the door to the town police officers.

They came inside and looked at the broken window. One of them made a quick survey of the house, checking to make sure all the windows and doors were still locked, while the other radioed in to the station.

Big doings in a small town. Annie sighed. She went into the kitchen and put on a pot of coffee. Something told her this was going to be a long night.

Peterson woke up instantly and answered the phone after only one ring.

"Yeah," he said, looking at the glowing numbers of his clock: 3:47. He ran one hand across his face. "This better be good."

"It's Scott. Can you talk?" Whitley Scott said in his flat New Jersey accent.

"Yeah, I'm awake," Pete said, sitting up and turning on his light.

"No, I mean...are you alone?"

"Yeah, I'm alone." Pete rubbed his eyes. "If you check my file, you'll see that I haven't been involved with anyone since last March."

"I've already checked your file," the FBI agent said easily. "And *it* says you've got something of a reputation as a tomcat."

Pete was silent, thinking about that new administrative assistant in the New York City office. Carolyn something. She had curly brown hair and legs a mile long. And eyes that made it more than clear that she was interested in him, no-strings-attached. She'd invited him out for a drink last night. If he had gone with her, she'd probably be lying here right now, next to him.

But he'd turned her down.

Why? Maybe because, regardless of the fact that he'd be using her the exact same way, he was tired of being the flavor of the month for ambitious, upwardly mobile women.

Even though he wasn't overly tall, he knew that with

his black hair and his dark brown eyes, he had the dark and handsome part down cold.

For years, he'd used his good looks to his advantage, but recently it had been rubbing him the wrong way. His relationships, which usually lasted a month or two, were getting shorter and shorter. And when he'd looked at that administrative assistant last night, he hadn't felt the usual heat from knowing that she wanted him. If he'd felt anything at all, it had been disdain.

More than once over the past few months, the thought of retiring from the agency had crossed his mind. The closer he got to his fortieth birthday, the more aware he seemed to become of an emptiness in his life.

He couldn't figure out what he was looking for. He was far too jaded to believe in true love—hell, he was too jaded to believe in any kind of love. And if he stopped having relationships based on animal attraction, on sex, he was in for a whole lot of cold, lonely nights....

"You still there?" Whitley Scott asked.

"Yeah."

"We've found a way for you to get close to Anne Morrow," Scott said. "She practically handed it to us on a platter."

Pete listened intently as Scott explained. It would work. It would definitely work.

After he hung up the phone and turned the light off, Pete stared up at the dark ceiling, feeling a wave of anticipation so charged that it was almost sexual. In a sudden flash of memory, he saw black lace against pale skin, and a pair of wide, blue eyes....

"The note said what?" Cara's voice rose sharply.

"It was stupid," Annie said, clearing some of the clutter off her desk. "I can't believe the police took it seriously."

"When someone bothers to send a message via a rock through a window," Cara said tartly, "it should probably be taken seriously."

"But, God, did they *have* to notify the FBI?" Annie said. "You know, the Federal agents got over here really quickly. I'm wondering if they weren't somehow responsible. I mean, they've been hassling me every other way imaginable. Why not a rock through a window?"

"With a note saying 'Prepare to die'?" Cara asked. "I doubt it, Annie."

"And *I* seriously doubt that a Native American group, no matter *how* radical or fringe, would resort to this kind of petty threat," Annie said. "The FBI can go ahead and investigate, but they're just wasting their time." She sat back in her chair, her normally clear blue eyes shadowed with fatigue. "I just don't need the FBI's garbage on top of everything else. You know, they wanted to provide me with round-the-clock protection. Surveillance is more like it. I told them I could protect myself perfectly well, thank you very much."

"I don't suppose you told them that the likeliest suspect is a ghost called Stands Against the Storm," Cara said. "Maybe we should've called Ghostbusters instead of the police." She sang the familiar horn riff to the original movie theme.

Annie laughed, searching for something on her desk to throw at her friend. She settled for an unsharpened pencil.

Cara dodged the pencil and grinned. "Of course, if a ghost isn't a freaky enough suspect, there are always Navaho witches."

Annie tiredly closed her eyes. "I see you finally read the background information I gave you."

"'Quantum Leap' reruns weren't on last night," Cara said. "So I had some free time. Fascinating stuff. I particularly liked the part that said the Navaho believe some people—who appear to be normal during the day—are really witches. And if plain old witches who can cast spells and wreak havoc aren't bad enough, these witches can transform themselves into giant wolves at night and roam the countryside. Very pleasant."

"Most cultures have some version of bogeymen that stalk the night," Annie said. "Werewolves are nothing new."

"Yeah, but *these* werewolves are neighbors, relatives even," Cara said. "And they start doing their witchy business when they get jealous of another person's wealth or good luck or— Hey, that's it." Cara grinned. "Call the FBI off. I've figured it out. Alistair Golden is really one of these witches, and he's cast horrible bad-luck spells on you because you're starting to steal away some of his business. Although, actually he'd make a better weasel man than a wolf man."

"There's a big hole in your theory," Annie said. "Golden's not Navaho."

"Good point." Cara's eyes narrowed, taking in the pale, almost grayish cast to her friend's face. "The guy fixing the window won't be done for another hour or so," she said. "Why don't you go upstairs and take a nap? I can hold down the fort."

The phone rang.

"That's got to be my call from Dallas," Annie said. "I called Ben Sullivan but he's out of touch for a while. He's on a dig in Turkey, so my contact for the death mask is the buyer, Steve Marshall."

Cara picked up the phone. "Dr. Morrow's office. MacLeish speaking." She listened for a moment, her eyebrows disappearing under her bangs. "One moment, please," she said. She covered the speaker with her hand as she gave the handset to Annie. "What, are you clairvoyant, now, too? It's Steven Marshall. Calling from Dallas."

Annie smiled wanly as she took the phone. "Hello?"

"Dr. Morrow," came the thick Texas drawl. "My secretary tells me you've been trying to reach me?"

"Yes, Mr. Marshall," Annie said. "Thanks for getting back to me so quickly. We're having a little problem."

Briefly she described both the threatening phone call and the follow-up note that had come through her window.

"I don't think there's any real danger," Annie said. "But I felt I had to notify you and give you the opportunity to have the artifact authenticated by an establishment with higher security."

There was a moment of silence. Then Marshall said, "But...you're the best, aren't you, darlin'?"

"Well, yes, I like to think so," Annie said.

"I'm more concerned with your personal safety," he said. "Are you frightened? Do you want to get out of this contract?"

"Not at all. It's just that I may not be set up to provide security at the level necessary to protect the piece," she explained.

"Oh, that's just a little bitty problem," Marshall said with the easy nonchalance of the very wealthy. "We can solve that, no sweat. *I'll* provide the security, darlin'. I'll send a man over later this afternoon. He'll be responsible for the safety of the death mask. He'll also act as your bodyguard."

Oh, great, just what she needed. A pair of biceps following her around. She took a deep, calming breath. "Mr. Marshall, that's not necessary—"

"No, no, darlin', I insist."

"But I'm backlogged," Annie protested. "It's going to be weeks before I even get a chance to *look* at the artifact. And the tests I need to perform will take that much time again. My contract states an estimated completion date of mid-December. That's over *two months*—"

"I'll tell the guy to be prepared to stay for a while."

"But—"

"I gotta get back to work now," Marshall said. "Nice talking to you, darlin'. I'll be in touch."

"But—"

He hung up.

"But I don't *want* a bodyguard!" Annie wailed to the buzz of the disconnected line.

"A what?" Cara asked.

Annie hung up the phone with a muttered curse. "I'm going to take a nap," she said, stalking toward the door. "Maybe when I wake up, this nightmare will be over."

"Did you say *bodyguard?*" Cara's voice trailed after her.

Annie didn't answer.

Cara's face broke into a wide grin. A bodyguard. For Annie. This was going to be an awful lot of fun to watch.

Chapter 3

Annie stretched, luxuriating, enjoying having spent the day in bed. It was a real self-indulgence, particularly since she had so much to do in the lab.

But she wouldn't have gotten a whole heck of a lot done if she'd tried to work. Her concentration would've been way off because of her fatigue, and she would have ended up having to do everything over again. So instead she'd slept hard, and now felt much better. And hungry. Boy, was she hungry.

She pushed back the covers and went into her bathroom to wash her face, deciding against a shower. Why bother? Cara would be leaving for home in an hour or so. And the artifacts Annie had to run tests on didn't care if she worked in her pajamas. She brushed the tangles out of her hair and put some moisturizer on her face.

The sky outside the window was dark, she realized suddenly. It must be later than she thought.

She went down the stairs barefoot, calling, "MacLeish! Are you still here?"

"No, she went home."

Annie stopped short at the sight of the stranger standing in the shadows of the foyer. How did he get in? What was he doing here? Fear released adrenaline into her system and, heart pounding, she stood on the stairs, poised to turn and run back up and slam the door behind her.

He must have realized that he had frightened her, because he spoke quickly and stepped into the light. "Steven Marshall sent me," he said, his voice a rich baritone with a slight west-of-the-Mississippi cowboy drawl. "My name's Pete Taylor. I'm a security specialist. Your assistant let me in. She didn't want to wake you...."

He was not quite six feet tall, with the tough, wiry build of a long-distance runner. His hair was black, and cut almost military short. His face was exotically handsome, with wide, angular cheekbones that seemed to accentuate his dark eyes—eyes of such deep brown, it was impossible to tell where the iris ended and the pupil began. His lips were exquisitely shaped, despite the fact that he wasn't smiling. Somehow Annie knew that this was not a man who smiled often.

He held out his wallet to her, opened to reveal an ID card encased in plastic.

Annie couldn't keep her hand from shaking as she took the smooth leather folder from him, and she saw a flash of amusement in his dark eyes. He thought it was funny that he scared her. What a jerk.

She sat down on the steps as she looked at the ID. Peter Taylor. Age 38. Licensed private investigator and security specialist. The card gave him a New York City address, in a rather pricey section of Greenwich Village. Across from the ID card was a New York State driver's license.

She lifted the plastic flaps and found an American Express Gold Card for Peter Taylor, member since 1980, a MasterCard, a Visa and a Sears credit card. He was carrying over five hundred dollars cash in the main compartment, along with several of his own business cards.

She tossed the wallet back to him and, as their eyes met, she saw another glint of humor on his otherwise stern face.

"Do I pass?" he said. As he tucked the wallet into the inside left pocket of his tweed jacket, she caught a glimpse of a handgun in a shoulder holster.

Annie nodded. "For now," she said, working hard to keep her tone formal, polite. "But just so that it's out in the open, I think you should know that I don't want you here. I consider your presence an imposition, and I intend to speak to Marshall about it tomorrow. So don't bother unpacking—you'll be leaving in the morning."

"When I spoke to Mr. Marshall this afternoon, he was adamant that I remain," he said. "Apparently he's concerned for your safety. Somehow I don't see him changing his mind so quickly."

Annie stared at him. His feet were planted on the tile floor, legs slightly spread, arms crossed in front of his chest. His jeans were tight across the big muscles in his thighs. His belt buckle was large and silver and obviously Navaho in origin. Annie couldn't see it clearly, but there was a silver ring on his right hand that also looked Navaho. He wore a necklace, but it was tucked into his shirt. She would bet big money that he was at least half Native American, and probably Navaho.

"Where did you grow up?" she asked.

He blinked at the sudden change in subject. "Colorado," he said. "Mostly."

His shoulders stiffened slightly. So very slightly, he

probably didn't even realize it. But Annie noticed. Something about the question had made him feel defensive, wary. Was it that she'd asked a personal question, or did his wariness have something to do specifically with Colorado, or the "mostly" that followed it?

She was instantly fascinated. It wasn't because he was outrageously handsome, she tried to convince herself. Her attraction toward him—and she *was* attracted, she couldn't deny that—was more a result of his quiet watchfulness, spiced with a little mystery. He had something to be defensive or at least wary about. What was it?

"You ride horses, don't you, Taylor?" she asked, head tilted slightly to one side as she looked at him, hooked into trying to solve the puzzle, hoping for another clue from his reaction.

She was watching him, Pete realized, studying him as if he were an artifact, memorizing every little detail, searching for his flaws and weaknesses.

Her hair was down around her shoulders, parted on the side and swept back off her face. It gleamed in the light. She wore a too-large pair of men's pajamas, with the legs cuffed and the sleeves rolled up. There was no makeup on her face, and instead of giving her that naked, vulnerable look most women have without cosmetics, she looked clean, scrubbed and fresh.

Her eyes were a brilliant blue, and she met his gaze steadily, as if she were trying to get inside his head.

"Yeah," he finally said.

"I figured it was either horses or a bike," she said. "Don't you feel odd, carrying around a gun?"

"No."

"What do you know about death masks?" she asked.

"Not much." She was firing off questions as if this were some kind of interview. He decided to play it her way. It might make her start to trust him. It certainly couldn't hurt—he wasn't going to tell her anything he didn't want her to know.

"How about art authentication?"

"Ditto."

"A Navaho leader from the nineteenth century named Stands Against the Storm?"

"Only the information that Marshall faxed me this morning," he said.

"Have you read it?"

"Of course."

She watched him thoughtfully. "Where did you go to school?"

He shifted his weight. While most people would have been loath to admit their ignorance, it hadn't bothered him one little bit to tell her he knew next to nothing about death masks and art authentication. But *this* question about himself, about his background, made him uncomfortable, Annie thought. Now, why was that?

"NYU," he said. The bio the agency had created for Peter Taylor had him attending New York University from 1973 to 1977. Truth was, he hadn't even set foot in New York until 1980. But he'd been Pete Taylor so many times, on so many different assignments, he almost had memories of the imaginary classes....

"Are you aware that I'm currently under investigation by the FBI and the CIA?" she asked, her blue eyes still watching him.

He was caught off guard by the directness of her question and had to look away, momentarily thrown.

"They think I'm involved in some kind of international art-theft conspiracy," she said.

He glanced up at her and saw that her lips were curved in a small smile. "Are you?" he asked.

He made a good recovery, Annie thought. He *had* known about the investigation. She was willing to bet he had done a full background sweep on her before coming up from New York City. It didn't surprise her one bit. Marshall wouldn't have hired anyone who was less than outstanding.

"Are you hungry?" she said, standing and stretching, arms pulled up over her head, ignoring his question. "I haven't eaten all day, and if I don't have something soon, I'm gonna die."

Pete found his eyes drawn to the gap that appeared between her pajama top and the loose bottoms that rode low on her slender hips. "I ate already, thanks," he said. "Besides, I have an expense account that Mr. Marshall is covering. It's not fair that I should cost you money. After all, you don't even want me here."

"It's nothing personal," Annie said, climbing up the stairs, heading for the kitchen.

"I know," he said, following her.

She turned on the light in the kitchen and opened the refrigerator. She pulled an apple from the crisper drawer and took it to the sink, where she washed it quickly, then dried it with a towel.

The kitchen was a small room, just barely large enough to hold a table in one corner and a counter with a sink, stove, refrigerator and dishwasher in the other. It was decorated in black and white, with a tile floor that reminded Pete of a chessboard.

"I'd like to do a complete walk-through of the building," Pete said, watching her take a healthy bite of the apple. "I checked out the first floor and the basement while you were asleep. Your safe location is good. It would take a significant explosive charge to blow it open.

But your general security is—'' He broke off, shaking his head.

"Bush-league?" Annie supplied, leaning back against the counter, ankles and arms crossed, watching him as she ate her apple.

It didn't rate a smile, but there was a flicker of amusement in his dark eyes. "Definitely. A professional could get into this house without triggering the alarm system— no problem. Don't you read *Consumer Reports?* The system you have is known for malfunctions. It's unreliable. It's easily bypassed, and it goes off spontaneously."

Annie shaved the last bit of fruit from the core of the apple with her teeth, licking her lips as she looked up at him. "I've noticed." She opened the cabinet door beneath the sink and tossed the apple core into a compost container, then rinsed her hands.

His expression changed slightly. Most people might not have picked it up—it was just a very small contraction of his dark eyebrows. But Annie was trained to pay attention to details, and on a face as expressionless as he kept his, the movement stood out. "What?" she asked.

He blinked. "Excuse me?"

"Something's bugging you. What is it?"

She was standing only a few feet away from him, and he breathed in her natural fragrance. She smelled sweet and warm, with a little bit of baby shampoo, some rich-smelling skin lotion and tart apple thrown in for good measure. Although her pajamas were boxy and made of thick flannel, he was well aware of the soft, feminine body underneath. He felt his desire for her sparking, and he tightened his stomach muscles. Man, his entire office believed that she was a thief....

"I was wondering if that's all you're going to eat," he said levelly. Through sheer force of will he stopped his desire for her from growing. He forced it back, down, deep inside of him, willing it to stay hidden. For now, anyway. "It doesn't seem like very much, considering that you were so hungry. You should eat something more filling."

Annie laughed, her white teeth flashing. "This is great," she said. "A bodyguard who gives nutritional advice. How appropriate."

He smiled. It was actually little more than the sides of his mouth twitching upward, but Annie decided it counted as a smile. Shoot, with a full grin, he'd be as handsome as the devil. *More* handsome...

"Sorry," he said. "But you asked."

"You're right," she said, leading the way onto the landing, "I did. Look, I've got to get some work done."

She flipped her long hair back out of her face in a well-practiced motion, and hiked up her pajama bottoms. Pete wished almost desperately that she would put on some other clothes. It wasn't like him to be so easily distracted, but every time she moved, he had to work hard to keep from wanting her.

For a long time now, he'd gone without sex. Not because it wasn't available, but because he simply hadn't wanted it. Didn't it figure that his libido should suddenly come to life again out here, in the middle of nowhere, while he was alone in this big house with this beautiful woman? Man, as soon as he got back to the New York office, he'd have to look up Carolyn what's-her-name, the administrative assistant with the long legs....

"It *would* help if I could take a look at the top floors of the house," Pete said.

Annie shook her head. "Taylor, I don't mean to be rude," she said, "but I'm already two days behind in my work schedule. Frankly, there's no point in my showing you around, because after I talk to Marshall tomorrow, you're going to be catching the next train back into the city."

"I drove up," he said expressionlessly.

"I was speaking figuratively," she said.

"It's going to be hard for me to do my job without your cooperation," Pete pointed out.

She started down the stairs to the lab. "Why don't you use my phone to call your answering machine," she said, not unsympathetically. "Maybe someone called with a different job for you. You can work for them and get all the cooperation you could possibly want."

Annie stayed in the lab until shortly after two-thirty in the morning. She finished all but the last set of purity tests on a copper bowl that had been found at a southwestern archaeological dig site, believed to have been left by early Spanish conquistadors. That last test would take another two hours, and the thought of spending that much more time under Peter Taylor's unwavering gaze was far too exhausting. Besides, even if she finished the testing, she wouldn't have any conclusive evidence until the sample results came back from the carbon-dating lab.

She switched off the equipment and put the bowl back in the safe, turning to find Taylor still watching her.

He was sitting in a chair by the door. He didn't look tired despite the late hour. He didn't look uncomfortable or put upon or...*any*thing.

Christmas, he was making her nervous.

She thought about just breezing past him, out the door and up the stairs, but her conscience made her stop.

"There's a spare bedroom upstairs," she said. "You can sleep——"

But he was shaking his head. "No."

"Oh," she said. "I suppose you want to stay down here, to be near the safe—"

"The safe's secure," he said, pulling himself out of the chair in one graceful, fluid motion. "You'd need a crane to move it, and a ton of dynamite to get into it. If I sleep at all, it's going to be in your bedroom."

Annie stared at him, shocked. In her bedroom... But his words had been said matter of factly, expressionlessly, without any hint of sexual overtones. Either he had no idea of his physical appeal, or he was so confident, he didn't doubt that any woman would be grateful to share her bed with him. "I don't think so," she said.

He raised one eyebrow, as if he knew exactly what she'd been thinking. "I meant, on the floor."

Annie willed herself not to blush. "You'd be much more comfortable in the guest room," she said.

"But you would be much less safe," he countered. "Your alarm system is nearly worthless—"

"I'll be fine," Annie protested. This was starting to get tiring. Why wouldn't he just accept his defeat and sleep in the guest room?

He was blocking her way up the stairs, his arms crossed stubbornly in front of his chest. "Will you please let me do my job?"

"By all means," she said. "Do your job. Just do it in the guest room tonight."

He wasn't going to move, so Annie pushed past him, starting toward the stairs.

But he caught her arm, stopping her. His fingers were long and strong, easily encircling her wrist. The heat from his hand penetrated the flannel of her pajamas.

Her heart was pounding from annoyance, Annie tried to convince herself, not from his touch. She tried to pull away, but his grip tightened.

"I *am* going to protect you," he said. His face remained expressionless, but his eyes were like twin chips of volcanic glass.

He had pulled her in so close that she had to crane her neck to look up at him. "Maybe so," she said, and to her chagrin, her voice shook very slightly. "But who's going to protect me from you?"

Pete dropped her arm immediately.

"I don't know you from Adam," Annie said, stepping back, away from him, rubbing her arm. "For all *I* know, you're really the guy who's been making the death threats. For all *I* know, you've done in the real Peter Taylor."

"My picture's on my ID, *and* my driver's license."

"Everyone knows picture IDs are easy to fake—" She broke off, staring in fascination at his necklace. She'd noticed earlier that he wore silver beads around his neck, but until now she hadn't caught a glimpse of the necklace. It was clearly Navaho, with small coin-silver hollow beads, and five squash blossoms decorating the bottom half, along with a three-quarter circle design pendant, known as a *naja*.

Ignoring her trepidation, she took a step toward him, lifting the *naja* in her hand. "This is beautiful," she said, glancing up at him before studying it more closely. Two tiny hands decorated the ends of the *naja*. "Navaho. It's quite old, too, isn't it?"

All of her anger, all of her uneasiness was instantly forgotten as she was caught up, examining the carefully worked silver. She looked at the necklace with real interest, real excitement sparking in her eyes.

Pete laughed, and Annie looked up at him in surprise. It was a rich, deep laugh complete with a grin that transformed his face. She had been right—with his face unfrozen, he *was* exceptionally handsome.

"Yeah," he said. "It's Navaho."

She was standing so close to him, mere inches away, holding the *naja,* but looking up at him. As he gazed into her wide blue eyes, he could feel the heat rising in him. What was it about her that made his body react so powerfully? He wanted to pull her into his arms, feel her body against his. He could imagine the way her lips would taste. Warm and sweet. Man, it would take so little effort....

Pete shoved his hands deep into the pockets of his jeans to keep from touching her.

"Your belt buckle is Navaho, too," she said. "And the ring on your hand, I think... I didn't really get a good look at it."

He pulled his right hand free from his pocket, glancing down at the thick silver-and-turquoise ring he wore on his third finger.

"Do you mind?" Annie asked, letting go of the pendant and taking his hand. She looked closely at the worn silver of the ring, at the delicate ornamentation. "This isn't quite as old as the necklace," she said. "But it's beautiful."

Her slender fingers were cool against the heat of his. She kept her nails cut short but well-groomed, and wore no jewelry on her hands.

"I thought you were a specialist in European metalworks," he said. "How come you know so much about Native American jewelry?"

She turned his hand over, looking at the other side of the ring. "When I was a kid, I spent about six years at sites in Utah and Arizona, one year in Colorado. Out of all the places we ever lived, my favorite was the American Southwest. When I went to college, I even considered specializing in Native American archaeology."

"Why didn't you?"

"I don't know," she said. "I mean, there were a lot of different reasons." She looked down at his ring again. His hand was so big, it seemed to engulf both of hers. He had calluses on his palm, and two of his fingers had healing abrasions on the knuckles—as if he'd slammed his fist into a wall. Or a person, she realized. In his line of work, it could very well have been a person.

He was looking down at her, making no attempt to take his hand away. Their eyes met, and for the briefest of instants, Annie saw the deep heat of desire in his eyes. Fire seemed to slice through her as her body responded, and she dropped his hand, noticing with rather horrified amusement that he had let go of her with as much haste. What had he seen in her eyes, she wondered. Was her own attraction for him as apparent?

She looked away, taking a step back from him, once again heading for the stairs. "Good night," she said, her voice sounding strange and breathless.

But he was in front of her, leading the way up to the second floor. "At the very least, I want to check out your room," he said. "Make sure all the windows are locked—"

"I can do that," Annie protested.

"Yeah, I know," he said as he went into her bedroom. "But I have to see it for myself."

The bed was still unmade from Annie's afternoon nap, and she saw him glance at her bright blue and green patterned sheets before crossing to the bay windows on the other side of the big room.

He pulled back the curtains and looked at each window carefully, checking to see that the locks were secure and the alarm system was working.

Annie stood in the middle of the room, arms crossed

in front of her as she watched his broad, strong back. With his conservatively short black hair, she wouldn't have expected him to be wearing jeans with his tweed jacket, but somehow it didn't look out of place. The jacket was well tailored, fitting his broad shoulders like a glove. His jeans were loose enough to be comfortable, yet managed to show off the long, muscular lengths of his legs. Legs that went all the way up to—

She pulled her eyes away, not wanting to be caught staring at Taylor's butt. It *was* exceptional though, she thought, grinning, glancing back at him. Even with his hair cut so short, Taylor would have no trouble qualifying for one of those hunk-of-the-month calendars....

"What's so funny?" he asked, pulling the last of the curtains closed again and walking toward her.

"Nothing," Annie said, backing away.

"Look," Pete said. "I'd really feel a whole lot better if I could sleep in here tonight." He paused for a moment. "You won't even know I'm here," he added.

Oh, sure, Annie thought. And they're expecting heavy snow this year in the Sahara desert. She forced herself to stay in control of what was rapidly becoming a ludicrous situation.

"No," she said. "Maybe I'd feel different if I thought I was in any kind of real danger. But I just don't buy it."

She walked him to the door. He hesitated before stepping out of the room, but finally he did.

"Feel free to use the spare room," Annie said. "It's across the hall. The bed's already made up."

He didn't say anything. He just watched her from behind his expressionless mask.

"See you in the morning," she finally said, closing and locking the door.

Pete stood out in the hall, listening as Annie got ready for bed. The water ran for a while in the bathroom, the toilet flushed and finally the lamp clicked off.

And still he stood there, just listening and waiting.

Chapter 4

Annie woke up at nine o'clock, before her alarm went off. Regardless of the fact that it was Saturday morning, she had work to do down in the lab. And wasn't today the day that Jerry Tillit was bringing in his latest finds from South America? *That* meant that Cara would be downstairs, despite it being a weekend. And there was that pickup she had to make at the airport....

She closed her eyes briefly. Damn, damn, damn. Six hours of sleep *used* to be enough. Five, really—she hadn't been able to fall asleep right away last night. She'd been thinking about...work. Yeah, right. Work. She was so far behind schedule, she had absolutely no time to spend thinking about anything or anyone else.

So why did Pete Taylor's dark eyes seem to penetrate her dreams?

Because his presence was a pain in the butt, Annie decided. And as soon as the sun came up in Texas, she'd give Steven Marshall a call and get this bodyguard business straightened out once and for all.

Rolling out of bed, Annie tiredly pulled her pajama shirt over her head, then pushed her hair out of her face as she walked toward the bathroom.

Oh, Christmas, Taylor was sleeping on her floor.

She quickly covered herself with her flannel top, holding it against her body, slipping the fabric under her arms.

He was fast asleep, on some kind of thin sleeping bag with a blanket over him. He'd taken off his jacket and shirt, and even in repose, the hard muscles in his arms and shoulders stood out underneath his tanned skin. His face looked younger, softer, less fiercely controlled as he slept. Annie stared in fascination at the way his long dark eyelashes lay against his smooth cheeks.

He *was* a very good-looking man.

And he was leaving this morning, Annie reminded herself. So why the heck was she admiring his eyelashes? She should be angry with him—God, he'd broken into her room while she was sleeping. She wondered how long he'd stood watching *her* sleep. He had no right....

She reached out a toe to nudge him awake.

It happened so quickly. One moment she was standing up—the next she was on the floor, on her back, with Pete Taylor's heavy body on top of her, his arm pressed up, hard, against her windpipe, cutting off her air.

Her first instinct was to fight, but he had her so thoroughly pinned down, she could do little more than wiggle against him. He was breathing hard, as if prepared to fight as he pulled his arm away from her throat. Gratefully, she sucked in a breath of air as he stared down at her.

"Don't *ever* do that again," he said sternly, his eyes hard, his face harsh.

"*Me?*" Annie sputtered. "What did I do? I only woke

you up. *You're* the one who tackled me and nearly choked me to death. *You're* the one who was asleep on my floor after I specifically told you I didn't want you in here, pal.''

She glared up at him, straining against him, trying to get free.

Although he had taken off his shirt while he slept, he had kept his necklace on. Now it hung down between them, the pendant brushing her neck and shoulders and—

Oh, God, she'd dropped her pajama top.

Annie saw from the sudden flicker in his eyes that he realized it the same moment she did. His bare chest was against hers, skin against skin, hard against soft.

They both froze.

She could feel his heart beating against her. Or was it her own heart? Whoever's heart it was, it was starting to beat faster.

''I think you'd better get off of me,'' Annie whispered.

Silently Pete pulled back, sliding away from her. Man, she was beautiful, he thought, watching her grab for her pajama top and pull it over her head. Her breasts were soft and full, with large dark pink nipples that had hardened into firm buds at the tips.

Pete sat on his bedroll, leaning back against the wall, glad that he was wearing his jeans, that she couldn't see how badly he wanted her. Man, what a way to start the morning.

''I'm going to take a shower,'' she said, her cheeks faintly pink. ''If that's all right with you.''

''Yeah,'' he said.

''Sure you don't want to check the bathroom out first?'' she asked, standing up and looking down at him, hands on her hips. ''You never know—maybe there's a bad guy hiding in the toilet tank.''

Pete stood up gracefully and walked past Annie into the bathroom.

"I was *kidding,*" Annie said, following him, trying not to stare at the rippling muscles in his back.

The bathroom was decorated in sea greens and blues. There was a claw-footed tub in one corner. Another corner held a large shower stall. The sink had a marble counter-top, and it was cluttered with Annie's makeup, lotions, soaps and shampoos.

There was a small window in the room, with frosted glass in the panes. Pete glanced at it, then tried the lock. It was secure.

He opened the door to the shower stall and looked inside.

"Oh, come on, Annie scoffed. "The window was locked. How could someone have gotten into my shower?"

Pete looked at her levelly. "Last night the door to your bedroom was locked. That didn't keep me from getting in. Hasn't it occurred to you that if I could do it, someone else could, too?"

She stared at him. Well, actually, no, it hadn't....

He went back into the bedroom. Annie followed him to the bathroom door and watched him roll up his blanket and sleeping bag. "If that's the case," she said, "why should I bother locking the door at all?"

Pete used a piece of string to tie the sleeping bag up. "Locks on doors and windows will keep most people out," he said. He stood up then, folding his arms across his broad chest. "And as for the people determined to get in... That's what I'm here for."

"That's very good," Annie said. "You should write that down and use it on your business cards. Just the right amount of macho with a little superhero thrown in. I think it'll sell. Unfortunately, I'm not interested in buying.''

She went back into the bathroom, not bothering to lock the door behind her.

The water in the teakettle had just begun to boil when Pete came into the kitchen. His hair was still wet from his shower, and he'd changed into a plain black turtleneck that hugged his muscular chest and was tucked neatly into his jeans.

Annie poured steaming water on top of the tea bag in her mug. "I don't have much to offer you in the way of breakfast," she said apologetically. "I usually don't do much more than eat some fruit myself, and even that's running low—"

"I'm eating on Mr. Marshall's expense account, remember?" Pete said, sitting down at the kitchen table. "But if it's not any trouble, would you mind if I kept some supplies in your refrigerator?"

Annie leaned against the counter, holding her mug in both hands. "In theory, I don't object," she said. "But remember? After I talk to Marshall this morning, you're going to be leaving."

"No, I don't think so," he said.

"Well, I *do* think so," she said.

"Sorry, you're wrong," Pete said, unperturbed. "Mr. Marshall is very anxious to avoid bad publicity. Did you know that he's facing racketeering charges out in Dallas?"

"Steven Marshall?"

Pete nodded. "Call him if you want," he said. "But I know he's going to insist that I stay. If something happened to you, it would be *very* bad publicity for him."

"But what about *me?*" Annie said, putting her mug on

the counter. Her bangs were pulled back from her face
with an Alice in Wonderland-like headband. She wore a
bright white sweatshirt over her jeans, and a pair of black
lace-up boots. She sat down at the table, across from Pete.
"I don't *want* a bodyguard. No offense, but...I *like* being
alone."

"I'll try to stay out of your way," he said. "You won't
even know I'm around."

"Yes, I noticed how well you stayed out of my way
this morning, particularly when you pinned me to the
floor," Annie said. "I can't wait to see what the rest of
the day brings. Maybe a little kick-boxing?"

She noticed that he didn't even have the grace to look
embarrassed as she left the room.

She *had* to talk to Steven Marshall.

Annie hung up the phone with a crash and an oath,
making Cara look up.

"Old Steven M. didn't go for your 'I can take care of
myself' routine, huh?" Cara said unsympathetically.

"He is *such* a jerk!"

"Things *could* be worse," Cara said.

"Yeah," Annie muttered. "You could start telling me
exactly how they could be worse."

Cara ignored the comment. "You could have been
stuck with one of those no-brain, mountain-of-muscles-
type bodyguards with a shaved head and equally shaved
intellect. If someone told *me* that I'd have to spend the
next few weeks with a guy as gorgeous as Peter Taylor
watching my every move, you wouldn't hear *me* complaining."

"But I like my privacy," Annie said, sitting down at
her desk for about four seconds before popping up and
pacing again.

"Hey," Cara asked, "did you catch sight of his necklace?"

"Navaho," Annie said. "Looks like it dates around 1860, maybe even earlier. You see his ring?"

"And the belt buckle? Yeah. You're gonna try to buy 'em, aren't you?" Cara finished clearing the files off her desk, uncovering a paperweight made of petrified wood, three framed pictures of her nephews and nieces and a plastic Homer Simpson doll with his head attached by a spring. She looked up at her friend. "Aren't you?"

Annie shook her head.

"You're kidding. Why not?"

"Because it's none of your business," Annie said crossly, throwing herself down into her chair again. "Since when do I have to justify myself to you? You work for me, remember?"

"You're not going to try to buy it off him because you like the man," Cara said triumphantly, making Homer's head bob wildly. "You like him, I knew it. You don't want to take advantage of him."

Annie put her head down on her desk. "Oh, MacLeish, he's going to be here for weeks and weeks and *weeks*. What am I going to do?"

"At least he's handsome," Cara said. "Imagine if you had to stare at some guy with no neck all day and night—"

Annie stared up at her. "Yeah, terrific. Great. Wonderful. He's handsome. He's gorgeous. To tell you the truth, I'd prefer staring at some guy with no neck. Taylor's so good-looking, it's distracting as hell, and he's...standing in the door, listening to me say this," Annie said, looking over at Pete, who was leaning against the door frame, amusement in his dark eyes.

"We were talking about you," Cara said unnecessarily. She smiled happily. "How embarrassing for us."

"It's not embarrassing," Annie said to Cara. "I mean, the fact that he's gorgeous shouldn't come as big news to him. He knows what he looks like. And the fact that we were discussing him also shouldn't put him into shock. He's invading my life, and I deserve a chance to bitch and moan about it—about *him*." Annie gestured toward Pete.

Still smiling happily, Cara said, "Annie just spoke to Marshall—"

"The bastard," Annie interjected.

"—on the phone," Cara finished. "Looks like you might want to get your suitcase in from the car and put it someplace a little more permanent."

"Oh," Pete said.

"Don't gloat," Annie snapped.

His eyebrows moved a millimeter. "All I said was—"

"I'm *so* annoyed," Annie said. "Marshall—"

"The bastard," Cara supplied.

"—doesn't think a woman can take care of herself," Annie sputtered. "I asked him to hire a female body-guard—no offense, Taylor—"

"None taken," he said.

"—and Marshall—"

"The bastard." This time Pete interjected, his lips twitching up into a smile.

"—laughed that obnoxious wheezing laugh of his." Annie demonstrated it, sounding an awful lot like a circus seal in mortal terror. "And he said that he'd *still* have to pay Taylor—to protect the female bodyguard! He said being a bodyguard is a man's job! Of all the stupid, chauvinistic things to say! *And* he topped it off by calling me 'little lady!' As if '*darlin*'' weren't bad enough. So I told him I quit. I told him he could take the stupid artifact and have it authenticated by a stupid *man*."

"And?" Cara asked, grinning in anticipation.

"Marshall—"

"The bastard—" Cara and Pete said in unison.

"Laughed again and said—" Annie imitated Marshall's heavy Texan accent "—'It's typical of a woman to try to break a written, binding contract.' Then he suggested we talk again when it was a better time of month! I wanted to reach through the phone, grab his nose and twist it—hard!"

"So?" Cara asked.

"So *nothing*. I've still got a contract *and* a bodyguard," Annie muttered, with a black look in Pete's direction.

"You know—" Pete started to say.

"You might not want to be talking right now," Annie interrupted him. "I'm starting to feel the urge to vent some of my hostilities, and you're looking like an extremely attractive target."

"Extremely attractive, eh?" Cara smiled, leaning back in her chair and putting her feet up on the desk.

"That's *not* what I meant," Annie said dangerously. "You're fired, MacLeish. Go make some copies or do whatever else it is that I pay you to do."

The phone rang, and Annie swooped toward it.

"Maybe it's Marshall," she said. "Maybe he changed his mind...." She picked up the receiver hopefully. "Hello?"

She'd pulled her headband out while she was pacing, and now she pushed her hair back from her face with one hand as she used the other to hold the receiver to her ear. As Pete watched, she stared into the distance, her eyes temporarily unfocused as she concentrated on the call. He saw surprise, then shock flash across her face. Then her blue eyes narrowed.

"Who is this?" she demanded. "You want to do those things to me? I *dare* you to try. Why don't you show yourself? Come here in person, instead of hiding behind threatening phone calls and rocks thrown through windows—"

Pete leapt toward her, grabbing the telephone out of her hand, trying to activate the tape recorder the FBI had left behind. But the connection had been broken, and the line buzzed with a dial tone.

"Damn it," he swore, hanging up the phone. "What the hell is wrong with you? Why didn't you record that call? And what the hell possessed you to say those things? You really want this guy to come out here?"

She was shaking. "Don't you shout at me!" she said, her eyes blazing. "I just listened to some crackpot describe some incredibly sick fantasy of his in detail, and I happened to have a major role. You can't expect me not to tell him off—"

"I expect you *not* to goad him on," Pete said, his own eyes glittering chips of obsidian. He stood with his hands on his hips, effectively pinning Annie in against her desk.

She wanted to move, but in order to do that she'd have to push past him, or climb over her desk. So she stayed where she was and tried to hide her shaking hands by sticking them into the back pockets of her jeans.

Pete picked up a pad and a pen from her desk. "You have to tell me what he said to you," he said brusquely. "Word for word."

Annie shook her head. "Sorry, I can't."

"If you don't remember exactly—"

"That's not it," she said. "I can remember. I just...can't repeat what he said. It was too awful."

She tried to meet his gaze challengingly, but her eyes suddenly welled with tears. She swore softly and blinked them back. "I'm having a really bad day," she said.

Pete turned away, shocked at his emotional response to the tears in her eyes. He wanted to pull her into his arms, tell her everything was going to be okay and kiss her until her hands shook for an entirely different reason. He wanted to tell her he'd take care of her, protect her.

But he couldn't tell her that, and he certainly couldn't protect her without her cooperation.

Annie took the opportunity to move around to the other side of her desk and sit down. She wished that Taylor would leave her alone. God, wasn't it bad enough that she'd been subjected to that obscene phone call? She wanted to forget about it. The thought of having to tell him exactly what that creep had said to her made her cheeks burn.

Out of the corner of her eye, she saw Taylor pull up a chair across from her desk. He sat down, then looked over her head, across the room to where Cara sat. Annie glanced at her friend, who was watching them both with unabashed interest.

"Would you mind...?" Pete said to Cara.

Cara stood up uncertainly.

"Set up the final test for that copper bowl, please, Mac-Leish," Annie said. "I'll be out in the lab in a minute."

Cara hated being left out of anything, but she went out of the office. Pete stood up and closed the office door behind her.

Annie looked up at him as he sat back down across from her. To her surprise, his eyes were soft, kind even.

"The reason I wanted to record this call," he said quietly, "was to help us track the caller. And I'm not just talking about locating him—most of these people call from public telephones, so that doesn't do much good. But the FBI can use their computers and try to match phrasing or word choice or even sentence structure, in the event that this is a repeat pattern offender.'' He pushed the pad and pen toward her. "And that's why I need to know what he said to you. As exactly as you can remember. Maybe it would be easier for you to write it down.''

For a long time she didn't move. She just stared at him. Then, suddenly, she picked up the pen and paper and began to write.

Pete sat back in his chair, watching her.

Sunlight was streaming in the window, and it lit her from behind, creating an auralike glow around her. Pete remembered the words he had overheard her saying to Cara. He distracted her. *He* distracted *her?* Not half as much as she distracted him, he was willing to bet.

He was carrying around this tight feeling of need all the time now, Pete realized. It no longer was triggered only by her quick smile, or her walk, or her low, sexy laugh. All he had to do was see her.... Man, all he had to do was *think* about her and, whammo, he wanted her. And when he wasn't with her, he sure as hell was thinking about her.... This could turn out to be one hell of an uncomfortable two months.

Annie finished writing, put the pen down on top of the paper and stood up. "I'll be in the lab,'' she said shortly and left the room.

"Thanks,'' Pete called after her.

She didn't respond.

He reached across the desk and picked up the pad she'd written on. As he read the words that the phone caller had said to her, his jaw tightened. The threats had a horrific, nightmarish quality to them. They were all violently sexual and graphically explicit.

He read it over and over, each time his sense of uneasiness growing. It was entirely possible that these were not idle threats meant only to frighten Annie. It was entirely possible that her life really was in danger.

He reached for the telephone and dialed Whitley Scott's number.

"One of us has to run out to the airport," Cara said to Annie as they finished up the test on the copper bowl. "We've got that package from France coming in."

Annie looked at her blankly.

"Remember, the package coming in to Westchester Airport?" Cara said. "The job you aren't going to get to for a decade? Subject of a conversation we had two days ago?"

"Right, right," Annie said. She had put her hair back into a ponytail while they were working, but now she pulled it free, and it swung down around her shoulders. She sat down on one of the wooden stools that were scattered throughout the lab. "MacLeish, when's the last time we took a vacation?"

Cara pushed her glasses up higher on her nose and frowned. "You mean, like a trip to Easter Island and two weeks of crashing through the underbrush and staring at giant rock heads from some distant, ancient culture? Or are you talking about Thanksgiving at the parents' house? *Or* do you mean Club Med—lying on the beach in bikinis while handsome men bring us daiquiris and margaritas?"

"I mean Club Med. I *definitely* mean Club Med."

Cara chewed her lip as she thought hard. "I've worked for you for...how long now?"

"Forever," Annie answered.

"Right. And the last time we took a vacation was... Never?"

"That decides it," Annie said. "We need a vacation. When we're through with what we've got—when's that gonna be?"

Cara shrugged. "End of December, beginning of January?"

"We're taking January off," Annie said. "Don't accept any more work unless the clients can wait until February for us to start the project."

"Thank you, Lord," Cara said to the ceiling. "Club Med, here we come! Bless you, master!"

Annie stood up. "Back to work, slave," she said. "I'm heading for the airport."

She quickly ran upstairs and grabbed her jacket and car keys. "See you later," she called out to Cara as she ran lightly down the stairs.

Outside, the air was crisp and cold, and she buttoned her jacket, thinking it was time to dig her scarf out of her closet—

Pete Taylor was standing next to her car.

"Ready to go?" he asked.

She looked at him blankly.

"I'm your bodyguard," he said patiently. "That means when you go someplace, I go, too."

Annie closed her eyes. *Please, God*, she thought, *when I open my eyes, make him be gone. Make this all just be a bad dream....*

He was still there. Damn, damn, *damn*.

"I'll drive if you want," he said.

"I *like* to drive," Annie said. But her car was piled high with books and papers and empty seltzer cans. And *his* car was a sporty little Mazda Miata.... Her eyes slid toward his shiny black car.

"We can take mine if you want," Pete said, as if he

could read her mind. He held out the keys. "You can drive."

Slowly she reached for them. "What's the deal? Is it rented?"

He shook his head. "No," he said with one of his rare smiles.

"You'd trust me...?" Annie asked.

"You're trusting me with your life," Pete said. "I'll trust you with my car."

Annie got in behind the steering wheel and adjusted the mirrors. She didn't realize just how little the car was until Pete got in and nearly sat down on top of her. He was so close, they were practically touching. Maybe they should've taken her car instead....

She turned the key and the engine hummed.

"I faxed the FBI your transcript of that phone call," he said.

"Oh, great," Annie said sourly. "I'll bet they get a good laugh out of *that*." She eased the sports car out of the driveway, feeling the power in the engine.

"They're checking a number of different leads," Pete said, ignoring her sarcastic comment. "There are a couple of radical groups who have already lodged ownership claims to Stands Against the Storm's death mask. And another group has sent a formal complaint, claiming it should be returned to the Navaho people in New Mexico."

"Don't tell me. None of those groups is actually connected to the Navaho," Annie said, glancing at him, already knowing the answer.

"You're right." A white flash of teeth made her turn quickly back to the road. His smile was a killer. It was a good thing he didn't do it more often. "The Navaho don't want anything to do with the death mask. As far as they're concerned, they were happier with Stands Against the Storm's bad spirit safely across the Atlantic Ocean in England."

"How do *you* feel about it?" Annie asked. "Having the death mask in the house?"

She risked another look at him. He wasn't smiling, but his eyes were lit with humor.

"You don't really think it would bother me, do you?" he said.

"You are at least *part* Navaho," Annie said. "Aren't you?"

"Yeah," he said. "Half. Is it that obvious?"

"Actually, no. But your necklace gave you away. It's so valuable. I figured it must have sentimental value to it, that it must be an heirloom and that's why you wear it. Because if you were just a collector, you'd keep it locked in a case."

"My grandfather gave it to me," Pete said. "His grandfather made it. My great-grandfather made the ring and the belt buckle. They were all made to be worn—not locked away."

She glanced at him again. When she met his gaze, she felt a jolt of warmth that was different from the attraction that always seemed to simmer between them. This was friendly and comfortable. Oh, brother, she was actually starting to *like* this guy.

She pushed the Miata up to seventy.

"So what do you think?" she asked. "Who's really after this death mask? If it's not the Navaho..."

Pete shrugged. "Maybe the FBI's right and it's one of these radical Friends of the Native Americans groups."

"But you don't think so." She glanced over at him. He was watching her, his eyes warm. What would he do, she wondered suddenly, if she reached over and took his hand?

He'd assume she'd fallen for him—the way every woman who'd ever crossed his path had no doubt done. But she didn't want to be just another notch on his belt. No way. If she was going to be stupid enough to fall in love with this man, she was going to make damn sure he fell in love with her, too.

Something told her she'd better work fast. She already liked him, and Lord knows she was attracted to him. Her heart was ready for some bungee jumping. It had been a long time since she'd met a man she wanted to get to know better, a man she could imagine becoming involved with. And she could imagine being involved with Pete Taylor. Oh, baby, could she imagine it.

With very little work at all, she could imagine the way his strong, hard-muscled body would feel against hers. She could imagine his mouth curling up into one of his rare, beautiful smiles before he kissed her. She could imagine him in her bed, his hair damp with perspiration, his naked body slick and locked together with hers. She could imagine his dark eyes watching, always watching, learning all of her secrets, giving away none of his own.

She glanced at him again, then quickly looked away, afraid if he gazed into her eyes too long, he might somehow read her mind.

But he managed to anyway. When she looked up at him again, there was a moment when she could see deep hunger in his intense, dark eyes. But he turned away before she did, as if he, too, were fighting the attraction.

Annie cleared her throat, focusing all her attention on the exit ramp that led to the local airport.

Pete tried to wipe his damp palms inconspicuously on

his jeans. Man, this woman disturbed him. One of these days, he was going to lose the last bit of his control.

Annie was following the signs leading to the main terminal parking lot. She slid the car into an empty parking space and shut off the engine. She turned in her seat and looked at him.

"How much danger am I really in?" she asked him point-blank. "Isn't it true that most of the creeps who make crank phone calls only intend to frighten their victims?"

"Yeah," Pete said. "But even if the odds are one in a million, why take that risk?" And the transcript she'd written from the last phone call had really bothered him. His gut reaction was that there was something to worry about here. It couldn't hurt to err on the side of caution.

"There's better than a one-in-a-million chance that I'll be killed in a traffic accident, isn't there?" Annie said. "But I take that risk every day."

Pete was silent, just watching her as they sat in the car. What was he supposed to tell her? "I got a bad feeling about this," he finally said.

She smiled. "You and Han Solo."

He blinked. "What?"

"*Star Wars,*" she explained. "Didn't you see that movie?"

"Yeah?"

"Well, that was what Han Solo kept saying," she said, then drawled, "'I got a bad feeling about this, Chewie.'" She laughed at the expression on his face. "Lighten up, Taylor, will you?"

"If memory serves me, Solo's premonition was on the money," Pete pointed out. "His ship was tractor beamed into the death star, right?"

"Yeah, well, you win some and you lose some," Annie

said with a smile. "And they won in the end, when it really mattered."

Pete was watching her, and she looked back at him, examining his face as carefully. There was a small scar interrupting the line of his left eyebrow, but other than that, his features were the closest thing to perfection Annie had ever seen. His nose was straight and just the right size for his face. His eyes were large, with thick, long lashes that would put any mascara company to shame. They were framed by cheekbones of exotic proportions, making him not merely good-looking, but stunningly, dangerously handsome. His lips were neither too thick nor too thin, and sensuously shaped. But he held them far too tightly, giving himself a serious, almost grim expression. Although his hair was cut too short, it was dark and luxuriant. If it had been another few inches longer, Annie would have been sorely tempted to run her fingers through it. As it was, its length served to remind her who he was, and why he was here.

But looking into his eyes was like staring into outer space on a moonless night. Dark, endless, mysterious, exciting. With a hope and promise for adventure, and a consuming, beckoning pull.

Annie wondered why he didn't try to kiss her. As soon as the thought popped into her mind, she berated herself. Kissing her wasn't in his job description. She was a job, not a date.

On the other hand, there was no denying this attraction between them. Annie had seen it in his eyes before, just a flash here and there, but enough to make her catch her breath. It was there now as he looked at her—a hint of slow burning embers of desire, ready to leap into flames at the slightest encouragement.

A significant part of her wanted to give him that encouragement. But she'd had a relationship based on sex before, and it hadn't lasted. Shoot, wasn't her aversion to casual sex the reason she hadn't gone to bed with God's gift to women, Nicholas York? Except, as attractive as Nick was, he couldn't hold a candle to Pete. It had nothing to do with physical appeal—Nick was as handsome as Pete, but in a golden blond, blue-eyed way. In fact, with Nick's easy smile and cheerful facade, many women would find him the more attractive of the two men. But Annie could trust Nick only about as far as she could throw him. Sometimes she wondered if deception was a sport for him, or maybe a way of life.

Pete Taylor was mysterious, but her instincts told her that the man was honest. If pressed, he might lie, but it certainly wouldn't be a game to him. Not the way it would be for Nick.

And Pete Taylor wasn't entirely selfish. Or unreliable. Or as unfaithful as they come....

Of course, she hadn't realized Nick was any of those things when she first met him. And even though her instincts told her Pete was good and kind and honest, her instincts had been wrong before.

No matter how strong the chemistry was between them, Annie wasn't going to do anything rash or stupid. At least not intentionally, she told herself with an inward smile. Pete was going to be hanging around for nearly two months. That was plenty of time for them to get to know each other, to become friends. And after they were friends, if she still felt this nearly irresistible gravitational pull toward him, well, that's when she'd do something about it.

"You know what I think?" she finally said.

Silently, still watching her, Pete shook his head.

He didn't try to speak because he wasn't sure he could

utter a word. In fact, Pete wasn't sure he could move. Somehow, during the last few minutes, the interior of the car had shrunk. Without either of them moving a muscle, they were now so close that all he'd have to do was lean forward to kiss her.

Pete forced himself to look into her eyes, not at her mouth. Not at her soft moist lips...

He had to get out of this car, or he was going to do something stupid. But he couldn't get out, because just looking into her eyes had turned him on so much, he couldn't even stand up without embarrassing himself. Damn, what was *wrong* with him? He felt seventeen again, and desperately out of control.

"*I* think the FBI is behind this whole thing," Annie was saying. She climbed out of the car, then leaned down, sticking her head through the open door. "I think they made those phone calls and threw that rock through my window. I think this is just more of their intimidation technique."

Pete's face was expressionless. "I guess you think I'm FBI, too."

"Are you?"

He met her eyes squarely. "No," he said. "No, I'm not."

She nodded, her eyes never leaving his face. "This is stupid. You know, I have no reason to, but I actually believe you." A wry smile turned up one corner of her mouth. "I guess I sound pretty paranoid, huh? Come on, Han Solo, let's go inside."

Pete slowly climbed out of the car, and stood looking at her across the roof. He felt as if he were balancing on top of eggshells. So far he was okay, but he had to take a step, and it had better be a careful one....

"It must be rough," he said, "when no one believes you."

"Damn straight," she said.

"Tell me about the whole art-theft conspiracy mess," he said. "Maybe I can help."

She was looking at him, her blue eyes wide and vulnerable. Was she involved? He didn't have a clue. But maybe she'd tell him about it. *Trust me, Annie*, Pete thought. *Trust me, trust me, trust me—*

"Can you help make the FBI believe that I'm innocent?" she asked almost wistfully. Then she shook her head. "I'm innocent, but I can't prove it, so I'm being hounded. Whatever happened to innocent until proven guilty, Taylor? *That's* what I'd like to know."

She glanced at the terminal, then at her wristwatch. "MacLeish said air freight is only open 'til three. We better hurry."

Pete watched her walk briskly toward the low brick building. Did he believe her? He wanted to.

Slowly he followed her into the airport terminal, watching the life in her quick step, the unconscious sexiness in the sway of her slim hips.

Yeah, he wanted to believe her, because he wanted her.

Normally he didn't allow sex to complicate things. Sex was...sex.

But he liked Annie. He really, truly liked her. And, strange as it might seem, he didn't sleep with women that he liked. Unless, of course, it was a totally mutual, honest relationship.

Well, they had the mutual part covered—Pete had seen the reflection of his own desire in her eyes. But honest? Mentally, he sounded the loser buzzer. Not much honesty here, at least not on his side of the relationship.

No, there was no way on earth that he was going to

sleep with her. Even if she came to him and begged, he wouldn't.

Yeah, and my mother's the queen of England, he thought morosely.

Pete watched Annie sign all the papers releasing the valuable package into her custody. He slid the box closer to the edge of the air freight counter and lifted it. It was heavier than he'd imagined, he thought, frowning, and much too ungainly to carry with only one arm.

"We're going to need someone to carry this out to the car," he said to the man behind the counter.

Annie looked at him in surprise. "It's not *that* heavy," she said.

Pete actually looked embarrassed. "Yeah, well, I have this policy of never carrying anything that ties up both my hands at once. I need to keep at least one hand free, in case I need to go for my gun."

"Good point," Annie said dryly. "You never know when you'll need it to blow away some evil spirit."

"Sam's on a break," the man behind the counter said, unfazed by neither the mention of a gun or evil spirits. "He can help you, but he won't be back for another twenty minutes."

"We can wait," Pete said.

"No we can't," Annie said, exasperated, picking up the box herself. Pete opened his mouth to protest, but she cut him off. "What do I look like?" she asked. "Some kind of weakling? I'll carry it. I would have if I'd picked it up a couple of days ago, before you started following me around."

She started for the exit, aware of Pete's discomfort. He was a gentleman, she realized as he held the door for her.

It really, truly bugged him to see her straining to lug something he could have carried easily.

"Okay, look," he said when they were outside. "I'll carry it."

Annie kept walking. "Absolutely not," she said. "You should stick to your rules. You always have, haven't you?"

He nodded slowly.

"That's probably why you're so good at what you do," she said.

"Yeah, but I feel like a jerk."

"The very fact that you feel like a jerk proves that you're not," Annie said with a smile. "So relax. You're a nice guy. Don't beat yourself up for sticking to your guns—no pun intended."

She thought he was a nice guy. Pete felt warmth and pleasure spread through him at her words. Sixth grade, he thought suddenly with an inward groan. He hadn't felt like this since sixth grade.

Chapter 5

Annie let Pete drive home. She sat in the front seat with the heavy package on the floor at her feet. She opened it carefully. There were two silver statues inside, wrapped in bubble pack and newspaper, stuffed into a box filled with big foam beads.

The statues glistened, a mournful shepherd kneeling and a Virgin Mary, both faces decidedly Byzantine. They had been cast from a mold, their seams worn with age, seemingly ancient.

Her heart began to beat faster as she examined them. These could be real. Boy, she loved it when the artifacts were genuine. She loved holding the smooth metal in her hands, knowing that other hands had held these the same way over the course of hundreds, even thousands, of years. She loved wondering about the people who had poured the metal, people turned to dust centuries ago....

Annie packed them back into the box, sighing with contentment, and looked out of the car window.

Traffic on Route 684 was heavy for a Saturday afternoon. Pete had the Miata all the way to the left, moving well above the speed limit. Still, a drab gray sedan pulled up alongside them, in the middle lane of the highway. Annie glanced over at the other car's driver.

He had thick, bushy brown hair that looked as if it hadn't been combed since the late 1980s. A full, shaggy beard covered most of the lower half of his face.

Annie pulled her eyes away, afraid to be caught staring. But the sedan didn't pass or fall back. Instead, it kept pace, right next to them.

Annie looked up again, and this time the driver looked over at her and smiled.

Her mouth dropped open in shock.

His teeth had all been filed into sharp-looking fangs. And his eyes...! His eyes were an unearthly shade of yellow-green.

Like an animal's eyes. Like some kind of cat or... Or a wolf.

Wide-eyed, Annie watched with revulsion as the man made an obscene gesture with his tongue. Then he lifted a bright orange squirt gun to the window and she realized the back of his hands were covered with the same thick brown hair—or fur!—that was on his head. He squeezed the trigger.

A stream of red sprayed the inside of his window, hanging on the glass, thick and bright as fresh blood.

"God!" Annie cried, jumping back and slamming into Pete's hard shoulder. "Did you see that?"

"What?"

"That car!" Annie said. But the gray sedan was already falling back, merging into the right lane. "That guy! He had a gun—"

Suddenly she was being shoved down, hard, her head

pushed into Pete's lap, her ribs pressed into the gearshift. "Which car?" he shouted.

"The gray one," Annie said, her cheek against the worn denim of his jeans. She tried to sit up, but his arm was pinning her down.

Taylor swore. "I don't see it. Are you sure it was gray?"

The muscles in his thighs flexed and tightened as he drove. He smelled good, Annie thought suddenly, like fresh air and leather, a fading remnant of smoke from an open fire, and a warm, spicy sweet smell that she already recognized as being his own. It definitely wasn't fair. A man who looked as good as Taylor shouldn't be allowed to smell so good, too.

"Gray, four-door," Annie said. "Midsize. I think it might've been a Volvo." She twisted her neck to look up at him. His eyes were narrowed in concentration, his mouth an even grimmer line than usual. She pushed against him again. "Taylor, let me up!"

"Don't fight me," he snapped.

The muscles in his legs moved again, and Annie could feel the car slow. Pete moved his hand then, to downshift as he took the exit ramp off the highway.

She pulled herself up, sweeping her hair back from her face as she looked at him. He pulled into the lot of a 7-Eleven and parked, turning toward her.

"Are you okay?"

She nodded. There was real concern in his eyes. Pete took his job seriously—that much was clear.

"Did you get a good look at him?" he asked.

Annie nodded again. "I sure did," she said. "He could have been anywhere from twenty-five to sixty years old. His hair was brown and shaggy, he had a full beard and bushy eyebrows that grew together in the middle. He looked like he hadn't showered or shaved in about ten years, and he was skinny.... More than skinny— gaunt...you know, hollow cheeks. He had yellow eyes and black claws at the ends of his...paws."

"Paws," Taylor repeated expressionlessly.

"Did I mention the fangs?" Annie asked. "He had fangs. A complete set."

He sighed, looking away from her, out the front windshield. "Are you sure?" he finally said, turning back to look at her. But even as he asked, he knew from the set expression on her face that she meant exactly what she had said.

"I'm sure. I notice details, and I remember them," she said. "It's my job, it's what I do. And you know, pal, details like fangs and paws aren't easy to forget." She ticked off the other details on her fingers. "The outside of the car was dull gray, the inside was beige, vinyl seats. His rearview mirror had a crack on the upper-right corner, and the driver had fangs. His left lateral incisor was filed shorter than the other teeth. He had a small mole next to his left eyebrow. I didn't get a clear look at the right side of his face. Presumably it was covered with as much hair as the left side of his face."

Taylor's eyebrow had twitched a fraction of an inch upward. "Anything else?"

"His gun wasn't real."

His eyes narrowed very slightly. "That's not always easy to tell," he said. "Even for someone who's good with details."

"This detail was kind of hard to miss," Annie said. "The gun was orange."

She was grinning at him, her blue eyes sparkling with humor. "It was a water pistol, Taylor," she said. "The only danger I was in was from you—and the gearshift."

She rubbed her side. "I think I've got one hell of a bruise. If I'd known you were going to go all macho on me, I would've told you about the gun a little bit differently."

She gave Pete a quick description of the bloodlike liquid the man had sprayed on the inside of his window. "It was probably just a coincidence," she said. "It's getting close to Halloween. It probably didn't have anything to do with me."

"I don't believe in coincidences," Taylor said.

"*I* don't believe in werewolves or ghosts or witches, Navaho or otherwise," Annie said. "I seriously doubt the spirit of Stands Against the Storm drives a gray Volvo. And no self-respecting Navaho witch is going to leave the Southwest, let alone cruise the highways of suburban New York City in wolf form on a Saturday afternoon. If this wasn't a coincidence, I'd say it's a sure bet that someone is trying really hard to make it look as if the Navaho are behind the death threats. But if that's the answer, it leaves an even bigger question. Why?"

Jerry Tillet was in the office, perched on the edge of Annie's desk, smiling at Cara.

His reddish hair had grown long, and he wore it pulled back into a ponytail at the nape of his neck. He had a thick beard and mustache, and he wore a battered Red Sox baseball cap on his head. His skin was sunburned on top of a deep tan, and his clothes looked as though they hadn't seen a washing machine in weeks.

"Is it safe to stand downwind of you, Professor?" Annie asked from the doorway. "That *is* you under all that hair, isn't it, Tillet?"

"Hey, Doc," Jerry said cheerfully. "Cara was telling me about the evil spirits. Bummer. So where's your little shadow?'' His gaze flickered over Annie's shoulder. ''Big shadow,'' he corrected himself.

Annie turned to see Pete standing behind her. She introduced the two men. ''Peter Taylor, Jerry Tillet.'' Pete leaned past her to shake Jerry's hand, and she could feel the heat radiating from his body.

Why am I fighting this? she thought suddenly. *Why do I even bother when it would be so easy to give in?* But she knew the answer. She didn't know Pete at all. And if she slept with him just because her hormones were urging her to, and he turned out to be a real yuck or some kind of Attila the Hun, she'd feel mighty stupid. But still, there was something to be said for surrendering to the animal attraction.

Annie smiled, picturing the look on Cara's face if she suddenly said, ''Excuse me, guys, but Taylor and I have to go upstairs and have sex now....''

Instead, Cara had her ''I'm dealing with the village idiot'' look on her face. ''Well?'' she asked Annie.

''Well, what?'' Annie said. ''Were you talking to me?''

''I asked if it was all right with you if Jerry and I left now. We were hoping to catch a double feature.''

''Sure, I've just about had it myself,'' Annie said, straightening up, reaching her arms over her head, stretching out her back. She stopped, midmotion, aware of Taylor's dark eyes on her, aware that her sweatshirt was riding up, exposing several inches of bare stomach above the waistband of her jeans. With a quick tug, she pulled the sweatshirt back down.

''It's getting late,'' Pete said. ''We have to go upstairs.''

Annie froze. Then laughed nervously. Upstairs? There was no way he could have read her mind.... Was there? ''Why?'' she asked.

If he noticed any suspicion or hostility in her voice, he ignored it. "I need to check out the security system on your top floors. I need to know what has to be fixed or added to make this place secure," he said.

"I've got to lock this in the safe," Annie said, motioning to the box that she'd brought in from the car.

"Well, we're outa here," Cara said, grabbing Jerry's hand and pulling him toward the door. "See you on Monday, Annie."

Annie started to lift the heavy box, but Pete was there. "I'll get it," he said, picking it up.

She raised her eyebrows and he smiled. "I think I can probably risk carrying it all the way to the safe," he said.

Pete followed Annie down the hall and into the lab. "I've got the same alarm system upstairs as I do down here," she said, returning to their conversation. "You know, the kind that doesn't work real well? It also doesn't work real well upstairs, too."

Annie opened the door to the safe and Pete put the box on the shelf next to the crate containing Stands Against the Storm's death mask. She closed the door tightly, spinning the combination lock.

"You know how the alarm system works," she said. "So why do you need to look at it?"

"I need to do a window count," Pete said. "As long as Marshall's willing to foot the bill, you might as well let him upgrade your security."

"How? By putting bars on the windows?" she asked. "Then what? A barbed-wire fence and a pair of Dobermans? No thanks. I have no intention of turning my house into a high-security compound."

He shifted his weight, crossing his arms, still watching her steadily. *This,* Annie thought, *is what it feels like to be a specimen under a microscope.*

"Invisible bars," Pete answered. "Motion detectors to start. We can go from there."

"My neighbors are going to *love* this," Annie muttered, following him up the stairs. "Every time a moth bumps against my window, the alarm's going to go off. I won't get any sleep—except when I'm in jail for disturbing the peace."

She trailed along after him as he went from room to room, checking the windows and recording information in his little pocket notebook. He finally paused in front of two closed doors on the second-floor landing.

"What's in here?"

"A linen closet," Annie said, opening the door to reveal her haphazardly stashed collection of sheets and towels.

He pointed at the second door. "And here?"

"Stairs to the attic."

Taylor opened the door, flicking on the light.

"There's nothing up there," Annie said.

He started up the dusty stairs. They creaked and moaned noisily under his weight.

Lit only by one bare bulb, the big attic was full of shadows—and junk. An old rocking horse sat in one corner with a broken television set. A collection of cross-country skis and poles and a child's wooden sled were in another. Boxes and boxes and boxes of books and clothing and stuff were everywhere, some of their contents spilling out onto the wooden floor.

"Nothing up here?" Pete said, a glint of amusement in his eyes as he watched Annie climb the last few stairs into the attic.

She smiled sheepishly. "Nothing important," she said.

But Pete's eyebrows had dipped slightly down in the

closest thing she'd seen to a frown on his face as he crossed from one window to another.

"You don't have your alarm system connected to these windows," he said, a note of disbelief in his voice. "Not a single one."

"Well, it would've cost nearly double," Annie explained. She moved toward a window, looking down through the dusk at the ground three distant stories below. "There's no way someone would climb up here. I mean, they'd be crazy—"

"I've known some cat burglars who wouldn't hesitate to scale seventeen stories for an easy target," Pete said. "This would be a cakewalk."

"No way." Annie shook her head, glancing down again. The lawn was *so* far away. She couldn't imagine climbing up this high. The shingles on the roof were slippery and some were loose. One wrong step, one misjudged placement of a foot, and there'd be nothing but air. Air and then the bone-breaking earth.

Pete reached up to lean his arms against the rough wooden rafter, the muscles moving under his trim black turtleneck as he looked down at her. "I guess you're not a climber," he said with a small smile.

"A climber?" she echoed, trying not to melt under his warm gaze.

"People are either climbers or not," he explained. "The not-climbers are more comfortable on the ground. It's not that they're afraid of heights, they just have a healthy respect for gravity. Too healthy. As a result, they doubt the very existence of climbers."

"I'm definitely a not-climber," Annie admitted.

"Climbers were born knowing about toeholds, and wanting to touch the sky," Pete said. "And climbing up to the attic of a three-story house wouldn't even get them half the way there."

"Which are you?" Annie asked.

Before he had a chance to answer, she launched herself at him, screaming like a banshee. His hands automatically came down to catch her, but he lost his footing, and he and Annie tumbled to the dusty attic floor.

His body responded instantly, his arms going around her, his fingers threading into the fine, golden-brown hair that he'd so often imagined touching. Silk. It felt like silk. Softer.... Oh, man—

"Oh, man," Annie wailed, pushing herself away from him and scrambling to the stairs.

He heard her stumble in her haste, and then the solid slam of the door.

With a groan, Pete lay back on the floor, feeling as if he'd been run over by a truck. What the hell had just happened? She'd tackled him, out of the *blue*, for crying out loud....

He saw it then.

It was a small black shadow, flitting up near the eaves. A bat.

Annie was afraid of bats.

She had leapt on top of him not from unrestrained attraction, but out of fear.

He tried to convince himself that the feelings flooding him were relief, nothing more. But he couldn't contain the laughter that bubbled up, laughter mostly aimed at his own overinflated ego.

He pulled himself up off the floor and opened one of the attic windows. Gently he herded the tiny bat in that direction, until it noticed the obvious path of escape and disappeared into the cool night air. Pete closed the window and looked around, dusting himself off.

* * *

Annie sat at the kitchen table, her hands wrapped around her mug of tea, as if for warmth. She glanced up as Pete came into the room, meeting his eyes only briefly before looking away, embarrassed.

"You okay?" he said.

"Yeah, I'm sorry," she said. "I'm, um…a little freaked-out by bats."

"A little," he agreed, amusement lighting his eyes.

She looked up at him again as he sat down across from her. A rueful smile slowly spread across her face. "You probably didn't know what hit you," she said.

"I *was* a little confused at first," he replied with an answering smile. "I got the bat out of there and found where he must've gotten in. I stuffed a rag in the hole. It's not a permanent fix, but it should keep him from coming right back inside."

"Thanks." She paused for a moment, then said, "Don't tell anyone. Please?"

"That you're afraid of bats?" Pete asked, surprise in his voice.

"Yeah. Cara doesn't even know."

"What difference does it make?" he asked curiously.

"I'm an archaeologist," Annie said. "Bats and I tend to hang out in the same places. I would be teased mercilessly if my colleagues knew I was afraid of them. And I'm really okay around bats if I'm expecting them to be there," she said. "It's when I'm not expecting them that I suddenly become nine years old again."

He was watching her with that funny little half smile on his handsome face, and Annie had an extremely vivid memory of the way his body had felt against hers. The man was all muscles, all hard, solid strength. But his hands had been so gentle as he touched her hair….

"Promise you won't tell," she said.

Her blue eyes were wide, watching him with such hopefulness, such trust and such innocence. She actually believed that if he told her that he wouldn't tell anyone, then he wouldn't. Pete had to look away, wishing he deserved that trust, knowing he didn't. Not by a long shot.

"I'd think at least you would've told Cara," he said. "You two seem pretty tight."

She shook her head.

"Why not?" he asked.

Her eyes narrowed slightly as she met his gaze. "Can you honestly tell me that *you* don't have some deep, dark secret that no one knows—not even your best friend?"

He laughed, but there was no humor in it. "I have way too many secrets," he said.

"Well, good. You tell me one of your secrets," Annie said, "and then we'll be even. You don't tell anyone that I'm a baby when I see a bat, and I won't tell anyone that…you secretly watch old Doris Day movies whenever they're on television."

Pete raised an eyebrow. "How did you guess?"

Annie laughed. "Do you really?"

"How many secrets do you want me to give away?" he countered.

He was flirting with her, Annie thought with a sudden flash of pleasure. "Just one," she said. "You know what I'd really like to know?"

"I can't begin to guess," he said.

"I want to know your real name."

Pete stopped breathing. She knew. How the hell could she know?

"You *do* have a Navaho name, don't you?" she asked.

He understood with a flash of relief. God, for a second there, he'd actually thought she knew he was undercover…. "Yeah," he somehow managed to say.

Annie looked across the table at him. He was watching her, his face suddenly guarded, expressionless. She wondered if perhaps she was prying too deeply. "I'm sorry. You don't have to tell me if you don't want to."

"Hastin Naat'aanni," he said. His voice was so soft, it was almost a whisper as he spoke the language of his grandfather. "That's what I was called."

Intrigued, Annie leaned forward. "What does it mean?"

He stood up. "It doesn't translate well," he said, obviously hedging.

"Roughly, then," she said. She stood up, too, testing her legs, checking to see that the wobble had truly gone away.

He turned to watch her closely, making sure she was okay. When had it stopped being annoying? Annie wondered. When had his presence changed from interfering to nice, to making her feel safe and protected?

"Roughly, it means 'Man Speaking Peace,'" he said. His lips curled up into a sardonic smile; then he turned and left the kitchen.

"That's a great name," Annie said, following him down the stairs. "Who gave it to you? How old were you? Why were you named that?"

At the bottom of the stairs he stopped and faced her, bringing them nose to nose.

"That's another secret entirely," he said.

They were standing close enough for him to kiss her. It would take very little effort on his part. She wanted him to kiss her, she realized suddenly. She actually *wanted* him to. Was she crazy?

But he didn't move.

"I'm going to use your phone," he said, "to call

Steven Marshall. He'll authorize me to have your security system updated and rewired to include the third floor.''

Annie felt the first sparks of anger. But that was good—anger was better than whatever it was that she'd just been feeling. Wasn't it? "But I don't want my system updated," she said, turning and going back up the stairs. "I'm happy with everything exactly the way it is."

"Then you better get used to me camping out on the floor of your bedroom every night," Pete said. He followed her back into the kitchen. "Because until we get motion detectors and a laser security system installed, that's exactly where I'm going to be."

"Oh, come on, Taylor," Annie said. "You don't really think I'm in any kind of danger, do you?"

"I've been hired to protect you," he said evenly, crossing his arms and leaning against the door frame. His dark eyes watched her as she took a loaf of bread from the cabinet, and jars of peanut butter and jelly from the refrigerator. "What I think is irrelevant."

Annie pulled a clean plate out of the dishwasher and set it on the kitchen table, then selected a dinner knife from the utensil drawer. She folded one leg underneath her as she sat at the table, opening the bread bag and pulling out two slices of thick, dark whole wheat bread.

"I don't enjoy sharing my bedroom," she said, frowning down at the chunky peanut butter she spread on one of the slices of bread. "Particularly since I don't believe someone really wants to hurt me."

"Maybe not," Pete said. "But maybe you're wrong. If I were you, I wouldn't want to find out the hard way that I was wrong."

He was watching her as if he were memorizing the way she put jelly on bread. "You hungry?" she asked suddenly. "Want a sandwich?"

Pete shook his head, a small smile playing about the corners of his mouth. "No, thanks," he said. Then he added, "Is this your dinner?"

She shrugged, taking a bite. "Believe it or not, it's healthy," she said around the peanut butter in her mouth. "The peanut butter is natural—just a little salt added—and the jelly's that all-fruit stuff. I got the bread at the health food store. You sure you don't want some?"

"I'll send out for something, thanks," he said dryly.

"I still don't think anyone would be able to climb up to the third floor of this house," Annie argued after she swallowed a bite. "Even if someone managed to get up there, the neighbors would see them and call the police."

Pete stepped into the kitchen, sitting down across from her at the table. "But what if someone *could* get up there?" he said. "What if they could gain access to your house that way? Then what? Your artifacts are locked in the safe. They're secure. But the lock on your bedroom door wouldn't keep anyone out."

"I can take care of myself," Annie said. "I'm not defenseless, you know."

"So you could defend yourself," Pete said. One eyebrow went up a half a millimeter. "With that plastic gun you had in the lab—the kind that says Bang! on a little flag when you pull the trigger? Very effective."

Annie actually blushed, then couldn't keep a smile from spreading across her face. "I was improvising," she said. "Gimme a break. It was the middle of the night and the alarm system went off."

"Look, I'll make a deal with you," Pete said. "Lock me out of your house. Then give me five minutes to get back inside without triggering your alarm system. If I can do it, then you stop complaining about updating the system, and you let me sleep on the floor of your bedroom until I'm convinced the house is secure.''

Annie had started to take another bite of her sandwich, but she pulled it out of her mouth. ''There's no way you can get back inside in five minutes,'' she said. ''No way.'' She bit down on the sandwich as if for emphasis.

''So is it a deal?''

''What do I get if you can't do it?''

His dark eyes rested warmly on hers. ''You get whatever you want,'' he said. Even with his face expressionless, his words had a faintly suggestive quality.

I'm imagining it, Annie thought, turning away from him. *I'm reading things that aren't really there.*

Nodding, she stood up, gesturing toward the hallway. Sandwich in one hand, she followed Pete down to the front door. He opened it, and looked down at her before opening the storm door.

''Lock the door and turn on your security system,'' he said. ''Then check the ground floor to make sure all the windows are locked.''

''Can I turn on the outside lights?'' Annie said, peeking out into the already dark evening.

Pete shrugged. ''Whatever you like.''

He pushed open the storm door.

''Hey, you better take your jacket,'' Annie said. ''It's cold out there.''

His eyes shone with that inner amusement she'd come to recognize. ''I'm not going to be outside that long.''

He vanished into the shadows.

Holding her peanut-butter-and-jelly sandwich in her mouth, Annie used both hands to quickly shut and lock the front door, activate the alarm system and turn on all the outside lights, including several spotlights that illuminated her stately Victorian house. She then went through the lab, and then the office, eating her sandwich and checking all the windows on the lower floor. They were all locked. There was no way he could get in that way.

Satisfied, she climbed the stairs. She would go into the kitchen, get the second half of her sandwich, then go down to the lab and— Oh, Christmas!

Pete Taylor was sitting at the kitchen table.

Annie felt her mouth drop open, and she looked at her watch. It hadn't even been three minutes, let alone five.

"How the hell did you do that?" she finally said.

"I climbed up to the attic," he said. "Came in the window."

"But—"

"I think I've proved my point," he said. "Now, can I use your phone?"

Annie was staring at him, her blue eyes troubled. "You just climbed up...that quickly?" she asked. "It was that easy?"

"Yeah," he said, all amusement gone from his eyes. "It was that easy."

She nodded, looking away and frowning thoughtfully. She met his eyes and nodded again. "Use the phone down in the office," she said.

Pete stood up.

"So you're a climber, huh?" she asked.

He nodded. "Yeah."

"You ever touch it? You know, the sky?"

He smiled then. "Not yet."

Annie lay in the darkness, listening for any sound at all from Pete Taylor.

Nothing.

No movement, no breathing, nothing.

But she knew he was there. He'd been there, lying on his bedroll, next to the wall by the bathroom when she'd turned out the light.

"Taylor—you awake?" she finally whispered.

"Yeah."

His voice was soft and resonant, thick, like the darkness that surrounded her.

"This is weird," Annie said. "Kind of like the first night of college, when my freshman roommate was still a stranger."

From where Pete lay on his bedroll, he could hear the rustling of her sheets as she sat up in bed.

"Except we didn't go to sleep," Annie's musical voice said, cutting through the darkness. "Instead, we stayed up, talking until dawn. It was my first all-nighter."

She was silent for a moment, then she asked, "You ever pull any all-nighters, Taylor?"

All the time, over in 'Nam. And twenty-four hours without sleep was a breeze. More often, it was seventy, eighty hours with nothing but caffeine and nicotine to keep him awake, to keep him alive— But Peter Taylor had supposedly gone to NYU, not Vietnam. "Yeah," Pete said softly. Still, it wasn't really lying, was it?

"I suppose in your business you still do it all the time," she said.

"Yeah," he agreed. That was closer to the truth.

"When's your birthday?" she asked.

"February 6th," he said.

"How old are you going to be?"

"Thirty-nine."

"What's your favorite color?"

Pete had to think about it. "Blue," he said finally. Yeah. Blue. The color of the sky, the color of the ocean. The color of Annie's eyes....

"Mine's red," she said. "Who's your favorite singer?"

He shook his head in the darkness. "I don't have one," he said. "I don't listen to music much these days."

"Why not?"

"I don't know," he said honestly. "I used to be into the Beatles...."

"I hate to break it to you," Annie said, "but they split up."

His laughter rolled through the darkness. "I said I didn't listen to music. I didn't say I didn't know what was going on."

"When you were a little kid," Annie said, "what did you want to be when you grew up?"

Pete was quiet for a moment. "Honestly?"

"Of course."

"I wanted to be a priest."

Annie didn't laugh, the way most people would have. "What happened?" she asked.

He sat up, leaning back against the wall. She could barely see him in the darkness, but despite that, his quiet strength seemed to radiate out into the room.

"I found out about the restrictions that went with the job," he said, laughter in his voice. "So I changed my career goals—I decided I'd be president."

"Of the United States?"

"Yep."

She saw the white flash of his teeth as he smiled, and she lay back in her bed, afraid to look at him, afraid of the reaction her body had to him.

"How about you?" he asked. "You must've always wanted to be an archaeologist, right?"

"Well, no," Annie said, lacing her fingers behind her head as she stared up at the dark ceiling. "When I was eight, we came back to New York for a few months and

I realized that most kids didn't live out of suitcases, in tents. I discovered that most kids didn't speak five different languages or have a monkey for a pet, and I developed a rather strong longing for what I now call 'TV normal.' It has nothing to do with reality, but, well, to make a long story short, I wanted desperately to grow up to be Mrs. Brady."

"You mean, the mother in 'The Brady Bunch'?"

"Bingo. I wanted suburbia, lots of kids..."

"A maid named Alice," Pete said.

Annie laughed. "A tall, handsome husband who kissed me on the forehead and called me 'dear' as he left for work," she said. "Fortunately for my parents, my fascination with a 'Brady Bunch' life-style lasted only a few months. I think after that I wanted to be an astronaut. Yeah, that was when we moved to Greece, and I caught reruns of 'Star Trek.' You know, I can say 'Beam me up, Scotty,' in seven different languages."

"Very impressive."

"Thank you. I've always been easily influenced by television and movies. I saw so little of them, and they seemed so magical. You know, I'm still affected by movies. I just saw *A Few Good Men*, and it made me want to go back to school and become a lawyer."

Pete laughed again. "That would be a major career switch," he said.

"Not as major as trying to be a suburban housewife," Annie said.

They were both quiet for a moment; then Annie said, "It's fantasy, you know? I mean, I love what I do. I really love it. It's not work to me. It's play. But still, I can't help but wonder what it would be like to do something different."

She was silent again for a moment. "Do you like your job, Taylor?" she asked.

Pete didn't answer. He couldn't answer. Yeah, Pete Taylor liked his job. He loved his job, since it meant lying there in the dark with Annie Morrow, talking to her, finding out that he liked her and that he wanted to keep finding out more about her.

But he wasn't Pete Taylor. He was Kendall Peterson. He was sent to spy on this woman, to uncover her secrets and betray her confidences. And Kendall Peterson had never hated his job more in his entire life.

Chapter 6

The morning passed quickly. Annie stretched and, for the first time in hours, looked up from the test she was running. She caught Pete's eye and smiled at him. He didn't smile back, but that was okay—she hadn't expected him to. Instead, he pulled off the headphones of the Walkman she'd lent him, and pushed the button that stopped the tape he was listening to.

"Lunchtime," she said.

"Does this mean you're actually going to eat?" Pete asked, his eyebrows moving slightly upward. "Or is this going to be a replay of breakfast where you just wave a mug of tea in front of your face?"

Annie's smile turned into a grin. "I'm starving," she admitted. "I better get a chance to actually eat. Although, first I've got to hit the office, check the fax machine and return all the phone calls I didn't take this morning."

Pete trailed down the hallway after her.

"You must be going nuts," she said. "Sitting there

watching me all morning. Not too stimulating, I'm afraid.''

On the contrary, Pete thought. He'd had an entirely enjoyable morning just watching her and listening to her collection of cassette tapes. He'd heard everything from Bach to a band called the Spin Doctors, and he'd enjoyed it all. It had been a long time since he'd taken the time to listen to music. The headphones Annie had didn't cut out the room noise, so he felt secure knowing he could hear everything that was going on around him.

And watching Annie was never a chore. Even when she was sitting, she was in motion. A foot was always jiggling, a pencil tapping, fingers moving.... He'd particularly enjoyed memorizing every little worn spot in her faded jeans. There was a place on her left hip where the seam was starting to tear....

It was Sunday, and Cara was spending the day with Jerry, so the answering machine had been on all morning. Annie pushed the message button, then went to the fax machine. Something had come in. She tore the sheet of paper free and looked at it as the messages played.

There were three calls from people whose names she didn't recognize, then Nick's familiar English accent came on, reminding her of their date at the Museum of Modern Art bash. He wanted her to call him. No doubt he had some new find that needed to be authenticated with utmost haste and great urgency. And gratis, as a favor to an old friend, of course. He wasn't a client, but somehow he always brought her work. He would ask her to squeeze it in, offer to stay up late into the night with her as she ran the tests, ply her with wine and promises of dinner....

There were messages from the buyer and the seller of the copper bowl she was working on, and five other messages from other clients.

Annie dialed the first of the clients who had called, and after saying hello, spent the next ten minutes listening to questions he had about her latest report on a piece he was trying to sell.

So much for lunch.

Annie's stomach growled. "Can you hold on a sec?" she asked, and pushed the hold button.

Annie looked up at Pete. "Will you do me a big favor?" she asked. "Will you go up to the kitchen and get me the bread, the peanut butter, the jelly, a plate and a knife? I'm never going to get off this phone."

"I'll do even better than that," Pete said. "I'll make you a sandwich."

"You don't have to do that," she said, surprise in her voice.

"I know," he said and smiled. "And believe me, I wouldn't do it for just anyone."

But he'd do it for me, Annie thought, a shiver going down her spine as she looked into his dark eyes. The guy had a killer smile, on top of his being drop-dead handsome, and so far, she'd only found things to like about him. He couldn't possibly be perfect, could he? As unrealistic as it seemed, she found herself praying that he was. Peter Taylor, security consultant, a.k.a. bodyguard, had appeared in her life totally out of the blue. Was it possible to hope that he might be here to stay?

He backed out of the door, his eyes not leaving hers until the last possible moment. Annie found herself listening to his footsteps on the stairs as she reconnected the line to her client. She glanced at her watch. Quarter to one. She was actually looking forward to tonight—to locking herself in her bedroom with Pete Taylor. And talking, she reminded herself. Just talking.

Ten minutes later, Annie stared at the telephone. One

down and five to go. She exhaled fully, and glanced up at the calendar on the wall. October. It was only October. Could she really keep up this pace until December?

A flash of movement at the window caught the edge of her vision, and she turned.

What the heck...?

Something was hanging from the tree right outside the window. Something red, and...

Very dead.

A carcass.

A very dead, very skinned carcass of an animal hung gruesomely from the tree, and she caught another streak of movement, as if someone were running away.

"Pete!" she shouted, rocketing out of her chair and scrambling toward the window. Whoever had been out there disappeared around the side of the house. She saw only the back of a black jacket. Or was it long black hair? "Taylor!"

She ran toward the front door, but Pete was already down the stairs, moving down the hall toward her with speed normally reserved for smaller, more compact men. He caught her in his arms to keep from plowing her down as he skidded to a stop on the slippery hardwood floor.

"What is it?" he said sharply. "Annie, what's wrong?"

"Someone was outside," she gasped. "Hurry! Maybe you can still catch him."

"Stay here," Pete ordered, then ran for the door. He drew his gun from his shoulder holster as he went out into the crisp afternoon air. Orange, yellow, brown and red leaves blanketed the wide lawn, and he could see the path the trespasser had made through them as he ran away from the house. That path led directly into one of the neighbors' yards, through a windbreak of tall bushes.

Pete raced up to the bushes, peering through them. The other yard was empty—no sign of anyone. He glanced back at the house. He didn't like leaving Annie alone, unprotected. What if this were only a diversion, designed to draw him away from the house, away from Annie?

She stepped out onto the front porch, and he felt a flash of annoyance. He trotted back toward her. "I thought I told you to stay inside," he said coldly. But his anger melted instantly as he saw the look on her face.

"I'm sorry," she said, hugging her arms across her body, trying to stay warm in the chill air. Her blue eyes looked even bigger than usual. "I, um, got spooked all alone in there."

Pete reholstered his gun. "Come on," he said, not unkindly. "It's cold out here. Let's get back inside."

But Annie was walking determinedly around to the other side of the house. "We have to cut it down," she said. "We can't leave it there."

Puzzled, Pete followed her, then stopped short at the sight of the animal hanging from the tree. He swore under his breath.

"I think it's a rabbit," Annie said, swallowing hard. "*Was* a rabbit, I mean. Do you have a knife?"

"Wait," Pete said. "We can't cut it down."

"Why not?"

"It's evidence," he said.

Annie stared at the skinned animal, blinking back the tears that suddenly appeared in her eyes. "It's hanging right outside my office window," she said, unable to keep her voice from shaking.

"I'll call the FBI," Pete said gently. "Hopefully they can send someone down to take care of it right away."

"And if they can't?"

"Annie, we've got to do this by the book."

"I don't know which is worse," she said. One tear escaped, rolling down her cheek before she brusquely wiped it away. "The fact that someone hung that thing there, or the fact that I can't cut it down when I want to."

"I'm sorry," Pete said, stepping toward her. He reached out toward her, well aware that this was exactly what he'd been so carefully avoiding—all physical contact. He wouldn't be able to hold her in his arms without wanting to kiss her. And if he kissed her, he'd be lost. He reached for her anyway, wanting only to stop her tears.

But she pushed past him, heading back into the house.

He followed her into the lab, where she ignored him completely, concentrating intently on the work at hand.

Pete went into the office and called the FBI, then brought Annie the sandwich he had made for her.

It lay on the counter, untouched, all afternoon.

Annie lay soaking in her bathtub with her eyes closed. The water turned from hot to warm to tepid, and she was considering letting some of it out and running in some more hot when a knock sounded at the bathroom door.

"You all right in there?" Pete's husky voice asked.

She sighed. "Yeah. I'll be out in a minute."

"Take your time," he said, but he heard the sound of water spilling down the drain.

Five minutes later the bathroom door opened, and Annie came out, dressed in a pair of plaid pajamas. Her face was scrubbed, and she was brushing her hair. Her eyes found Pete, who was standing by the bedroom door.

"Can I lock this?" he asked.

She nodded, sitting cross-legged on her bed, still brushing her long, shiny hair. "How long till the motion detectors are installed?" she asked.

Pete knew that what she meant was, *How long till*

you're out of my room? "With any luck, they'll be up in a couple of days," he said.

She nodded.

He used the bathroom quickly, washing up with the door open, so he could hear her if she needed him. He hung his towel on the rack next to hers. Annie's towel was damp from her bath, and smelled like her. The entire bathroom smelled like her—fresh and clean and sweet.

Pete turned out the bathroom light and went into the bedroom. He sat down on his sleeping bag, leaning back against the wall.

As he watched, Annie put her hairbrush on the small table next to her bed, then turned off the light.

Darkness.

It surrounded him completely, and he waited patiently for his eyes to adjust. He took advantage of the privacy the darkness provided and pulled off his T-shirt and slipped out of his jeans. He'd slept in his clothes the night before, and woke up much too hot. He lay back against his pillow, listening to the rustling of sheets as Annie moved about, trying to get comfortable.

There was silence then for several long minutes before he heard Annie ask, "Taylor, you still awake?"

He smiled into the darkness. "Yeah."

"I was wondering…"

"Mmm?"

"When do you get a day off?" she asked.

"I don't," he said. "Not until after the job's finished."

"But that's probably going to be at least six more weeks," Annie said. "Doesn't that get a little intense? You watch me all day, *and* all night. Aren't you going to burn out?"

"No."

It was said so absolutely, Annie had to believe him. "Is

your job always like this?'' she asked. ''You know, round-the-clock? What about your social life?''

''I don't have a social life.''

''By choice?'' she asked.

He was quiet for a moment. ''Yeah, I guess so,'' he said. ''How about you? You work all the time, too.''

''I have a social life,'' Annie said defensively. ''I go…places, and do…things.''

Who was she trying to convince? she wondered. Pete or herself?

She frowned up at the dark ceiling. When *was* the last time she'd had a date? It was when Nick had last been in town. He took her out to a little Italian restaurant in the city and tried to convince her to come back to his hotel room afterward. She'd had too much wine, she remembered, because she'd almost given in.…

''Annie, I'm sorry about this afternoon,'' Pete said, the faint Western drawl of his rich voice making all thoughts of Nick vanish from her mind. ''I wish it could've been handled differently.''

''It wasn't your fault,'' Annie said tiredly.

''Yeah, well, I still wish…'' His voice trailed off. Man, he wished this whole investigation had been handled differently. He wished Annie hadn't turned out to be so friendly and funny and charmingly sweet. He wished he could allow himself to care what happened to her. *Too late,* a little voice spoke in his head. *Too late, you already do care…*

On the other side of the room, he heard Annie sit up. ''What?'' she asked, her voice little more than a whisper. ''You wish what?''

Pete pushed himself up on his elbows, sensing her sitting there in the darkness, afraid she was going to get out of bed and move toward him. Disaster. That would be a disaster. If she as much as touched him, he would go up in flames. Spontaneous combustion. A life, a solid career reduced to little more than a sensational headline on the front of the *National Enquirer.*

He remembered running down the stairs that morning, adrenaline sweeping through his system after she'd shouted his name. He'd held her in his arms then. True, it had only been for a few short seconds, but he could take that memory, play it on slow motion and... Dangerous. Man, that was way too dangerous.

"What do you wish?" Annie asked again. He heard a noise, as if she were moving down to the foot of her bed, down where she could see him if she peered through the darkness.

"Too many things," Pete said. "Go to sleep, Annie."

The noise stopped.

Pete prayed, sending a few words up to the gods of his grandfather, as well. *Please don't make this temptation worse than it already is....*

There was silence for several long minutes.

Annie swore choicely, her voice breaking through the darkness. "I can't sleep. I'm exhausted, but my brain won't slow down. And I have to get up early tomorrow, and—"

"Are your eyes closed?" Pete asked.

"Well, not exactly—"

"Close your eyes," he said in his tone of voice that left no room for argument. "I'm going to teach you a relaxation technique, okay?"

"Okay," Annie said, doubt in her voice. "But I've tried this kind of thing before, and it doesn't work."

"This one does," Pete said. "Do you have a favorite place? Somewhere you can go and feel totally calm?"

Annie squinted up at the ceiling, thinking. "Monument

Valley," she said decidedly. "I loved it there. Sunrises were *incredible*. Except... No, maybe the beach on Tahiti would win. *That* was fabulous." She sat up. "I *really* loved it there. Although, there was something about the pyramids in Egypt that made me feel like I was on another planet, which was surprisingly calming—"

"Annie."

"Yes?"

"Lie down."

She lay back against her pillow, pulling her sheet and the comforter up to her chin.

"I'm going to tell you about *my* favorite place, okay?" Pete's voice was soft but clear.

"Okay," Annie said.

"Close your eyes," Pete said, "*and* your mouth, or else it won't work."

She was obediently silent.

"My favorite place was a beach," Pete said. "It wasn't Tahiti, but it was the Pacific Ocean. Usually when I got there, I was tired and hot and dirty, so the first thing I'd do was take off my boots and walk straight into that clear blue water." He would come out from the jungles of Vietnam, and wash all the blood and death away from him in the ocean. "Picture yourself doing that. Picture yourself in the water, letting everything that happened today just get washed away. Out where you are, behind the break, the ocean's calm, with gentle swells that lift you up. You can look out toward the horizon, and it's all blue water, as far as you can see. It just goes on and on and on, almost forever."

Annie lay in the darkness with her eyes shut, letting Pete's soft voice wash over her. His twang was more pronounced as he himself relaxed and his voice grew lazy.

She liked it. The drawl suited him far better than the clipped accentless voice he assumed when giving orders.

"You climb out of the water," he was saying. "And up onto the beach. The sand's fine and soft and hot under your feet. It feels real good. There's a blanket already spread out, and you lie down on it. It's warm and the sun feels great on your face. There's no one else on the entire beach—you've got the whole place to yourself—so you take off your wet clothes."

Pete paused a moment, unable to get the picture of Annie lying naked on the beach out of his mind. Damn, this was supposed to be relaxing....

"You lie back against that blanket, and feel that hot sun on your skin. The sky is the bluest you've ever seen it, and the sand is so white. You close your eyes, though, and listen to the sounds of the waves, and to the seabirds. It's like music, with its own special rhythm and rhyme. It's soothing, and soon you're so relaxed, you seem to be floating...."

He could hear Annie breathing, slow and steady as he let his voice trail off. She was asleep.

She trusted him. Another few nights like this, and he'd ask her about what she'd done in Athens—who she talked to, where she'd gone. He'd ask her if maybe she was in too deep....

Although he couldn't believe she was involved with any kind of conspiracy. He smiled to himself. She didn't seem to have the ability to lie. Another few nights and he'd know for sure....

Except the alarm system was scheduled to be updated starting tomorrow afternoon, and he'd soon be sleeping in the guest bedroom, away from her.

Pete lay awake, staring up into the darkness for a long time before he finally fell asleep.

* * *

Pete called Whitley Scott in the morning, while Annie was in the shower.

"Can you talk?" Scott asked.

"For maybe three minutes," Pete said. He stood in the office doorway, listening for Annie, and looking down the long hallway, watching the front door for Cara. "I need you to delay the installation of the motion detectors. Have the alarm installers call Annie and tell her it'll be at least a week before they can get the system out here."

"Annie, huh?" Scott said meaningfully.

Pete ignored the comment. "Will you do it?"

"Sure."

"What have you found out?" Pete asked.

"You mean about the phone calls?" Scott asked.

"And the rock through the window, and the wolf man in the car, *and* the carcass hanging—"

"Right, right," Scott interrupted him. "Not much. It's not our main concern right now—"

"Push it up a little higher on the priority list," Pete said, his tone leaving no room for argument.

But Scott argued anyway. "Come on, Captain," he said. "You know those nutball groups. This could be any one of them. We don't have the manpower to waste an investigation on a threat that's not real—"

"I think it *is* real," Pete said tersely. "Get a team working on it immediately."

Silence. Whitley Scott didn't like being ordered around. But Pete waited him out, and Scott finally sighed with exasperation. "I'll see what I can do," he said grouchily. "So what's happening up there? Are you getting somewhere with Morrow?"

"She's starting to trust me," Pete said. "She's starting to think of me as a friend."

"A friend?" the head of the FBI division scoffed. "What's this *friend* crap, Pete? Seduce her, for crying out loud. Women naturally trust the men they sleep with. She'll tell you all her secrets then."

"I've got to go," Pete said brusquely, even though he could still hear the water coursing through the house's old pipes, and there was still no sign of Cara. He hung up the phone, Scott's words echoing in his mind. *Seduce her.*

Why should Scott's nonchalant words make him so angry?

Because Annie was…well, *Annie*. She was special. Pete liked everything about her. He liked her a lot—way too much to take advantage of her that way.

He sat down heavily at Annie's desk, massaging the tense muscles in his neck and shoulders. The ironic thing was, if he really *were* Pete Taylor, if he really *were* plain and simply Annie's bodyguard, with no ulterior motives or hidden agendas, he would have been working hard to get into her bed long before this.

Life was too damn strange.

"Yo," Cara said, breaking into Annie's concentration. "You've got a phone call I figured you'd want to take. It's the burglar-alarm guy."

Annie looked up from her equipment, stretching her stiff shoulders and back, and working out the kink in her neck with one hand. "Thanks," she said to her assistant. "I'll take it in here."

She crossed to the white lab phone that hung on the wall next to the door. It was late afternoon, and the light was already starting to fade. She picked up the phone and flicked on the bright overhead lights.

"Anne Morrow speaking," she said, glancing over at Pete. He sat leaning back in a chair, his feet up on a stool.

His relaxed position was only a sham, she realized. He was watching her as intently as ever, no doubt noticing the way she couldn't keep her eyes from running the long, lean lengths of his jean-clad legs. Shoot, the man was just too good-looking. She turned her back, trying to focus on the voice speaking to her over the phone.

"We gotta little problem with scheduling," the man with the heavy New York accent said, after identifying himself as being the owner of the burglar alarm installation company Pete had called to put in the motion detectors. "The earliest I'm going to be able to send a crew out is next week. End of next week. Thursday, Friday at the earliest. Maybe not even till Monday."

"Oh, shoot." Annie chewed her lip. "You were supposed to be here today."

"Sorry, miss," the man said, not sounding remotely remorseful. "It's that time of year. Halloween. You can try calling another alarm company, but it's the same all over. Everyone's backlogged."

Annie stared out the window into the deepening twilight. Another week and a half of Pete sleeping in her room at night. Now, why didn't that news bother her the way it would have a day or two ago?

"You still wanna keep your name on our list?" the man asked.

"Yes," Annie said. "Yeah, thanks. Thanks for calling."

Slowly she hung up the phone and told Pete about the call. He took the news with his normal lack of expression. Was he disappointed? Pleased? She couldn't begin to tell.

"Is this an official break?" Cara asked cheerfully, coming back into the lab. "It's time. You've been hard at it all afternoon. I, for one, have finished inputting all that data from the dread phony copper bowl, so I'm ready to celebrate."

"You're always ready to celebrate." Annie smiled.

"Yes, but this time I have an excuse," Cara said. "Jerry's coming over in a little while. What do you say we all go out and have Chinese food?"

"I don't know," Annie said.

"Oh, come on," Cara urged. "You know how weird you get when you don't leave the house for days on end. A little fresh air and some moo goo gai pan'll be good for you."

Annie glanced at Pete. "Whaddaya say, Taylor? Do you want to go?"

"I go where you go," he said.

"I know that," she said impatiently. "I asked you if you *wanted* to go."

He pulled his worn-out cowboy boots off the stool and stood up. "I would love to," he said, a smile breaking across his face as he steadily met her eyes.

Annie watched Pete as Jerry talked about his latest exploits in South America, telling stories across a table that was littered with the remains of their dinner. As the busboys began to clear away the dishes, Pete looked over at Annie and smiled. She felt the now-familiar warm rush of attraction and had to look away.

This was not a date, she reminded herself for the hundredth time that evening. Pete was her bodyguard. He was there only to protect her, despite the fact that his eyes sometimes burned with an intensity that could take her breath away.

In the few short days that he'd been protecting her, he'd done nothing to make her think she meant anything to him besides a reason for employment. True, he was friendly, kind even, generally polite, but in short, he wasn't acting like a man who was going crazy, longing for her touch.

The way she was longing for him to touch her.

Damn, damn, damn, Annie thought. When had she crossed the line between *This is a guy I'd like to get to know,* and *This is a guy I must have?* When had it happened?

Last night, probably, when she'd drifted off to sleep listening to his soft, husky voice. Or it might've been earlier that day, when he'd offered to make lunch for her. Or maybe it was the night before, when they first lay awake, talking....

"You're awfully quiet tonight," Jerry said to Annie. "And you barely ate anything. What gives?"

Annie could tell from the way he and Cara were sitting that they were holding hands underneath the table. Cara looked so happy.

"She's had a bad week," Cara answered for her. "She lost a couple of days' work by going to England to pick up old Stands Against the Storm's death mask, and then when she came back, she got hassled by the feds while she was going through Customs. They detained her *six* hours."

"Why?" Jerry asked. "Whatd'ya do this time, Morrow?"

Annie glanced at Pete, who was watching her intently. "After I picked up the artifact from the English Gallery, the place was bombed and robbed," she said.

"You're kidding," Jerry said with shock.

"I wouldn't kid about something like that," Annie said ruefully.

"God, you have the worst luck," Jerry said, shaking

his head. "Maybe you should stay stateside for a while. I mean, another coincidence like that and—"

"No thank you," Annie said with a flash of anger in her eyes. "My job requires international travel. I'm not going to let myself get bullied into changing my life."

"Maybe you should've been more cooperative with the Athens thing," he said, frowning.

"How much more cooperative, Tillet?" Annie said tartly. "You mean, like giving them a signed confession? Because that's what they want." She turned to look at Pete. "We better get going. I've got more work to do tonight."

"Does she ever not work?" Jerry asked Pete. He turned to Annie. "You must be disgustingly rich. Maybe I should be hitting *you* up for funding for my latest project. See, I found a site in Mexico—"

"I know, I know!" Annie said, rolling her eyes. "I've heard it…what? Five thousand times this week already."

"You know that you're interested," Jerry said. "You could come along." He shot a sideways glance at Cara. "You, too," he added. He looked back at Annie. "When was the last time you participated in a dig?"

"It would be fun," Annie said, "but I *really* don't have the money."

The waiter brought the dinner check, and she reached for it, but Pete grabbed it first. "This one's courtesy of Mr. Marshall," he said with a smile.

"I'll drink to that." Jerry grinned.

Annie watched Pete bring the check to the cashier. She stood up, pulling on her jacket. Pete's leather jacket was on the back of his chair, and she picked it up. God, it was heavy. "See you guys tomorrow," she said, giving Cara an overobvious "have fun" wink.

Pete met her at the door and took his jacket. "Thanks," he said.

"What are you carrying in your pockets?" Annie said, leaving the warmth of the restaurant and going out onto the sidewalk. "Your jacket weighs a ton."

Zipping her own jacket up, she shivered slightly in the cold autumn night.

"It's armor," Pete said. "In case I have to throw myself in front of any speeding bullets."

Annie laughed.

"I'm serious," he said. "It's bulletproof."

He was watching her in the dim light from the street lamp on the corner. His dark eyes were soft and warm, luminescent. If any other man had looked at her like that, she would have bet her life savings that he was going to kiss her. But not Pete Taylor. He broke the eye contact, looked down at the ground and took two solid steps backward, away from her.

Hiding her exasperation, Annie turned, and they walked to his car in silence.

Chapter 7

Annie threw her jacket over the back of her chair in the office and pressed the playback button on her answering machine.

The first voice on the tape was Nick. He didn't even bother to identify himself, assuming that she'd recognize his voice. Which, of course, she did.

"Sweet Annie," he said in his proper English accent. "I'm beginning to consider taking your answering machine to the party at the museum instead of you. I've spoken to it more often in the past few weeks. Where are you? MacLeish says you're busy, but you've never been too busy for me before. What's going on? Call me."

Pete had assumed his regular position, leaning in the doorway.

"That was Nick York," she told him.

"I know," he said. "Why don't you call him back?"

Annie sighed, temporarily stopping the tape. "Because he's going to ask me to authenticate some very tiny, but

very important, archaeological find for him. It'll be really
easy, he'll tell me, it'll only take a few hours of my time,
I can surely squeeze him in. Except something will go
amazingly wrong—there'll be some glitch in the test, and
I'll end up working until dawn four nights in a row." She
sighed again. "Somehow Nick always talks me into doing
things. This time I really *don't* have the time, so it's easier
to avoid him." She met Pete's eyes and smiled ruefully.
"I know it's the coward's way out. I also know that he's
going to catch up with me sooner or later. At the fund-
raiser at the Museum of Modern Art, at the very least."

Pete kept his face expressionless, afraid that the flash
of jealousy he'd felt at the sound of York's voice would
still somehow show. Jealousy? Man, what the hell was he
doing feeling *jealous?* He had no right. No right at all.
So just stop it, he ordered himself.

He cleared his throat. "What other messages are on
there?" he asked, motioning toward the answering machine with his head.

Annie started the tape rolling again.

Another message was from the Westchester Archaeological Society, asking if Dr. Morrow had any free time
in the next few months to come and give a lecture at one
of the group's monthly meetings.

"Free time," Annie laughed. "If they only knew...."

There were four hang-ups in a row, then a voice spoke.

"I am calling on behalf of Stands Against the Storm."
Annie looked sharply up at Pete. He hadn't moved a muscle, but he was instantly a picture of intensity, his dark
eyes burning into hers as they both listened. The voice
belonged to a man and was accentless and soft.

"You must surrender the death mask," he said, almost
mildly. "Return it to the Navaho people. It is for your
own good that I tell you this. The evil spirit within the

mask will awaken if you disturb it. Do not touch it, do not hold it—or be ready to face the spirit's wrath. Your life as you know it will crumble. Await further instructions.''

There was a click, and the answering machine beeped twice, signaling that there were no more messages, and shut off.

Annie sat so still at her desk that Pete could hear the wall clock ticking as its second hand jerked around the dial. But as if her energy couldn't be contained, she stood up suddenly, pushing past him out of the room and down the hallway. He followed her into the lab, where she switched on the bright overhead lights and crossed directly to the big safe.

It only took several quick spins to the combination lock, and the heavy door swung open. Without a word, Annie took out the heavy crate from England and carried it to the wide lab counter. She set it down and got a hammer from one of the cabinet drawers.

Pete didn't ask what she was doing—he already knew.

"You know," Annie said evenly, "this thing is such a pain in the butt, and I haven't even taken a good look at it yet."

She used the forked end of the hammer to pry the top of the crate up and off.

The crate was filled with large foam peanuts. Annie dug through them, finding the top of the heavy artifact about six inches down. She pulled it out, careful to keep the foam chips in the box.

The death mask had been wrapped in layers of bubble pack. She peeled them back to find the artifact surrounded by a soft cloth. Carefully she unwrapped it, setting it on the counter on top of that same piece of fabric.

It was amazing. The gleaming, golden face of Stands

Against the Storm sat in front of her, every wrinkle, every sagging muscle in the old man's face recorded forever by the casting that had been done shortly after his death. His eyes were closed, and he looked so tired, so sad. Annie wondered what his eyes had been like, wondered if he'd had eyes like Pete's—dark and burning with intensity and life.

Annie glanced up at Pete. "Curses, shmurses," she said, and picked the death mask up, holding the cool metal in her hands. Nothing happened. She wasn't immediately struck by lightning or attacked by a flock of screaming evil spirits. And as far as her life crumbling...well, it couldn't really get *that* much worse. Could it?

She carried the death mask to the other side of the lab, to a big magnifying glass that was clamped to the counter with an accordion-like arm. She turned on another, even brighter, light and held the artifact under the glass, looking at it closely.

Pete pulled up a stool and watched.

Annie examined the casting marks, moving slowly across the piece for several long minutes. Finally she looked up at Pete.

"Is it real?" he asked.

She didn't answer at first. Instead, she brought the artifact up to her mouth and licked it. She grinned at the way his eyebrows moved upward. "Well, it's real gold, at the very least," she said.

"You can tell that by tasting it?"

Annie nodded. "Yes."

"That doesn't seem too scientific," he said. "All these high-tech instruments in this lab, and you end up using your tongue."

"That was just a preliminary test," she said. "I'll get a full metal content when I have more time. But I think the final outcome is going to have to be decided by carbon dating."

"Why?" asked Pete, watching her.

She had put the death mask down on the counter, and now she gathered her long hair away from her face, pulling it easily into a ponytail and using a rubber band to hold it back. She was wearing her worn-out jeans and a red sweater that was textured, designed to be touched. Pete hooked his thumbs through his belt loops and tried to concentrate on what she was saying.

"Well, it certainly passes a quick inspection," Annie said. "The casting marks all look comparable to what was being done in England in the nineteenth century. But without written records—you know, receipts or bills of sale, something to document it—the only way to be sure it wasn't cast last month in Liverpool is to carbon-date it."

Pete leaned in for a closer look. "So, how long will that test take?"

She turned and found herself nearly nose to nose with him. Up close, his eyes were beautiful. They were exquisitely shaped and surrounded by thick, black lashes. But his expression was so closed, so guarded, he might have been a statue. He didn't seem to notice that he had long since invaded her personal space, that he was sitting at a distance more appropriate for an embrace than a conversation.

She swallowed, moistening her dry lips with the tip of her tongue. "Even if I start the tests now, it will probably be weeks before I get the results. I have to contract out for carbon dating."

There was a flash of relief in his dark eyes, and Annie's heart leapt. He was glad. He wanted to stick around for a while. More than ever, she wanted him to kiss her. *Kiss me,* she thought, staring into his eyes, hoping he could read her mind.

But he didn't move.

She was going to have to do it, she realized. She was going to have to kiss him. She looked away, gathering her courage. The worst he could do was laugh at her, right? So she should just do it—

Pete straightened up, pushing his stool back, out of range.

Damn, Annie thought. The moment had passed. What was wrong with her? she wondered. Wasn't she making her interest in him obvious enough? Or maybe it was Pete, she thought glumly. Maybe he had a reason to fight the attraction that sparked between them every time they were together in a room. Maybe he was in love with someone else. Shoot, maybe he was married....

She sat at the lab counter for a long time, pretending to study the death mask, but in truth thinking long and hard about Peter Taylor.

Annie turned off the light on her bedside table, determined to follow the resolution she had made while she was brushing her teeth in the bathroom just a few moments ago. She was not going to chase this man. She had let him know—subtly, of course, but Pete Taylor was a smart man—that she was interested in him. It had been up to him to do something about it. Or not.

Obviously, he'd chosen "or not."

Well, okay. That was fine. She was a grown-up; she could deal with that.

But it wouldn't do her any good to lie in the dark, talking to him until the early hours of the morning. It wouldn't do her any good at all to share more secrets with him. And it certainly wouldn't do her any good to fall in love with him.

She lay in the dark, in silence, hoping that it wasn't already too late.

Minutes passed. Long, endless minutes, during which she tried to organize and prioritize the work she had to do tomorrow. Then she tried to think of all the songs she knew that started with the word *I*. "I Think I Love You," "I Wanna Hold Your Hand," "I Had the Craziest Dream," "I Do," "I'm Dreaming of a White Christmas"—no, that was the first line, not the name of the song.

She gave up. "Taylor, are you awake?"

"Yeah."

On the other side of the room, Pete closed his eyes briefly. Annie had been quiet for so long, he had been afraid that she had broken her pattern and was already asleep.

"Do you think that guy on the phone meant he's going to call again and tell me to bring the death mask someplace, when he said, 'Await further instructions?'"

Pete knew exactly which guy she was talking about. "Probably," he said. "But first I think he and his buddies are going to try to scare you badly enough so you won't want to get the police involved."

"The police are already involved," Annie said. "What do these guys think I'm going to do? Simply hand them a piece of gold that's worth tens of thousands of dollars? And that's ignoring any possible historical value. Even if I do hand it over, then what? I call up Ben Sullivan and say, 'Oops. Lost your artifact. Sorry'?"

"*I* know you're not about to do that," Pete said. "But these people don't know you. They don't realize you don't scare easily."

"Maybe you don't know me, either, Taylor." Annie's voice was soft. "Sometimes I think I'm scared of everything."

"It's one thing to be scared," he said, "and another thing entirely to let it affect you."

"Like my fear of bats," Annie said wryly.

"Obviously you've dealt with that pretty damn well," he said, "since I'm the only one who knows about it."

"Aren't you afraid of anything, Taylor?" Annie asked.

Pete stared at the outline of the windows for a long time before he answered. "Yeah," he finally said. "I get afraid when the line between right and wrong isn't clear. Lately it seems it never is. It's been scaring the hell out of me."

There was silence for a moment, then he laughed, but there was no humor in it. "I'm also afraid I haven't lived up to the name my grandfather gave me."

Pete hadn't wanted to go to Vietnam and had seriously considered losing himself up in the Rocky Mountains, much in the way his ancestors had when they'd received orders from the federal government that they hadn't liked.

But he obeyed the draft, and he went to Vietnam. At first he wondered what the hell someone named Man Speaking Peace was doing stalking through a foreign jungle with an automatic weapon in his hands and camouflage gear on his back. But it didn't take him long to realize that he was good at staying alive, and especially good at keeping the men around him alive, too. And somehow, when the real war was over and the American troops were shipping out of Saigon, he'd remained behind, part of the exclusive force assigned to locate and rescue the massive numbers of POWs and MIAs still in the jungles.

Ever since the summer that he was drafted, when he

was barely eighteen years old, not even old enough to drink in Colorado, he'd always carried at least one gun. He felt it now, a hard lump, tucked under his bedroll where he could reach it easily if he needed it.

"A man of peace needs no weapon," he could remember his grandfather telling him. "Only a conscience, a will and a voice loud enough to carry."

"Man Speaking Peace." Annie's voice cut into his thoughts. "Why were you named that?"

He was silent for so long, she thought maybe he wasn't going to answer.

"I haven't thought about any of this in a really long time," Pete finally said. "I'm not sure I want to...."

"I'm sorry," Annie said. "I was just— I shouldn't have—"

"I was thirteen years old," he said, interrupting her. "It was the summer that my aunt died—my mother's sister. It really messed my cousins up. They came to stay with us at the ranch. There were five of them—Jack was the oldest, he was twelve. Then there was Wil, Thomas, Eddie and Chris, who was just a baby really. He couldn't have been more than five. He missed his mother something fierce. They all did, but Chris was the only one who would cry. He would cry, and Tom would taunt him, saying boys didn't cry, only babies cried. Then Jack would beat the hell out of Tom, and soon they'd all be fighting.

"Well, I spent all of July being a mediator, keeping the peace between those five boys. I was older than them, and they looked up to me. But more often than not, as soon as my back was turned, *wham,* someone would end up with a fist in his eye.

"After a few weeks, I began to realize that there was a pattern to when little Chris would cry about his mother. He usually cried first thing in the morning, and at a certain

time in the afternoon—about one o'clock, I think it was—
because that was the time his mom had set aside a half
an hour every day to read to him and play with him—
with *just* him, giving him her full attention, while the
other boys were off at school.

"So I started distracting him. I'd be the one to wake
him up in the morning, and I'd keep him so busy, he'd
never really notice the emptiness. And I did the same
thing in the afternoon, and his bouts of crying happened
less and less often."

Annie listened, realizing she was almost holding her
breath. Pete had never spoken at such length in the entire
time she'd known him, and certainly never about himself,
about his childhood.

"Unfortunately, the same couldn't be said about the
fighting," he said, with a low laugh. "Even when Chris's
crying stopped, the older boys found other reasons to set
themselves off. I couldn't figure out what had gotten into
them. They'd never fought before—not like this."

He paused. *Don't stop,* Annie thought. She could picture him as a thirteen-year-old boy, tall and serious, with
those same intense, dark eyes. "So what happened?" she
asked softly.

"I went and talked to my grandfather," Pete said. "I
asked him why my cousins were fighting. He told me it
was their way of grieving for their mother. Well, I thought
about that for a couple of days. But after I watched Wil
give Jack a broken nose, and after Jack damn near broke
Tom's arm, I decided that those boys needed to find a
different way to deal with their mother's death.

"I took the whole pack of them out on a hike, up into
the mountains, to a place I knew about where you could
see down into the whole valley," Pete said quietly. "It
was like heaven up there. You could look out across my

father's ranch, at the fields laid out like squares on a patchwork quilt. Everything was alive and growing. There were so many different shades of green, and the sky was so blue, it hurt to look at it.

"We sat down on some rocks, and the boys were quiet for once, just taking it all in," he said. "I sat there, thinking about my aunt Peg, their mother. I thought about her, and it didn't take me long to start to cry. So I sat there, with tears running down my face, and one by one those boys noticed I was crying. They were shocked, really shocked, because, as Tom was so fond of pointing out, boys weren't supposed to cry.

"Wil asked me why I was crying, and I told him it was because I missed his mother. I told them that sometimes even men had to cry, and if it was okay for a man to cry, then it was surely okay for a boy to cry. And they believed me, you know, because I was older than them. Soon Chris started in—it never took much to set him off—but then Tom broke down, and Wil and Eddie, and finally even Jack was crying. We all just sat there and cried for about an hour. Then I told them that this place that we had climbed to was my special place, but that they could use it whenever they needed it.

"We went back down that mountain, and from that day on almost all the fighting stopped," Pete said. "It was at the end of that summer my grandfather gave me the name Hastin Naat'aanni, Man Speaking Peace. It was the name of a great Navaho leader, back more than a hundred years ago."

He had been so proud, so young and full of hopes and dreams. Pete didn't have to wonder what had happened, what had changed him. He knew damn well. Vietnam.

"That's a great story," Annie said, her voice soft in

the darkness. "Thanks for telling me. Your grandfather sounds like he was really cool."

"Yeah," Pete said, closing his eyes, remembering. "He was a full Navaho. He must've been in his sixties back then, but he still had long, black hair that he kept out of his face with a headband. He was a silversmith and he traveled all the time, selling his jewelry at fairs and rodeos. When he was visiting, he'd set up a workshop in the barn. He didn't want me to go."

"Go where?"

To Vietnam. His eyes snapped open. Oh, man, what was he doing? Had he actually forgotten who he was, why he was here? Peter Taylor hadn't gone to Vietnam. "To New York University," he said, glad he had a ready answer.

"Why *did* you go?" she asked, her voice slipping through the dark of the room as if it were something he could reach out and touch.

"I had to," he said simply.

"You didn't *have* to," she said. "Nobody *has* to do something if he doesn't want to."

"Not true," he said. "There are some things that you have no choice about."

He had to get back on track, Pete thought. They had to stop talking about him, and focus the conversation on her. He had to get her talking about Athens, about England and about the people she had met with there. But how?

"Annie."

She closed her eyes, loving the way he said her name, and knowing that she shouldn't. "Mmm-hmm?"

"If you ever find yourself in any kind of trouble," he said slowly, searching for the right words to say, "I hope that you'll come to me and let me help you."

The room was suddenly silent. The little sounds Annie

made—all the restless movement, the whisper of sheets, even the sound of her breathing—all stopped. Fifteen seconds, twenty seconds, the silence stretched on and on....

"Taylor, I can't figure out what you're trying to say," Annie finally said. "Why don't you do me a favor and just say it?"

Pete laughed, unable to hold it in. Man, this woman was too much.... "Okay," he said. "I guess what I'm trying to say is, if you're somehow involved with this art robbery thing, and you're in too deep, I wish you would tell me, because I can help you."

There were another few seconds of silence. Then Annie said, "Thanks, Taylor, that's really sweet. Good night."

Chapter 8

Waffles. Annie woke up wanting waffles. It didn't happen too often—only about twice a year—but when the urge came upon her, she'd get the waffle iron down from the top shelf of the kitchen cabinet, pull out the one-hundred-percent pure maple syrup and actually spend more than her usual five minutes in the kitchen.

She climbed out of bed, pulled her bathrobe on over her pajamas, found her slippers and shuffled into the kitchen.

A short time later, the batter was nearly entirely blended, and the waffle iron was heating and Annie was rummaging through the refrigerator, looking for the maple syrup. She spotted the glass bottle way, way in the back. Almost diving in headfirst, she triumphantly pulled it out, only to discover it was nearly empty.

"Oh, shoot," she said crossly. She turned the waffle iron down to the very lowest setting, and went back into her bedroom.

Pete was in the bathroom. Annie could hear the sound of the shower running, so she quickly pulled on her jeans and a sweatshirt and slipped her feet into her sneakers. She ran her brush quickly through her hair, and pulled it back into a ponytail, then grabbed her purse and her car keys.

She was nearly out the front door when she realized she should probably leave a note for Pete. She quickly scrawled one on the back of an envelope, and left it at the bottom of the stairs.

Her car started grouchily in the cold morning air, and Annie found herself wishing that she'd taken the time to grab her jacket from where she had left it in the office. It was only a few minutes' ride to the grocery store, though, so she didn't go back for it.

She parked in a space close to the store, and ran to get inside quickly. The automatic doors opened with a mechanical swish, then closed behind her. She didn't bother to get a shopping cart or even a basket, going straight to the aisle that held the boxed pancake mixes and the syrup. There were shelves and shelves of the cheap, imitation syrup, but only one brand of the real stuff. It was from Vermont, no less. She took the glass bottle to the express line and was standing there, cheerfully reading the headlines on the sensational gossip newspapers, when she was roughly grabbed.

Startled, she let out a yelp before she realized who had grabbed her.

Pete.

He was barefoot, wearing only his jeans and an unbuttoned shirt. His hair was wet and he brushed a drop of water from his nose as he glared angrily at her.

"What the hell did you think you were doing?" he

said, his voice getting steadily louder until the very last word was practically roared.

The cashier looked at him curiously, and rang up Annie's maple syrup.

"I had to get this," Annie said, wide-eyed, motioning to the syrup. "You were in the shower, so—"

He was holding her tightly, his fingers encircling her upper arm. "So you should've waited until I got out, dammit," he spat out.

He was furious, and he wasn't trying to hide it. She could see the muscles in his jaw working, the force of his anger in his eyes. She had never seen such emotion on his usually carefully controlled face.

"Four dollars and seventy-nine cents," the cashier said, snapping her gum and watching them with unconcealed interest.

Before Annie could take her wallet from her purse, Pete threw a five dollar bill down on the counter and snatched up the bottle of maple syrup. He pulled her toward the door with him. "You are to go *no*where without me," he said, his voice harsh. The mechanical door didn't open fast enough for him, and he slammed it with the palm of his hand, pushing it, accentuating his words. "*No*where."

As they stepped out into the parking lot, out into the cold, crisp air, Annie pulled free of him, taking the maple syrup possessively and stashing it in her purse. "Oh, come on, Taylor," she said, getting angry herself. What gave him the right to drag her out of the store and shout at her in front of the entire town? What gave him the right to tell her what to do, anyway?

"No. *You* come on, Annie. You're a smart lady." Pete made a tremendous effort to lower his voice, and his words were clipped, spoken through tightly clenched teeth with a quietness that sounded far more dangerous than his outburst. "Nowhere means *no*where. I don't want you stepping outside of the *house* without me, do you understand?"

When he couldn't find her in the house, he had been so scared, he could barely breathe. There was some kind of electric frying pan in the kitchen, and the power had been left on. There was a mixing bowl filled with something on the counter, eggs and flour all over the place. The first thing he thought was that somehow she'd been snatched right out from underneath his nose. Her car keys and purse were missing, but her jacket was right where she'd thrown it last night. He had been damn close to calling the FBI when he found her little scribbled note at the foot of the stairs.

And the fear that had tightened his chest had turned instantly to anger. White-hot, burning, seething anger.

But fear gripped him again as he raced to the grocery store without even taking time to pull on his boots. What if someone had been watching, waiting for the moment when she was alone, unprotected...?

"Aren't you getting a little carried away, Taylor?" Annie said, her own eyes flashing with anger now, her breath making a white mist in the cold air. "I only went to the grocery store, for crying out loud."

She turned on her heel and started toward her car. But Pete caught her arm, spinning her around, hard, to face him.

"What, you think you can't get killed in a grocery store?" he said roughly. "Think again, Annie. I've seen more victims of assassins' bullets than I care to remember—every one of them killed because they were careless, because they didn't think they needed protection while they ran to the bank or the pharmacy. *Or* the grocery store."

She tried to pull free, but his hands were on her shoulders, and he wouldn't let go.

"You can *not* go out by yourself," he said, his eyes burning with intensity as he tried to make her understand how important this was. "Annie, there's someone out there who says that he wants you *dead*." His voice broke with emotion. "Damn it—"

She was staring up at him, her lips slightly parted. Her long hair had come free of its restraint, and it hung down around her face, moving slightly in the chill wind. Pete didn't notice the cold air blowing against the bare muscles of his chest. He was unaware of the cold, sharp pebbles of the parking lot underneath his bootless feet. All he could see, all he could feel, was Annie. He was drowning. Drowning in the shimmering blue ocean of her eyes...

He wasn't sure how it happened, but suddenly she wasn't trying to pull away from him anymore. Suddenly she was in his arms and he was kissing her.

He wasn't supposed to be doing this.

Her lips opened under his, and he plundered the sweetness of her mouth desperately. He wanted more than just a taste, he wanted to consume her, totally, absolutely, utterly.

Her mouth was softer and sweeter than he'd ever dreamed, so soft, yet meeting the fierceness of his kisses with an equally wild hunger. She clung to him, one hand in his hair, pulling his head down toward her, the other up underneath his shirt, exploring his muscular back, driving him insane.

He shouldn't be doing this.

He groaned, pulling her even closer to him, pressing her hips in tightly against him, kissing her harder, deeper, longer. He kissed her with all the frustration, all the pent-up passion of the past few weeks. Man, he'd wanted to kiss this woman since he first set eyes on her from behind the one-way mirror in the airport interrogation room.

He shouldn't be doing this.

She moved, rubbing against his arousal, and he heard himself make a sound—a low, animal-like growl in the back of his throat. Oh, man, he wanted her more than he'd ever wanted anything in his life. He wanted to bury himself deep in her heat, deep inside of her. He wanted to make love to her and never stop, never stop, never...

Stop.

He shouldn't be doing this.

It wasn't right.

He couldn't do this.

Kendall Peterson, a.k.a. Pete Taylor, was a strong man, but he didn't know how strong he was until he pulled away from that kiss.

Annie stared up at him, her eyes molten with desire, her cheeks flushed and her lips swollen from the force of his mouth on hers. He watched her chest rise and fall rapidly with each breath she took, saw the pebbled outline of her taut nipples even underneath the thick material of her sweatshirt.

"Pete," she breathed, reaching for him.

Somehow he kept her at arm's length. "Get in your car," he said hoarsely. "I'll follow you home."

For the hundredth time that afternoon, Annie found herself staring sightlessly at her lab equipment, unable to concentrate. She looked across the room to where Pete was sitting and pretending to read a newspaper. He had to be pretending—he hadn't turned the page in over an hour.

As she watched him, he glanced up, meeting her eyes. His expression was so guarded, he might have been carved from stone. In a flash, she remembered the way his face had looked after he had kissed her. She'd read so many things in his eyes. She'd seen desire, but no, it was more than mere desire. It was hunger—a burning, scorching need. But she'd also seen confusion and uncertainty. And fear.

Annie sighed, glancing over to the other side of the room, where Cara was working. Cara had been in the office when they'd come back from the grocery store.

Pete had just kissed Annie like no other man in her life had ever kissed her, and she had a million things to say to him, only they had no chance to talk, no privacy to continue what they'd started. And she got the feeling that he was relieved about that.

That feeling turned to certainty as the day wore on and Pete made a point to keep Cara around, like a chaperon at a high school dance. And those rare times when Cara was out of the room, he managed to be on the telephone.

Annie restarted the test she was running, a test to check the purity of a bronze knife blade, and sighed again. He'd kissed her, and suddenly it all seemed so clear to her, so obvious. Sure, they were friends. It was true that she liked him on that level. But there was no way she would've reacted the way she had to a kiss from a mere friend. That kiss had been more disturbingly intimate, more earth-shatteringly intoxicating than anything she had ever felt before.

No, there was more than mere friendship here.

Truth was, she was falling in love with this man.

And he was scared to death of her.

Annie looked at Cara across the office. "Well, shoot," she finally said with a smile. "It's about time."

Cara nervously fiddled with the toys on her desk. "It

still seems so sudden to me," she said. "I mean, marriage..."

"MacLeish, you've known the man for three years." Annie shook her head.

"But as friends," Cara said. "We were just friends."

"I can't think of a better way to start," Annie said quietly. "Have you set a wedding date?"

Cara grinned. "Jerry wants us to fly to Las Vegas this weekend."

"Good old Jerry," Annie said, rolling her eyes. "Always the romantic."

They both were quiet for a moment, then Annie asked, "So, are you trying to work up the courage to give me notice?"

Cara looked up, shocked. "No!" she said. "I mean, I don't know.... You know, Jerry's trying to get funding to go to Mexico in February...."

"You're irreplaceable, MacLeish," Annie told her. "But don't worry, somehow I'll muddle through."

"I'll definitely stay until the end of December," Cara said. "Remember, we were going to take January off anyway...."

Annie turned away, not wanting her friend to see the sadness that she knew must be on her face. January was looking to be a very cold, very lonely month, with both MacLeish and Taylor leaving for good.... She managed to smile at Cara as she left the room, though. "Congratulate Tillet for me, will you?"

Chapter 9

From the lab, Annie heard the sound of the door closing as Cara left for the evening. She heard Pete slide the bolt home and turn on the alarm system.

This was it. They were finally alone in the house, just the two of them.

She heard the sound of Pete's cowboy boots on the hardwood floor of the entryway, and her heart went into her throat. Turning, she saw him standing in the doorway. His face was carefully expressionless, but there was a tenseness about the way he was standing, an infinitesimal tightness in his shoulders. He was as nervous as she, Annie realized.

"I'm sending out for a pizza," he said.

It was the first full sentence he'd spoken to her since they'd gotten home from the grocery store, since that kiss.

"Want to split it?" he asked. "There's a place in town that delivers. Tony's. Unless you know someplace better...."

He was trying to pretend nothing had happened, Annie thought. He was standing there talking about the best place in town to get a pizza, when they should have been addressing the fact that that morning he had taken her into his arms and nearly kissed the living daylights out of her.

His casualness didn't come as a surprise—not after the way he'd avoided her all day. He was telling her, not in so many words of course, but he *was* telling her that he regretted the kiss, that it had been a mistake.

Disappointment shot through her, and she turned away, not wanting him to see it in her eyes.

"You know, if you're not done working, I can wait to call," Pete offered. "'Course, it'll be about forty-five minutes before the pizza's delivered even if I call now."

Her composure regained, Annie looked at him. From the tips of his boots to the top of his short, dark hair, the man was extremely easy on the eyes. Faded blue jeans cut loose, but not loose enough to hide the taut muscles of his legs—long, strong legs—stretched way up over narrow hips. His plain brown leather belt with the shining buckle encircled his trim waist. He was wearing a heavy white canvas shirt, the kind with snap fasteners instead of buttons, open at the throat, sleeves rolled up to just below his elbows. He drove his hands deep into the pockets of his jeans, and the tanned, sinewy muscles of his forearms strained the fabric of his shirt. His shoulders were broad, his chest powerful.

And that was just his body.

Inside that perfectly shaped head, behind those intense dark eyes, underneath that thick, black hair, beneath the movie-star features, was a mind and a soul that Annie couldn't help but like, couldn't help but fall in love with.

But he didn't want her. Not the way she wanted him.

If he did, he wouldn't be acting so business-as-usual, would he?

"Pizza sounds great, Taylor," she said, keeping her tone light. "Forty-five minutes'll give me just enough time to finish up in here."

He turned so that his face was in the shadows. "I'll call from the office," he said, and disappeared.

It was clear, Annie thought later as they ate their pizza, that to Pete, the morning's kiss had been an aberration, a slipup, a mistake. Their conversation wasn't as stilted or awkward as Annie had feared it would be, but Pete's face never lost its carefully guarded expression. And his eyes never even once lit with the heat she'd seen that morning—not even when they accidentally collided in the small kitchen as they prepared a salad to go with the pizza. He'd reached out to steady her, and she'd looked up into his face. But his eyes were distant, emotionless.

After dinner, Annie spent several restless hours in her office, putting little more than a small dent in the paperwork that sat on her desk. As she sat there, buried in files, Pete's eyes seemed to haunt her. Even though he wasn't in the room, she could still see his eyes, so detached, almost cold.

Oh, Christmas, she thought suddenly, sitting up straight in her chair. *What if it was me? What if I threw myself at him this morning?*

How exactly had it happened? Who kissed who first? She closed her eyes, trying to think back.

Pete had been so angry, holding her arms tightly enough to bruise her. She'd been trying to pull away from him, hadn't she? But he just held on to her; he wouldn't let go. She remembered staring up at him, intrigued by the sparks of anger that seemed to fly from his eyes, startled by the raw emotion displayed on his face. She remembered seeing the fire in his eyes change to a heat of an entirely different kind. And then she remembered him bending to kiss her.

He kissed her. Yes, she thought with relief, he definitely kissed her. Thank goodness she could remember. It wasn't that she necessarily minded making a fool of herself. But she hated the thought of not being aware she'd made a fool of herself. *That* was too much to take. But it was okay. She *hadn't*—

"You working or sleeping?" Pete's husky voice cut into her thoughts and her eyes flew open. He was leaning in the doorway, with his arms crossed in front of him, watching her.

Annie grinned wryly. "Would you believe neither?" she said.

"It's nearly midnight," he said quietly, his eyes following her movements as she shut off the computer and restacked the files, putting them into her in basket. As she pushed her shining hair back behind one ear. As she unconsciously moistened her lips with the tip of her tongue...

Oh, damn, thought Pete. He'd spent the entire day and evening trying to fool himself into believing he was unaffected by that kiss. He'd tried to ignore the fact that when he kissed her, she'd kissed him, too. She wanted him. Even now, even though she was trying to hide it, he could see it in her eyes.

All he had to do was say the word, and he could have her.

But while making love to her would certainly solve tonight's immediate and pressing problem, it would generate a vast array of other, even more difficult future problems. If he slept with her without telling her who he really was, she would hate him. On the other hand, if he told her who he was *before* he slept with her, she wouldn't sleep with him, *and* she would still probably hate him.

But maybe not as much.

Pete followed Annie up the stairs and checked the windows in the bedroom while she went into the bathroom and got ready for bed.

Maybe if she didn't hate him quite so much, he'd still have a chance....

To what?

To have a future with her?

Ruthlessly, he crushed that thought, pushing it away, out of sight.

Pete refocused his attention on the sound of water running in the bathroom. Annie was brushing her teeth. She'd be out any minute now.

He locked the door to the bedroom and sat down heavily on his bedroll.

Tomorrow would be easier, he thought. All he had to do was get through tonight. He closed his eyes, hoping, praying to whatever gods were listening, that Annie wouldn't try to talk about that kiss.

He'd been waiting for her to say something all through dinner. He'd never even tasted the pizza, he'd been wound so tight. He'd half expected her to reach out for him, to touch him, to try to finish what they'd begun.

Expected? Or hoped?

No, he couldn't hope for it. As much as he wanted to kiss her again, he couldn't even allow that much to happen.

Because if she touched him, she'd know. And how the hell was he going to explain why he wouldn't make love to her when he wanted her so badly, it was making him shake?

The bathroom door opened and Annie came out.

She was wearing her oversize plaid flannel pajamas, and she was brushing her hair.

Pete couldn't watch. He lay back against his pillow and closed his eyes.

It didn't help.

Annie set the brush on her bedside table, the same way she did every night, and turned off the light. She pulled the covers up over her and curled onto her side.

"Good night, Taylor," she whispered, but Pete didn't answer.

For once she could hear his breathing. It was slow and steady, as if he already were asleep.

She sighed, flipping onto her back, trying to get comfortable. She stared up at the dark ceiling, willing herself to relax.

Picture yourself on a tropical beach, she told herself, closing her eyes. Remembering the way Pete had talked her through it just a few nights ago, Annie pictured herself wading out into the warm Pacific Ocean. She imagined the clear water washing all her problems away. She imagined herself coming out of the water, taking off her silly plaid pajamas as she walked up to a beach blanket that had been spread out upon the sand. She imagined Peter Taylor lying on it, as naked as she was. He smiled up at her, reaching for her hand and pulling her down next to him, covering her mouth with his own—

Annie's eyes opened. What the heck was she doing? This was supposed to be a relaxation technique, not self-torture. How could she possibly rub salt into her own wounds by fantasizing about a man whom she *knew* wasn't interested in her?

But...

Annie squinted up through the darkness at the ceiling. Wait a minute.

She didn't really *know* he wasn't interested in her. She was only assuming it. He never actually *said* that he only wanted to be friends. He never actually *said* that he didn't want their relationship to progress any further.

Shoot, she was supposed to be some kind of brilliant scientist, and here she was *assuming* a whole hell of a lot of unproven facts....

"Taylor, you awake?"

The sound of Annie's voice came slicing through the darkness. Pete almost jumped. Almost. Instead he continued to breathe slowly and deeply, pretending to be asleep.

Coward, he silently accused himself.

"Taylor?" she said again. Then, "Pete?"

The sound of her voice saying his first name nearly did him in. But somehow he didn't move, and he didn't answer.

Come on, Annie, he thought. *Roll on over and go to sleep.*

The sheets rustled, but she wasn't pulling them up. She was pushing them back. He heard the sound of her bare feet on the hardwood floor. Oh, damn, she was out of bed. She was walking toward him—

"Pete, wake up," she said, her voice next to him in the darkness.

He opened his eyes to see her crouched down beside him. He could just barely make out her features in the dim light from the windows.

"Go back to bed," he said. But he didn't sound very convincing, even to his own ears.

Annie sat down, cross-legged, next to him. It was obvious that she wasn't planning on going anywhere. At least not real soon. "We have to talk," she said.

Pete pushed himself up so that he was sitting, his bare back against the coolness of the wall, putting several more inches between them. Man, she was still sitting much too close. He could smell her gentle fragrance, see the pulse beating at the delicate juncture of her neck and collarbone. His gaze was drawn to the deep-V neckline of her pajama top. He made himself look away.

"Annie, go back to bed," he said, louder this time. His eyes met hers and locked. "Please," he added, but it was little more than a whisper.

He turned his head away, but not before Annie saw it. It was only a flash, only a glimmer in his dark eyes, but it was there. The same deep hunger she'd seen that morning before he'd kissed her....

"Pete, why did you kiss me?" she asked, her voice husky.

"I shouldn't have," he said. "I was out of line." He braced himself to look up at her, steeling himself to remain expressionless. "I'm sorry."

"But I'm not," she said. She frowned very slightly. "You didn't answer my question. See, I just can't seem to figure out why you'd go and kiss me, and then act like I've got the plague. What's the problem? Are you married?"

"No."

"Involved?"

He was involved more than he wanted to be, and it was getting worse every second. "No. Annie, please—"

"So why did you kiss me, Taylor?"

"Let's just drop this—"

"I don't want to *drop* this," she said fiercely. He was saying one thing with his words, but his eyes were telling her something entirely different. "If there's a problem, tell me what it is. If there's not a problem—'' She waited until he looked up at her. "Kiss me again."

Pete drew in a long, shaky breath. "You don't know me—who I really am," he said, caught in the depths of her eyes.

"I know enough," she said. Her hair was shining in the pale light from the windows, her eyes colorless and mysterious. She reached up to touch the side of his face, but he caught her wrist.

"You wouldn't like me," he rasped.

"Isn't that for me to decide?" Annie asked.

It would have been so easy to kiss her. She was leaning toward him, inviting him....

"I can't get involved with you," he said harshly, releasing her wrist as if it burned him. "It's not possible. It's not smart—"

He saw the flash of hurt in her eyes, and it did him in. "Annie, believe me, I have no choice," he said, his voice gentler. "It's damn near killing me, but I care too much about you to start a relationship that I know won't go anywhere." He reached out, turning her chin so that she looked up at him. "You'll see, it's better if we just stay friends."

This time Annie moved toward him first, thinking that if he still told her he only wanted to be friends after she kissed him, then she'd believe him. So she kissed him.

He groaned, his voice a note of despair, as his lips and then his tongue met hers in a long, deep kiss that sent fire racing through his body.

His arms went around her, pulling her toward him, closer, closer, until she was on his lap, pressed against him, and still that wasn't close enough.

He kissed her, again and again, almost frantically now as his need for her increased with each pounding beat of his heart. She received him feverishly, her hands sweeping down his back, over his chest and arms, as if she couldn't get enough of touching him.

And still he kissed her.

So much for his words. So much for his good intentions.

She was straddling him now, and his hands explored the strong muscles of her thighs. Moving upward, he found the soft flannel edge of her pajama shirt and swept one hand underneath it. Annie shuddered with pleasure as his roughly callused hand caressed her back. His fingers moved down, slipping under the elastic waistband of her pajama pants, stroking the soft, smooth skin of her buttocks.

Slowly, so slowly, he tightened his grip on her, pulling her hips forward until she was positioned directly on top of him. It was exactly what he knew he shouldn't do, but he couldn't seem to stop. It was an invitation, a silent question. Did she want more?

She gave him her answer by pressing herself down against the hardness in his jeans, by moving against him.

Yes, she wanted him.

And despite his resolve, despite knowing that he shouldn't, he was going to take her. He knew now that all along he'd been fooling himself. He had no choice—that much had been true. He was aching for her, dying for her. He reached for her, and she was there, her sweet mouth against his.

You're weak, a small voice in his head accused. But he had to protest. The odds weren't exactly in his favor. It was two against one—his body and her body against his resolve to stay away from her. He didn't stand a chance.

But it wasn't right. She didn't know the truth about him.

He kissed her, determined to ignore the tiny disapproving voice that chastised him. *Don't think,* he told himself. *Don't think....*

Annie pulled her pajama top over her head, and Pete stopped thinking.

In one movement, he flipped them both over, so that he was on top of her. Her blue eyes sparkled as she smiled up at him, and he kissed her again. He started at her mouth and moved down her long, slender neck. He traveled slowly across her collarbone and kissed his way down to her breasts, taking first one and then the other firm nipple into his mouth, caressing it with his tongue until she cried out.

He lifted his head then, gazing down at her. The sparkle in her eyes had been replaced by liquid fire. Man, he'd fantasized about her looking at him like that. He'd fantasized about having sex with her. What he *hadn't* fantasized was that sex with Annie would be the best he'd ever had in his life. But it was. He'd never felt like this before. Never. And he still had his pants on....

She smiled at him again and lifted her mouth to be kissed. He met her lips slowly, a gentle, lingering kiss that grew into an earth-shattering touching of souls.

Suddenly Pete knew what was different. Shaken, he pulled back. He rolled off her and scrambled to his feet.

Annie sat up. "Pete?"

He'd done something really stupid. Outrageously stupid. He ran his fingers through his hair. When had it happened? How could he have let it happen?

"Pete?" Annie said again. She got to her feet and took a tentative step toward him. "Are you all right?"

He'd gone and fallen in love with her.

That's what was so different. Sex with Annie wasn't simply sex, it was making love. Oh, man, he *loved* her....

She took another step toward him, concern on her beautiful face.

He had to get out of here. He had to think. He had to figure out what the hell he was going to do.

"I'm sorry," he whispered to Annie. "I'm—"

He spun on his heels, nearly leaping for the door to the hallway, leaving Annie alone in her bedroom for the first time in a week.

Pete leaned his head back against the wall and stared at the closed door that led to Annie's bedroom. This was crazy. This was ridiculous. He had never even believed in love before. He thought it didn't exist. But all the symptoms were undeniably there. He was in love with Annie, no doubt about it. It felt so much like what was described in all those silly songs he'd scoffed at for so many years, it was almost laughable. Except he didn't feel very much like laughing right now.

For the first time since he was a kid, he knew exactly what he wanted. He wanted Annie. He wanted her to fall in love with him. He wanted a chance at a future together. He wanted...forever.

Forever. Now *there* was a good joke. What were the chances that she'd want to spend forever with him after she found out he was a government agent sent to gather evidence against her?

Pete ran his fingers through his hair for the hundredth time and looked at his watch. Three-fifteen. Man, was this night never going to end?

He swore under his breath, knowing that he was in too deep. He was emotionally involved. He should be on the phone with Whitley Scott right now, making arrangements to be taken off this case.

But if he were removed from the case, who knew who

they'd assign to take his place? What if the replacement agent wasn't able to protect her? There was no way he was going to trust her life to someone else. No way.

He closed his eyes for a moment. Damn, he ached all over.

He put his head in his hands, remembering the look on Annie's face as he bolted for the door. Talk about coitus interruptus, he thought with a strangled groan. She must think he was nuts, the way he jumped up like that, right in the middle of such serious foreplay.

He groaned again. She must not be very happy with him right now. He doubted if Miss Manners had a book on sexual etiquette, but he was willing to bet if she did, she would frown heavily upon a gentleman heating a lady up and then leaving her out in the cold.

But if Pete had made love to Annie, if they'd gone all the way, he'd have blown his chance at a future with her. When she found out he was CIA, she would assume he'd been assigned to seduce the art robbery information out of her. Which he had. Which was why he couldn't... This was *way* too complicated.

Annie woke up to the clock radio, and lay in bed for at least half an hour, listening to the country station and wishing that Pete was lying next to her.

But Pete didn't want her.

A tear slipped out and slid down her cheek, and she wiped it quickly away.

Why hadn't she listened to him? It was the same question that had kept her tossing and turning all night long, and the only answer she could come up with was that she was a fool. He had told her in no uncertain terms that he only wanted to be friends. But no, she had to go and throw herself at him. She had to go and try to show him how wrong he was. But she was the one who had been wrong.

It wasn't fair, but love never was. There was never a guarantee that two people would feel the same way about each other. In fact, it seemed like happy, mutual love was the exception rather than the rule. Why else would there be so many songs about unrequited love? Four out of seven of the country songs she'd heard that morning had that age old "you-don't-love-me-as-much-as-I-love-you" theme.

Another tear escaped, and Annie brushed it away. What was it Cara always said? Look on the bright side.

She stared up at the ceiling, trying to find the bright side as another song started. Look on the bright side, she thought. At least this had happened before she let herself fall in love with him.

But deep down inside, she knew that was a lie.

That night, Pete lay on his bedroll in the dark, waiting for Annie to ask him if he was awake.

The day had seemed endless, with Annie avoiding him when she could and being distantly polite when she couldn't.

He'd apologized, and she'd shrugged it off, telling him to forget it, it was her fault.

Pete frowned. She'd seemed so flip, so casual. Was it possible she didn't care? Was it possible that all she'd wanted was a quick roll in the hay?

No. He'd seen the hurt in her eyes, hurt that she couldn't hide. He closed his eyes, flooded by a wave of shame and remorse. His only comfort was knowing that he would be feeling equal amounts of shame and remorse if he *had* made love to her. Not to mention an additional dose of guilt.

Come on, Annie, he thought, lying there on the floor of her room. *Talk to me.*

But she didn't say a word.

Chapter 10

Cara looked at Annie speculatively. "Why?"

"Does it really matter why?" Annie asked.

"You're asking me to spend all my waking hours over the next three days virtually locked in the lab," Cara said, crossing her arms. "Is it so strange for me to want to know why?"

With a sigh, Annie got up and closed the office door. "If we work overtime, we can get a sample of Marshall's death mask ready to go to the carbon-dating lab by the end of the week. Then it'll only be another week, maybe two before we get the results. *Then* both the death mask *and* the people making those threats will be out of my hair."

"Pete Taylor will be out of your hair, too," Cara commented.

"Yes," Annie agreed. "Taylor, too."

Cara leaned back in her desk chair, eyes narrowing. "I thought you were starting to really like this guy."

"Yeah," Annie said, looking away. "I was."

"So why do you suddenly want to get rid of him?" Cara asked, lazily reaching out to bob the spring-attached head of her Homer Simpson doll. "What happened?"

"Nothing," Annie said.

"What, did he put the moves on you?" Cara asked, grinning. "Did he come on too strong, too fast?"

Annie put her head down on her desk.

"Give the guy a break," Cara said. "You should see the way he looks at you. It's like he's been struck by lightning—"

"He's just embarrassed," Annie said, looking up at Cara, her own cheeks flushing slightly from the memory. "I...well, I sort of...I tried to seduce him. But he just wants to be friends."

"You're kidding," Cara said, looking very shocked. "You mean you...? And he *didn't...?*"

Annie buried her face in her hands. "You got it."

"But I've seen him look at you like he's totally in love with you," Cara protested.

"Well, you're wrong," Annie said sadly. "He's not."

The front doorbell rang, and Pete put down his book. He went out into the foyer, checking the gun in his shoulder holster before opening the door.

Three men stood on the front porch. A van was in the driveway behind them; a colorful sign on the side read Mt. Kisco Security Systems.

"Dr. Morrow?" the older of the three men said.

"No," Pete said.

"We're here to install a burglar alarm," the man said, glancing at his clipboard, checking the address.

"Wait here," Pete said, and closed and locked the door, leaving them outside.

He swore silently to himself as he walked down the hall to Annie's office. This was really going to mess things up. With the system upgraded, he'd have no reason to sleep in Annie's room. And if he didn't sleep in her room, they'd never get back to the same friendly, easy-going relationship they'd had before.

He knocked on the office door.

"Come in," Annie's musical voice called.

He opened the door.

She was sitting at her desk, wearing a long-sleeved, flower-print T-shirt and her faded jeans. Her long hair was pulled back into a ponytail, making her look more like a college coed than a Ph.D. As she looked up at him, there was apprehension on her face.

Pete swore to himself again, but for an entirely different reason. "There are some guys at the door," he managed to say expressionlessly. "From Mt. Kisco Security. Did you call them?"

She stood up. "Yeah," she said. "I thought it would be a good idea to get the new system installed as soon as possible." Her cheeks flushed slightly, but she met his eyes solidly. "I thought it would make it easier...for both of us."

"What kind of system are they going to put in?" Pete asked, following her down the hallway.

He wasn't happy about this. Annie wasn't sure how she knew since his face betrayed nothing. But she did know. "The same kind you wanted that other company to install," she answered. "I wrote down the model number and the manufacturer's name. This company had the equipment in stock, and the manpower to do it today...."

"All right." Pete nodded and turned to open the door.

Later that afternoon, he called Scott to inform him of the setback to the investigation. Scott told Pete to get what he needed, and then get out. When he hung up the phone, Pete cursed softly.

The days sped past with Annie and Cara spending nearly three straight days and nights in the lab. Cara often didn't leave before midnight, and Annie frequently worked until two or two-thirty in the morning.

With the new alarm system installed, Pete slept in the guest bedroom. He moved the bed so that he could clearly see the new secondary burglar alarm control panel that had been installed next to Annie's bedroom door. If he woke up in the night, he could look over across the hall and be reassured. A red light meant the system was on-line and working. Green would mean it had been shut off.

Regardless of the new security system, Pete insisted that both bedroom doors be left open. But despite the fact that Annie was just across the hall, it seemed as if she were miles away.

He was no closer to finding out about her involvement in the art robberies than he'd been before. And he was slowly going crazy, wanting to hold her, wanting to make love to her....

Pete was plagued by the notion that if he *had* made love to her that night, she probably would have opened up to him by now and told him if she was involved in anything illegal. And if he had made love to her, he wouldn't have to face that flash of hurt confusion that even now still sometimes crossed her face. And, if he had made love to her that night, he probably would have made love to her the next night, and the next, and the night after....

Instead, he sat with her as she ate her lunch and dinner, telling her stories about his grandfather, about his childhood. They were pieces of himself he hadn't shared with anyone, secrets he'd kept locked away since Vietnam. In Vietnam, he hadn't talked about himself; he never got personal, he hadn't made friends. In Vietnam, if you made friends, you had to watch those friends die.

And after the war, when he'd joined the agency, he was always on assignment, always undercover. His past was fictional, part of an assigned bio.

Pete Taylor hadn't grown up on a ranch in Colorado. But Kendall Peterson had, and despite knowing better, despite being unable to tell her his real name, Pete wanted Annie to know who he was, who he *really* was.

And he wanted to make her smile again.

On Thursday, the doorbell rang, and Annie peeked through the window to see a stranger on the front porch. She pushed the button on the intercom that had been installed with the new security system and buzzed Pete, who was up in the kitchen.

"Yeah," he said, his voice sounding surprisingly clear over the cheap speaker. "What's up?"

"There's an unidentified male Caucasian outside the door," she reported. "He's approximately forty-five years old, wearing a dark business suit and a black overcoat. He hasn't smiled yet, but he doesn't quite seem the fanged wolfman type...."

The doorbell rang again.

"Just the facts, ma'am," Pete said, coming down the stairs and smiling at her. "No speculation, please."

Annie's heart flipped until she remembered that his smile was only a smile. He wanted to be friends, nothing more. "He *does* look like a thug," she said. "And *that's* a fact."

Pete's tweed jacket had been casually draped over the end of the banister, and he picked it up and slipped it on over his T-shirt, hiding the brown leather straps of his shoulder holster.

"Stay back, okay?" Pete said, and Annie nodded. He pushed the override button that would allow them to open the front door without shutting down the entire system. The light on the control panel still glowed red, but now there was an additional orange light signaling that the front door could be opened without triggering the alarm.

He opened the door. "Can I help you?" he asked the man politely, but with no nonsense in his tone. He adjusted the lapels of his jacket, pulling it back slightly on the left side so that his gun was briefly, but quite clearly revealed. It was no accident, Annie knew.

If the man standing on the porch was at all disturbed by the sight of the gun, he didn't show it. "You must be the butler," he said dryly.

"Something like that," Pete said.

The man held out a business card. "I'm looking for Dr. Anne Morrow," he said. "She at home?"

Pete took the card. He glanced down at it, then handed it back, behind the door, to Annie. "Joseph James," it said. "Antiquities Broker." There was a New York City address and telephone number.

"What's this in reference to?" Pete asked.

"I'm afraid I can discuss that only with Dr. Morrow," James replied smoothly.

Pete's gaze flicked back to James's face. The man's nose was flat, as if it had been broken many times. There were several small scars up by his eyebrows, and a longer one on the left side of his jaw. Antiquities broker and knee breaker, he thought.

"So. May I come in?" James asked.

"No," Pete said pleasantly. "We're not inviting anyone inside these days." He leaned closer and added almost conspiratorially, "We're having a little problem with evil spirits."

"Lookit, I have a business matter to discuss with Dr. Morrow," James said. "So if you don't mind...?"

Pete looked back at Annie, who told him with a shrug that she didn't recognize the name on the card.

"If you want to talk to her, I'm going to have to search you first," Pete explained in that same pleasant tone.

James stared at him. "You're kidding, right?"

Pete stepped out onto the porch, pulling the door most of the way shut behind him. "Hands on the top of your head, legs spread," he said. "Please."

"Lookit," James said. "I'm carrying. But I've got a license, it's legal."

"Hands on your head, legs spread," Pete said again.

James crossed his arms, his patience obviously flagging. "I know you're just doing your job, buddy, but why don't you let it go. I didn't come out here to shoot Dr. Morrow. I came to talk."

"Hands on your—"

"Will you give me a break?" he said. Annoyed, James moved past Pete, reaching for the door.

It happened so fast, Annie realized that if she had blinked she would have missed it. One second James was heading toward the door, and the next, Pete had him backed up against the porch's sturdy wooden pillar, his gun dangerously close to the broker's face, his other arm pressed up under the man's chin. Annie rubbed her neck, remembering how unpleasant that felt.

"Taylor, is everything okay?" she called out, stepping into the doorway.

"Hey, lady," James squeaked. "Call off Fido, will you?"

Pete released James, but still held his gun trained unwaveringly at the center of the man's chest. "Please keep your hands on your head," he said calmly.

"You wanted to talk to me, Mr. James?" Annie asked.

James rested his hands reluctantly on the top of his thinning hair. "This wasn't exactly what I had in mind," he said crossly.

"I'm sorry," Annie apologized. "There've been a number of threats to my life recently. Taylor likes to err on the side of caution."

"Does he do this to all your customers?" James asked. "It must be great for business."

"Please get to the point," Pete said. "Dr. Morrow is very busy."

James gave Pete a black look, then turned toward Annie. "In that case, I'll be as brief as I possibly can. I have a client, Dr. Morrow, who is interested in purchasing the gold death mask owned by one Benjamin Sullivan that is currently in your possession. This client will pay four million, sight unseen, uncertified."

Annie's mouth fell open. "You can't be serious."

"I'm quite serious," James said. "My client is willing to give you a broker's fee of ten percent if you submit this offer to Mr. Sullivan and convince him to sell."

With great difficulty, Annie closed her mouth. "But I haven't authenticated it yet," she said. "It may not be genuine."

"My client wants this artifact, authentic or not," James said. "In fact, my client has a personal relationship with another authenticator, and would prefer that authenticator check the piece out instead of you."

Annie nodded slowly. "What's so special about this death mask?" she asked.

James smiled. Annie was reminded of a shark. "My

client is...shall we say, eccentric? I'm afraid I'm not at liberty to discuss his motives any further.''

"Ten percent of four million, huh?" Annie asked. "I'm assuming the transaction will be legal, with contracts and taxes paid...."

"Of course," James said, sounding affronted.

"Why can't you broker this yourself?" she asked, direct as usual.

James shrugged. "I've tried. Mr. Sullivan won't take my calls."

"What makes you think he'll take mine?"

"My *client* thinks he'll take your call," James said. "I think it's a gamble, just like anything else. Except this is one sweet gamble for you. You stand to lose nothing, or gain four hundred G's."

Annie thought about that for several long moments. "All right," she finally said. "I'll talk to Sullivan, and get back to you."

Annie and Pete watched in silence as Joseph James got into his Cadillac and pulled out of the driveway.

"Four hundred thousand dollars," Annie said wistfully as Pete closed and locked the door, and turned off the override to the alarm. The control panel glowed with a single red light.

"That's a lot of peanut butter and jelly," he said.

She smiled. "I could finance one hell of a field project with that much money," she said, warming to the subject. "I could back Tillet's dig in Mexico. I could cohead the excavation, get my hands dirty for a year or so, learn something new.... Do you know how long it's been since I've been camping?"

Pete shook his head, smiling at her excitement. "No."

"*Too* long," she said with a grin and disappeared into the office.

* * *

Benjamin Sullivan was back in town, and he greeted Annie warmly when he picked up the phone. "You know," he said, in his upper-crust Bostonian accent, "I had dinner with your parents two evenings ago."

"How are they?" Annie asked. "*Where* are they?"

"Fine and Paris." Sullivan chuckled. "I was on a stop-over, they were on their way to Rome. Their book is coming along quite nicely. They've finished a first draft."

"Now *that's* good news," Annie said. She took a deep breath and plunged right in. "Mr. Sullivan—"

"Please, call me Ben," he interrupted. "Mr. Sullivan makes me feel so old, and I'm only in my seventies."

"Okay, Ben." Annie briefly outlined the offer for the death mask.

Ben didn't answer right away. "Well," he finally said. "This is a bit unfortunate, isn't it? The contract with Mr. Marshall has been signed. Even though it's only for a tenth of what the other collector is offering." He sighed. "I suppose we might be able to try to wriggle out of the deal," he said, "but that's just not for me. I guess being honest costs a bit of money, but in the long run, it's worth it. At least I hope it is." The old man laughed, then went on. "Strange, though, that this offer didn't come until now—I had put the word out that the piece was for sale some time ago." He paused for a moment. "No matter. I can't do it."

"I see," Annie said.

Ben chuckled. "You sound disappointed, Annie. What was your take going to be? Ten percent?"

Annie laughed. "Yeah. The money could have come in handy. I have a friend who's looking for funding for a project in Mexico, and ten percent of four million would've been perfect."

"Anyone I know?" Ben asked, interest evident in his voice.

"Do you know Jerry Tillet?" Annie said.

"Haven't met him," Ben said. "But I've heard only good things. Mayan specialist, if I remember correctly."

"That's him. He's found a site that he believes was a major trading center. The dig's scheduled to start in February, if he can find the backing."

"Sounds exciting," Ben said. "I'll have my accountant look into it, see what I can do to help out."

Annie laughed. "Oh, that's terrific."

"I've got to get back to work," he said. "I'm sorry I can't accept Mr. James's client's offer."

"Let me know if you change your mind," Annie said and hung up the phone.

She looked up to find Pete standing in the doorway, watching her. She made a face at him. "Sullivan won't sell," she explained, "but he's thinking about backing Tillet's project, so it wasn't an entire washout."

She shuffled the papers around on her desk, searching for Joseph James's business card. She quickly dialed his number and left a brief message on his answering machine, then tossed the business card into the top drawer of her desk.

Pete came into the office and sat down across from her. Annie looked up to find his dark eyes on her. She couldn't look away, trapped by his gaze. He was looking at her as if he wanted...what? She knew he didn't want her, so what did that heat in his eyes mean? Damn, damn, *damn*—she couldn't figure this guy out for the life of her.

The phone rang, loud and shrill.

Annie jumped. "Excuse me," she said to Pete, then picked up the receiver.

Pete watched her glance up at him, then swivel her chair so that she turned slightly away. "I haven't been avoiding you," he heard her say. She was talking to Nick York. It had to be him. Pete resisted the urge to clench his teeth.

"All right," Annie said, laughter in her voice. "Yeah, you're right. Okay! I give in. I *have* been avoiding you." She paused, then laughed. "Yeah, but if you bring anything with you, it had better be flowers, not some archaeological find you want me to test." She laughed again. "Don't count on it, pal."

Pete stood up, unwilling to listen to Annie being flirted with over the telephone. Particularly not by someone who was probably far better suited for her than he was....

Annie watched Pete leave the room. Before he closed the door, he glanced back at her, briefly meeting her eyes.

It was that look again, Annie realized. He wanted something, and he wanted it badly. Too bad it wasn't her.

Chapter 11

Friday morning dawned bright and clear—a perfect autumn day. Despite working late the night before, Annie woke up early and pulled on her rattiest pair of jeans, an old sleeveless T-shirt and a sweater whose collar was starting to come undone. She rummaged in her closet, searching for a moment before she located several pairs of work gloves.

Whistling, she crossed the hall to Pete's room.

The door was open as usual, but he was still in bed. His hair was getting longer, and it was rumpled. He needed a shave, and his night's growth of beard made him look dangerous, particularly with his shirt off and so much hard muscle showing.

Annie steeled herself against the attraction that threatened to overpower her whenever they were together. She tossed the larger pair of gloves onto his chest.

Pete stared down at them for a moment, then up at

Annie, one eyebrow quirked. "If you're challenging me to a duel," he said, "you missed."

Annie grinned. "It's leaf-raking day," she said.

Pete rolled over to look at his alarm clock. "Didn't we just go to sleep?" he asked.

Annie crossed to the window and pulled up the shade. Sunlight flooded the room. "How can you sleep on a day like today?"

Pete squinted from the brightness. "Leaf-raking day, huh?"

"Hurry up and get dressed," Annie said. "I want to go outside. If we work fast, we can get most of the lawn done before Cara even gets here."

She turned to leave, but Pete's voice stopped her. "Annie."

He was pulling on his jeans, and her eyes were drawn to his hands as he fastened the button and pulled up the zipper. *Oh, Christmas, stare, why don't you,* she chastised herself, feeling her cheeks flush.

"I'm not sure if this is such a good idea," Pete said, gracefully ignoring her discomfort. "You're much safer inside the house. Out in the yard, you're a target. It's harder for me to protect you."

"You know, Taylor," Annie said, "a perfect day like this doesn't come along all that often. I'm sorry, but I can't let it pass me by. I'll wait for you downstairs."

When Cara's car finally pulled into the driveway, Annie and Pete hadn't finished raking half of the big yard. The day was unusually warm, and Annie had long since stripped off her sweater. Even with only her old T-shirt on, she had sweat running down her back and trickling between her breasts.

"Darn," Annie said. "Guess I miscalculated how long this would take."

Pete leaned on his rake and looked at her. It was that look again, Annie thought, nervously tucking a loose strand of hair behind her ear. Why did he watch her that way? With his shirt off, and his upper body glistening with perspiration, she couldn't bear to look at him. Instead, she turned and watched Cara climb out of her car.

"If you promise to keep the alarm on after you go inside," Pete said, "I'll finish up."

"Oh," Annie said, glancing back at him. "No..."

"I don't mind," he insisted. "In fact, it feels good to be out here. But you've got to promise to let the answering machine pick up all the phone calls. And if anything strange happens—anything at all—you call me. Immediately. Is that clear?"

She smiled. "Yeah."

He reached out, and for one heart-stopping moment, Annie thought he was going to touch her, to pull her in close to him. But he only plucked a leaf from her hair and tossed it to the ground. She turned quickly then, and nearly ran back to the house, hoping that he hadn't seen the hope that she knew had briefly flared in her eyes.

She tried to comfort herself by counting the days until the carbon-dating test results on Stands Against the Storm's death mask would come in. Eight more days at the most, maybe even less. Eight more days, and then he would be gone.

Now, why didn't that make her feel any better?

Annie took a gallon of ice tea and a pile of peanut-butter-and-jelly sandwiches out to Pete at lunchtime. She sat and ate with him, then closed her eyes and let the sun warm her face.

She'd showered and changed earlier that morning, and she now wore a bright yellow T-shirt with her jeans. Her hair was down loose around her shoulders, shining as it moved slightly in the gentle breeze.

Pete lay on his back in the grass, pretending to watch the clouds, but in truth watching Annie. Just when he thought he'd memorized every angle and plane of her face, he'd see her in a different light. With her eyes closed, her face held as if in worship up toward the sun, she looked angelic and serene—two characteristics Pete didn't normally associate with Annie Morrow.

He ached from wanting her. But every time Annie called him Taylor, he was slapped in the face with the magnitude of the lies he had told her—was continuing to tell her.

And the worst part of the situation was that he no longer doubted her innocence. Annie Morrow was not involved in an art conspiracy. Pete would bet his life on that. He'd been with her every moment for weeks now, and she'd neither received nor made one single suspicious phone call. No one had tried to contact her any other way. She left her mail opened and out on her desk—there was nothing she was trying to hide.

Except her feelings for him.

Pete knew that it was only a matter of time before he gave in to his own feelings, his own needs. Man, when she looked at him, when he saw that longing in her eyes—

Annie opened her eyes slowly and caught him staring at her.

Embarrassed, she looked away. When she glanced back at him, he'd sat up and was scraping some dirt off the well-worn toes of his cowboy boots.

"I have a date tonight," she said.

His dark eyes flashed toward her, and for an instant, Annie thought she saw surprise on Pete's face. But it was quickly covered up, if it was ever even there.

"Tonight's the fund-raiser at the Museum of Modern Art in the city," Annie said. "All kinds of backers and grants people and just plain rich folk are going to be there." She smiled wryly. "Along with every museum and university and private researcher vying for any extra cash that might be lying around. It'll be a real schmooze-fest."

"Who's the lucky guy?" Pete asked.

Annie looked at him blankly.

"Your date," he said. "Who is he?"

"Nick York," Annie said.

Pete nodded slowly.

Annie fought a wave of disappointment. But what did she expect? she scolded herself. Did she really expect Pete to be jealous? In all likelihood, he was probably relieved. If she was with Nick, she wouldn't be at home, mooning over Pete like a star-struck teenybopper.

"I'd better get back to work," she said, standing up and brushing off the seat of her jeans. She started toward the house.

"Annie."

She stopped, turning slowly back around.

Pete was standing there, looking like an ad for Levi's, with his snug jeans riding low on his hips, and his tan muscles gleaming in the sunshine.

"Thanks for the lunch," he said.

His eyes seemed to drill into her, burning with that same, unmistakable intensity. It was that look again.

Annie shook her head, letting all the air out of her lungs with an exasperated laugh. "Taylor, what do you want from me?"

He blinked. "What?"

"Why do you look at me that way?"

Pete looked down at the ground. "What way?" he

asked, knowing damn well exactly what she was talking about.

"Oh, forget it," she muttered and stalked back to the house.

"Keep the alarm system on," he called after her, and without turning around, she held up one hand, signaling that she'd heard him.

He watched as she went inside, then picked up the rake and went back to work.

What did he want from her?

He should have told her. What would she have said, he wondered, if he'd told her the truth?

At one-thirty in the afternoon, the phone rang. Annie was in the office, and she answered it without thinking, remembering only after she said hello that Pete had told her not to answer the phone.

"Sweet Annie!" came a familiar voice. It was Nick York. "What are you wearing?"

"Jeans," Annie said. "Why?"

"No, not right now, you darling idiot." Nick laughed. "Tonight. What are you wearing tonight?"

Outside the office window, Pete carried a bundle of leaves toward the compost pile. Annie followed him with her eyes, trying not to crane her neck too obviously as he passed out of view. "I don't know," she said. "I haven't thought about it yet."

"Go all out tonight, will you, love?" Nick said. "Wear something tiny, with lots of leg and cleavage. Maybe something blue, to match your eyes. I want 'em drooling."

"And *I* want to preserve my reputation as a legitimate scientist," Annie protested.

"You're the best in your field," Nick murmured.

"Everyone knows that. Promise me you'll wear high heels?"

"I promise I'll wear blue," Annie said. "Tiny or high heels I can't guarantee."

"Fair enough," Nick said cheerfully, "though if you love me, even just the teeniest little bit, you'll wear high heels tonight. I'll pick you up at seven."

Annie hung up the phone, mentally reviewing the clothes that hung in her closet. Blue, she thought. What did she have that was blue? She had a new pair of blue jeans. She snickered, imagining the look on Nick's face if he came to pick her up and she was wearing jeans—and her navy-blue high-top sneakers. *That* would be perfect.

But how often did she get a chance to dress up? She wore jeans all the time.

Outside the window, Pete was almost finished raking the leaves. Annie imagined coming down the stairs, wearing something tiny, with high heels showing off her long legs. She imagined breezing past Pete to kiss Nick fondly on the cheek. She and Nick would get into his sports car and drive off, leaving Pete openmouthed and jealous.

Well, probably not openmouthed, Annie thought. She sighed. And probably not jealous. Pete wouldn't even notice.

She stood up. Pete might not notice what she was wearing, but Nick sure as heck would. And maybe that would give her bruised ego a well-needed boost.

Annie took the stairs up to her apartment two at a time. Somewhere, in the back of her closet, was the perfect little dress for this particular occasion.

The door to her bedroom was closed, and Annie hesitated, her hand on the doorknob. That was funny, she thought. She hadn't closed the door. It had been open a few hours ago when she brought the plates back from lunch....

Maybe Cara had been up here.

She retraced her steps back down the stairs, and went into the lab where Cara was painstakingly cleaning the rust from an ancient iron pot.

"MacLeish, have you been upstairs?" Annie asked.

Cara looked up, thinking for a moment. "Nope," she said. "Not today."

"How about Jerry?" Annie prodded. "When he was here at lunchtime, did he go up?"

"No," Cara said, putting down her brush. "Why? Is something wrong?"

But Annie had already gone into the foyer. She overrode the alarm system, allowing the front door to be opened, and went outside.

Pete was by the toolshed, folding the tarp. He still wasn't wearing his shirt, and he still was gorgeous. He looked up as she approached. "What's the matter?" he asked, dropping the tarp immediately and crossing toward her.

He'd picked up on her tension, Annie realized. His dark eyes raked her face, narrowing slightly, trying to read her mind.

She swallowed, and smiled weakly. "This is probably silly," she said, "but my bedroom door is closed, and I'm sure I left it open. Cara didn't close it, Jerry wasn't even upstairs when he was here, and..." She shrugged. "It was probably just the wind."

Pete looked up at the house, his sharp eyes quickly locating Annie's bedroom. "Your windows are closed," he said. He gave her a quick, fierce smile. "I'm proud of you. You didn't open the door. You came and told me. That was the right thing to do."

He took her by the arm and hustled her around the side of the house to the front door. He had already pulled his gun from its holster in his back pocket, Annie realized, and held it in front of them as they went inside.

Pete looked up the long staircase, then back at Annie. If an intruder was in the house, it didn't necessarily mean he was behind that closed door. She would be safer if she was near him.

"Stay right behind me," he said quietly.

Annie nodded, and Pete started up the stairs. He glanced at her over his shoulder. "Closer," he whispered, reaching back with his left hand to pull her in toward him, almost pressing her against his back.

She put her hand out to keep her nose from bumping into his solid shoulder blades. Her fingers touched the heat of his back and the hard smoothness of skin stretched tightly over his well-defined muscles. She resisted the urge to press her lips against him, to taste the saltiness of his skin with her tongue.

Pete positioned them against the wall next to her door, out of any possible line of fire. Slowly he reached out and turned the doorknob. He gave a push, and the door swung open.

The bedroom was dark inside, all the curtains drawn. There was no sound, no movement.

"I left the shades up after my shower," Annie breathed, her mouth close to Pete's ear.

He nodded once. "Stay back," he whispered, checking his gun, making sure the safety was off.

She caught his arm. "Be careful, Pete," she said softly.

His eyes moved down to her mouth, and for a heart-quickening instant, Annie thought he was going to kiss her. Instead he smiled, touching her cheek briefly with his work-roughened fingers.

Without warning, he leapt in front of the open door. His arms were outstretched, his left hand supporting the gun he held in his right. Startled by his sudden movement, a cloud of bats erupted from Annie's room.

Bats!

Pete swore, ducking as the bats fluttered and screeched around him.

Annie was flat against the wall, panic in her eyes. He grabbed her and pulled her down to the floor, covering her with his body. With one hand he reached out and caught the bottom edge of the door, yanking it shut.

"Cara, close the door to the lab!" he shouted.

He heard the thump of the downstairs door slamming closed, then Cara's voice raised in a plaintive wail, "Oh, yuck, are those *bats* out there?"

There were hundreds of them. They fluttered and swooped, dazed and confused by the bright sunlight.

Pete pulled Annie toward the stairs, half carrying, half dragging her down with him. He had to get her out of there, more than just her fear motivating him. Bats carried rabies. He couldn't let her get bitten, but there were so many of them, and they were *every*where....

He pulled her toward the front door, pulling it open. As if sensing the freedom, a bevy of the bats rushed toward the open door.

Annie ducked, desperately trying to get out of their way. But she wasn't quick enough. Its radar off kilter, one of the bats swooped too low.

Annie felt the tug as the bat became entangled in her hair. Panic engulfed her, and she swatted at it, breaking free from Pete and running for the open air of the front yard. The bat struggled, equally frightened, but only became more firmly ensnarled.

"Pete!" Annie screamed, and he was instantly at her

side. His strong fingers plucked the bat from her hair, throwing it onto the ground. Rabies, he thought. What if the bat had rabies? He crushed it with the heel of his boot.

Annie's knees buckled. But Pete's arms were around her, holding her. Gently he lowered them both down, so that he was sitting on the ground with Annie on his lap. He could feel her trembling as she clung tightly to his neck.

He held her close for several long minutes, until he felt her heartbeat start to slow. Then gently he tried to pry her fingers loose. But she wouldn't let go of him. "Come on, sweetheart," he murmured. "I've got to make sure it didn't bite you."

Annie released him and sat quietly with her eyes closed, letting Pete run his fingers through her hair, meticulously checking every square millimeter of her scalp and neck.

By the time he was done, the paramedics Cara had called had arrived, followed closely by the police and a fire truck. The FBI even pulled up, glaringly obvious in their big, unmarked car and dark suits. Last but not least to make the scene was a pest control van. As the paramedics checked Annie, a man and a woman dressed in sturdy protective gear went into the house and rounded up the rest of the bats. Pete pulled on the T-shirt he had discarded on the lawn while he was working.

The police bagged the dead bat that had been in Annie's hair, to send it to the county lab to test for rabies. As far as anyone could tell, Annie hadn't been bitten. But if the bat turned out to be rabid, the police officer told her, she'd probably still want to look into having a series of rabies shots—better safe than sorry.

It was after five by the time the pest control folks finished locating and removing all the stray bats. By then the burglar alarm company van had appeared in the driveway. The same man who had installed the system was in the foyer, deep in argument with Pete, insisting that if the motion detectors had been operational and on-line, there was simply no way an intruder could have gotten into the house without triggering the alarm.

"Maybe the bats made their way into the house through a hole in the roof," Annie heard the alarm specialist suggest as she approached the two men.

"Did they also close my bedroom door and pull down the shades?" she asked tartly.

Pete glanced at her. Her face was still a shade or two too pale, but she'd bounced almost all the way back, and the fire had returned to her eyes.

"The system was on all day," Pete added, crossing his arms as he brought his attention back to the man. "Occasionally we bypassed the front door, but I was in sight of that door each time, and believe me, no one unauthorized entered or exited that way."

The alarm specialist shrugged. "I'll check the system again," he said, returning to the control panel.

Pete turned to Annie. "I'm so sorry about this," he said, emotion in his voice.

"I have to wash my hair," she said, then shuddered. "Lord, I hate bats."

Pete's face darkened. "*I* hate knowing that someone was in here with you while I was out in the yard." He rubbed his forehead, then ran his hand through his hair as if he had a headache. "If they'd wanted to kill you," he said, his voice harsh, "they could've. And I wouldn't have been able to do a damned thing. Annie, I wouldn't have even *known*."

She put her hand on his arm. "It didn't happen," she said. "It's all right."

"It's *not* all right," Pete said. He looked down at her

hand, her fingers pale and smooth against his tanned skin. He took a step back, and her hand fell away from him. "We can't stay here tonight. It's not safe."

"It was a prank," she protested. "They only wanted to scare me." She smiled ruefully. "They succeeded."

"If they got in once, they can get in again," Pete said.

"You said yourself that if they wanted to kill me, they could've," Annie said. "Obviously, they don't want to."

"Yet." Pete shook his head. "I'm authorizing a further upgrade of your security system. Until it's installed, we're not going to stay here. We're going to a hotel. I've already talked to the FBI team about additional protection."

Annie crossed her arms. "What about the artifacts? I've got over two million dollars' worth of antiquities in my safe. I'm not just going to leave them here."

"I'll post a guard," Pete said. "Round-the-clock, outside the house. I've also made arrangements to have all your locks changed."

Annie stared at him. "Did it occur to you to ask me if I *wanted* my locks changed?" she asked, annoyance in her voice. This was just too much....

"I assumed you'd want to stay alive," Pete said.

Annie glanced at her watch. It was nearly six o'clock. She had only an hour to get all these people out of her house, shower and change. "Where's Cara?" she said suddenly, noticing that the front lab was empty.

"She's in the office, being questioned by the FBI," Pete said.

"Questioned?"

"She's a suspect, Annie," he said. "She and Tillet are the only ones who have keys to this house besides you and me. If Tillet's as desperate for money as he says he is—"

Annie's eyes were shooting fire. She took an angry step

toward him. "You go in there," she said, "and you tell them that Cara is *not* a suspect."

Pete held up his hands as if to placate her. It didn't work. "Annie, you've got to admit, Cara had access to your bedroom all day. There's no proof that she's not somehow involved—"

"I don't need proof," Annie said hotly. "Now, are you going to tell them to stop harassing her, or am I?"

Before Pete had a chance to reply, the office door opened, and Cara came out, looking dazed.

"Are you okay?" Annie asked, her eyes filled with concern for her friend.

Cara's lower lip trembled. "Annie, *you* don't think I had anything to do with putting those bats in your room, do you?"

"I know you didn't, MacLeish," Annie said, forcing herself to make light. "I just can't picture you handling two hundred bats."

"Yuck," Cara said, smiling shakily.

"I'm giving you two weeks' paid vacation," Annie said.

Cara frowned. "You can't afford that right now—"

"Courtesy of Mr. Marshall," Annie said with a grin. Her smile faded. "MacLeish, I'm not going to let you get blamed for everything that goes wrong around here. Do us both a favor. Leave tonight and don't come back for two weeks."

"I'll feel like I'm deserting you," Cara protested.

"You're not," Annie said. "I'll see you at the museum tonight, all right?"

"What?" Pete asked.

"Oh, no, look at the time," Cara said. "I should've been home an hour ago. Jerry wanted to get there early...." She hugged Annie. "See you later."

Pete's jaw tightened as he watched Cara let herself out of the house. He turned to Annie. "You're not going to that fund-raiser."

Annie raised her chin. "Oh, yes, I am."

Pete ran both hands down his face, and took a deep breath, trying to calm himself. "Annie." He shook his head. "We're both exhausted. This isn't the best time to go out into a crowd. It's too dangerous."

Maybe if he had talked to her before changing the locks, maybe if he had stood up for Cara, maybe then she would have agreed with him. She *was* exhausted. But she was angry—angry that things had gotten out of control, angry that her life seemed to be no longer her own, angry at Pete...

"I've got a date," Annie said coolly. "I've got to go get ready."

She started up the stairs. When she reached the top, she turned and looked back at Pete. He was standing where she had left him, looking up at her. His jeans were dirty, his T-shirt was stained with sweat and grass and he hadn't shaved or showered all day. "Please tell the FBI agents to leave," she said. "I don't want them here when Nick shows up."

Annie was putting on her stockings when she heard a soft knock at her bedroom door. She slipped into her bathrobe and opened the door. Pete stood in the hall.

"York's here," he said expressionlessly. "He's waiting in the living room."

Annie nodded, unable to meet his eyes. "Thanks."

She started to close the door, but he stopped it with his hand. "I'm going to take a shower," Pete said. "Don't leave without me."

Annie crossed her arms. "Taylor, I'm going on a date.

Somehow I don't think Nick's going to appreciate it if you tag along."

Pete smiled, and Annie had to look away. "Understandable," he said, watching her study the floorboards. "But I'm going to protect you. From Nick York, at the very least."

Annie looked up sharply. "What if I don't *want* to be protected from Nick?"

Pete didn't say anything; he just looked at her. "Don't forget to pack a change of clothes," he finally said. "We might as well spend the night at a hotel in the city."

Annie felt a stab of annoyance. "What if I decide to go home with Nick?" she said, then instantly regretted saying it.

Pete looked stunned. He covered it almost immediately, but he couldn't hide the hurt that lingered in his eyes. "I'm sorry," he said. He shook his head. "I...didn't know you and York were..."

"No," Annie said quickly. "We're...*not*. I don't know why I said that. It was stupid. I—" She looked away from him, embarrassed. "I was just trying to make you jealous," she admitted in a low voice. "I'm sorry."

"It worked," he said.

She met his eyes, and shook her head. "I still don't know what you want from me, Pete. It would've been really nice if things had worked out between us, but, look, they didn't, and tonight I'm going out with Nick. If you've got to come along, be inconspicuous, okay? Do you have something to wear? This is a formal event...."

"I can handle it," Pete said, releasing the door.

Great, thought Annie, closing the door tightly. *But can I?*

Chapter 12

It was twenty after seven before Annie, walking carefully in her high heels, went into her living room.

Nick, resplendent in his tux and black tie, got to his feet. The gleam in his blue eyes was almost as bright as the light reflecting off his golden hair as he came toward her, arms outstretched. He kissed her, first on one cheek, and then on the other, before he nuzzled her neck.

"Perfect," he said, his quick grin showing off a white flash of teeth. "I couldn't have dreamed up a better dress. You look good enough to devour, sweet Annie. All of New York City will be salivating. I love it when you wear your hair up, darling—you look like a little girl playing dress-up."

Pete stood quietly in the doorway, looking at Annie. York was right, he realized. With her hair elegantly swept up off her neck, with those wispy bangs in the front, with her wide blue eyes and generous mouth, Annie actually looked younger than when she wore her hair down. But her dress revealed a body that was all grown-up. It was blue velvet with an off-the-shoulder neckline that plunged down between her breasts. Short stand-away sleeves further framed her long neck and smooth shoulders. The bodice of the dress was tightly fitted, sweeping down into a short skirt that hugged her every curve. Sheer stockings covered elegantly shaped legs that went on and on and on, tucked into a pair of black-velvet high-heeled pumps. Her only jewelry was a pair of dangling coin-silver earrings. They were Navaho, Pete noticed.

"Hel-lo." Nick had spotted him. "Who's this?"

Annie's eyes widened at the sight of Pete. His tuxedo was perfectly tailored, fitting his trim body exactly. With his hair slicked back and his cheeks freshly shaven, the only similarity between him and the dangerous-looking man who'd so recently raked her yard without a shirt was his dark, glittering eyes.

Pete couldn't help himself. Involuntarily, his gaze swept down and then back up her body, lingering on her long legs and the soft, exposed tops of her breasts and throat. His eyes met hers, and he knew from the look on her face that he wasn't able to hide his desire, his need from her any longer. Hell, he'd given himself away. Turning, he tore his gaze away from her, staring blindly down at the Persian rug that covered the floor.

Annie had to work to catch her breath, wondering if she'd only imagined the raw desire she'd seen in Pete's eyes. But no, she knew what she had seen. She just couldn't begin to explain it.

"Nick, this is Pete Taylor," Annie said, trying to cover her sudden breathlessness. "He let you in, remember? Pete, Dr. Nicholas York."

The two men shook hands. Annie could see Pete quietly

sizing Nick up. Nick was a little less subtle, giving Pete an obvious once-over.

"I thought you were the gardener," Nick said. "Apparently I was mistaken." He turned to Annie. "Darling, you didn't tell me you'd gotten a new research assistant."

"Taylor's my bodyguard," Annie explained.

"A bodyguard," Nick said, turning to look at Pete again. "You're kidding."

"Annie's been getting death threats," Pete said, his gentle Western drawl a sharp contrast to Nick's clipped English accent. His eyes met Annie's again for only the briefest of instances before he looked away.

"*Annie* has, has she?" Nick said, exaggerating Pete's use of her first name. He looked at Annie. "You know, that's the problem with you Americans. You're so focused on equality, you let the servants call you by your first names." He turned back to Pete. "Take the night off, old boy. I can protect her just as well as you can. Better, no doubt—my IQ's probably twice as high as yours."

"Don't be a jerk, Nick," Annie said sharply.

Nick put his arms around her waist, pulling her in close to him. "I had a *very* romantic evening planned," he whispered. "I intended to seduce you in the back of the limo on the way into the city."

Pete clenched his teeth. It wasn't hard to squelch the urge to grab Nick York by the front of his white tuxedo shirt and rearrange his perfect, golden-tanned features, but the fact that Pete had had the urge in the first place was alarming. Pete had no claim on Annie. He'd had his chance, but he'd declined, he'd passed, and now, God help him, he had no right to do or say anything at all.

"A *limo?*" Annie said, pulling away from Nick.

Nick grinned. "I'm in desperate need of funding," he said. "Down to my last nickels and dimes. But there's going to be quite a bit of money floating around tonight. And I figured, people like to back a winner, right? And winners arrive in limos. Speaking of arriving, we should get going. We don't want to miss the buffet—it may be my one square meal all week.''

"I'll be right there. I just want to check to make sure everything's locked up.'' Annie headed down to the lab with Pete and Nick trailing after her.

As Nick went toward the front door, Annie went into the office and turned off the lights. She then checked the lab. The instruments were put away, the sinks were clean, the counters were cleared off. Everything was in order, the safe was securely locked. She turned back to the door, coming face-to-face with Pete.

Their eyes met and again she saw heat. This time he didn't look away.

"You look beautiful,'' he said softly.

Annie stared up at him, hypnotized by the look in his eyes. "Thank you,'' she murmured.

Pete couldn't stop himself. He took a step toward her, and another step. As he watched, she nervously moistened her lips, and he felt desire slice through him, hot and sharp and very painful.

God help him, he had to kiss her—

Nick's voice floated in from outside. "Darling, I hate to be a nag, but we really must be on our way.''

Pete turned abruptly away, nearly consumed by a wave of anger and frustration. He wasn't sure who he was angrier at—York, for interrupting them, or himself for nearly giving in to his weakness.

Annie turned off the lights in the lab, then hurried past Pete, heading out the door.

"Ready then, are we?'' Nick smiled, taking her arm and leading her toward the waiting limo.

Pete carried out Annie's overnight bag and his backpack and put them in the trunk. He was about to join Annie in the main body of the car when Nick stopped him.

"Servants go up front," Nick said, his eyes cool. "You can sit with the driver."

Pete kept his expression carefully neutral. "Not this time," he said and climbed into the back. He sat down across from Annie, sinking into the soft leather seat.

As Nick climbed in beside Annie and the limo rolled slowly out of the driveway, Pete stared out the window, steeling himself for the long night ahead. He could feel Annie's eyes watching him. Her confusion was nearly palpable, and he knew he shouldn't look into her eyes again—it would only make things worse.

But he couldn't help himself. He looked up. He'd meant only to glance in Annie's direction, but her gaze caught and held him.

As he stared into the bottomless blue depths of her eyes, he knew for damn certain he was out of control.

Inside the Museum of Modern Art, the party was in full swing. An orchestra played music in the main lobby, and people were dancing. A buffet table had been set up, and it was loaded with wonderfully aromatic food.

Pete left Annie's jacket and their two bags at the coat check, keeping a careful eye on her the entire time.

Nick had whisked her out onto the dance floor where they moved gracefully to an old song. "Stardust," Pete thought. It was called "Stardust." He moved to the edge of the crowd, where he could see Annie and Nick clearly.

Annie stood out in the crowd. With her gleaming hair, her long, graceful neck, those creamy white shoulders contrasted by the deep blue of the dress... She looked as if she belonged here, amid the glitter of New York society. And Nick York looked as if he belonged at her side.

Pete watched York bend down and say something in Annie's ear. She smiled distractedly. She was looking around, searching the crowd.... Her eyes landed on Pete, and he realized with a sudden breathlessness that she'd been looking for him.

Even across the room, the charge that their locked gaze generated seemed to spark and crackle with heat. But then York spun Annie around, turning her so that her back was to Pete.

Pete took a deep breath and glanced around the room, looking for any sign of trouble, anything out of the ordinary. It wouldn't be too difficult in a crowd like this for an assassin to get up close and do some real damage with a knife. One quick thrust, and the victim wouldn't even fall, held up by the crush of people. Man, what he wouldn't give to be next to Annie, to be able to shield her with his own body. What he wouldn't give to be able to dance with her, to hold her in his arms....

The orchestra ended the song, and the dancers applauded. Pete watched York lean close to Annie's ear again and gesture toward the food.

Annie let Nick lead her by the hand to the buffet table. She glanced back through the crowd to where she'd last seen Pete, but he was gone.

He'd been standing there through the entire dance, watching her, looking at her the way he had back at the house, and for most of the limo ride. What was going on? By running out of her room that night, Pete couldn't have told her any more clearly that he didn't want her. So why was he suddenly looking at her as if he did? Was this some kind of macho possessive thing? Annie wondered, frowning slightly. Maybe even though Pete didn't want her, he simply didn't want Nick to have her, either. Or maybe he just liked the idea of jerking her around. Maybe he liked having her panting after him. Maybe—

Pete was standing by the buffet table, looking at her as if *she* were the main course. His dark eyes swept her face, lingering on her mouth a heartbeat or two longer than necessary. Silently, he offered her a plate, but she shook her head.

"No, thank you," she said. "I'm not very hungry."

Through the throng of party-goers, she spotted Jerry Tillet. "Excuse me," she murmured to Nick, and slipped her hand out from his arm. As she approached Tillet, she saw that he was talking earnestly to a tall, broad-shouldered man who was wearing a cowboy hat. It wasn't until she was closer that she realized it was none other than Steven Marshall—the buyer of Stands Against the Storm's death mask, and Pete's employer. She greeted both men with a smile.

"Dr. Tillet, I didn't realize you knew Mr. Marshall," she said.

Despite his smile, Jerry looked uncomfortable. "Yeah, well," he said, "in this business, everyone knows everyone else. You know how it is...."

Marshall shook Annie's hand, then brought it up to his lips. "How's it goin', darlin'?" he asked. "Everything okay?"

Annie extracted her fingers from his grip. "To be perfectly honest, things are getting a little out of hand."

Marshall's light brown eyes sparkled in amusement. "Dr. Tillet told me about the bats," he said. "That musta really shook things up."

A waiter with a tray of champagne glasses passed, and Marshall deftly removed two, handing one to Annie with a flourish. She took a sip, glancing around the room—and directly into Pete's eyes. He stood about fifteen feet away, leaning against the wall, watching her. Deliberately, she turned her back to him.

"I bumped the death mask up on my list," Annie told Marshall. "I should be getting carbon-dating results back any day now."

Marshall's smile broadened. "Well, all right," he said. "Your rainy day makes my garden grow. But that's the way life is, isn't it?"

"Yeah, that's life," Annie agreed.

Tillet looked positively antsy, and Annie realized she'd broken into the conversation before he'd had a chance to hit Marshall up for funding. "Has Dr. Tillet told you about his latest Mayan project?" she asked him. "It's fascinating."

With a grateful smile, Tillet launched into his well-rehearsed patter. Annie had heard it too many times before, so she let her attention wander, sipping her champagne and looking around the room.

Pete Taylor had moved, planting himself once again directly in her line of sight.

Annie tried to stare him down, but the heat in his eyes only intensified. *It's a mind game,* she told herself. *He's just toying with me.* She held on to her anger, trying not to give in to the molten feeling of desire that was forming in the pit of her stomach.

She turned away abruptly, heading back to the buffet table in search of Nick and safety. She had to laugh at the thought of that. Nick would be highly offended to find out she considered him safe.

But he was deep in conversation with three wealthy-looking women, no doubt trying to charm them into making a sizable donation to the Nick York fund.

Annie frowned down at the table that held the food, wishing that she had stayed home, thinking sourly about the way her colleagues had to scrape and grovel for money to support their scientific research. Ever since government funding had virtually disappeared, brilliant scientists were forced to spend nearly all their free time begging and scratching for money to keep their projects alive. And not just their free time, Annie realized, but also much of the valuable time they should have been spending doing research.

Still frowning, she stabbed a black olive with a toothpick, popped it into her mouth and turned away from the table.

"Don't tell me that's all you're going to eat."

Startled, Annie looked up, directly into Pete's obsidian eyes. He was standing much too close, only inches from her.

She backed away. "You're not being very inconspicuous," she accused him.

He moved closer. "Do you want me to get you a plate?" he asked. "There are some tables free, if you want to sit down."

Annie was staring up at him, an odd mixture of disbelief and longing on her face. Still, he moved toward her, stopping when there was only a hint of space between them. If she took a deep breath, he realized, her breasts would brush his chest.

"Pete, why are you doing this?" she asked softly.

It was a good question. Why *was* he doing this? He knew damn well that if he made love to her tonight, the way he wanted to, he would be risking everything. For one brief moment, he thought crazily, fleetingly, of taking Annie and running away. They could leave the country, leave behind the art conspiracy charges, leave behind

Captain Kendall Peterson. He could spend the rest of his life as Pete Taylor. Annie would never have to know; he would never have to tell her who he really was, tell her that he'd lied to her.

"What do you want from me?" she whispered.

"Dance with me, Annie," he said, his voice husky.

Annie felt her throat tighten, and she steeled herself, ordering herself not to cry. "Don't do this," she said, her voice shaking slightly despite her attempts to keep it steady. "Don't play with my feelings, Taylor. You know full well that I..." She closed her eyes, and took a deep breath. "...want you. There. I admitted it. You win. Now leave me alone."

She turned, nearly diving for the other side of the room. She could feel the sting of unshed tears on the backs of her eyelids, but she forced herself to smile brightly at the faces she recognized in the crowd. How she wanted to go home. But home was off-limits, unsafe until a new, more elaborate security system could be installed.

She caught sight of the bar, stretching across one entire end of the gaudily decorated lobby, and headed for it. She'd get a tall, cool glass of seltzer, then hunt for Cara. They could hang out in the ladies' room together, away from Pete Taylor....

"Dr. Morrow! What a pleasant surprise!"

Annie turned to find a small man with brown wavy hair standing before her. He wore a thick gold chain around his wrist and a white carnation in the lapel of his tux. It was Alistair Golden, her chief competitor.

"Dr. Golden," she said, taking the hand he had extended.

"How's work?" he asked, his startling green eyes probing.

Talking to this man was a lot like being interrogated,

Annie thought. It wasn't his words, but rather the penetrating way he had of staring. He reminded her of a frog eyeing a fly it was going to eat for dinner. And she was the fly.

"Fine," she lied. "And how are things with you?"

"Fine," he said, and she wondered if he was lying, too. "I heard you're having some security problems lately. Something about...evil spirits?"

"News does travel," Annie murmured, looking longingly at the bar.

The man's gaze focused over Annie's right shoulder, and she turned to find Pete standing there.

"I don't believe we've met," Dr. Golden said.

"Dr. Alistair Golden, Pete Taylor," Annie said briefly. The two men shook hands.

"Taylor works for me," she said, intentionally labeling him as mere hired help. "He's a security guard." She didn't call him a bodyguard, not wanting to make their relationship even that personal. "Excuse me," she added, taking the opportunity to escape both from Golden's inquisitive eyes and Pete's presence.

She was still twenty feet from the bar when a hand caught her arm. She froze, knowing without turning around that it was Pete.

"Annie, we have to talk," he said, his soft drawl somehow cutting through the noise of a thousand people talking and laughing, through the sound of a twenty-piece orchestra playing an old romantic song.

She turned, then. "No, we don't," she said. "Give me a break, Taylor. Please? I don't feel like talking."

"Then dance with me."

Her eyes flashed with anger. "Read my lips, pal. No. Get it? *No*—"

She turned away, but he caught her wrist and pulled

her back. "Then *listen* to me," he said. "You don't have to talk, you don't have to say anything."

"I don't want to listen—"

"Annie, have mercy on me—"

"Sweet Annie!" Nick York bounded up, startling them both. "They're playing our song!"

Nick pulled her out onto the dance floor and wrapped his arms around her. Annie looked over his shoulder. She could see Pete shake his head slightly with frustration. When he looked up and met her eyes, Annie caught her breath, recognizing that same look, the one that had been confusing her for weeks now.

Why now, out of the blue like this, did Pete suddenly want to dance with her? It didn't make sense. *None* of this made any sense at all.

A wave of fatigue washed over her and she stumbled. Only Nick's arms around her kept her from falling.

"Nick, I'm exhausted," she said, looking up into her friend's eyes. "I'd like to leave."

"Shall I call you a cab?" he asked, then, realizing how callous he sounded, added, "I can't leave now, Annie." His eyes were serious and he actually had the decency to look ashamed. "I'm sorry, darling, but I've got a few leads on some backers and—"

"It's all right," she said. And it was. She hadn't really expected Nick to leave this party three hours early. She'd hoped, but not expected. "I'll get a cab my—"

"Oh, Lord, there's Mr. and Mrs. Hampton-Hayes," Nick said. "And they're heading for the door. Annie, they're richer than God and I've *got* to talk to them. Call me, darling."

He was gone, leaving her standing alone in the midst of all the dancers. Good old Nick. If there was one thing you could count on, it was that you couldn't count on him.

"I was going to ask if I could cut in, but it looks like your partner already cut out."

Pete.

Annie turned to find him standing behind her, and before she could say anything, before she could move, he'd taken her into his arms.

It was heaven.

He held her so close, she could feel his heart beating. His arms were strong, yet he held her gently, one hand at her waist, the other holding her hand.

Annie closed her eyes, leaning against him. This had to be a dream. Certainly she'd dreamed about Pete holding her like this often enough. In a heartbeat, all her resistance had vanished. She pulled her hand free and slipped it up around his neck, pulling him even closer, running her fingers through the softness of his hair.

His arms tightened around her waist, and she looked up to see desire growing in his eyes. He slid one hand up to the deep-V back of her dress, letting his fingers trail lightly across her bare skin, up to her smooth shoulders, and back down again.

Pete felt, more than heard, the small sound she made as he touched her, and it was almost too much for him to take.

"Annie," he breathed. "Annie..."

He'd lost his mind—there was no doubt about it. He'd told her that they had to talk, but really, what was he going to say to her? He couldn't tell her he was CIA; he couldn't do that.

He could tell her that he loved her.

He could pray that she loved him, too—enough to forgive him for all the lies, all the half-truths, all the deception.

His thighs pressed against her as they rocked back and forth, pretending to dance, and Annie looked up at him again, losing herself in the bottomless depths of his eyes.

Why didn't he kiss her?

She couldn't stand it another second. Standing on her toes, she pulled his head toward her and brushed his lips with hers. "Kiss me, Taylor," she said, her lips parted invitingly.

He gave a sound that was half like a laugh, half like a groan. "I can't."

She pulled back, as far as she could with his arms still around her. "Why not?"

Pete could see frustration in her eyes, frustration and questions and a shadow of hurt. She didn't understand. She thought he didn't want to kiss her. Man, if she only knew...

He reached up and touched the side of her face, gently tracing her lips with his thumb. "Annie, I want to," he said softly. "But I'm supposed to be protecting you. How can I watch for trouble if I'm kissing you?"

He could feel her trembling in his arms. "Kiss me with your eyes open."

"Not a chance." Pete shook his head. "When I kiss you, I'm going to do it right."

Their eyes locked and for several long seconds, Annie couldn't breathe. *Why now?* The question kept popping into her head. He'd run away from her the night she'd offered herself to him. He could have had her, but he'd turned her down. So why did he want her now?

Don't think, she ordered herself. *Don't wonder, don't ask questions, don't ruin this. And maybe whatever 'this' is could last forever....*

She nervously wet her lips. "If you won't kiss me with your eyes open, then we should go someplace you feel is safe enough to close your eyes."

His fingers were at the nape of her neck, gently stroking her soft skin. "That sounds like a great idea to me," he said.

He took Annie's hand and led her off the dance floor, knowing full well that leaving the lights and the crowd was a mistake. Tonight they would share a hotel room, and unless he got a sudden burst of self-control, he'd share her bed.

Pete looked at the woman following him, looked at her soft, smooth skin, her beautiful face, her blue eyes, so wide and trusting— He swore, silently, harshly, knowing his self-control was long gone, and praying she'd forgive him when she found out the truth.

Chapter 13

The city streets were crowded even though the night air was cold.

Pete had his backpack and Annie's overnight bag slung over his right shoulder. His other arm was wrapped tightly around her shoulders. She looked up at him and tried to smile. Pete realized she was as nervous as he was.

"Where are we going?" she asked.

"I know a place over on the west side," he said, looking casually over his shoulder. But his eyes were sharp, his swift gaze missing no detail of the people and cars around them.

"Are we going to walk? Usually I don't mind walking. It's just these shoes aren't exactly cut out for— Hey!"

In a flash, Pete scooped her up in his arms.

"I was thinking more along the lines of a cab," she said, looping her arms around his neck. "But this is nice." She closed her eyes, leaning her head against his shoulder. "Yeah, I could get real used to this."

"We're going to get a cab," Pete said, carrying her across the street. "I didn't want to find one too close to the museum. We'll be harder to trace this way."

He gently set Annie down on the sidewalk, but she kept her arms around his neck. "I feel very safe," she said. "Are you sure you can't kiss me yet?"

"Definitely not yet." He glanced down at her, a smile softening the lines of his face. "I feel like we're targets at a shooting range. If I kiss you now, it would have to be over quick," he said, looking boldly into her sweet blue eyes. "And, Annie, when I finally do kiss you, it's going to last a long, long time."

Annie smiled. "I like the sound of that, Taylor."

Taylor. Right. Pete had to look away. Would she still smile at him that way after he told her who he really was, and why he'd been sent to play the part of her bodyguard? *Please,* he prayed to his vast collection of deities. *Please let her forgive me....*

When he glanced back, she was still smiling at him. "Think maybe it'll be safe enough in the cab for you to kiss me?" she asked softly.

Pete's arms went around her, and he pulled her in tightly. "It better be," he murmured into her soft hair.

He reluctantly detached Annie's hands from his neck and stepped toward the curb. Down the block, the light turned green, and a wall of headlights approached. They were too far away for Pete to distinguish the cabs from the regular vehicles, but there was one car traveling faster than the others. It moved to the right lane, as if the driver had spotted them. Pete lifted his hand, signaling that they needed a cab.

He saw that there was no taxi roof light at the same instant that he realized the car was speeding up, not slowing down. Something was wrong. Something was really wrong....

He turned, and fear hit him like a solid punch to the gut. Annie wasn't next to him! God, where was she?

Searching wildly, he spotted her several yards away, leaning against an open-air telephone booth. She stood on one foot, serenely unaware of any danger. Her shoe was in her hand as she gracefully bent her leg to examine a rubbed spot on her heel.

Pete dropped her overnight bag, and went for Annie at a dead run, catching her around the waist as the speeding car jumped the curb and came onto the sidewalk. Around him, everything switched into slow motion. Out of the corner of his eye, he could see the startled look on Annie's face, and her shoe pinwheeling from her hand. There was a storefront ahead of him, with a door set back from the sidewalk. If he could make it there, they'd be safe. But the distance he'd have to cross, the actual sidewalk itself, seemed to stretch, to lengthen into an impossibly unattainable goal.

As the car came closer, he could see the face of the driver. The man's teeth were bared in a grimace of concentrated rage; his eyes were wild. Pete's training kicked in, and he glanced down at the car's license plate, instantly committing the three numbers and three letters to memory. Memory, yeah, right. As if he'd even have a memory after this was over....

Pete had been faced with his own probable death before, but it had never angered him the way this did. No way was he going to let Annie die. And no way was *he* going to end up dead, either. Not now. Now when he'd finally found the best reason he'd ever had for staying alive.

With herculean effort he pushed his straining muscles

harder, and threw both Annie and himself into the store-front. The car missed them by mere inches, but hit the phone booth, knocking it down and dragging it several hundred feet before driving away, tires squealing.

Pete turned instinctively into the fall, to cradle and pro-tect Annie. With a tearing sound, the left sleeve was torn off of his tuxedo jacket as he skidded on the rough con-crete. His shoulder was badly scraped, but he felt nothing but relief as he pulled Annie onto his lap.

He ran his hands quickly down her arms and legs to reassure himself that she was still in one piece. Her right knee was scraped, the stocking destroyed, but other than that she was all right.

"Pete, you're bleeding," she said, her voice remark-ably clear.

As he looked up, he realized she was checking him over as carefully as he had checked her. His elbow was a mess, along with his left knee, and blood stained the fine fabric of his tux. He couldn't see his shoulder—didn't want to see it.

"Still feel safe?" he asked her hoarsely.

To his surprise, she smiled. It was shaky, but it was definitely a smile. "If you're with me," she said, "then I'm safe."

Man, she was giving him an awful lot to live up to. Painfully, he stood up, pulling Annie to her feet. There was a crowd gathering, and he wanted to get away from all the curious eyes.

"We've got to get out of here before he comes back," he said. His pack was still on his back, but he'd dropped Annie's bag on the sidewalk. Miraculously, it hadn't been stolen; it still lay where it had fallen. Wincing, he bent to pick it up. There was a distinct tire track on the soft leather.

Someone in the crowd handed Annie her missing shoe.

She thanked them politely, calmly, as if this sort of thing happened every day.

Several cars had stopped at the accident scene, one of them a cab. Its off-duty light was lit, but Pete pulled several twenty-dollar bills from his wallet, and the driver was happy to get back to work.

"Where you heading?" the cabbie asked as they got in.

"Madison Square Garden," Pete said. "And I'll give you another fifty bucks if you keep the off-duty light on."

"But that's illegal—"

"A hundred."

"You're the boss."

As the cab pulled away from the curb, Pete pulled Annie down with him so that they were both lying on the seat, hidden from view. Her face was illuminated in spurts by the streetlights they passed under, and she stared up at him, her eyes wide.

"You okay?" he asked.

She nodded, looking into his eyes as if he were a lifeline. "That was no accident," she said. "Someone tried to kill us, didn't they?"

"Yeah."

Annie nodded again, still looking into his eyes. "Are *you* okay?" she asked him.

"I'm fine."

"Really?"

The cab's suspension system squeaked as it hit a pothole. Annie's hair had all but fallen down around her shoulders, and he pushed a lock off her face. "Ask me that same question in a minute," he murmured. "Something tells me I'm going to be even better than fine."

He kissed her gently, just a slight brushing of his lips

against hers. She smiled, then lifted her mouth to his for more. He kissed her again, a long, slow, sweet kiss that made his heart pound and sent his blood racing through his veins.

"Madison Square Garden," the cabbie announced. "Uh, you folks want me to go around the block a few more times?"

Annie grinned. "What does he think we're doing back here?" she whispered into Pete's ear.

"Probably exactly what we *are* doing," he whispered back, kissing her neck. "Yeah, keep going," he said in a louder voice to the driver. He lifted himself up slightly, so he could peek out the back window.

After the cab made three right turns with no cars following them, Pete had the driver pull over, and he and Annie climbed out.

The cab had no sooner pulled away from the curb when Pete flagged down another taxi. They quickly climbed in.

"La Guardia Airport," Pete directed the driver.

An hour and a half later, they ended up in an expensive hotel overlooking Central Park. The room was large and elegant, decorated in hushed shades of rose and burgundy, with a beautiful floral-printed wallpaper that reminded Annie of an English garden. A table and chairs sat in the corner by the window, a couch and several overstuffed chairs were positioned around a cold fireplace and a big bed was against the wall. One bed. Annie pulled her eyes away from it and looked at Pete.

"You know, when you told that cabdriver to take us to the airport," she said, "for a while there, I thought you wanted to catch the next flight out of town."

Pete slipped the chain on the door and fastened a deadbolt. "Would you have gone?" he asked.

"Yes," she said without hesitating even a second. "If that's what you wanted."

She trusted him. It was clear from her eyes and her voice. Perfect, Pete thought grimly. She trusted him absolutely, yet he'd told her nothing but lies and half-truths. She would have every right to be furious with him when she found out the real story, every right never to trust him again.

Annie watched as he pulled the desk chair over and wedged it tightly underneath the doorknob. He seemed more silent and expressionless than ever, as if he were hiding something. Were they really safe here? Maybe they *should* have taken a flight out of New York, away from the city....

"Does that work?" she asked, gesturing to the chair.

"It's not going to stop anybody who's determined to get in here," Pete said. "But it makes me feel better."

"Are we safe?" she asked.

His eyes met hers, and electricity seemed to crackle between them.

Safe.

If they were safe, Pete could relax. He could close his eyes and kiss her. And if he could close his eyes and kiss her...

"Yeah," he said. "For now."

His gaze was so intense, Annie had to look away. Her overnight bag was on the floor, and she looked at it, seeing for the first time the tire mark that marred its leather surface. Her eyes were very wide and very blue as she looked back up at Pete. "I nearly got you killed. Didn't I?"

Pete shook his head. "*You* didn't try to run me over," he said, painfully shrugging out of what was left of his tuxedo jacket, depositing onto the table a small gun that he'd somehow concealed up his sleeve. "Don't go doing the guilt thing on me, Annie. I knew exactly what I was getting myself into when I took this job."

He pulled another gun out from where it had been tucked into the back of his pants.

"Did you really?"

He turned to glance at her, and froze. Annie had taken off her evening jacket, too, and she stood in front of him, her sexy blue dress wrinkled, her stockings torn, her makeup smudged, her hair disheveled and down around her smooth shoulders. She was gorgeous, perfectly, mind-numbingly gorgeous. Desire slammed into him, running him down and crushing him so that he could barely breathe.

"No," he managed to say, his voice sounding raw. "I didn't have a clue."

He couldn't hide how badly he wanted her—he knew it was written clearly across his face. He turned away abruptly, unfastening his shoulder holster and putting that gun with the others. He knew he should wash the scrape on Annie's knee, and maybe take a look at his shoulder in the bathroom mirror....

Annie walked slowly toward him, hoping for another glimpse of that exhilarating fire she'd seen burning in his eyes. "Do me a favor, Taylor," she said, her voice even lower and huskier than usual. "Unzip me?"

She turned, sweeping her hair in front of one shoulder, exposing her slender neck and smooth back, waiting. For several long seconds, she was afraid he wasn't going to do it. Then his big, gentle fingers found the tiny zipper pull and tugged it slowly down. Annie heard Pete take a deep breath.

"You should take a shower," he said on the exhale.

Pete briefly closed his eyes, willing her to walk away

from him. But she didn't. When he looked again, she was still standing in front of him. And he couldn't resist.

Annie sighed with pleasure as she felt Pete touch her shoulders, his callused fingers stroking her soft skin.

"Annie," he breathed close to her ear. "*I* should take a shower—a cold one."

"I have a better idea," she said, turning to face him. The heat in her eyes left him no doubt as to what she had in mind.

He knew that he should stop touching her, he should stop tracing the line of her delicate collarbone, he should keep his fingers out of her silky hair....

She took a step toward him, closing the shrinking gap between them, and suddenly his arms were around her and he was kissing her.

This was not like the sweet kisses they'd shared in the back seat of the taxi. This was an explosion, a scorching, turbulent eruption of emotion and desire held far too long in check. He molded her body against his as their mouths met hungrily, frantically. He welcomed her tongue into his mouth, pulling her inside him, as if he wanted to devour her whole. She moaned, a soft, sensual sound that nearly brought him to his knees, and he swept his tongue past her lips, piercing her, possessing her, claiming her as his own.

Annie heard herself moan again, as Pete's hands moved down to her buttocks, pressing her tightly to the ironlike hardness of his arousal. Feeling herself flood with even more heat, Annie wrapped one leg up around him, fitting herself against him. She could feel his hand slide up the silky nylon that covered her thigh, slipping underneath her dress.

Suddenly, violently, Pete pulled away from her. He crossed to the other side of the room, as if to put as much distance between them as possible. Not again, Annie thought with frustration, watching him lean against the far wall, pressing his palms to his forehead. She took a deep breath, trying to calm her ragged breathing. At least he didn't run away, she told herself. This was definitely a step in the right direction....

"Annie, I'm dying to make love to you," he said. "But we have to talk first. You need to understand that there are things I can't tell you—"

Annie slipped out of her dress, kicking her shoes into the corner of the room. She wore a black bustier that ended in a point just above the black silk of her panties. Pete watched, almost hypnotized, as she peeled off her tattered stockings and tossed them into the wastebasket.

She walked toward him then, saying, "We were attacked by a flock of bats *and* nearly run over by some maniac, all in the space of a few hours. Maybe this is just a day's work for you, pal, but I've had it. I don't want to talk. I don't want to deal with any problems. And I don't want to have to wonder if I'm going to get killed before I get a chance to make love to you."

"Annie—"

She pressed her fingers to his lips. "Tell me tomorrow," she said, her blue eyes beseeching him. "Please?"

The last time Pete had seen her dressed in only her underwear, she'd stood this close to him, but she'd been on the other side of a thick pane of glass. This time, with no barrier between them, he couldn't help himself, and he reached out for her.

She went into his arms willingly, thankfully, kissing him as his hands swept over her body, stroking, touching, exploring. Her fingers fumbled as she unbuttoned his shirt, but finally it was open, and she ran the palms of her hands up and down the hard, smooth muscles of his chest. "Make love to me, Pete," she whispered.

In one sudden movement, he scooped her into his arms and carried her to the big bed. Still holding her with one arm, he grabbed the covers and wrenched them back. He sank down onto the clean white sheets, pressing himself on top of her, kissing her eyes, her mouth, her neck, sliding lower and lower until his mouth found her breast. Her nipples were already hard with desire, and he took one into his mouth, sucking and pulling through the delicate lace of her bra. His hands found a hook and eye at her back and he undid it, but it was just one of a whole long row of fasteners. Growling with frustration, he rolled her onto her stomach. With his fingers and eyes working together, the bra was easy to remove, and he quickly tossed it onto the floor.

He sat back to pull his shirt off, uncaring of the pain in his scraped shoulder and elbow, knowing only that he had to feel his body against hers with no barriers in between. He watched Annie sit up, her breasts round and full, her nipples invitingly taut.

He knew that it was a mistake to make love to her like this, before she knew the truth about him. But he also knew that mistake or not, it was too late to turn back—his need for her possessed him. The only way he'd be able to turn away from her now was if she begged him to stop. Pete groaned as her slender fingers unfastened the button at the waist of his pants. No, she definitely didn't want to stop.

He took her hand, pulling it down and pressing it against the hard bulge in his pants. Their gazes locked, and they both smiled, quick, fiery grins of recognition at the need for haste that they saw in each other's eyes. Pete pushed off his shoes as Annie tugged at his pants. He lifted his hips and yanked both his pants and his shorts down, then groaned with pleasure as her hand closed around his shaft. He rolled on top of her, pinning her with his body as he kissed her almost feverishly.

His hand slipped underneath the thin black silk of her panties, finding the heat between her legs, finding her moist and ready for him. He slid his fingers into her tightness, and she moaned, lifting her hips and pressing against him.

"Pete," she whispered huskily, looking up at him with passion in her eyes. "Please…"

Her soft words ignited him, and the black panties joined her bra on the floor. He scrambled for his pants, searching the pockets for the condom he'd put in his wallet weeks ago, back when Annie was only a suspect to be investigated. He'd put that condom there in anticipation of good sex—nothing more than physical pleasure with a beautiful adversary. But it was more than sexual desire that made his hands shake as he put it on now. It was knowing that he wanted Annie in ways that he'd never wanted anyone before. It was love, pure and simple, and oh, so complicated. Too complicated for words.…

Pete turned back to Annie and kissed her as if the world were coming to an end. His body covered hers, and she put her arms around his sleek, strong back, pulling him even closer to her, opening herself to receive him. But he paused, his muscles tight in his arms and chest as he looked down at her.

"I love you," he breathed. "Annie, I love you so much—"

Beads of sweat stood out on his forehead and he was breathing hard, as if holding back was a test of endurance. But while his eyes blazed with the intensity of his desire, they also held another flame, the softer, smoldering fire of love that promised to burn forever.

Annie felt her eyes fill with tears. He loved her....

"Promise me you'll never forget that," he said, his voice husky with emotion.

"How could I ever forget?" she asked, pulling his head down, meeting his mouth with her lips. She kissed him, drinking in his sweetness, pulling him toward her, wanting more, more. She lifted her hips up, pressing against his hardness, wanting him, needing him, now and for all time.

He entered her with one smooth thrust and they both cried out, their voices intertwined in the hushed stillness of the room.

Harmony. There was perfect harmony in the way their bodies moved together, harmony in the emotions that seemed to charge the very air around them, harmony in the love Pete felt for her, a love he knew she felt, too, just from looking into her beautiful eyes. It was like the sonorous consonance of nature, the perfectness of marriage between a Colorado mountain peak and the blue sky above it. Two bodies, two hearts, two souls joined in the ultimate collaboration. They were one, part of each other forever.

Annie exploded, swirling in a barrage of colors and sounds and sensations that focused on the man in her arms, this man she held so tightly, this man who had stolen her heart. Through the waves of her pleasure, she heard him call out her name, felt the shudder of his own tremendous release.

She held on to him tightly, feeling the pounding of both their hearts begin to slow. Spent, he lay on top of her, and still she clasped him to her, holding his body against hers, wanting to freeze time, keep them in this special place forever.

Pete's breathing became slow and steady, deep and relaxed.

"Taylor, are you awake?" Annie whispered.

He lifted his head to find himself staring directly into Annie's blue eyes. "Yeah," he said, then smiled, a slow, satisfied smile that made Annie's heart turn a quick somersault.

"I love you, too, you know," she said, and Pete closed his eyes briefly, feeling the warmth of her words surround his heart. She loved him.

"Pete, why did you leave my room that night?" she asked softly. "You know, I wanted you to stay."

"I couldn't," he said, tracing her eyebrows with one finger. "I wanted to, but I couldn't."

"Why not?"

He shook his head, uncertain of the best way to explain. "I wanted—I *still* want—more than just a sexual relationship," he finally said. "I want more than just a night or two or even two months of nights. I want forever, Annie. I want you to marry me—"

"Yes," she said, interrupting him.

Pete laughed. "But I wasn't— That wasn't—" He took a deep breath and started over. "There are things you need to know about me before I can even ask you to marry me."

He was looking at her with such love in his eyes, such emotion on his face. Annie shook her head. "I love you, Pete," she said simply. "And there's nothing you can tell me that will make me stop loving you."

He rolled onto his back, pulling her with him and holding her close. "I hope so," he said. "I hope so."

Chapter 14

Morning dawned cold and gray, but Annie was warm and secure, wrapped in Pete's arms in the hotel bed. She slept soundly, her long hair fanned out against the pillow, her legs comfortably intertwined with Pete's.

Pete watched her as she slept. He'd watched her sleep before, but this was the first time he'd watched her as he held her in his arms.

She loved him.

She'd told him that over and over last night, with more than just words.

Pete studied the freckles on her nose and the way her eyelashes lay against her cheek, hoping against hope that she loved him enough to handle the truth, to understand why he'd intentionally misled her.

What he couldn't figure out was how the hell he was going to find the right time, the right moment to tell her who he really was. He had to wait until the investigation was over, of course. But that wouldn't be long—not after

Whitley Scott received Pete's report, which stated that, in his opinion, Annie Morrow was not involved in any kind of conspiracy.

How long would it take to get the report filed and the investigation dropped? A week, maybe two. By then they'd have this death mask mess cleared up, too. They'd track down whoever it was who had tried to kill them—

He'd come so close to losing her last night. Pete stared at the ceiling, holding Annie tighter. He couldn't bear the thought of losing her.

But when he imagined himself telling Annie he was CIA, it was so easy to picture her anger, to picture her storming out the door.

But she loves you, he reminded himself. Or did she? She loved Peter Taylor. Maybe she wouldn't feel the same about Kendall Peterson.

He closed his eyes, willing himself to stop thinking, letting sleep wash over him.

"Annie." Pete's lazy drawl whispered in her ear. "Wake up."

She awoke to the sensation of his roughly callused hands sweeping across her body. His thumb gently flicked her nipples to life, as his other hand moved lower, starting that now familiar surge of fire through her body. He pulled her hips toward him, entering her slowly.

She opened her eyes to find him watching her, his eyelids half-closed, a small smile on his handsome face. He moved languorously, unhurriedly, deliciously.

"Morning," he said.

"Well, this sure beats an alarm clock," Annie said with a smile. She stretched, lifting her hips and joining his rhythmic movements. "I could get used to this."

"You and me both," Pete said, rolling onto his back, pulling her on top of him. She leaned forward to kiss him, and the telephone rang.

Annie froze. "Nobody knows we're here," she said. "Do they?"

She moved to get off him, but he held her in place, reaching with his right hand to answer the phone. "Yeah," he said into the receiver, tucking it between his ear and shoulder. He looked up into Annie's eyes and pushed himself more deeply inside of her. She swallowed a sound of pleasure that almost escaped, and glared at Pete in mock outrage. He grinned at her. *Oh, yeah?* thought Annie. *Well, two can play this game.*

She began to move on top of him. His eyelids slid halfway down again and he smiled, his dark eyes molten with desire.

"Yeah, that's fine," he said into the telephone. His gaze strayed downward, caressing Annie's body. "Really fine," he said to her.

But she wanted to see him squirm. She leaned forward, leaving a trail of light, feathery kisses up his neck to a little extrasensitive spot she'd found right underneath his ear—

"Uh!" Pete said, then covered it with a cough. He wiggled away, pushing her back up, keeping her at arm's length. "No, no, I'm all right," he said into the telephone, flashing Annie a look of surrender. "Okay, but we need an hour." There was a pause, then he said, "Tough. Go eat a doughnut. I'll see you in an hour."

He hung up the phone, then pulled Annie down, kissing her hard on the mouth.

They made love slowly, tenderly, in the morning light.

"Who was on the phone?" she asked later, lying back, satisfied, in his arms.

He kissed the top of her head. "A guy named Scott, from the bureau."

Annie sat up, turning to look at him. "Bureau? As in Federal Bureau of Investigations? As in the FBI?"

Pete nodded. "Yeah. I called them last night while you were in the shower. I thought they might like to know the plate number of the car that tried to flatten us. At the same time, I figured we could use 'em for a safe ride up to Westchester this morning. That was what they were calling me about. They've got a car ready, down on parking level one."

"You actually got a look at the license plate of that car last night?" Annie said, her eyes wide. "*And* you remembered it? I'm impressed."

"Just doing my job, ma'am," Pete said a little too modestly. He swung Annie up, pushing her out of the bed. "In about twenty-five minutes, there's going to be a swarm of FBI agents knocking at the door, ready to escort us down to the car. I recommend taking a shower now, because when we get back to your house, we're going to have to give them a detailed account of the hit and run attempt. It could take some time."

"Don't I know," Annie muttered under her breath.

She took a quick shower, then eased her blue jeans on over the scrape on her knee. She sat on the bedroom floor and rummaged in her overnight bag, pulling out a well-worn T-shirt and a pair of socks and her sneakers, and quickly got dressed.

There was a pile of weaponry on the table—Pete's guns. Bemused, she counted three different guns. Why so many? she wondered. In case he dropped one?

A loud hammering at the door made her jump. Startled, she scrambled to her feet, backing toward the bathroom door.

Pete was still in the shower; she could hear it running. But the water shut off as the pounding was repeated.

The door to the bathroom was ajar, and Annie pushed it open. "Pete?"

Steam swirled in the small room, fogging the mirrors, curling around Pete as he stood naked on the bath mat, drying his lean, athletic body. He looked up at her, reading her face swiftly and accurately as usual. "What's wrong?"

"Someone's at the door."

He swore under his breath, giving himself a few more swipes with his towel before he wrapped it around his waist. Annie followed him out into the bedroom, and Pete motioned for her to move to one side as he grabbed one of his guns and approached the door. Obediently hanging back, Annie watched as he looked out into the hallway through the door's peephole. The tension in his shoulders and neck visibly decreased, and he pulled the chair away from under the doorknob and opened the door a crack.

"You're early," Annie heard him say.

"Brought ya breakfast," she heard a man's voice say. "A bag of doughnuts and coffee. Figured you could probably use the extra energy more than I could."

"Give me ten minutes," Pete said, "and we'll be ready to go."

"Take all the minutes you need," the man said. "No one's going anywhere for a long time."

The tightness returned to Pete's shoulders. "What's going on?"

"You'd better open the door, Captain," another, different voice said.

Captain, thought Annie. *Now why the heck would they call Pete that?*

He shot a quick look over his shoulder at her, then

moved closer to the door, saying something in a low voice.

"To hell with your cover, Captain Peterson," the first man said. He pushed his way through the door, into the room, his eyes falling on Annie. "This entire investigation's over," he said, waving a folded document in the air. "I'm holding a warrant for the arrest of Dr. Anne Morrow."

Annie stared. "What?" she said. She looked at Pete. "Pete, what's going on? Who is this man?"

"It's simple, lady." The man smiled at her from behind a thick pair of glasses. "I'm Whitley Scott, with the FBI. You're already familiar with Captain Peterson, here. He's CIA."

Pete had taken the paper from Scott's hand and was reading it, his eyes quickly skimming down the pages. He looked up to meet Annie's shocked gaze.

"No," Annie breathed. But she knew it was true. She could see the guilt in Pete's dark eyes.

"And you," Scott continued, "are busted. We're charging you with five different felonies, including robbery, conspiracy, felony murder." He turned to Pete. "You wanna Miranda her?"

"Oh, God," Annie said. Pete was CIA....

"No," Pete said, his voice low.

"Collins," Scott addressed one of the other men who had come into the room with him. "Read her her rights and frisk her."

"No," Pete said, his voice sharp. "She's clean."

"You know it's gotta be done," Scott said.

"You have the right to remain silent," Collins began to drone.

"I'll frisk her," Pete said.

"Anything you say can and will be used against you in a court of law."

"Nice room," said Scott. He looked at the unmade bed, at the condom wrappers that still lay scattered on the floor. He smirked. "Must've been one hell of a night, eh, Peterson?"

"Oh, *God*," Annie said. Pete was *CIA*....

Pete took her arm, and she looked up at him, startled by his touch. "You son of a bitch," she said, pulling away from him.

"You have the right to an attorney," Collins said.

"Annie, I don't know what this is all about," Pete said, talking low and fast, "but I'm going to find out. Right now you need to stay calm."

"If you cannot afford an attorney," Collins said, "one will be appointed for you at no cost."

On the other side of the room, Scott opened the curtains and the gray light of a rainy October morning did little to illuminate the room. "Nice view of the park," he said.

"This has to be done," Pete told Annie, "and I'll do it as quickly as I can, but you've got to help me."

"Do you understand these rights as I have read them to you?" Collins said.

"Spread your legs apart and put your hands on your head," Pete said.

Woodenly, Annie obeyed him.

"Dr. Morrow," Collins said. "Do you understand these rights?"

"Yes," Annie whispered. She closed her eyes as Pete's hands moved methodically and impersonally over her body. Oh, *God*...

"She's clean," she heard him say, his voice tight, clipped.

Everything he had told her was a lie. His name was

Peterson, not Pete Taylor. He wasn't a bodyguard. He probably wasn't even half-Navaho, probably had never even been to Colorado. He'd only been using her to get information.

He didn't love her.

It was all a lie. He didn't love her....

"I'm going to be sick," Annie said, lunging for the bathroom.

Collins and the other FBI agent moved to follow, but Pete blocked the door. "I'll handle it," he said.

He went into the bathroom, closing and locking the door behind him.

Annie knelt on the floor in front of the commode. Her face was pale. Taking a washcloth from the towel rack, Pete ran it under cool water and handed it to her.

"Pete, how could you?" she asked, reproach in her eyes. "How could you use me this way?"

His clothes lay in a pile near the shower. He pulled his shorts on under his towel, then used the towel to dry his hair. "There's something really wrong here," he said, almost to himself.

"Captain Peterson," she said, looking at him with new horror in her eyes as he pulled on his jeans. "You're that horrible man who was behind the mirror window at the airport, aren't you? And I *slept* with you. You *bastard*—"

"Annie, I meant it when I said that I loved you," he said. "You've got to believe that. And you've got to trust me until I figure out what's going on."

She laughed, a dull, hollow sound. "You're kidding, right?"

He grabbed her by the shoulders, pulling her up to her feet. "You made me a promise," he said, shaking her slightly. "You promised not to forget that I love you, so don't forget, damn it."

She pulled away from him. "I made that promise to Pete Taylor, and you're obviously not him." Her eyes filled with tears, and she fought them back. "You can go to hell, Captain Peterson."

She turned and walked out of the bathroom, closing the door tightly behind her.

Chapter 15

The interrogation room held one table and some stiff-backed wooden chairs. The walls were a dull, ugly shade of beige, and the floor was cheap, industrial linoleum tile. *This is what hell looks like,* Annie thought, fatigue washing over her as she looked around the table at the myriad of FBI agents that sat looking back at her. She was even willing to bet that Satan wore a dark suit exactly like the ones these men had on.

She clasped her hands tightly in front of her on the table. "If you can't get more specific with your charges," she said tightly, "then you better release me."

Scott leaned back in his chair. "So you're saying that you've never been in possession of these artifacts, and you don't know how they got into your house."

Annie glanced down at the pictures for the hundredth time in the past few hours. They were antiquities—some she recognized, most she didn't. But none had ever been near her house, much less in her possession. "I told you

I don't know how any of this happened,'' she said, not for the first time.

Scott nodded, obviously not believing her.

She leaned forward. "Tell me, Scott," she said. "Why in God's name would I become involved in some idiotic art robbery? Why would I bomb museums? I've got an impeccable reputation, I make a decent living, I'm respected by my peers—why would I risk all that?"

"You tell me."

The door opened and Pete came in. Captain Peterson, Annie corrected herself, trying to numb the pain that seeing him brought. He was wearing a conservative dark suit exactly like all the other agents, and Annie almost didn't recognize him. Almost. He looked around the room, and one eyebrow went down very slightly in his version of a frown. Annie's stomach hurt. She could read his face so well, even now. How was it that she hadn't picked up on his lies?

"Where's your lawyer?" he asked Annie.

Scott answered for her. "She's waived her right." He grinned. "She says she's not guilty, so she doesn't need an attorney."

"Get her one," Peterson said coldly.

"She doesn't want one," Scott said. "I can't force one down her damned throat."

Annie was looking at Pete as if he were something that had crawled out from under a rock. "I don't want him in here," she said to Scott. "Make him leave."

Scott shrugged, obviously enjoying her discomfort. "Can't do that," he said. "Captain Peterson's as much in charge here as I am."

Pete set a file down in front of Scott and sat down across from her. Annie turned away, not looking at him.

"All right," Scott said to Annie, opening the file and

shuffling through the papers. "You want to get specific?" He pulled out a piece of paper, and began to read it.

"'Two packages were observed on a counter in the laboratory of the suspect's house. They were open, and contained articles numbered one through eight. The articles, in plain view of the investigating officers, matched the description of those articles missing from the English Gallery. The packages were seized in accordance with the warrant blah blah blah.'" He pushed the report across the table to her. "Read it and weep," he said.

The room was spinning. Annie leafed through the pages of the report, describing the room-by-room search, the description of the artifacts...

"What gave you the right to search my home?" she asked quietly.

"The warrant was obtained as a result of evidence gathered over the course of this investigation, and a tip—"

"Who?" Annie demanded. "Who gave you this *tip?*"

"This information came to us anonymously," Scott said.

"Oh, terrific!" Annie threw up her hands. "Obviously a reliable source—"

"It certainly turned out to be, didn't it?" Scott said, leaning across the table. "Especially when we found materials to construct explosives in a desk drawer in your office."

"What?" Annie gasped. Her eyes moved involuntarily to Pete's face. He was expressionless, his dark eyes watching her steadily. "This is some kind of setup," she said. The enormity of the situation crashed down around her, and she realized for the first time that she was in serious trouble. The stolen artifacts, the explosives... "I want a lawyer."

She looked back at the report in front of her. "Two

packages were observed on a counter in the laboratory of the suspect's house.''

On a counter in the laboratory of the suspect's house.

In the laboratory!

Yes!

Pete had been in the lab with her before they left for New York City. He'd seen that the counters were clean, everything put away. He had locked the place up as they left the house, and had been with her ever since. He could confirm her story. He would tell them she had nothing to do with this!

Yes!

"Pete," she said, excitement vibrating through her voice. She handed him the report. "You were with me when I went into the lab to turn off the lights before we went out last night, remember? The lab was all cleaned up—the counters were clear. You were right there in the doorway."

Pete glanced up from the report. His eyes were expressionless, his face guarded.

"Remember?"

He had to remember. Of course he'd remember.

"Nick was waiting for us outside. You told me I looked beautiful." Suddenly she looked down at her hands, and blushed at the memory. But she had to go on; she desperately needed him to stand with her now, no matter how humiliating. "You were looking at me—" she swallowed and looked up at him "—like you wanted to kiss me."

Pete met her gaze for only a second before looking back at the report, his eyes narrowing as if in concentration.

"Remember?"

He handed the paper back to Scott, glancing briefly at Annie, his eyes cold, detached. "No."

She stared at him, shock draining the blood from her

face, leaving her pale. Oh, God, he was part of it, part of the setup....

Pete stood up, careful not to meet her eyes. "I'll go make arrangements for a lawyer," he said, leaving the room.

Annie stared down at the table, forcing herself not to cry as what was left of her heart shattered into a billion tiny pieces.

Annie walked up the driveway to her house. Her thin formal jacket was wrapped tightly around her, but it did little to keep out the rain on the long, cold walk from the train station. There were no lights burning in her windows, nothing to welcome her home.

Home. Lord, she couldn't believe she was actually here. Once her attorney had arrived, the endless interrogation had stopped and bail was set. She'd been ready to call her parents to ask for help in posting the quarter-million-dollar bail when she found out that bail had already been paid by an anonymous source. Her father, she thought gratefully. Somehow he had found out she was in trouble even before her call, and he'd come to her rescue.

The trial date was set for three months from now, and her license was revoked until that time. She couldn't work, couldn't even finish the work she'd started.

With a disparaging laugh, she remembered the phone call that had told her not to touch the golden death mask, warning her that Stands Against the Storm's evil spirit would harm her if she did. As a result, her life would crumble.

You win, Stands Against the Storm, she thought. Her life had indeed crumbled.

Keying her authorization code into the outside alarm control panel, she waited for the light to go from red to green. Unlocking the front door, she sighed. First thing in the morning, she'd have to pack up everything in her safe, ship it back to all the owners....

She turned the alarm back on and climbed the stairs in the dark and went into her bedroom. Was it only last night that she'd been so happy? Dancing with Pete, making love to him— How could she have been so stupid? He must be laughing at her now.

She dumped her bag on the floor. Shivering, she went into the bathroom, turned on the light and quickly stripped off her wet clothes.

Steam from her hot shower soon fogged the mirror, and she washed herself, washed off the very last trace of Pete's scent. Closing her eyes, she let the water run over her face, disguising the tears that she couldn't hold back any longer.

"Annie, wake up."

She opened her eyes to find Peterson sitting on her bed, looking down at her. She didn't move, she just stared.

"Are you awake?" he asked. The morning light coming in behind the curtains dimly lit his face. He looked tired, his eyes red and bleary, as if he hadn't slept. He had changed out of that dreadful dark suit and back into his familiar blue jeans and T-shirt.

"No," she said. "I better not be. I better be dreaming. You better not be sitting here in my room like this."

He tried to smile, but it came out as a wry twist of his lips. "Sorry," he said. "I'm really sitting here."

A host of different emotions flew across her face, but anger won. Her eyes blazed. "Get out."

"Annie, I had to—"

"I don't want to hear it, *Captain Peterson.*" She said his name sarcastically, her teeth clenched in barely controlled rage. "You son of a bitch. You set me up. Get out of my house!"

"I didn't know about—"

"You really expect me to believe that?" she seethed. "I know damn well you remember coming into the lab with me when I turned off the lights that night. You *know* that stuff from the English Gallery wasn't there."

"Annie—"

She kicked him, hard, her foot against his back, but the bed covers broke the force of the blow, and he didn't even flinch. "You bastard," she shouted. "The FBI decided that I was guilty five months ago. But they couldn't prove it, so they had to frame me. And you're just going to go along with it, aren't you? Because you're one of them, you creep!"

He gave up trying to explain. He sat there, watching her quietly, letting her vent her anger.

"Tell me," she said, her voice biting, "do you get extra points for sleeping with me, Captain? Four times in one night! You probably got stud points from the other guys for that. Oh, yeah, and once in the morning. A nice touch. Make your buddies wait out in the hall while you make it with the suspect one last time before you arrest her—"

He couldn't hold it in. "I didn't know they had a warrant—"

"Do you *really* expect me to believe *anything* you say?" she said, as her eyes accused him of terrible crimes.

He looked down at the floor, knowing that he was guilty. He'd kept the truth about his identity from her for all those weeks, even after he knew he was in love with her, even after he knew she couldn't possibly be involved in any kind of crime. He *was* guilty. "No," he said quietly. "No, I don't."

"You were so good," she said, her voice breaking.

"All those stories you told about when you were a kid, living out in Colorado, about your Indian grandfather—You probably grew up in the Bronx, right?"

"Not everything I told you was a lie," he said, meeting her gaze. "Those stories were all true. And I was telling you the truth when I said that I love you." He looked down at his hands, clenched tightly into fists on his lap. "I know you don't believe me...."

"Yeah, you're right. I don't," Annie said, watching him close his eyes against the harshness of her words. "What do you want from me? Why are you here?"

Pete stood up and walked across the room. "You're being framed," he said, his back to her as he composed himself.

She laughed, a harsh exhale of air. "Tell me something new, Captain America."

"I want to help you," he said, turning to look at her.

"*Now* you want to help me?" she said, tight anger in her voice. "Yesterday, you could have told them that those things weren't in the lab—"

"Annie, I'm here because you're not safe," he interrupted. "Someone on the inside is in on this frame, and I don't know who it is."

Annie stared at him.

He smiled, a tight, satisfied smile. "Yeah, I *was* there that night, Annie. And I *do* remember. I saw the lab. I know you're being set up."

She kept staring at him, the tiniest seed of hope fluttering in her stomach.

"Why didn't you say something yesterday?" she asked, her voice low. "You could have saved my reputation."

"I thought it was more important to save your life." His dark eyes held her captive. "Until I know how many people are in on this thing, you're safer if they think no one believes you.''

''But the FBI? How—''

''All I know is too many things don't add up. How did someone get into the house to put those bats in your room? How did they get in to plant that stolen art? Nobody had the codes to the security system except you, me and Cara...*and* anyone who had access to your case file.''

''But what about all those fringe groups the FBI was going to investigate?''

He shook his head. ''There's no way one of those groups is responsible for bombing and robbing two European art galleries—or disarming a professional alarm system to plant bats in your bedroom and stolen art in your lab.''

Pete was pacing now. ''There's just too much that's wrong about this.'' He stopped in the middle of the room and faced Annie again. ''Why would someone want to kill you? Or why would they want you arrested, in jail, out of the picture?''

Annie stared at him and Pete smiled grimly. ''There's a lot of things we don't know. And it's about time we started finding out.''

Pete sifted through the pile of file folders that were out on Annie's desk. He ran his fingers through his hair, then leaned back and stretched. Man, they were getting nowhere....

''*Here* it is,'' Annie called from the floor in front of her file cabinet. ''June 4, 1989. Back before I started using my computer system. That was the last time I tested anything for the English Gallery. It was a gold ring from ninth-century Wales. Wanna see the file?''

''Sure, why not?'' Pete said. He spun in his chair to

face her as she brought the folder to the desk. "How come it's been such a long time? Recession hitting them, too?"

Annie shook her head. "No. Alistair Golden's pretty much got that gallery locked up for sales coming into the United States. They use him exclusively. If it hadn't been for Ben Sullivan, I never would have gotten this job."

Pete frowned. Then reached for the telephone. As Annie watched, he dialed a number. "Yeah," he said, into the phone. "This is Peterson. I need access to a list of all sales of artwork and other artifacts brought into the U.S. via the English Gallery."

"But I've got that information," Annie said.

He looked at her in surprise. "Let me call you back," he said into the phone. He hung up and looked at her questioningly.

"I'm tied into a computer network that keeps track of current sales of artwork and artifacts—anything from a Picasso to a Stone Age ax," Annie said. She came around to his side of the desk and turned on her personal computer and her modem. "It's useful information for art brokers to have. Using this list, I can track down and access a buyer for just about anything. Take your necklace, for instance. If you wanted to sell it, I could find a buyer simply by calling up the names of all the people who have made multiple purchases of Navaho jewelry over the past several months."

Pete leaned back in his chair to give her better access to the keyboard. She narrowed her eyes slightly in concentration as she keyed in the commands to sign on to the network.

"All we have to do is request a specific list where the gallery was the English, and point of shipping equals U.S.A...."

She was close enough for him to reach out and touch

her, but Pete didn't dare. Just over twenty-four hours ago, she'd told him that she loved him. But he could still see the look on her face when she found out he was a government agent, sent to investigate her. He remembered her eyes as her love for him died. His heart ached. It was his own damned fault....

"Here we go," she said.

A list of dates and items scrolled down the computer screen. Pete forced his thoughts back to the task at hand and leaned forward for a closer look.

"It's chronological," Annie said, turning toward him. They were nearly nose to nose, and she quickly straightened up. "The most current shipments are at the very bottom."

She sat on the edge of the desk and watched Pete from a safe distance as he moved the cursor down the long list. His handsome face was lit by the amber light from the computer screen. He looked exhausted, overtired, but there was a glint of determination in his eyes. He glanced up, feeling her watching him.

"Why are you doing this?" she asked.

"Because I know you're not guilty," he said, looking back at the computer.

"You paid my bail, didn't you?"

"Yeah."

"Where did you get that kind of money?" Annie asked.

"I borrowed it. If you skip town, I lose everything. My car, my condo..." He looked up at her again, and the familiar glint of humor in his eyes made her heart twist. "Who knows? The guys I borrowed it from would probably even break my legs."

"Why would you risk all that for me?" she asked.

"I'd risk everything," he said simply, squinting at the computer screen. "Even my life...."

"Why?"

Pete looked up at her. "It's not that hard to figure out," he said. "I'm in love with you, Annie."

She stared down at him for several long moments, wishing that he hadn't turned into this stranger sitting before her—a stranger she somehow knew so well. But that was just an illusion. She only thought she knew him. Pete Taylor had been only a cover, a charade. He was gone as absolutely as if he had died. Annie felt a stab of grief so sharp and painful that she almost cried out.

"Is there..." Pete said, then cleared his throat and started again. "Do I have any chance at all? With you?"

He looked like Pete Taylor. He sounded like Pete Taylor. He even acted like Pete Taylor. But he wasn't Pete Taylor. He wasn't—

Annie pushed herself off the desk, unable to meet his eyes. "No."

Pete nodded, as if that were the answer he had been expecting. With the muscle in his jaw working, he turned his attention back to the computer, as though his last hopes hadn't been dashed to bits.

Chapter 16

When Annie went back into the office, Pete was on the phone again.

He had printed out a list of names, dates and transactions from the computer, and she glanced over his shoulder, trying to make some sense of it.

He hung up the phone and turned toward her.

"Any luck?" she asked.

"You know this guy Steadman?" he asked, pointing to the list. He was a buyer, and his name appeared repeatedly.

Annie shook her head.

"He buys things from the English Gallery like it's a K mart end-of-the-season sale," Pete said. "There are also a couple of other partnerships and corporations whose names come up frequently."

"But these were all legitimate transactions," Annie protested, looking at the list again. "Some of these pieces are well-known, and these prices are all fair...."

Pete spent the rest of the morning and most of the afternoon on the telephone, trying to gather more information.

Annie went upstairs and cleaned the last of the mess the bats had made out of her bedroom and tried not to think about Peterson. But as she scrubbed the floor, she kept hearing his voice as he asked her if he still had a chance with her. No, she told herself over and over. Absolutely not. She didn't love him. She refused to love him. Sure, she still found him physically attractive....

She closed her eyes for a moment, remembering the night they'd spent together, the night they'd made love. Had it been only two nights ago? It seemed as if a million years had passed since he'd held her in his arms....

"Are you all right?"

Startled, Annie opened her eyes to find Pete standing in the doorway. "Yeah," she said, attacking the floor with renewed vigor. "What did you find out? Anything?"

Pete squatted down next to the bucket, pulling out a second sponge and going to work beside her. "Something," he said. "I'm waiting for a few more calls that should give me the rest of the information I need. Apparently, Mr. J. J. Steadman is buying most of the stuff that comes out of the English Gallery one way or the other. He's an owner or a partner in every single one of the companies on that list of buyers."

Annie stopped scrubbing the floor. "Quite the busy little collector."

Pete smiled and Annie had to look away. "Quite. And quite the mediocre one, too, it seems. He rarely holds on to the pieces for more than a couple of months after he buys them, and he often sells them at a small loss."

"Big deal," Annie said. "There's no law that says that rich people can't be stupid."

"Yeah," Pete said. The muscles in his back and arms rippled as he rubbed the sponge across the dirty floor. "But get a load of this." He smiled at her as he rinsed the sponge in the bucket. "Guess who else owns a piece of J. J. Steadman's companies. Give you a hint. Funny green eyes, gold bracelet, kind of like a rattlesnake in a tux?"

Annie had to smile at him. "Let's see... Could it be Alistair Golden?"

They smiled into each other's eyes; then Annie looked away, her expression suddenly guarded, distant.

They scrubbed for several minutes in silence; then she leaned back on her heels. "You know, Peterson, I don't even know your first name."

Pete looked up. "Kendall," he said. "But nobody calls me that. Everyone calls me Pete."

"Even your mother?" Annie asked.

"She calls me Hastin Naat'aanni."

Man Speaking Peace, his Navaho name.

"That really happened?" Annie said. "It was true, that story you told me, about your cousins, when your aunt died?"

Pete threw his sponge in the bucket and sat cross-legged on the floor, his elbows around his knees. "With the exception of my name, my career and my college, I lied to you only by omission," he said. "Everything else I told you was the truth. I just didn't tell you enough."

Annie was quiet for a moment. "Why did you lie to me about going to New York University? Where *did* you go to school?"

"I didn't," Pete said. "I went to Vietnam. I was drafted when I turned eighteen."

"*That's* where your grandfather didn't want you to go," Annie said, sudden comprehension lighting her eyes.

Pete nodded, looking into the bucket of soapy water. "He didn't understand why a kid named Man Speaking Peace had to go fight a war on the other side of the ocean. He didn't like war," he said. "I didn't, either." But he smiled, and Annie was chilled by the hardness in his eyes. "I was good at it, though. I was good at staying alive, too. And I was good at search-and-rescue raids. I spent most of my time in enemy territory, finding the guys who'd been shot down and bringing them out of the jungle. In '75, after they pulled the troops out, I was asked to stay behind."

"Stay behind," Annie repeated, horror in her voice. "Why on earth would you want to do that?"

"I didn't *want* to. But they asked me to become part of an agency team that was working to locate and free POWs and MIAs," Pete said quietly.

"So you stayed."

"I stayed. I spent about four more years in southeast Asia, doing what I did best," he said. "Making war."

"You were saving lives," Annie protested. "How many men did you help set free?"

Pete looked at her in surprise. She was actually defending him. His heart skipped a beat and he tried to control it. It didn't mean a thing.... "I never knew the exact figures," he said. "But it was in the hundreds."

"After that you joined the CIA?" she asked.

She wanted to know about him. Was it mere curiosity, or... Pete couldn't dare to hope. He nodded. "As a field operative."

"So you've spent most of the past two decades risking your life," she said, shaking her head.

"Not all the time—"

"Oh, I suppose you get a weekend off every few years

or so," she said. "How can you live that way, with your life always in danger…?"

"Look at it from my perspective," Pete said. "If I'd stayed in Colorado, I would never have met you."

Annie's eyes narrowed. "Then you definitely should have stayed in Colorado," she said sharply. She stood up suddenly and carried the bucket into the bathroom, flushing the dirty water down the toilet, watching it swirl away.

Pete followed her. "In my life, with my job, I have to get things right the first time around," he said, his voice low and intense. "If I don't, I'm dead. Every now and then I'll blow it, though. I'll make a really bad decision, make a major mistake. After I get over the surprise that I'm still alive, I grab that second chance and I don't let go. And I'm damn sure I don't mess up the second time around."

She was looking at him, her eyes so wide, so blue. He couldn't help himself—he took a step toward her, and then another and another. Before he could stop himself, he'd taken her into his arms. She was shaking, but at least she didn't pull away. "Annie, give me a second chance," he whispered. "I love you— God, please, I need you in my life.…"

And still she didn't pull away. Her breasts were rising and falling with each breath she took, as if she had just run a mile. Pete felt his own pulse pounding as his fear of driving her away wrestled with his need. Need won, and he kissed her.

Her mouth was soft, warm and as sweet as he remembered. He felt her arms tighten around him as she responded to him, and he prayed—hell, he *begged* the gods for that second chance.

She opened her mouth under his, and he nearly wept—

until she struggled to break free. He released her immediately, and she stared at him, her eyes accusing.

"No," she breathed. "I can't."

Annie ran from the room, leaving Pete alone.

The phone rang shrilly, quickly pulling Annie out of a restless, uneasy sleep. The clock on her bedside table said it was after 2:00 a.m., but there was a light on in the kitchen, shining in through her bedroom door. She could hear Pete talking on the phone, his voice lowered so as not to disturb her.

He was on the phone, sitting at the kitchen table, writing in his little notebook. His T-shirt was off and his hair was rumpled. His eyes were rimmed with red, as if he still hadn't gotten any sleep.

"Yeah, I got it all," he said into the telephone, looking up at Annie. She stood in the doorway, squinting at him, letting her eyes adjust to the bright light. "Thanks, I owe you one."

Pete stood to hang up the phone, and Annie saw that he wore only a tight pair of white briefs. She looked away, embarrassed at her body's instant reaction to his masculinity, afraid to be caught staring.

He immediately noticed her discomfort. "I'm sorry," he apologized quietly. "I was lying down when the phone rang. I wanted to answer it before it woke you."

Annie went to the stove, putting on a kettle of hot water for tea. "What did you find out?" she asked, her back to him.

"Let me put on my jeans," he said. "Then I'll tell you."

"Do you want a cup of tea?" Annie asked as Pete came back into the kitchen, tucking his T-shirt into the waistband of his jeans. Now *she* felt underdressed, standing there in her flannel pajamas.

"Thanks," Pete said gratefully.

She got a second mug down from the cabinet and dropped a tea bag into it, then leaned against the counter, arms folded across her chest, waiting for the water to boil.

Pete took a lemon from the refrigerator, grabbed the cutting board from the shelf and opened the knife drawer. He was at home here in her kitchen, Annie realized. He knew where everything was; he knew where to find the plates and the glasses, he even knew where she hid a chocolate bar for those times when nothing else would substitute. *He* knew all those things. Captain Kendall Peterson, formerly of the U.S. Army, currently of the CIA, knew all sorts of private and personal things about her. Because everything that Peter Taylor had seen and heard, Kendall Peterson remembered.

"How do you do it?" Annie asked.

He glanced up at her, then finished cutting the lemon neatly into eighths. "Do what?"

"How can you take on someone else's identity for such a long period of time?" Annie asked. "Don't you start to lose your own self?"

Pete shook his head. "Annie, it's not like I'm an actor," he said. He turned toward her, trying to make her understand. "I just take a different name, a different label. It doesn't matter whether you call me Captain or Peterson or Taylor or Hastin Naat'aanni, or whether my driver's license says I'm from Colorado or New York City. I am always the same man. I am me—I'm Pete."

"You think of yourself as Pete," Annie said, "not Hastin Naat'aanni, Man Speaking Peace?"

Pete was silent for a moment, looking down at his bare

feet against the black-and-white tile floor. "I *am* Hastin Naat'aanni. I always will be. But in Vietnam, the men in my platoon called me Machine—short for War Machine. I'm that, too."

The teakettle whistled, and Annie turned toward the stove, shutting off the gas. She filled both mugs with steaming water, then set them down on the table. Pete brought the plate of lemons over and sat down across from her.

Annie bobbed her tea bag up and down in her mug, watching as the hot water was slowly stained brown.

"Want to hear what I found out?" he asked.

"Is it good news or bad news?" she countered.

"It's strange," Pete said.

"Fire away."

"Okay. So far, we've got J. J. Steadman—whoever he is—and Alistair Golden as partners in some pretty lame art-collecting companies. And we already know Golden authenticates everything that comes out of the English Gallery—everything except for this one artifact, the death mask." Pete thought for a moment, and then asked, "Does it make any sense that Golden should fly to England *before* every single transaction?"

"Hardly," Annie said, taking a sip of her tea, testing to see if it was strong enough. "But Golden isn't exactly what I'd call sensible. Apparently he insists on packing the artwork or artifacts himself. I think he's kind of anal retentive."

She was silent as she fished the tea bag out of her mug and put it in the garbage. She squeezed a piece of lemon into her tea, then took another sip. "I called Ben Sullivan and told him about this mess I'm in," she said, taking a sip. "I told him I'd be shipping the death mask back to him, and he asked me to recommend another authenticator besides Golden. Seems Golden threw a little bit of a fit when he found out he wasn't going to do the work, and he called up Ben and screamed in his ear. Ben was not impressed.''

Shipping the death mask back.

The death mask.

Somehow it was connected to Annie's being framed.

And although Pete couldn't say why, returning the death mask to Sullivan seemed even more dangerous than keeping it.

Chapter 17

The next day, Alistair Golden called.

"He said that he wants to come by and discuss taking over some of my work," Annie said. "Since my license has been revoked, *some*one has to do the jobs. And suddenly he's my best friend...."

Pete listened silently.

"He says he'll pay me a referral fee," Annie continued, "and, of course, he'll get all the necessary approvals."

Pete nodded. "Squeaky-clean."

Annie shrugged. "I told him it was okay with me. I mean, I've got to do something with all this work I'm supposed to be doing. I can't just sit on it until my trial."

"Yeah, I know." Pete stood up. "When's he coming?"

"Sometime around three this afternoon."

"I'd like to talk with him when he gets here," Pete said. "On the record."

* * *

At around noon, Annie watched as Pete carefully taped the tiny microphone to his chest, just under his collarbone. Then he buttoned his shirt back up and shrugged on his heavy leather jacket. He picked up the set of headphones he had placed on the desk in the office and handed them to Annie. "This whole surveillance unit is mobile. You can hook the recorder to your belt and carry it with you wherever you go. If you want to hear what's going on, just listen in on the headphones."

"What do you expect him to do, confess to framing me?" Annie said. "We don't even know he's involved."

"Maybe he's not, but maybe he is," Pete replied. He headed downstairs, and Annie followed. "I'm going to go outside and walk around the house to check the range on this thing. When he comes, I want to meet him outdoors and see if I can find out anything before we let him in."

He accessed the alarm system bypass and opened the front door.

"I'll keep talking as I walk around outside," Pete said. "You keep the headphones on, and if you can hear me, flick the outside floodlights on and off."

She looked up at him and said, "I know it's silly, and Alistair Golden is about as dangerous as a worm, but this cloak-and-dagger stuff really gets me nervous."

Annie stared into Pete's bottomless dark eyes, searching for what, she wasn't sure. Dishonesty, maybe. Or deceit. But all she could see was love. He loved her. He really, truly loved her. He looked away, as if embarrassed by her scrutiny.

"I'd better get out there," he said.

"Pete," she said.

He stopped and turned back, his face carefully revealing no emotion. "Yeah?"

"No matter what happens, you're going to be careful, right?"

He didn't answer right away, but his heart showed in his eyes as a seed of hope took root and bloomed all in the space of a few short seconds. "Yeah," he finally said, his voice huskier than usual. "You bet I'm going to be careful."

She looked so worried, her blue eyes darkened with anxiety. He reached out and pushed a lock of hair back from her face, stroking her soft cheek with his thumb. "Everything's going to work out," he said gently.

Annie's blue eyes filled with tears. "Everything but us," she said. "I just can't forgive you, Pete."

"Have you really tried?" he asked softly.

Annie slipped the headphones over her ears.

"Okay, I'm out here," Pete said as he stepped off the porch. He turned to see the floodlights switch on and then off again. "I'm heading around to the side of the house now."

The lights flicked on and off steadily as he made his way around the house, talking all the while. When he got to the front of the house he went onto the lawn and said, "I'm in the front yard now, and believe it or not, it looks like the lawn could use another raking." He looked back at the house, and for a moment, the lights did not come on. Then they did, and quickly went off again. He then spoke softly. "And I'd very much like to help you rake it, Annie." And again the lights stayed unlit for several moments, finally flashing on for a brief second before being extinguished again.

Finally Pete squared his shoulders in the middle of the

yard and faced the house head-on. Looking directly into the darkened floodlights, he tried to speak, but his voice broke. He bowed his head, looked up again at the big house he had come to think of as his home, took a deep breath and said, "I'm talking really quietly now, I can barely hear my own voice. Can you hear me? I love you, Annie. And I'm going to win you back if it's the last thing I do."

The floodlights never came on.

Annie brusquely wiped at the tear that had escaped and was running down her cheek. She was about to pull the headphones off when she heard Pete curse under his breath, and then say, "Annie, our guest has arrived three hours early. How rude of him. Of *them*."

At that, Annie hurried to the front of the house to look out the window. Golden, impeccably dressed in a dark blue suit and a maroon tie with accent handkerchief, was getting out of his car, and that broker, Joseph James, or James Joseph, or whoever he was, wearing jeans and a light jacket, was getting out of the other side of the car. Pete was running across the lawn toward them as they came up the porch steps. Pete was whispering to her as he ran.

"Annie, lock the door and don't open it, *no matter what happens.* Turn on the alarm, get the death mask out of the safe and hide it in the attic somewhere. Then get out the back door, and get to a safe place. Do you understand me?"

Even as he said the words, she was locking the door, turning on the alarm. As she ran to the safe, got the death mask and hauled the heavy box up to the attic, she muttered under her breath, while another tear ran down her cheek, unchecked, "You be careful, do you understand *me?*"

"Well, lookee here, if it isn't Fido," Joseph James said to Pete, an unpleasant smile on his unpleasant face.

"You gentlemen might want to get someone to check your watches. You appear to be a little early." Pete smiled. "What's the rush?"

"We decided to come for lunch," Joseph James said, folding his arms across his broad chest with a smirk. "On account of our busy schedules."

Joseph James.

It came to him in a flash.

Pete eyed the two men and decided to take a chance. If he was right, he had to keep them talking and out of the house. If he could get them to say something stupid, the tape would prove Annie was innocent, even if he messed up and they killed him.

Pete smiled broadly at the taller of the two men. "Well. We were expecting only Dr. Golden, not you, Mr. James. Or is it Mr. Joseph? Or maybe…Mr. Steadman?"

At that, the man took a step toward Pete, until his face was inches away. "Maybe you should shut up," he snarled.

Jackpot.

Pete looked steadily at Steadman, unperturbed. "My mistake. Your name is undoubtedly Grumpy." He turned to Golden. "And that must make you Sleazy."

Pete was banking on Steadman's anger. He knew that Joseph James Steadman wanted to take a swing at him, to get back at Pete for having been roughed up the last time he was out here. That was good. Angry people didn't think clearly. Angry people weren't careful about what they said, and the mike inside Pete's jacket was ready to pick it all up....

"We're here to see Dr. Morrow," Dr. Golden said, his green eyes a little too bright in his face. "I'd like to get this over with."

"That's a pity," said Pete. "She just went into town. She said she wouldn't be back for a few hours."

Golden smiled, and Pete was reminded of a lizard. "I don't think so," he said. "Her car is still in the driveway."

Inside the house, Annie had called Whitley Scott at the FBI. Scott had said they were on their way. They'd arrive in twenty minutes, maybe less. She now stood at the top of the stairs, listening through the headphones to the conversation outside.

"In fact, I'll bet she's standing on the other side of these windows, listening to us talk," she heard Golden say.

"Maybe," she heard Pete drawl, his Western accent more pronounced than usual. "Maybe not. Why don't you just tell me what you want, and then maybe I can help you." He paused. "Maybe."

Outside, Steadman was starting to lose his cool. "Maybe you'd better be quiet before I use this to blow your head off your neck, smartass," he said as he reached into his jacket pocket and pulled out a huge automatic pistol. He jammed it under Pete's chin.

A vein bulged in Golden's forehead, and Pete thought the man was going to have a stroke.

"It's certainly big enough," Pete said with a cocky smile. "Fire this sucker, and the entire neighborhood will come running to see what happened."

"Keep the gun under your coat," Golden snapped nervously at Steadman.

Inside the house, Annie's fingers clutched the banister. They were threatening Pete with a gun! *Where* was the FBI? According to her watch, they were still over fifteen minutes away. For the first time in a long time, she found herself wishing they would show up early. Slowly she crept down the stairs, closer to the front door.

"Why don't you tell me what you want," Pete offered. "I'm listening." Me and the FBI, he thought. "Maybe we can make a deal."

"You give us the death mask," Steadman said, "and we don't kill you. How's *that* for a deal?"

Pete pretended to think about it. "I guess you're going to have to try to kill me," he finally said. "Though, I've got to warn you, I don't die very easily."

Oh, Pete, what are you doing? thought Annie.

"Or, you guys could crawl into whatever hole you came out of," Pete said. "And come back when you're ready to make a real deal."

Steadman pulled the gun away from Pete's head. With an angry look, he began to attach a large silencer to the barrel.

Unconcerned, Pete sat down on the top of the porch steps and looked up at the two men. "Using a silencer is illegal, you know," he said. "Shame on you."

"Tell Morrow to open the door," Golden said.

"Tell me," Pete said pleasantly. "Do I look that stupid?"

"I would really like to shoot you," Steadman snarled.

"Gee, what a coincidence. I'd like to shoot you, too," Pete said to Steadman, still in the same pleasant tone.

"Put your hands on your head," Steadman snapped, a touch of panic in his voice. He glanced at Golden. "Check his pockets. He's carrying."

Golden was nervous as hell, but he pulled Pete's gun out of his jacket pocket, holding it like a dead mouse.

"I'm not cut out for this," Golden said. "Let's get that crate and go."

"Dr. Morrow," Steadman called, his voice angry. "Open the damned door."

"Annie, I know you're not even in there, but if you are, don't open the door," Pete said calmly.

From inside the house, Annie watched as Steadman backhanded Pete across the face. With a gasp, she saw Pete skid along the porch, hitting the side of the house with a solid thud.

"Open the door, Annie," Steadman called. "Or I'm gonna kill this bastard."

Pete came up smiling. "I hate to break it to you guys," he said, "but I'm Navaho. And you know what happens when a Navaho dies. Sure you do—you did your research before you made those threatening phone calls to Annie. But in case you need a refresher course, I'll tell you. A dead Navaho returns to avenge the wrongs made against him in life. Kill me, and my evil spirit will kick you straight to hell."

Steadman didn't look worried. "I'm gonna count to three, *Annie,*" he said, "and then I'm going to shoot him. One…"

"She's not going to open the door," Pete said. "She knows that you're bluffing."

Annie stood at the door, her hands on the deadbolt. His leather jacket was lined with a bulletproof vest, she reminded herself, trying to force back the panic that threatened to overpower her. Even if they shot him, he'd be okay, wouldn't he? Oh, God, unless they shot him in the head. If they shot him in the head, he'd die. The panic was back full-force. If she didn't open the door, and Pete died, she'd never be able to live with herself, knowing that she could have saved him.

"Two," shouted Steadman. "I'm not bluffing."

She didn't want Pete to die. She desperately didn't want him to die....

"Yes, he is," Pete said. "Annie, don't open the door!"

Because, dammit, she loved him. She yanked the headphones off her and pushed the alarm system's front door override.

"Three!"

Annie jerked the door open.

"No!" Pete shouted. God, no! He'd told her to keep the door shut no matter what!

Steadman's gun swung toward Annie.

Pete moved fast, letting his backup gun drop from his sleeve into his hand. He blocked Annie with his body, shooting Steadman cleanly in the right arm and in the leg. Steadman's shots went wild, hitting the roof of the porch, the side of the house.

Then three more gunshots rang out. Bullets from the gun Golden was holding hit Pete, the force knocking him back into the house and slamming him into the foyer wall. He fell like a stone onto the floor.

Annie slammed the door shut and threw the deadbolt, leaving Golden and Joseph James Steadman out on the porch. They pounded on the door, and it strained beneath their combined weight. Much more of this, and they were going to break through, taking the old door right off its hinges.

Pete didn't move.

"Pete," Annie said. "Get up!"

She'd seen the bullets hit him in the chest. That meant he was all right, because his jacket was bulletproof.

But he still didn't move.

"Pete!" she shouted. It was only natural that he be dazed. He probably had the air knocked out of him. He probably needed to lie there a minute and catch his breath. But she was starting to get scared. Golden and Steadman were going to bust through the door any second....

"Pete, come *on!*" she yelled, turning to look at him.

Blood.

Pete's blood.

Bright and red, it seeped out from underneath him, running in the cracks on the hardwood floor....

With a cry, she ran toward him. Oh, God, he was bleeding. "Please don't be dead. Please, God, don't let him be dead!"

She turned him over onto his back, oblivious to the door breaking open, oblivious to Golden and Steadman as they shouted and waved their guns at her. Annie was only aware of Pete, of the blood.

There was so much blood, leaking out from underneath the waistband of his jacket, staining the front of his jeans.

He wasn't breathing. God, he wasn't breathing....

"Pete," Annie cried, touching his face, his hair, his arms. Arms that had held her, lips that had kissed her... "No! God, no! Pete, I love you, don't be dead—"

Rough hands pulled her up, off the floor, away from Pete's body. She struggled, sobbing his name, trying to get back to him, uncaring of her safety. Golden hit her, and she fell to the ground, not feeling the pain, not feeling anything but grief. Oh, God, Pete was dead....

He was lying sprawled on the floor, one arm trapped underneath the weight of his body, the other flung out, his fingers spread wide as if he were reaching for something, reaching for her....

"He's dead," Golden said, nudging Pete with his foot. His green eyes looked almost feverish in his white face. He looked frighteningly inhuman, his nervousness frozen away by whatever coldness now inhabited him. "Open the safe, or you will be, too."

Annie sat very still. She didn't care. By killing Pete, Golden had already killed her.

Swearing, Golden began to drag her into the laboratory.

"For crying out loud, give me a hand," he finally said to Steadman.

"Which hand do you want, Al?" Steadman said, his voice pinched with pain. "I got a bullet in my right arm, and I think it's broken, and I'm bleeding like a stuck pig from this gash in my leg—"

"Shut up," Golden said, finally pushing Annie down in front of the safe. He held the gun to her head. "Open it."

Woodenly, she pulled herself up and began to open the safe. He was going to kill her. She knew he would, as soon as she gave him the death mask. He'd killed Pete, and he was going to kill her.

But he wasn't going to get away with it. If she stalled, Whitley Scott and the FBI would come. If she stalled long enough, she might even live to see Golden and Steadman rot in prison....

"You set me up, Golden," she said, suddenly feeling almost deadly calm, turning to look at him. "Didn't you?"

"Open the safe," he hissed.

"The death mask isn't in there," she said.

Steadman cursed loudly.

The panic in Golden's eyes deepened. "Where is it?"

"Tell me why you set me up," Annie said.

"Because it was so easy to do," he said. "The FBI was already investigating you. I just played into their hands."

"What are you talking about?"

"Do we really have to get into the details? The incident at Athens was just your bad luck. We didn't have anything to do with that—you came under suspicion because they couldn't find anyone else. So we staged a similar little event in England after you left. And then we planted the stuff in your lab. Are you satisfied? We gave the FBI what they needed, and now you're gonna give me what I need. Then I'm gonna burn this place down." Golden cocked his gun, pressing it against Annie's head. "Now, where is that crate?"

"Upstairs," she said, curiously unafraid of the gun, its cold metal barrel bruising her temple. "In the attic." Something still wasn't clear. What was the big deal about this artifact? Why did they have to frame her? She'd probably never know....

"I can't handle the stairs," Steadman complained. "You take her. And leave her up there, will you?"

Golden forced Annie's arm back behind her, twisting it upward so that she should have cried out from the pain. But the numbness was surrounding her so completely, she didn't make a sound.

Pete's body lay in the foyer with all that blood, and the grief tore through, slicing into her, cutting her in two. He never knew that she loved him. He had died before she had a chance to tell him. No, that wasn't true. She'd had plenty of chances, she had just been too pigheaded, too stubborn, too *selfish*, and now he was dead and he would never know.

Tears spilled down her face, and she stumbled on the stairs, looking back at him. His face was probably already growing cold to the touch. The puddle of blood had grown. There was even blood on the knees of his jeans....

Annie froze. Outwardly, she made herself keep going, but inwardly, even her heart had stopped beating.

Pete's fingers had been spread, reaching, but now they were clenched, his hand in a tight fist.

Breathe, she told herself. *Breathe.*

Around her, everything snapped into tight focus. She tried to appear to move at a normal speed, and still stall their inevitable climb up to the attic. They were walking up the stairs in slow motion. The light was on in the kitchen, and the black-and-white tiled floor became almost three-dimensional. There was a cobweb hanging from the light fixture in the hall. The banister at the edge of the second-floor landing was in serious need of dusting. And the secondary burglar alarm control panel that had been installed next to Annie's bedroom door was flashing green.

Green. The system had been shut down.

The motion detectors had been turned off. But when she opened the front door, she'd activated only the override, leaving the rest of the system on-line. If *she* hadn't turned off the alarm system, then...

Pete.

Pete was alive.

She started to shake, and Golden pushed her harder. "Scared?" he taunted her. "You better be. If that crate isn't up here, you're dead."

But she wasn't scared. She was happy, thunderously, joyfully happy. Pete was alive! God was giving her a second chance....

His clenched fist had been some sort of signal to her. He knew that she would notice—he knew she always noticed details.

He was trying to tell her something. But what?

They reached the top of the stairs and she pointed to the attic door, unable to speak. Golden motioned for her to open it.

The attic stairs creaked as they went up, up to the attic, up where Golden intended to leave her. Permanently.

Annie's heart was pounding.

She strained her ears, but she heard no sounds from downstairs. No struggle, no scuffle, nothing.

What was Pete trying to tell her?

Golden released her arm as they stepped up into the attic. He held his gun steady with both hands as he aimed it at her. "Get it."

Behind the old TV. She had put the crate behind the... The crate!

In a flash she remembered picking up a similar heavy package at the airport. Pete had lifted it up, realized he would need both hands to carry it and refused. *She* had ended up lugging it all the way out to the car because, he said, if something threatening happened while he was carrying it, he wouldn't be able to properly protect her. He wouldn't be able to go for his gun.

He couldn't carry the package and hold a gun at the same time!

And if *Pete* couldn't...

With a silent heave, Annie picked up the crate and placed it solidly in Alistair Golden's outstretched left hand. And she watched as he brought his right hand, his gun hand, over to support the bottom of the heavy crate.

Annie wasn't sure if the look of surprise on Golden's face was from the unexpected weight of the crate, or from the sight of Pete, covered with blood and looking as if he'd risen from the dead, crashing through the attic window, a gun in each hand.

"Freeze," Pete shouted. "Annie, get down!"

Annie dove for cover as Golden lunged toward Pete, futilely throwing the crate at him. She heard the sound of gunshots.

Then there was silence.

"You stupid son of a bitch," Annie heard Pete say. "I *told* you to freeze."

Slowly she poked her head out. Golden lay on the floor, his sightless eyes staring up at the rafters, but Annie could see only Pete.

Pete!

Standing in front of her, breathing, living....

"You're alive," she said, unaware of the tears that coursed down her face. "My God, you *are* alive."

She moved toward him, held by a gaze she'd thought she'd never see again, beautiful dark eyes filled with life. And pain.

"Careful," he said, "I'm covered with glass."

"I don't care," she said, touching his face, wrapping her arms around him. "I love you. I'm never going to let go of you again."

He kissed her, sweetly, softly.

Downstairs, a team of federal agents poured into the house.

"Well, if it isn't the cavalry," Pete said, swaying slightly in her arms. "About time." And then his knees gave out.

The next few seconds blurred together as Annie caught him, shouting, screaming for help. She didn't have the strength to hold him up, but she kept him from hitting the floor with force, lowering him gently down.

Whitley Scott was there in an instant. "Agent down!" he shouted. "We have an agent down! Get those paramedics up here—"

Someone unzipped Pete's jacket. There was a huge stain of bright red blood on his lower left side.

"The bullet went in under his jacket," Scott's voice said, "and angled up...."

Pete looked up at Scott. "Steadman—" he croaked.

Scott nodded. "We found where you left him," he said. "He hasn't come to yet, but he's cuffed."

"What's this on the floor?" someone asked. "Whoa, these aren't your everyday, average foam chips...."

"Peterson's lost an awful lot of blood," someone said.

Another voice swore softly. "How the hell did he manage to climb up the outside of the house in this condition? It's unreal...."

"Had to," Pete whispered. "Stairs creak...."

"Cocaine," Annie heard someone say. "This entire crate is *filled* with cocaine...."

"Hang in there, Captain," another man's voice said. "Paramedics are on their way."

"Get him downstairs," Scott ordered. "Lift him up and get him down and into a car. There's no time to wait. We can meet the ambulance halfway—"

This couldn't be happening, Annie thought, letting go of Pete's hand as five men lifted him. She couldn't get him back only to lose him again.

Miraculously, the ambulance had arrived, and the paramedics were in the foyer with their stretcher. The other agents laid Pete gently on it.

"Annie," he whispered.

She leaned over him, touching his face. His skin felt so clammy. "Don't you dare die on me, Peterson," she said fiercely. "Not twice in one day. I won't let you!"

"I have no intention of dying," he said, his voice little more than a rasp. His eyes were glazed with pain, his fingers gripping hers. "No way...."

"I love you," Annie told him. "You better not forget that."

Somehow he managed to smile. "I won't."

Chapter 18

Pete woke up.

Intensive care, he thought, staring at the massive array of monitors and machines that surrounded his hospital bed.

He was alive.

Yes, he was definitely alive. The pain in his gut was proof of that.

His throat was dry, his mouth was gluey and tasted like old socks. He tried to swallow, but it was a lost cause.

He had an IV tube in the back of his right hand.

His left hand was stuck in some kind of vise....

No, that was no vise grip, that was Annie! She held his hand tightly as she sat next to his bed, her head resting on the edge of the mattress, her eyes closed, her breathing even. She was asleep.

Gently he pulled his hand free, then touched the silky smoothness of her hair.

Her eyes opened slowly, and she sat up, looking at him.

"I was starting to wonder if you were ever going to wake up," she said, her eyes filling with tears. One escaped and slid down her cheek.

"Don't cry." Pete couldn't make his voice any louder than a whisper. "Everything's gonna be all right—"

Her eyes blazed with anger. "You should have told me that you were going to try to provoke Golden and Steadman. I had no idea what you were doing—I thought you'd lost your mind. And when Whitley Scott told me that you had intentionally been making them angry, that you wanted them to try for you, that you were fast enough to disarm them both by winging them and that *I* was responsible for your getting shot because I opened the door and distracted you—"

Huge tears fell from Annie's eyes, faster and faster. Pete reached out to touch her hand, but she jerked away. But then, as if on second thought, she took his hand, bringing it up to her lips, then pressing it against the side of her face.

"I'm really mad at you," she said.

"It wasn't your fault," he whispered. "I underestimated Golden, didn't think he would have the guts to shoot me—"

"If I hadn't opened the door, he *wouldn't* have," Annie said, "but, God, Pete, I was so afraid you were going to die."

"I didn't," he said.

"I love you," she said.

"I remember."

Pete rode in the wheelchair down to the lobby. Outside the big double doors, he could see the flash of Annie's shining hair in the bright autumn sunshine.

The nurse pushed him through the doors and out onto

the sidewalk. The morning air was cold, bracing. He took a deep breath, then smiled up into Annie's dancing blue eyes.

"Okay, Captain," the nurse said. "You can take it from here."

Pete stood up, still moving slowly, carefully. It would be a few more weeks before he was running any laps.

Annie was watching him carefully. "You talked to Whitley Scott this morning?" she asked.

"Yeah."

"Did they find out who was the inside contact?"

"Collins," Pete said. "He had access to the security codes—he got Steadman and Golden into your house."

"So this whole thing was about smuggling drugs?"

"That's it," Pete said. "Steadman put up the money to buy the art, and Golden would take on the task of authenticating it. But what he really did was fly out to England and pack the piece using special foam packing peanuts that he'd picked up wholesale in Colombia. The peanuts were loaded with cocaine, sometimes tens of millions of dollars' worth. Golden would bring the cocaine into the U.S. via England. He figured—correctly—that anything brought in from Colombia would be carefully searched, whereas England's not particularly known for its drug trafficking, so Customs tends to be more lax. As for the artifact, Steadman would turn right around and sell it—usually at a loss. He didn't care if he lost a few dollars on the art, he was making a bundle distributing the coke.

"When Ben Sullivan specifically called for you to authenticate the death mask, Golden had already packed it—gotten it ready to ship," he said. "He and Steadman stood to lose the whole shipment of cocaine." They had reached the car. Pete looked at the woman he had risked his life for, the woman he would gladly risk his life for a hundred times more. "They stood to lose millions. Or worse. You could have found the coke. So they made those threatening phone calls, trying to set up a Navaho group as the fall guy when they stole the piece from you. When *I* made the scene and security got too tight, they got desperate. They tried to kill you, and when that didn't work, they resorted to their back-up plan—they framed you. They were willing to do *any*thing to get Golden named as the authenticator again. Because then the crate—with the coke—would go back into his possession."

Annie shuddered. "I'm just glad the whole mess is over."

Pete let her help him into the car, then watched as she slid behind the wheel.

"Ready?" she asked.

"Very ready." Pete leaned over, pulled her toward him and kissed her, long and hard. They were both breathing heavily when he finally let her go. "Guess what I want to do first thing when we get home?"

Annie frowned in mock seriousness. "You promised the doctor no strenuous exercise."

"Who said anything about strenuous?" He smiled, tugging on her earlobe with his teeth.

She pulled away. "No, Pete, really," she said, all teasing gone. "You better ask the doctor first, make sure it's okay...."

"It's okay," he said, playing with her long, brown hair, running it through his fingers. "And I didn't even have to ask. The doctor brought it up himself. I think he noticed the way I look at you."

The way Pete was looking at her right now... It was heat, steam, fire, his eyes glowing with flames. He bent to kiss her again, and Annie closed her eyes, losing herself in the conflagration....

"Let's go home," he whispered.

Heart pounding, Annie pulled out of the driveway and onto the main road. After a mile or two, her pulse had finally returned to near normal, and she glanced over at Pete. "Jerry Tillet got funding for his Mexico project," she said. "Ben Sullivan came through."

"That's great news," Pete said. "Can't you drive any faster?"

Annie laughed. "We're five minutes from home," she said.

Pete's eyes told her that five minutes was five minutes too many.

"Cara's going to Mexico with Tillet," she said, trying to distract him—trying to distract herself. Would this traffic light *never* change? "Now I've got to find another research assistant."

"I thought you were thinking about going along," Pete said as the car moved forward. "You know, get your hands dirty for a change, do a little camping...."

Annie didn't answer, didn't even look up from the road. *What are your plans?* she wanted to ask. *When do you have to return to work?* But she didn't. She couldn't get the words out.

"I have a great idea," Pete was saying. "We can go out to Colorado first, then head down to Mexico—"

"We?" She couldn't hide her surprise.

Pete smiled at her. "Yeah. We. You. Me. You know. We could make it our honeymoon."

Annie pulled sharply off to the right, into a department store parking lot. She stopped the car, then turned to look at him. "Are you asking me to marry you?"

There was a spark of uncertainty in his eyes. "I thought I already did," he said slowly. "In the ambulance. On the way to the hospital?"

"You remember that?" Annie said in disbelief. "Pete, you were delirious."

"Well, yeah." He grinned. "Because you said yes...." His eyes were intense and his smile disappeared as he watched her. "*Will* you marry me, Annie?"

She moistened her lips. "I'm not sure I want to be married to someone who works for the CIA," she said softly. "I'm not sure I could handle it...."

The silence in the car stretched on.

Who was she fooling? Annie thought. It wouldn't be easy; she'd spend all her time worrying that he would be hurt, shot, killed even. She'd hate the long hours, the weeks away. But she loved him, and she was willing to take whatever he was willing to give.

"Yes," she said, at the exact same moment he turned to her and said, "I'll retire."

They stared at each other for a long time, then Pete said again, "I *will* retire."

"You don't have to," Annie said quietly. "I'll marry you anyway."

"But I want to," he said, taking her hand in his and kissing the tips of her fingers. "I've been thinking about it for a while. I just never had a good enough reason to retire before this."

"But what will you do?" Annie said. "You're awfully young to retire."

Pete smiled. "I've been thinking about a career change," he said. "I heard there's this really terrific position open—someone's looking for a research assistant. I don't have a whole hell of a lot of experience in a lab, but I'm really good at camping and digging in the dirt, or whatever it is you archaeologists do."

Laughing, Annie kissed him. And kissed him, and kissed him.

When they drew apart, her hands were shaking. "Well," she said. "I'm glad *that's* settled."

But Pete touched her chin, tugging her face toward him. "Wait," he said. His eyes were serious. "I need to ask you…" He looked down for a moment as if gathering his courage. "I know you love me." His eyes met hers. "But have you forgiven me?"

"Forgiven? Yes," she said. "Forgotten? Never. I'm not going to make *that* mistake twice."

His eyebrow moved slightly in the tiniest of frowns. He didn't understand.…

"I'm *never* going to forget that you love me," she said, and put the car into gear. "Let's go home."

* * * * * *

Look for Suzanne Brockmann's exciting
return to Silhouette Intimate Moments
in Summer 2001!

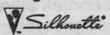

Silhouette —
where love comes alive—online...

eHARLEQUIN.com

your romantic books

♥ Shop online! Visit Shop eHarlequin and discover a wide selection of new releases and classic favorites at great discounted prices.

♥ Read our daily and weekly Internet exclusive serials, and participate in our interactive novel in the reading room.

♥ Ever dreamed of being a writer? Enter your chapter for a chance to become a featured author in our Writing Round Robin novel.

• • • • • •

your romantic life

♥ Check out our feature articles on dating, flirting and other important romance topics and get your daily love dose with tips on how to keep the romance alive every day.

• • • • • •

your community

♥ Have a Heart-to-Heart with other members about the latest books and meet your favorite authors.

♥ Discuss your romantic dilemma in the Tales from the Heart message board.

your romantic escapes

♥ Learn what the stars have in store for you with our daily Passionscopes and weekly Erotiscopes.

♥ Get the latest scoop on your favorite royals in Royal Romance.

Back by popular demand are

DEBBIE MACOMBER's

Hard Luck, Alaska, is a
town that needs women!
And the O'Halloran brothers
are just the fellows
to fly them in.

Starting in March 2000 this beloved series returns
in special 2-in-1 collector's editions:

MAIL-ORDER MARRIAGES, featuring
Brides for Brothers and *The Marriage Risk*
On sale March 2000

FAMILY MEN, featuring
Daddy's Little Helper and *Because of the Baby*
On sale July 2000

THE LAST TWO BACHELORS, featuring
Falling for Him and *Ending in Marriage*
On sale August 2000

Collect and enjoy each MIDNIGHT SONS story!

Available at your favorite retail outlet.

HARLEQUIN®
Makes any time special ™

Visit us at www.romance.net

PHMS

LINDSAY McKENNA

continues her most popular series with a
brand-new, longer-length book.

And it's the story you've been waiting for....

Morgan's Mercenaries:
Heart of Stone

They had met before. Battled before. And
Captain Maya Stevenson had never again
wanted to lay eyes on Major Dane York—
the man who once tried to destroy
her military career! But on their latest
mission together, Maya discovered that beneath
the fury in Dane's eyes lay a raging passion. Now she
struggled against dangerous desire, as Dane's command
over her seemed greater still. For this time, he laid claim
to her heart....

Only from Lindsay McKenna and Silhouette Books!

"When it comes to action and romance,
nobody does it better than Ms. McKenna."
—*Romantic Times Magazine*

Available in March at your favorite retail outlet.

Silhouette®
™ *Where love comes alive*™